Robert Henry McClellan

Practice in Probate Courts

Robert Henry McClellan

Practice in Probate Courts

Reprint of the original, first published in 1875.

1st Edition 2024 | ISBN: 978-3-38538-380-7

Verlag (Publisher): Outlook Verlag GmbH, Zeilweg 44, 60439 Frankfurt, Deutschland
Vertretungsberechtigt (Authorized to represent): E. Roepke, Zeilweg 44, 60439 Frankfurt, Deutschland
Druck (Print): Books on Demand GmbH, In de Tarpen 42, 22848 Norderstedt, Deutschland

qualifying, and after giving the notice in the next section required, with the aid of appraisers so appointed by the surrogate, shall made a true and perfect inventory of all the goods, chattels and credits of such testator or intestate, and where the same shall be in two different and distant places, two or more such inventories, as may be necessary." (2 R. S., 82.)

" § 3. A notice of such appraisement shall be served, five days previous thereto, on the legatees and next of kin residing in the county where such property shall be; and it shall also be posted in three of the most public places of the town. In every such notice, the time and place at which such appraisement will be made, shall be specified. (Id.)

NOTICE OF APPRAISEMENT.

To the legatees (or next of kin) of ...., deceased.
      Rensselaer county, ss.

Take notice, that the subscribers, with the appraisers duly appointed, will attend at the late dwelling house of deceased, in the ...... of ...., in the said county, on the ...... day of ...., 187..., at ten o'clock in the forenoon of that day, to estimate and appraise the personal property of the said deceased, and with the aid of the said appraisers take an inventory thereof.

      Dated, ..., 187....

                  ...., ⎫
                  ....⎭ *Executors.*

PRACTICE

IN

PROBATE COURTS:

BEING

A TREATISE ON THE JURISDICTION OF THE

SURROGATES' COURTS

AND

THE REMEDIES OFFERED THEREBY;

COMPRISING, ALSO,

THE LAW OF WILLS, EXECUTORS,

ADMINISTRATION,

LEGACIES, GUARDIANS AND DOWER,

WITH

COMPLETE FORMS FOR PRACTICE.

BY

ROBERT H. McCLELLAN,

COUNSELOR AT LAW,

AND FORMER SURROGATE OF RENSSELAER COUNTY.

ALBANY, N. Y.:

WILLIAM GOULD & SON.

1875.

PREFACE.

To most of the profession, the practice in the Surrogate's Court is a mystéry, passed over in their preparatory studies, and, in consequence, not followed in after years. Therefore the practice is confined very much to the court itself, and to a few of the profession in each county, few others caring to master a theory and practice differing so much from that laid down and regulated by the Code.

In the preparation of this work, I have assumed that my brethren do not want a treatise to give them elementary instruction, but a book of ready reference, in which, in each case, they can find clearly pointed out, the rights and remedies offered by the Probate Courts, with forms easily adapted. Such a work I have endeavored to prepare, and here present.

In the preparation of the forms, I have used those familiar to every surrogate, in the main, but have endeavored to render them more concise and pointed, and have given more, I believe, than were ever before printed. I bespeak especially a consideration of this feature of the book.

I trust that my professional brethren will find this book useful to them.

ROBERT H. McCLELLAN.

Troy, February 1, 1875.

TABLE OF CONTENTS.

TABLE OF CASES CITED.

FORM FOR WILL.

The last will and testament of A B, of the town of
...................., in the county of .... and state
of New York.

I, A B, make this my last will and testament as
follows:

First. I direct that my funeral charges, the expenses
of administering my estate, and my debts, be paid out
of my personal estate; and if my personal estate be
insufficient for those purposes, I expressly charge the
payment thereof, or of any deficiency, upon the real
estate whereof I may die seized, and for that purpose,
or for the payment of the legacies hereinafter bequeathed, I authorize my executors hereinafter named,
to sell at public or private sale, the whole, or such part
of my real estate, as may be sufficient for those purposes.

Second. I give and bequeath unto my beloved wife
if she shall survive me, the sum of .... dollars, to be paid to her, with interest from the time of
my decease, in lieu of her dower, and of her distributive share in my estate.

Third. I give and bequeath to my daughter C D,
wife of ...., one thousand dollars to be paid
to her by my executors, for her separate use.

And I further direct, that if she should die during my lifetime, leaving issue, and any of her descendants shall be living at my decease, said sum shall be paid to such descendants in the proportions that the same would be paid to them under the statutes of this state, if the said C D had died intestate, leaving said sum for distribution as a part of her personal estate.

Fourth. I give and bequeath unto ...., infant son of .... of ...., one hundred dollars; and I authorize my executors, if they shall deem it safe and prudent, to pay the said legacy to the father of said infant, and take his receipt therefor, and his agreement to hold the same in trust for the said infant, to be paid to him when he shall arrive at full age, with interest; or, if they shall think best, the said executors may deposit said legacy in some savings bank to be selected by them, to the credit of said infant, and proof of such deposit shall be a sufficient discharge to my said executors for the same.

Fifth. I give and bequeath to each of my brothers, A and B, the sum of five hundred dollars, and I direct that in case either of my said brothers should die during my lifetime, his legacy shall not lapse, but shall go to the survivor. If both of my said brothers shall die during my lifetime, then the legacies to them shall lapse into the residue of my estate.

Sixth. I give and bequeath my ten shares of one hundred dollars each, of stock in the Union National Bank of Troy, to my friend ....

Seventh. I give and devise to my beloved wife, the dwelling house and lot, in the village of ...., where I now live, for and during the term of her natural life; and from and after her death, I give and devise the same, to my son A R, his heirs and assigns forever.

Eighth. I hereby dispose of the custody and tuition of my infant children during their minority, and while they shall remain unmarried, to my beloved wife, so long as she shall remain my widow; but if she shall die, or marry during the single life and infancy of any of said children, then and in that case, I dispose of and commit their custody and tuition, to my friend R F.

Ninth. I give, devise and bequeath all the residue of my estate, real and personal, to my children, share and share alike, as tenants in common.

Lastly. I appoint my son S B and my friend A R, executors of this, my last will and testament, hereby revoking all former wills by me made.   '

In witness whereof I have hereunto subscribed my name this ...... day of ...., in the year of our Lord one thousand eight hundred and seventy-five.
(Signed), A B.

The foregoing instrument was, at the date thereof, subscribed by the said A B, in our presence, and he at the same time declared the same to be his last will and testament, and requested us to sign our names as witnesses which we do in his presence.
C D, Troy, Rens. Co., N. Y.
R M D, Troy, Rens. Co., N. Y.

Attestation Clause where the Execution was Acknowleged.

On the day of the date of the foregoing instrument, the above named A B acknowledged to us and each of us, that he had subscribed the foregoing instrument, and at the same time declared the same to be his last will and testament, and requested us to sign the same as witnesses which we do in his presence.

C D, Troy, Rens. Co., N. Y.
R M D, Troy, Rens. Co., N. Y.

Attestation Clause showing Execution, and good in any state except Louisiana. Three witnesses are required.

On this ...... day of ...., 1875, the undersigned being present and believing the above named A B, to be of sound mind and memory, saw the said A B subscribe the foregoing will, and at the time of such subscription, the said A B stated to each of the undersigned, that the paper so subscribed by him, was his last will and testament, and requested us and each of us to sign said will as witnesses. Whereupon we do in his presence and in presence of each other, attest and subscribe the same as witnesses, the day and year above written.

C D, Troy, Rens. Co., N. Y.
E F, Troy, Rens. Co., N. Y.
G H, Albany, N. Y.

Clause in a Will, limiting Certain Property to the Use of a Married Woman.

I give and bequeath to A B, and C D, the survivor of them or their successors appointed by the Supreme Court, the sum of two thousand dollars, in trust to receive the interest thereof during the joint lives of G H, and E H, his wife, and to pay the same to the said E H, and her assigns, notwithstanding her coverture, for her sole and separate use, from time to time, during the joint lives of the said G H, and E H, his wife, so that the said E H, shall not sell, mortgage, charge, or otherwise dispose of the same in the way of anticipation. And if the said E H shall survive her said husband, then upon trust to pay the said principal sum to the said E H; but in case the said E H shall die during the lifetime of her husband, then in trust, after the decease of the said E H, to assign and transfer the said sum of two thousand dollars, to such person or persons and in such shares and subject to such conditions, as the said E H, by her last will and testament in writing, or by any writing in the nature of, or purporting to be her last will and testament, shall limit or appoint, and in default of such appointment, upon trust to pay, transfer and assign the same to the next of kin, of the said E H, not including therein the said G H, her husband.

Clause in a Will, limiting Real Estate to the Separate Use of a Married Woman.

I give and devise to A B and C D, during the joint lives of E H and G H, her husband, all that parcel of land conveyed to me by R J, by deed dated Nov. 1st, 1873, and recorded in the office of the clerk of the county of ...., in book No. ...... of deeds, page ......, etc., upon trust to pay the rents, issues and profits thereof to the said E H, or to such person or persons as she shall by writing appoint to receive the same, during the joint lives of the said E H and G H, for her sole and separate use, so that the said E H shall not sell, mortgage, or otherwise dispose of the same in the way of anticipation. From and immediately after the decease of the said G H, then I give and devise said premises to the said E H, if she shall survive her said husband. But in case the said E H shall die in the lifetime of her husband, then I give and devise the same to her heirs at law, as tenants in common.

Legacy to Charitable or Religious Corporations.

I give and bequeath to the (American Bible Society) (stating the name, if possible, or otherwise clearly describing the society), the sum of one thousand dollars, to be applied to the uses of said society.

Codicil.

Whereas I, A B, did heretofore make my last will and testament dated the ...... day of ...., 1875. Now I make this a codicil to said will.

First. I give and bequeath to my beloved wife the further sum of five thousand dollars.

Second. Whereas I did in said will give and bequeath to my son R R the sum of one thousand dollars,
now I revoke said bequest, for the reason that I have
paid said sum to my said son.

Inasmuch as I contemplate advancing to my children sums of money hereafter, I direct that all moneys
which I shall advance to them, or which shall be owing
to me from any of them at my decease, shall be considered as a part of my residuary estate, and shall be
deducted from his, or her respective share.

In witness whereof I now hereunto subscribe my
name this ...... day of ...., in the year of our
Lord, one thousand eight hundred and seventy.........

A B.

The foregoing instrument was at the date thereof
subscribed by the above named A B, in our presence,
and he declared the same to be a codicil to his last will
and testament and requested us to sign the same as
witnesses, which we do in his presence.

J L, Troy, N. Y.
G S, Troy, N. Y.

PRACTICE

IN

PROBATE COURTS.

CHAPTER I.

OF THE SURROGATE'S COURT AND THE POWERS AND
DUTIES OF THE SURROGATE GENERALLY.

The Surrogate's Courts, are the courts of original
jurisdiction for the proof of wills and the issuing
of letters testamentary thereon and the granting of
letters of administration upon the estates of intestates, and with wills annexed.

They are provided for by the constitution (art.
VI), and their jurisdiction is regulated and restricted by the statutes of the state. They are not
courts of record but are among the "courts of
peculiar and special jurisdiction" (2 R. S., 220,
276), and attorneys, admitted to practice in all the
courts of the state, are not officers of these courts,
but when acting, represent their clients specially.
(*Coates* v. *Cheever*, 1 Cow., 463.)

The court is held by the county judge of each
county, or in the city and county of New York and

in counties having a population exceeding forty thousand, in which the board of supervisors have provided for a separate office, to perform the duties, by a surrogate.

The county judge acting as surrogate, or the surrogate, before entering upon the duties of his office, files his official oath and bond in the office of the clerk of the county, with two or more sureties approved by the clerk, for the faithful performance of his duties. In New York city and county, the surrogate holds office for three years, but in the other counties for six, and their salaries are fixed by the legislature, and can neither be increased or diminished, during their terms of office. (Cons., art. VI, § 14.) The surrogate may be removed by the senate on the recommendation of the governor, after service of the copy of the complaint against him, and after having had an opportunity of being heard in his defense. (Cons., art. VI, § 11).

In regard to the general powers of the surrogate, the Revised Statutes, title I, chapter II, of part III, as amended by chap. 460, of Laws of 1837, provide as follows :

"§ 1. Every surrogate who shall have duly qualified, by taking the oath, and executing the bond required by law, shall hold a court within the limits of the county for which he was appointed, and shall have power :

1. To take the proof of wills of real and personal estate, in the cases prescribed by law, and also to take the proof of any will relating to real estate situated within the county of such surrogate, when the testator in such will shall have died out of this state, not being an inhabitant thereof, and not having any assets therein;

2. To grant letters testamentary and of administration;

3. To direct and control the conduct and settle the accounts of executors and administrators;

4. To enforce the payment of debts and legacies, and the distribution of the estates of intestates;

5. To order the sale and disposition of the real estate of deceased persons;

6. To administer justice in all matters relating to the affairs of deceased persons, according to the provisions of the statutes of this state;

7. To appoint guardians for minors, to remove them, to direct and control their conduct, and to settle their accounts, as prescribed by law;

8. To cause the admeasurement of dower to widows;

9. To take proof of and certify as to the heirs at law of deceased persons." (S. L., 1872, ch. 680.)

"The surrogate of each county shall have jurisdiction exclusive of every other surrogate, within the county for which he may be appointed, to take the proof of last wills and testaments of all deceased persons, in the following cases :

1. Where the testator at, or immediately previous to his death was an inhabitant of the county of such surrogate, in whatever place such death may have happened ;

2. Where the testator, not being an inhabitant of this state, shall die in the county of such surrogate leaving assets therein ;

3. Where the testator, not being an inhabitant of this state, shall die out of the state, leaving assets in the county of such surrogate ;

4. Where a testator, not being an inhabitant of this state shall die out of the state, not leaving assets therein, but assets of such testator shall thereafter come into the county of such surrogate ;

5. Where no surrogate has gained jurisdiction under either of the preceding clauses ; and any real estate devised by the testator shall be situated in the county of such surrogate." (S. L., 1837, chap. 460, § 1.)

The Surrogate's Courts shall be at all times open for the hearing of any matters within the jurisdiction thereof; and particularly on Monday of each week, it shall be the duty of every surrogate to attend at his office, to execute the powers and duties conferred on him. (2 R. S., 221, § 2.)

Every surrogate shall have power :

1. To issue subpœnas under his seal of office to compel the attendance of any witnesses residing or being in any part of the state, and the production of any paper material to any inquiry pending in his court, the form of which shall be similar to that used by courts of record in like cases ;

2. To punish disobedience to any such subpœna, and to punish witnesses for refusing to testify after appearing, in the same manner, and to the same extent as courts of record in similar cases, and by process similar in form to that used by courts of record;

3. To issue citations to parties in all matters cognizable in his court, and in the cases prescribed by law, to compel the appearance of such parties ;

4. To enforce all lawful orders, process and decrees of his court, by attachment against the persons of those who shall neglect or refuse to comply with such orders and decrees, or to execute such process ; which attachments shall be in form similar to that used by the court of chancery in analogous cases ;

5. To exemplify under his seal of office all transcripts of records, papers or proceedings therein; which shall be received in evidence in all courts, with the like effect as of the exemplifications of the records, papers and proceedings of courts of record;

6. To preserve order in his court during any judicial proceeding, by punishing contempts which amount to an actual interruption of business, or to an open and direct contempt of his authority or person, in the same manner and to the same extent as courts of record. (2 R. S., 221, as amended by chap. 320, 60 of Laws of 1830.)

He may also issue a commission to take testimony in the same manner as a court of record. (Chap. 460, S. L., 1837, § 77.)

The surrogate shall keep books :

1. For record of wills and proofs;

2. For letters testamentary and of general and special administration;

3. For minutes of proceedings, for orders and decrees, and for the testimony taken by him in relation to the granting or revocation of letters testamentary or of administration;

4. For appointments of guardians and the revocation of such appointments and for their accounts;

5. For proceedings in relation to the admeasurement of dower. (2 R. S., 222, § 7.)

He shall carefully file and keep all papers belonging to his court, and such papers and the books kept by him, shall belong and appertain to his office, and be delivered to his successor. (2 R. S., 223, § 8.)

He may adjourn any proceeding pending before him, and administer oaths to witnesses and in all other cases where it may be necessary in the exercise of his powers and duties. (S. L., 1837, chap. 460, § 62.)

To give efficiency to the process of the court it is provided that every sheriff, jailor, coroner or other executive officer, to whom any citation, subpœna, attachment or other process issued by a Surrogate's Court, may be directed or delivered for the purpose of being executed, shall execute the same in the same manner as if issued by a court of record, and, for any neglect or misfeasance therein, shall be subject to the same penalties, actions and proceedings as if the same had occurred in relation to any process issued by courts of record. (2 R. S., 223, § 9.)

The surrogate may not be counsel, solicitor or attorney for or against any executor, administrator, guardian or minor, in any civil action, over whom or whose accounts, he could have any jurisdiction by law. (2 R. S., 223, § 13.) Nor shall he practice or act as attorney, counselor or solicitor in his court, nor in any cause originating in such court; nor shall any partner of or person connected in law business with any surrogate, practice or act as attorney, solicitor or counselor in any cause or proceeding before such surrogate, or originating before him. (S. L., 1847, chap. 470, § 51.)

Each surrogate may, by order, appoint a clerk, who shall have power to certify under the seal of the surrogate, copies of all official papers, and sign as clerk to the Surrogate's Court, all citations and other writs and process required to be issued therefrom, and to administer oaths and to certify the same for use in such court and the surrogate may revoke such power and make a new appointment. (S. L., 1863, chap. 362, § 9.)

CHAPTER II.

Of Wills, their Execution and Probate.

SECTION I.

Of Wills, who may make them, and who may take under them.

A last will and testament, whether consisting of one or several instruments, is a disposition of the estate of the testator, to take effect only on his death.

The distinction formerly existing between *wills* and *testaments*, the former relating to the disposition of personal property, and the latter to real estate, has become obsolete, together with the technicality that a testamentary paper not appointing executors, was not a will, but only a codicil or "unsolemn will," the term codicil being derived from the diminutive of *Codex*, a will. (Williams on Exrs., 7.)

The last will and testament may consist of several papers, the will proper, and one or more codicils, the latter term being now applied to the supplementary papers adding to or taking from, or changing the dispositions made in the will, and they all together when proved constitute one will.

The power to made a will and testament, in this age we would say, is founded in natural right, although the right as now possessed was for a long time not recognized by the law, as respects the disposition of real estate; while even in the reign of Henry II, a man could only dispose by will of one third of his personalty, one other third descending to his next of kin, and the remainder to his wife. (2 Bl. Com., 492.)

But now, speaking generally, and with the limitations to be noted, all persons except idiots, persons of unsound mind and infants, may devise their real estate by a last will and testament duly executed. (2 R. S., 57.)

Married women formerly disabled, are now enabled to devise real estate in the same manner and with the like effect as if they were unmarried. (S. L., 1868, chap. 782, § 3.)

Every male person of the age of eighteen years or upward, and every female of the age of sixteen years, or upwards, of sound mind and memory, may give and bequeath his or her personal property by will in writing. (S. L., 1867, chap. 282, § 4.)

Such wills shall be in writing, and executed with the formalities prescribed by statute, except in the case of a nuncupative will bequeathing personal estate, made by a soldier while in actual military service, or by a mariner while at sea. (2 R. S., 60.)

The limitations as to the power to dispose of

‚real and personal property, are, that a man cannot so devise his land but that it will be subject to the dower of his widow. (1 R. S., 740.)

And no person having a husband, wife, child or parent shall, by his or her last will and testament, devise or bequeath to any benevolent, charitable, literary, scientific, religious or missionary society, association or corporation, in trust or otherwise, more than one-half part of his or her estate, after the payment of his or her debts, and any such devise or bequest shall be valid to the extent of one-half and no more. (S. L., 1860, chap. 260. See also S. L., 1848, chap. 319, § 6.)

Every citizen of the United States may take lands by devise. (1 R. S., 719, § 8.)

And any person may take personal property by bequest under any will, except a witness thereto. (2 R. S., 65, § 50.)

SECTION II.

The Execution of Wills.

A will of real or personal property, may be in any form or language ; but its execution must be accompanied with certain formalities, to the intent that the court may be assured that the instrument was really a will, and that the testator was not imposed upon as to the character of the instrument

Every last will and testament of real or personal property, or both, shall be executed and attested in the following manner.   (2 R. S., 63, § 40.)

1. It shall be subscribed by the testator at the end of the will.

The name may be written by another person in the presence of the testator and by his express direction. (*Robins* v. *Coryell*, 27 Barb., 556 ; *Campbell* v. *Logan*, 2 Brad., 90, and cases cited.)

But in such a case the statute requires that the writer shall also affix his own name as a witness. (2 R. S., 63, § 41.)

But his omission to do so does not affect the validity of the will, it only exposes him to a penalty of fifty dollars.   (Id.)

Subscription may also be made by the mark of the testator. (*Kenney* v. *Whitmarsh*, 16 Barb., 141, and cases cited ; *Van Hauswyck* v. *Wiese*, 44 Barb., 494.)

Such subscription must be at the end of the will.   And this may be limited to mean the foot of the formal instrument, notwithstanding other papers such as maps are annexed to it, and so referred to as to constitute them a part of the will. (*Tonnele* v. *Hall*, 4 N. Y., 140.)

It was accordingly held, that where the decedent signed so much of the instrument as made a full disposition of his property, and then there was un-

derwritten an appointment of executors which was
signed only by the witnesses, which was followed
by a direction to the executors to pay debts and
personal charges, the instrument was not signed
at the end, and probate was refused; (*McGuire* v.
Kerr, 2 Brad., 244;) but in a similar English case,
(*In the Goods of Howell*, 2 Curt., 342, see Wms.
on Exr's, 66, 67,) although probate was refused
to the executors, the will as appearing above the
signature of the decedent was admitted to probate,
and it must be supposed that the question of incompetency to some extent affected the decision in
McGuire v. *Kerr*.

So there should not be an unnecessary or unreasonable space between the end of the will and
the signature of the testator. (Wms. on Exr's, 68.)

The statute in England is similar to our own
and the rule there seems to be (*In the Goods of
Anderson*, 15 Jur., 92; 1 Eng. L. and Eq., 634,
note), that where the testator has placed his name
below the dispositive part of the will, the signature will, generally speaking be well placed. The
same rule will apply, where the will is signed below
and on the same side with the *testimonium* clause.
But when the signature is below the attestation
clause but not on the same side with the conclusion
of the dispositive part of the will or *testimonium*
clause, the will is not duly signed, unless the at-

testation clause follow the conclusion of the dispositive part or *testimonium* clause immediately, and without leaving a space for the signature of the testator. (See 16 Jur., 178; *In the goods of Milward*, 1 Curt., 912; *In the goods of Martin*, 3 Curt., 754.)

2. Such subscription shall be made by the testator in the presence of each of the attesting witnesses, or shall be acknowledged by him to have been so made, to each of the attesting witnesses. (2 R. S., 63, § 40, sub. 2.)

Where the execution is attested by acknowledgment, the signature must be shown to the witnesses and identified and recognized by the testator, and in some apt and proper manner acknowledged as his signature (*Lewis* v. *Lewis*, 11 N. Y., 220), and this acknowledgment would be good of a signature written by a party other than the testator.

But it has been held that where the decedent stated to the witnesses that the instrument shown to them was his will, and they *saw his signature*, it constituted a sufficient acknowledgment under the statute. (*Robinson* v. *Smith*, 13 Abb. Pr. R., 359.)

In this last case however, the handwriting of the testator was proved, and this decision is in accordance with the English rule. (See Wms. on Exr's, 75, and notes.)

But where the witnesses did not see the signature and the decedent said, " I declare the within to be my freewill and deed," probate was refused and the decree affirmed. (*Lewis* v. *Lewis, supra*).

But the decedent may have signed the will in the presence of one of the attesting witnesses and acknowledged his signature to the other. (*Hoysradt* v. *Kingman*, 22 N. Y., 372.)

So the acknowledgment may be made in answer to a question or may be made by signs. (*Coffin* v. *Coffin*, 23 N. Y., 9.)

3. The testator, at the time of making such subscription, or at the time of acknowledging the same, shall declare the instrument so subscribed to be his last will and testament. (2 R. S., 63, § 40, sub. 3.)

This act is termed the publication of the will, and is no less necessary than the subscription. It need not be in words, nor in any particular form; but the testator must personally make the fact of his own understanding and intention, known to both of the witnesses, by such express words, or signs, as to leave no doubt in their minds, that the instrument was his will. (See various cases *Remsen* v. *Brinckerhoff*, 26 Wen., 325 ; *Torrey* v. *Bowen*, 15 Barb., 304 ; *Burritt* v. *Silliman*, 16 id., 198; *Nipper* v. *Groesbeck*, 22 id., 670 ; *Chaffee* v. *Baptist Missionary Convention*, 10 Paige, 85; *Exparte Beers*,

2 Brad., 163; *Campbell* v. *Logan*, id., 90; *Brown*
v. *De Selding*, 4 Sand., 10.)

There must be a mutuality as to the knowledge
of all the parties in respect to the nature of the
instrument, and it was accordingly held by Surrogate Bradford, that where the subscribing witnesses
gained their knowledge as to the nature of the
instrument, only by looking at the attestation
clause, there was not a valid publication. (*Hunt* v.
Mortrie, 3 Brad., 322; *Wilson* v. *Hatterick*, 2 Brad.,
163.)

Yet, had the testator requested them to read the
attestation clause, it would seem to have been sufficient. The decision in this last case affirmed by
the Supreme Court, was reversed by the Court of
Appeals on other grounds. (26 Barb., 252; 23 N. Y.,
394.)

So in making publication the word *declare* is not
essential; " I acknowledge " is sufficient. (*Seguine*
v. *Seguine*, 2 Barb., 385.)

A reading of the will in the presence of the testator and the witnesses, followed immediately by
execution, in a sufficient publication. (*Van Hooser*
v. *Van Hooser*, 5 N. Y. Surr., 365; *Moore* v.
Moore, 2 Brad., 261; *Campbell* v. *Logan*, id., 90.)

The declaration must, however, be in all cases
distinct and unequivocal, and nothing short of
this will prevent the mischief and fraud designed

to be reached by the statute. The fact must, in some manner, although no particular form of words is required, be declared by the testator in the presence of the witnesses, that they may not only know the fact, but that they may know it from him, and that he understands it, and designs to give effect to it as his will. (*Lewis* v. *Lewis*, 11 N. Y., 226; See also *Exparte Beers*, 2 Brad., 163, See also *Coffin* v. *Coffin*, 23 N. Y., 9.)

4. There shall be at least two attesting witnesses, each of whom shall sign his name as a witness at the end of the will, at the request of the testator. (2 R. S., 63, § 40, sub. 4.)

In most of the New England states, at least three witnesses are required to a will devising real estate, but in this state, two or more, and these must sign their names. But where the execution in other respects was sufficient, and one of the two subscribing witnesses made her mark opposite her name, which was written by the other witness, and she acknowledged it to be her mark and signature, it was held that she did, within the requirements of the statute, *sign* her name. (*Meehan* v. *Rourke*, 2 Brad., 385; *Morris* v. *Kniffin*, 37 Barb., 336.)

It will be observed that a like holding has been had in the case of a subscription by the testator, but in the latter case the testator must *subscribe* while as to the witnesses it is required that they must *sign* their names, and this decision can only be sustained upon the presumption that the legislature in each case meant the same thing.

The witnesses shall sign their names at the end of the will. In practice it is usual to write out an attestation clause, certifying as to the performance of the requirements of the statute, and the names of the witnesses are affixed below this clause.

The principles applying to the signature of the testator, already commented on, will apply to the place of the signature of the witnesses, with this allowance, that an interval taken up by the attestation clause is permissible.

The witnesses shall sign their names at the request of the testator.

The request must be no less unequivocal than the publication, and the witnesses and testator must concur in the act; the one must by signs, words, or actions, make the request, and the others must understand the intention to request.

It may be communicated by a third party acting for the testator, the testator positively recognizing and adopting the act (*McDonough* v. *Laughlin*, 20 Barb., 238; *Hollenbeck* v. *Van Valkenburgh*, 5 How., 281). So the request may be implied; as where a third party told the testatrix in presence of the witnesses that they had come to witness the

will and she bowed her head in assent and she and
they signed it (*Brown* v. *De Selding*, 4 Sand., 10.
See also *Coffin* v. *Coffin*, 22 N. Y., 9) ; and where
the witnesses were told in the presence of the testator that they had been called in to witness his
will (*Doe* v. *Roe*, 2 Barb., 200); but the request
must be actual or constructive, as to both, not to
one only. (*Rutherford* v. *Rutherford*, 1 Den., 33.)

It is not necessary that the witnesses sign in
presence of the testator, in terms, but all the formalities must be concurred in and be complied with,
in the same interview. (*Ruddon* v. *McDonald*, 1
Brad., 352; *Vernam* v. *Spencer*, 3 Id., 16.) But
the compliance may be only substantial and not
literal (*Gamble* v. *Gamble*, 39 Barb., 373), and the
order in which they are observed is not material
(Id.) ; and it is a sufficient compliance with the
requirements as to publication and the request to
the witnesses, if the testator, or some other party,
whose act he adopts, reads aloud an attestation
clause, stating the fulfilment of the requirements
(*Remsen* v. *Brinckerhoff*, 26 Wen., 336) ; or reads
the will and attestation clause; or, where the
witnesses signed before the testator, and the paper
so signed was read to him with their signatures ;
for the statute, although it demands a compliance
with all the requirements, demands only a substantial compliance, (*Vaughan* v. *Burford*, 3 Brad., 83 ;

Carle v. *Underhill,* Id., 101 ; *Gamble* v. *Gamble,* 37 Barb., 373.)

Nor is the order in which the several acts are done, at all material, although the statute requires that they be done at the same time ; certainly not at the same instant, for that is impossible, but at the same interview, the acts, irrespective of their order, following without special interruption. (*Vaughan* v. *Burford, supra.*)

The fulfilment of these requirements, implies the mutual concurrence of the testator and the witnesses, in all the acts, the signing or acknowledgment by the testator ; the publication of the will, the request to the witnesses, and the signing by them, and therefore, if but partially performed only during the testator's life, the instrument being imperfect at his death, cannot take effect as his will. (See *Vaughan* v. *Spencer,* 3 Brad., 29.)

SECTION III.

Nuncupative Wills.

Wills disposing of personal property before the passage of the statute of frauds (29, Car. II.) might be made without any writing, the testator simply declaring his purpose before a sufficient number of witnesses. (Williams on Exr's, 95.) But as wills of this description are liable to great impositions,

and may occasion many perjuries, that statute
which has been adopted in our revised statutes (2
R. S., 60), provides, that no nuncupative, or unwritten will, bequeathing personal estate, shall be
valid, unless made by a soldier, while in actual
military service, or by a mariner, while at sea.

This provision as to soldiers, has been held, in
England, to be restricted by the words, " actual
military service " to such when on an expedition,
and not when quartered in barracks. (See Wms. on
Exr's, 96.) And herein it agreed with the civil
law, which provides thus. (Institutes of Justinian,
lib. II, tit. XI, §3, Cooper's translation.) " This privilege was granted by the imperial constitutions,
to military men, to be enjoyed only during actual
service, and while they lived in tents. For, if
veterans after dismission (discharge), or soldiers
out of camp, would make their testaments, they
must pursue the forms required of all the citizens
of Rome."

The word *mariners,* is held to include the whole
naval force, marines, as well as officers and seamen,
in the navy, and all persons in the merchant service. (Wms. on Exr's, 97.) The question has also
arisen, as to what constitutes being *at sea,* within
the meaning of the act, and the English courts
have held, that where a commander in chief of
the naval force at Jamaica, lived on shore, at his

official residence, only occasionally going on board
of his ship, he was not at sea, within the meaning
of the act (*The Earl of Euston* v. *Seymour*, 2
Curt., 339) ; but in a case where a mariner being
temporarily on shore at Montevideo, in South
America, received a wound, and died on shore,
having first made a nuncupative will, probate was
allowed. (*In the Goods of Lay*, 2 Curt., 375.)

The right to make an unwritten, or informal
will, having been adopted from the civil law, it
would seem that the rules of that law should follow the right as allowed by our statute. Accordingly, Mr. Surrogate Bradford, held, that the will
need not be made in immediate prospect of death,
in extremis, admitting to probate a nuncupative
will made at the wharf at Bremen, two days before
the testator died at sea, out of that port. (*Ex parte
Thompson*, 4 Brad., 154.) This decision is adverse
to that of the Supreme Court. (*Hubbard* v. *Hubbard*,
12 Barb., 155, also *Prince* v. *Hazleton*, 20 John.,
502). The case last cited, was carried to the Court
of Appeals but was decided on other grounds (8 N.
Y., 196), nor was this point essential to the decision. It was held, however, that a master of a
vessel lying at anchor in a bay of the ocean, near
the land, where the tide ebbs, and flows was at sea.

The point as to whether the will should be made
in extremis was also considered in *Botsford* v. *Krake*

(1 Abb. N. S., 112), and decided in accordance with the decisions in *Exparte Thompson, sup.*

The proof of a nuncupative will should be explicit and clear, especially should it appear, that the person making it, intended it as his will. In this connection I quote again from the Institutes. (Lib. II, tit. XI, § 1.) "The Emperor Trajan wrote as follows in his rescript to Catilius Severus concerning military testaments. 'The privilege given to military persons, that their testaments, in whatreve manner made, shall be valid, must be thus understood; it ought first to be apparent that a testament was made in some manner; for a testament may be made without writing by persons not military (before seven witnesses). And therefore, if it appear that the soldier, concerning whose goods question is now made before you, did, in the presence of witnesses, purposely called, declare what person should be his heir, and to what slaves he should give liberty, he shall be reputed to have made his testament without writing, and his will shall be ratified. But if it is only proved that he said to some one, as it often happens in discourse, *I appoint you my heir, or I leave you all my estate,* such words do not amount to a testament. Nor are any persons more interested than the soldiery, that words so spoken should not amount to a will; otherwise, witnesses might without difficulty be produced after the death of any military man, who would affirm, that they heard him bequeath his estate to whomever they please : and the true intention might be defeated.'"

The same rules should be observed in our courts.

The Roman law required two witnesses, but it would seem that as to proof, the common law rule would prevail, that the will be so proved as to satisfy the conscience of the court, and one witness if credible, is sufficient. (*Exparte Thompson, sup.*)

On sufficient proof, the surrogate will record the testamentary words as the will, together with all the proofs taken.

SECTION IV.

The Revocation of Wills.

It is of the very essence of a will, that the testator may at any time, revoke or alter its terms, and that is only his last will, which is in existence and in force at his death ; but, by the revised statutes, a will can only be revoked, either in fact, or impliedly, in the manner provided (2 R. S., 64, §§ 42, 43 and 44).

It may be revoked or altered

1st. By some other will in writing, or some writing of the testator, declaring such revocation, or alteration, and executed with the same formalities, with which the will itself was required by law to be executed.

Where the revocation is express, in the latest instrument, no question can arise; but the question has arisen, as to what disposition, other than an express revocation, will amount to that; and it has been accordingly held, that a will disposing of all the testator's estate, is so inconsistent with any former wills, as to be a revocation of them, even if the last does not in express terms revoke the former. (*Simmons* v. *Simmons*, 26 Barb., 68.)

A codicil also is to be deemed a revocation only to the same extent, in the absence of express words of revocation; but is to be construed with the will, giving so much effect to the will as is possible. (*Kane* v. *Astor's Exrs.*, 5 Sand., 467; *Conover* v. *Hoffman*, 1 Bosw., 214.)

But while no man can leave more than one last will and testament, that one may be made up of many separate instruments. (*Campbell* v. *Logan*, 2 Brad., 90.)

And where the last will, in order of execution, was inconsistent with a former one, as to some of its provisions only, not expressly revoking it, the last, will amount to a revocation of the former only *pro tanto*. (*Brant* v. *Wilson*, 8 Cow., 56.)

When it is claimed that the testator executed a subs quent will, not only its due execution must be proved; but it must appear that its provisions are inconsistent with the former one; and where its contents are not proved, or they cannot be ascertained, it will not amount to a revocation of the former will. (*Nelson* v. *McGiffert,* 3 Barb. Ch. R., 162. and cases cited.)

A will may be revoked

2dly. By burning, tearing, cancelling, obliterating, or destroying the will, with the intent, and for the purpose of revoking the same, by the testator himself, or by another person, in his presence, by his direction and consent; and when so done by another person, the direction and consent of the testator, and the fact of such injury, or destruction, shall be proved by at least two witnesses.

These acts must be done with the intent of effecting a revocation, and not through mistake; as where a testator tears or partially destroys a will, supposing it to be a former one.

And it would seem, that the destruction need not be complete, where the intent is perfectly clear; for it was held, that where the testator tore the will but a little, and threw it on the fire; but, it rolling off, was preserved by a servant, it was nevertheless a revocation. (*Bibb* v. *Thomas*, 2 W. Bl., 1043.)

Where a will was written in ink, and the testator subsequently drew a line in pencil through a clause, it was held to raise no presumption of a revocation, but to have been merely deliberative. (*Francis* v *Grover*, 5 Hare, 39.)

And where a will was partly obliterated by the testator, it was held not to amount to a revocation of the unobliterated parts; and in a case of a devise to two, the striking out of one name was held only to effect a revocation *pro tanto*. (*Sutton* v. *Sutton*, 2 Cowp., 812; *Larkins* v. *Larkins*, 3 B. & P., 16. But see *Short* v. *Smith*, 4 East., 419, *Redfield on Wills*, 404, etc.)

It is believed however that the last cases would not be approved in our courts, for if it appeared that the obliteration was made *animo revocandi* our courts would hold it to be a revocation under our statute. (*McPherson* v. *Clark*, 3 Brad., 92.)

A will is revoked in law:

First. If after the making of the will, disposing of all his estate, the testator shall marry and have issue of such marriage, born either in his life time, or after his death, and the wife, or the issue of such marriage shall be living at the death of the testator, such will shall be deemed revoked, unless provision shall have been made for such issue by some settlement, or unless such issue shall be provided for in the will, or in such way mentioned therein, as to show an intention not to make such provision; and no other evidence to rebut the pre-

sumption of such revocation shall be received.   (2
R. S., 64, § 43.)

So it will be seen, that marriage alone, will not
raise a presumption of revocation, but there must
be both marriage and the birth of issue, and the
surviving of either the wife, or such issue; and if
it be claimed that there was an intention to provide for the issue, that intention must be gathered
from the will only.

Of a similar character is the partial revocation
provided for   ·

Secondly. Whenever a testator shall have a
child born after the making of his will, either in
his life time or after his death, and shall die, leaving such child so afterborn, unprovided for by any
settlement, and neither provided for nor in any
way mentioned in his will, every such child shall
succeed to the same portion of the father's real and
personal estate as would have descended or been
distributed to such child, if the father had died intestate, and shall be entitled to recover the same
portion from the devisees and legatees in proportion to, and out of the parts devised and bequeathed
to them by such will.   (2 R. S., 65, § 49.)

But in this case, the will will be proved and
distribution and payment made under it, and the
remedy of the afterborn child will be against the
devisees or legatees.

Thirdly. A will executed by an unmnaried wo-man shall be deemed revoked by her subsequent marriage. (2 R. S., 64, § 44.) Nor will the will be deemed re-published by the death of her husband and her restoration to her former condition. (*Cotter* v. *Layer*, 2 P. Wms., 624 ; *Doe* v. *Staple*, 2 Term Rep., 685 ; 4 Kent. Com., 528.)

A change in the pecuniary or family circumstances of the testator, will not work a revocation, except as provided for by the statute.

A bond, agreement, or covenant made by the testator, for a valuable consideration, to convey any property devised or bequeathed in any will previously made, shall not be deemed a revocation of such previous devise or bequest, either at law or in equity. (2 R. S., 64, § 45.)

Nor shall a charge or incumbrance upon any real or personal estate for the purpose of securing the payment of money, or the performance of any covenant, be deemed a revocation. (Id., § 46.)

A conveyance, settlement, deed, or other act of a testator, by which his estate or interest in property previously devised or bequeathed to him shall be altered, but not wholly divested, shall not be deemed a revocation of the devise or bequest of such property, unless in the instrument by which such alteration is made, the intention is declared, that it shall operate as a revocation of such previous devise or bequest.   But if the provisions of the instrument by which such alteration is made, are wholly inconsistent with the terms and nature of such previous devise, or bequest, as, where the testator conveyed the property, was receiving a bond and mortgage thereon in payment, such instrument shall operate as a revocation of such devise or bequest, unless such provisions depend on a condition or contingency, and such condition be not performed, or such contingency did not happen. (2 R. S., 65, §§ 47, 48 ; *Langdon* v. *Astor's exr's*, 16 N. Y., 9 ; *Vandermark* v. *Vandermark*, 26 Barb., 416.)

It would seem to us however, that the term, *revocation*, is not strictly correct as used in the statute last quoted, but that the cases provided for, are simply cases where the devise or bequest shall *fail*, because the property, as to which it was intended to operate, had passed from the testator.

Under the civil law (Institutes, lib. II, tit. XVII), a will was revoked first, by the testator becoming an adopted son in the family of another, or by adopting an heir; second, by the making of a subsequent legal will; third, by the testator's suffering diminution, that is, the change of his condition from liberty to slavery, or loss of the right of a citizen, as a punishment for some crime.

A partial revocation shall take place as to the devise or bequest to any person who shall be a subscribing witness to the execution of any will wherein any beneficial devise, legacy, interest, or appointment of any real or personal estate shall be made to such witness, and such will cannot be proved without the testimony of such witness, as where there are but two witnesses, one of whom is a beneficiary, such witness may be compelled to testify as to the execution of the will in like manner as if no devise or bequest had been made to heirs. (2 R. S., 65, § 50.) But in this case, if such witness would have been entitled as heir at law or next of kin, of the testator, the share or portion which would have descended or been distributed to him, if there had been no will, may be recovered by him from the devisees or legatees taking under the will, so established by him as a witness. (Id., § 51.)

CHAPTER III.

THE POWERS OF THE EXECUTOR AND OTHER PERSONS
BEFORE PROBATE.

Formerly, any person intermeddling with the
goods of a deceased person, beyond preserving
them, became in the language of the law an executor or administrator *de son tort*, or in other words
by such intermeddling he became liable as an executor or administrator to the extent of assets received by him, to any person interested in the
estate of the deceased. (See Williams on Ex'rs,
210.)

But under our statutes the learning on this
subject has become obsolete, and the powers of
executors before probate and the powers and liabilities of unauthorized persons before administration granted are limited and defined.

"No executor named in a will, shall, before
letters testamentary are granted, have any power
to dispose of any part of the estate of the testator,
except to pay funeral charges, nor to interfere
with such estate in any manner, further than is
necessary, for its preservation." (2 R. S., 71, § 16.)

From this we learn, that while the common
law as to the power of the executor before pro-

bate, as to the preservation of the testator's property is in force (see Williams on Exr's, 240), he is restricted by the statute from any further interference. And, while by the common law, an executor before probate, might do almost all the acts incident to his office, except only some of these which relate to suits, and could not only take possession of the testator's assets, but dispose of them, could release debtors, and pay debts (Id.); now, he can only dispose of the assets for the particular purpose of paying funeral charges.

For the purpose of preserving the property of his testator he may, though he is not bound to do so, take it into his own possession, and for that purpose, may peaceably enter into the house of the heir where the effects may be, and take them. And when the effects, at the decease of his testator, are in the possession of parties not interested in the preservation of them, there can be no doubt of the duty of the executor to take them and properly care for them.

It may be remarked here, that any one performing the Christian service of burying a deceased person, will be allowed reasonable funeral expenses out of his estate, without reference to the rights of the next of kin or creditors, and in preference to their claims. (*Hasler* v. *Hasler*, 1 Brad., 248.)

3

Our statute as to executors *de son tort*, provides that " no person shall be liable to an action as executor of his own wrong, for having received, taken or interfered with the property or effects of a deceased person, but·shall be responsible as a wrong doer, in the proper action, to the executors, or general or special administrators of such deceased person, for the value of any property or effects so taken or received, and for all damages caused by his acts to the estate of the deceased. (2 R. S., 449, §17.)

And where the goods of the deceased are taken from the executor, he may, even before probate, bring his action to recover possession, and need not make profert of letters, for his action is founded on possession.

The statute further provides, that every person who shall take into his possession any of the assets of any testator or intestate, without being thereto duly authorized as executor, administrator or collector, or without authority from the executor, administrator or collector, shall be liable to account for the full value of such assets, to every person entitled thereto, and shall not be allowed to retain or deduct from such assets for any debt due to him.   (2 R. S., 81, § 60.)

CHAPTER IV.

PLEADING IN SURROGATE'S COURT.

It has been frequently said, hastily said, as we think, that there are no rules of pleading in this court.

But the courts have held (see *Fortes* v. *Wilbur*, 1 Paige, 540; *Van Vleck* v. *Burroughs*, 6 Barb., 344, and *Carle* v. *Underhill*, 3 Brad., 101), that litigants in this court, shall present their cases in such form, as to give the court notice of the propositions which they seek to establish, or controvert; and the practice which has almost universally obtained in the several Surrogate's Courts of this state, is exceedingly uniform. From that practice, clear and simple rules of pleading may be deduced.

The court itself, is the successor in its functions of the Ecclesiastical Courts of England. These courts were established in the time of William I, by act of parliament, and it was ordained, that they should decide according to the canon law: that is according to rules established by the ordinances of the Catholic councils or the decretals of the several popes. The Ecclesiastical Courts, like the Court of Chancery, in the earlier times in that country, was officered by clerical persons, unversed in the common law, as it then existed, and adopting the canons, they adopted also the method of procedure, which had descended from the Roman Courts, or their successors on the European continent. (See an admirable and complete history of the Surrogate's Courts, by Daly, justice, acting as surrogate, 15 Abb., 12.)

This method of procedure was far more simple and inartificial than that built up in the common law courts, and abolished in this state by the legislature in the adoption of the Code of Procedure. Indeed that code is, practically, an adoption of the rules of the civil law, as to pleading.

In the Ecclesiastical Courts, and others governed by the civil law, as we understand it, the suitor applied by petition, stating the facts upon which he relied for the relief he sought, and asking for such relief; and, when the parties all were gotten into court, the other party stated the facts upon which he relied to defeat the claim for relief, or, to oust the Court of Jurisdiction. We see traces of this practice in the chancery pleadings in use in this state until 1848. The party now styled the plaintiff, was then called the complainant, and he styled himself, " your orator," *anglice*, petitioner, or one who prays, in his bill of complaint.

The Ecclesiastical Courts preserved more nearly the practice of the civil law, and upon the petition of the suitor, issued the process, summons, citation, or subpœna, as the case required, and the party defending, was required to state, in apt language, the grounds of his defense.

Keeping in mind, then, the origin of the Surrogate's Courts, we can readily see how a system of pleading has arisen, and has been continued, and how it has, in some cases, been embodied in the revised statutes of the state.

The theory, then, on which the practice of the court is founded, is, that the court in all cases, is moved by petition, stating the facts which confer jurisdiction of the persons or matter, upon the court, and asking for the process or relief appropriate to the facts. The court thereupon enters the proper order for the relief, or for process, and if process is asked, issues it. On the return of the process, the party cited or summoned, if there be a contest, states, in apt language, the facts upon which he relies, and, the issue being made up, a trial is had.

It does not follow, that the petition shall always be actually made in form, but in all cases, it is believed, it is presumed to have been made.

Viewed with this explanation, the system of pleading in this court, is harmonious and perfect, and assimilates the practice as a whole, to the practice prescribed by the code for civil actions.

It will be our endeavor to show the manner of using this system, in enforcing the rights, and taking advantage of the remedies afforded by the Surrogate's Court.

CHAPTER V.

PROOF OF WILLS AND ISSUING OF LETTERS TESTAMENTARY.

SECTION I.

Of the petition for proof, and the issuing and service of a citation.

The application for the proof of any last will and testament, may be made, by any executor, devisee, or legatee, named therein, or by any person interested in the estate of the deceased. (S. L., 1837, chap. 460, § 4, p. 524.) The practice is, to move for the proper order in each case, upon a petition which ought to contain a statement of the facts conferring jurisdiction upon the court, and a request for the relief or action desired.

The petition for proof should therefore show :

1. The residence of the testator and his death ;

(*a.*) That he was an inhabitant of the county of the surrogate ;

(*b.*) That not being an inhabitant of the state, he died in the county of such surrogate, leaving assets therein ;

(*c.*) That not being an inhabitant of the state, he died out of the state, leaving assets in the county of such surrogate ;

(*d.*) That not being an inhabitant of the state he died out of the state, not leaving assets therein, but that assets of such testator have since his death come into the county of such surrogate ; or,

(*e*). That some real estate devised by testator is situated in the county of such surrogate, and no other surrogate has gained jurisdiction under either of the preceding clauses :

2. That he left a last will and testament with a description of it, if it be not produced with the petition;

3. That it relates to real or personal estate only, or to both ;

4. The heirs at law or the widow and next of kin, of the testator, or that the same cannot, after diligent inquiry, be ascertained, and

5. A prayer for the issuing of a citation requiring the heirs at law ; or the widow and next of kin, or all of them, to appear and attend the probate of the will.   (S. L., 1837, chap. 460, § 5, and S. L., 1863, chap. 362, § 1.)

The heirs of a deceased person are those who would succeed to his real estate under the statute in relation to descents, and are :

1. His children lawfully begotten, if he have any, and the children of such as shall have died ;

2. His father, if he be living ;

3. His mother, if she be living, or,

4. His collateral relations. (3 R. S., 41.)

The next of kin are :

1. The children and descendants;

2. The father ;

3. The mother and brother and sisters, and the legal representatives of such as shall have died, or,

4. His collateral relatives, not beyond brothers and sisters children. (2 R. S., 96.)

The heirs at law and next of kin of an illegitimate are :

1. His descendants;

2. His mother ;

3. His relatives on the part of the mother. (S. L., 1845, chap. 236.)

And illegitimate children, born since 1855, in default of lawful issue, are heirs at law and next of kin of their mothers. (S. L., 1855, chap. 547.)

The following is suggested as a proper form of petition :

In the matter of proving the last will and testament of John Doe, deceased.

To Moses Warren, Esq.,

    Surrogate of the county of Rensselaer.

The petition of Henry Williams of the town of Brunswick, in said county of Rensselaer, respectfully

shows, that he is one of the executors named in the
last will and testament of John Doe, deceased; that
said John Doe died, from disease (or otherwise), on or
about the first day of January last, at said town of
Brunswick which was the place of his residence at the
time of his death (or, that said John Doe, not being an
inhabitant of this state, but of the town and county of
Kenosha, in the state of Wisconsin, died in said town
of Brunswick, leaving assets in said town; or, that,
said John Doe, not being an inhabitant, but of the
town and county of Kenosha, in the state of Wisconsin,
died at Kenosha aforesaid about the first day of January last, leaving assets in said town of Brunswick; or,
that said John Doe, not being an inhabitant of this
state, died (as aforesaid) not leaving assets in this state,
but that since his decease certain of his assets have
come into said county of Rensselaer; or, that said
John Doe, not being an inhabitant of this state but
(residence and death as before), and some real estate
devised by the will hereinafter mentioned is situated
in said county of Rensselaer, and no other application
has been made for the probate of his will); that the
instrument herewith presented, purporting to be the
last will and testament of the said deceased, and bearing date the 25th day of December, 1859, your petitioner verily believes to be such last will and testament,
and that it relates to both real and personal estate.

And your petitioner further shows that the said
deceased left him surviving, his widow Mary Doe,
his children .... and .... residing
in the town of .... in the county of ....
and state of .... and his grand children ....
and .... residing in the town of Randall, in
the county of Kenosha, and state of Wisconsin,
and .... whose place of residence is unknown,

and which, after inquiry of the mother of said ....,
cannot be ascertained, who are all, and the only heirs
at law and next of kin of the said deceased.

Your petitioner therefore prays that a citation may
issue to the said heirs at law and next of kin to the
deceased, requiring them to appear in this court on
such day as shall seem meet, to attend the probate of
said last will and testament according to law.

Dated Troy, February 22, 1874.

JOHN DOE.

State of New York, } ss:
  Rensselaer county }

John Doe being duly sworn says that the foregoing
petition by him subscribed is true.

JOHN DOE.

Sworn before me this }
    day of .... 1874, }

JAMES LANSING,
Commissioner of Deeds, Troy, N. Y.

This petition must be verified as above and the
oath can be administered by any officer authorized
to administer oaths.

The surrogate on the filing of the petition enters
an order that a citation issue. The following may
serve as a form. The order is recorded in his book
of special minutes.

ORDER FOR CITATION.

At a Surrogate's Court held in and for the county of .... at the Court House in the village of .... on the ...... day of .... 1874.

Present — Hon. ...., Surrogate.

In the matter of the will

of

..................., deceased.

On reading and filing the petition of .... duly verified, propounding for probate, a paper purporting to be the last will and testament of .... late of the town of .... deceased.

Ordered, that a citation issue to the heirs at law and widow and next of kin of said deceased, pursuant to the prayer of said petition, requiring them to appear in this court on the ...... day of .... 1874, at ten o'clock A.M. to attend the probate of said will.

..................., *Surrogate.*

A citation is thereupon issued and it shall state the name of the person upon whose petition the same is issued, and whether the will relate to real or personal estate, exclusively, or to both, and shall be directed to the proper persons by name. (S. L., 1837, chap. 460, § 7, as amended 1863.)

Under the act of 1837, the citation was directed to the general guardians of minors, if any such resided in the state, and before the issuing of the citation, a special guardian was appointed for

minors having no general guardians, and the citation was also directed to such special guardian.
But, since the statute of 1863, the petition need
not state whether any parties are minors, and no
special guardian is appointed until the return of
the citation.   (S. L., 1863, chap. 362.)

CITATION.

To Mary Williams and Sarah Boyd, of the town of
Brunswick in the county of Rensselaer and state of
New York, William Jones, Henry Jones, and Sarah
Jones, of this town of Randall, in the county of Kenosha, in the state of Wisconsin, and James Jones,
whose place of residence is unknown, and which cannot after diligent inquiry be ascertained, heirs at law
and next of kin of Henry Williams, late of the town
of Brunswick, in the county of Rensselaer, deceased.

You and each of you are cited and required to appear at the office of our surrogate in the city of Troy,
in the county of Rensselaer, on the tenth day of April,
1862, at ten o'clock, A. M., of that day, to attend the
probate of the will of said deceased, which will then
be offered for probate, by Henry Williams, an executor
named therein, and which relates to both real and personal estate.

In testimony whereof, we have caused the seal
[L. S.]   of office of our said surrogate to be hereto
affixed.

Witness, Moses Warren, surrogate of the county
of Rensselaer, the twenty-second day of
February, A.D., 1862.

MOSES WARREN,
Surrogate.

The time limited for the return of the citation, is practically regulated by the time required for service, which is not less than eight, nor more than ninety days, and the mode and time of service is prescribed by law.

The citation, shall be served on the persons to whom it shall be directed as follows : (S. L., 1837, chap. 460, amended S. L., 1840, chap. 1, and S. L., 1863, chap. 362.)

1. On such as reside in the same county with the surrogate, or an adjoining county, by delivering a copy to such person, at least eight days before the day appointed for taking the proof, or, by leaving a copy at least eight days as aforesaid, at the dwelling house or other place of residence of such person, with some individual of suitable age and discretion, and under such circumstances as shall induce a reasonable presumption in the mind of the surrogate that the copy came to the hands or knowledge of the person to be served with it, in time for him to attend the probate of the will ;

2. On such as reside in any other county (other than the county of the surrogate and the county adjoining thereto,) in this state, by delivering a copy personally to such person, or leaving it at his dwelling house or other place of residence in the manner and under the circumstances above men-

tioned, at least fifteen days before the day appointed for taking the proof;

3. On such persons as do not reside in this state, citations may be served by delivering a copy personally to such persons, or leaving it at his or her dwelling house or other place of residence not less than fifteen days, nor more than ninety days before the day appointed for taking proof of any will; and on such persons as do not reside in this state, or whose places of residence cannot be ascertained, by publishing a copy of the citation in the state paper for six weeks previous to the day appointed for taking proof.

If such citation be directed to a minor under the age of fourteen years, within this state, whose name and residence can be ascertained, a copy thereof shall be delivered to such minor personally, and also to his father, mother, or guardian, or, if there be no such father, mother, or guardian within this state, then to any person having the care and control of such minor, or with whom he shall reside or in whose service he shall be employed.

In all cases where the service is made by publication, a copy of said citation shall also be mailed to each person so served at his place of residence, or post office address, if the same can be ascertained, at least thirty days before the return day thereof. (S. L., 1863, chap. 362.)

In all cases where the service is made by leaving a copy with some person of suitable age and discretion, instead of the person named in the citation, the proof of service should show, not only the absence from home of the party served, but the probable duration of his absence, so that the surrogate may be able reasonably to presume that he had returned home in time to have received the copy, and attend the court on the return day.

Therefore, if it shall appear that the party was far from home and, at the time of service, not expected to return in due time to receive the notice, the surrogate will adjourn the proceedings and issue a new citation to the parties not properly served in the first instance.

Before proceeding to take the proof of any will, the surrogate shall require satisfactory evidence by affidavit, of the service of the citation in the mode prescribed by law. (S. L., 1837, chap. 460, § 9.)

This language can scarcely be considered imperative, but rather directory, and the practice has long been to admit as proof of service, the admission of service, signed by the parties served, and with their signatures proved by affidavit, and it is not doubted that the certificate of service made by a sheriff would give the court jurisdiction; for sheriffs are expressly charged with the duty of executing the process of this court in the same manner as if issued by courts of record. (2 R. S., 223, § 9.)

PROOF OF SERVICE OF CITATION.

Rensselaer county, ss :

Henry Williams of the town of Brunswick, in said county, being duly sworn, says, that on the first day of April, 1862, at said tow of Brunswi he served the withi citation on Mary William and Sa Boyd, therein named by deliverin to, and leavi with each a copy thereof; that at least thirty days before the tenth day of April, 1862, he served the same on William Jones, Henry Jone and Sar Jones, therein named, by depositi copi thereo in the post office in the city of Troy, in said county, each securely folded and enclos in an envelope, havi thereo a proper stamp for the prepayment of the proper postage, directed to each of them respectively at Rand Kenosha county, Wis.

[That at least fifteen days before the tenth day of April, 1862 he served the same on Henr Jone and Sarah Jone therein named, who are minor by delivering to each a copy thereof, in presence of John Jones, their father with whom the reside, in th town of Randal Kenos county, Wis. and at the same time by delivering to said John Jones, a cop of said citation for each of said minors.]

Henry Williams.

Sworn before me this 10th }
   day of April, 1872. }
       James Lansing,
          Com'r of Deeds, Troy, N. Y.

4

The appearance of a party of full age, either in person or by an attorney, is practically deemed a sufficient waiver of service.

On the return day, the surrogate will enter the appearances and the default of those not appearing, and if it then shall appear that some proper parties were omitted in the petition or citation, or, that the service is not complete, he will enter an order for an adjournment and for a new citation, making it returnable on the adjourned day. (S. L., 1837, chap. 460, § 9.) But in case it shall appear that some proper parties, heirs at law or next of kin, were, through ignorance of their names, or from any other cause, omitted from the first petition, the proper course undoubtedly would be, at any time, on discovering the omission, or on the return day, to make a supplementary petition, stating the omission and the cause of it, and giving the names of such parties, upon which a new citation would issue of course.

Should it be desired to save the time necessary for service, and all the parties interested are of full age, they may join in the petition for immediate proof of the will and the surrogate may then enter an order that the proof be taken without delay. (*Everts* v. *Everts*, 62 Barb., 577.)

But this course cannot be taken where minors are interested, for the reason that no special guar-

dian can now be appointed for them until the
return day of the citation, as will hereafter be
seen, and it is submitted that a special guardian
can in no case waive the formalities required by
law, he being appointed expressly to see that these
formalities are complied with.

The expenses of the executor or other person
who shall serve the citation, or the time of a person
employed for that purpose will be allowed as part
of the expenses of administration, without regard
to creditors, as well as the expense of advertising
in the state paper.

The rate as fixed by law for publication is seventy-
five cents per folio of one hundred words for the first
insertion and fifty cents per folio for each subsequent insertion. (S. L., 1869, ch. 831.)

At the time of the issuing of the citation, or at
any other time, a subpœna will issue signed by
the surrogate or the clerk of his court, to compel
the attendance of witnesses. This subpœna also
issues upon the order of the court which is entered
in the surrogate's minutes, and a clause may be
added to such subpœna, commanding any person
having the custody of or power over any will to
produce the same before the surrogate for the purpose of proof. Disobedience to the subpœna is
punished by commitment (see Contempts, *post*) ;
but if any person be committed for not producing

any will, he may be discharged on producing the same to the surrogate who committed him, by an order for that purpose.   (2 R. S., 58.)

The fees of witnesses are the same as in Courts of Record; fifty cents for each day's attendance and where the witness resides more than three miles from the place of trial, traveling fees of four cents per mile going and returning.

SECTION II.

Of the Proof of the Will.

The citation having been duly served, and due proof of the service having been filed with the surrogate, or, all the parties interested appearing, the surrogate enters in his minutes the proceedings and appearances, and shall ascertain whether any, and which of the parties interested as heirs, widow or next of kin are minors, or lunatic or an idiot (S. L., 1872, chap. 693), and the names and places of residence of their general guardians if they have any; and if there shall be no general guardian within this state, who shall have been served with the citation, the surrogate shall, by an order to be entered, appoint a special guardian for such minors, idiots or lunatics to take care of their interest, in the premises.   The special guardian shall, however, before his appointment, consent in writing to serve, and his consent shall be filed with the surrogate.

CONSENT TO BE APPOINTED SPECIAL GUARDIAN.

Surrogate's Court, Rensselaer county.

In the matter of proving the last
will and testament

of

...................., deceased.

I, William Lord, of the town of Brunswick, do hereby consent that I may be appointed by the surrogate of the county of Rensselaer, special guardian of Henry Jones, and Sarah Jones, infant heirs at law and next of kin of ...., late of the town of Brunswick, deceased, for the sole purpose of taking care of the interests of said infants in the matter of proving the last will and testament of said deceased.

Dated April 10, 1874.

WILLIAM LORD.

ORDER APPOINTING SPECIAL GUARDIAN.

At a Surrogate's Court, held in and for the county of Rensselaer, at the Court House in the city of N. Y., on the ...... day of .... 1874.

Present — Hon. Moses Warren, Surrogate.

In the matter of proving the last
will and testament

of

....,"deceased.

The citation in this matter having been duly served, according to law, and it appearing that ....

and ...., named in said citation, heirs at law and next of kin of said deceased, are infants.

Ordered that William Lord, of the town of Brunswick be and he is hereby appointed special guardian of said infants, for the sole purpose of taking care of the interests of said infants in the matter of proving the last will and testament of said deceased.

MOSES WARREN, *Surrogate.*

The special guardian shall appear in person in the proceeding before any evidence shall be taken in regard to the will. The testamentary guardian named in the will to be proved, shall not, for this purpose, be deemed a general guardian. (S. L., 1863, chap. 362, amending chap. 460, S. L., 1837, as amended chap. 1, 1840.)

The parties being all in court, if any of them desire to contest the probate, they now signify their desire and file their objections to the probate.

OBJECTIONS TO PROBATE.

Surrogate's Court, Rensselaer county.

In the matter of the will
of
..................., deceased.

To Hon. Moses Warren, Surrogate.

A B and C D, heirs at law and next of kin of the above named deceased, respectfully object to the probate of the paper writing propounded as the last will and testament of said deceased, and say that said paper writing is not the last will and testament of the said deceased.

A. B.

JAMES LANSING,   C. D.
        Proctor.

The above form puts in issue all the material allegations in the petition.

Legatees not named in the will propounded may ask to be admitted parties to the proceeding and act with the proponent in support of the probate. In like mannnr any person affected by the probate and not named in the citation may ask to be admitted.   This is called intervention, and for the purpose a petition should be filed. (*Walsh* v. *Ryan*, 1 Brad., 433; *Foster* v. *Tyler*, 7 Paige, 51.)

It has also been held, that a legatee, not one of the next of kin, named in a former will, may oppose the probate of a subsequent will and be permitted to intervene in the same manner. (*Matter of will of James Malcom*, Dayton's Sur., 3d ed., 159.)

PETITION FOR LEAVE TO INTERVENE.

Surrrogate's Court, Rensselaer county.

In the matter of proving the will
of
...................., deceased.

To Moses Warren, Esq.,

Surrogate of the county of Rensselaer :

The petition of ...., of the ....
of ...., in said county, respectfully shows :

That your petitioner is a legatee named in the will
of ...., deceased, proceedings for the proof
of which are now pending in this court. That your
petitioner is not one of the heirs at law or next of kin
of said deceased, and therefore has no standing in this
court, except by leave thereof.

Your petitioner's interests would be beneficially
affected by the proof of said will and he therefore
prays leave to intervene in said proceedings and appear therein, to the end that he may care for his own
interests.

Dated, April 15, 1874.

(Signed)   ....

Rensselaer county, ss :

.................., being duly sworn, says that the foregoing petition by him subscribed, is true.

(Signed)   ....

Sworn before me, this ...... }
day of April, 1874.   }

JAMES LANSING,
Com'r of Deeds, Troy, N. Y.

ORDER THAT PARTY MAY INTERVENE.

At a Surrogate's Court held in and for the county
of ...., at the ...., in
the .... of ...., on the
.... day of ...., 187...
Present — ...., Surrogate.

In the matter of proving the will
of
...................., deceased.

On reading and filing the petition of ....,
from which it appears that said petitioner is a legatee
named in the will of said deceased, and not being one
of the heirs-at-law or next of kin, of said deceased, and
it appearing that said petitioner is interested in the
proof of said will :

Ordered that said .... have leave to intervene in these proceedings, and appear therein, and
move in the matter as he shall be advised.

(Signed),

...................., *Surrogate.*

On the examination, at least two of the witnesses, if so many are living in this state, of sound
mind, and not disabled from age, sickness, or infirmity from attending, shall be produced and examined ; and the death, absence (from the state),
insanity, sickness, or other infirmity, of any of
them shall be satisfactorily shown to the surrogate
taking such proof. (S. L., 1837, chap. 460, § 10.)

And, in case the probate is contested, if any person having the right to contest the same, shall file with the surrogate a request in writing, that all the witnesses to the will shall be examined, then all the witnesses to the will, who are living in this state, and of sound mind, and who are not disabled from age, sickness, or infirmity from attending, shall be produced and examined; and the death, absence, insanity, sickness or other infirmity of any of them, shall be satisfactorily shown to the surrogate taking such proof. (Id., § 11.)

If any such aged, sick or infirm witness reside in the same county with the surrogate, it shall be the duty of the surrogate, after examining the other witnesses, to proceed, without unnecessary delay, to the dwelling house, or other place of residence of such witness, and there, in the presence of such persons as may choose to attend, proceed to take the examination of such persons in the same manner and with the like effect, as though such witness had attended and been examined before such surrogate on the return of the citation. (Id., § 12.)

If such aged, sick, or infirm witness reside in a different county from the surrogate, and it shall not be probable that his attendance can be procured within a reasonable time, to which the surrogate may, in his discretion, adjourn the proceeding for that purpose, the surrogate may, in such case, after having examined the other witnesses, make an order adjourning the proceeding in his court to some future day, and directing that such aged, sick, or infirm witness be examined before the surrogate of the county in which he resides, and specifying some Monday, on or before which the order shall be delivered to the surrogate directed to take the examination; a copy of which order, under the seal of the surrogate making the same, together with the original will, shall be delivered to the person applying for the probate, to be transmitted to the surrogate directed to take the examination. (Id., § 13.)

The following may serve as the order to be made.

ORDER FOR EXAMINATION.

At a Surrogate's Court held in and for the county of .... at the surrogate's office in the .... of ....
on the ...... day of .... 1874.
Present — Hon. Moses Warren, Surrogate.

In the matter of the application
for the proof of the will
of
...................., deceased.

Application having been made for the probate of the will of the above named deceased and it appearing satisfactorily to the surrogate, that .... one of the witnesses to said will is aged (sick or infirm), and resides in the town of .... in the county of .... and that it is not probable that his attendance can be procured within a reasonable time.

Ordered that said .... be examined before the surrogate of the said county of ....

It is further ordered that this order together with the will offered for probate, be delivered to said surrogate of said county of .... on or before Monday the ...... day of .... next.

    Witness Moses Warren surrogate and the seal
[L.S.]   of said court the day and year first above
    written.

                MOSES WARREN,
                    Surrogate.

The surrogate, by whom any such order and will shall be received, shall, on the Monday mentioned in such order, appoint a time and place for taking such examination and give notice thereof to any person who may attend such surrogate for the purpose of hearing such examination, and at the time and place so appointed, or at such other time and place as it may be found necessary to designate by adjournment, the surrogate, in the presence of such persons as may choose to attend, shall proceed to take the examination of such aged, sick, or infirm witness, in the same manner, and with the like effect, as though such witness had attended and been examined before the surrogate having original jurisdiction on the return of the citation. Such surrogate may issue subpœnas, under his seal of office, to compel the attendance of any such witness or witnesses for the purposes aforesaid, in like manner and with the like effect, as in cases in which he has original jurisdiction. (Id., § 14.)

This may serve as the order to be made by the surrogate delegated to take the proofs.

ORDER FOR EXAMINATION.

At a Surrogate's Court held in and for the county of Washington at the surrogate's office in the village of Salem, on the ......
of ...., 1874.

Present — Hon. Lonson Fraser, Surrogate.

In the matter of the application
for probate of the will
of
..................., deceased.

Application having been made to the surrogate of the county of Rensselaer for probate of the will of the above named deceased, and an order having been made by said surrogate of Rensselaer county that, ..., an aged witness to said will who resides in the town of Salem, in the county of Washington, bo examined before the surrogate of the county of Washington. Ordered that the examination of said ...., be

taken at his residence in the town of Salem aforesaid
on the ...... day of ...., next at ten o'clock
in the forenoon.

LONSON FRASER,

Surrogate.

Such examination shall be reduced to writing,
and be subscribed by the witness; and the examination, together with a statement of the proceedings before the surrogate taking the same, shall be
certified by him under his seal of office and be
returned without delay to the surrogate who ordered the examination.   (Id., § 15.)

The following is suggested as the return to be
made under the order :

In the matter of the application
    for probate of the will
            of
.................., deceased.

I, Lonson Fraser, surrogate of the county of Washington, do certify that an order having been made by
the surrogate of the county of Rensselaer, for the
examination of ...., an aged witness to the
above mentioned will, resident in the town of Salem,
which said order is annexed hereto marked A, I, on
the ...... day of ...., 1874, made an order,
that the examination of said aged witness be taken at
his residence in the town of Salem, on the ...... day
of ...., 1874, a copy of which last mentioned
order is hereto annexed marked B.

And I further certify that on the said .... day of
..................., 1874, I attended at the time and place
mentioned in said last mentioned order and took the
examination of said witness upon oath, which examination was reduced to writing and subscribed by said
witness and is hereto annexed marked C.

Witness my hand and the seal of this court this
[SEAL]   ...... day of ...., 1874.

LONSON FRASER,
Surrogate.

These provisions in relation to the examination
of aged, sick and infirm witnesses, are by chap. 129,
laws of 1841, entitled "An act concerning the
proof of wills," extended to all witnesses in the proceeding, under infirmity and resident in another
county, provided that the surrogate before whom
the will is propounded shall be satisfied that the
testimony of such witnesses is material.

The third section of the same act provides that
notice of the time and place of examining such
witnesses, shall be given to all the parties appearing
on the proof, for the same length of time as is required in case of trials of issues of fact in the
Supreme Court.

The application for the examination of witnesses,
not subscribing witnesses, should show under oath,
that the testimony of such witnesses is material.

A Commission may issue.

Where it becomes necessary to have the examination of a witness, out of the state, either a subscribing witness or any other witness, a commission can be obtained according to the provisions of the revised statutes. (2 R. S., 393.) The commission issues on motion based upon an affidavit, either of the party applying, or of any other person who can show the materiality of the testimony and the non-residence of the witness, and upon notice of ten days, specifying the terms of the order applied for. The granting of the motion is in the discretion of the surrogate, as is the similar proceeding in the Supreme Court in the discretion of that court, and the party opposing may show by affidavit, any fact tending to show the unfitness of any commissioner.

The commission will issue upon the order of the court which is to be entered in the special minutes.

Practically, the parties may meet, agree upon the commission and upon the interrogatories, and on appearing before the surrogate without notice the order for the commission will be entered and the commission issue in accordance with the agreement of the parties, or, if there be no parties appearing except the proponent for probate, a commission will issue upon the filing of the affidavit.

The following are convenient forms for the affidavit, notice, order, and commission.

AFFIDAVIT.

Surrogate's Court, Rensselaer county.

In the matter of the application
for probate of the will
of
John Doe, deceased.

Rensselaer county, ss:

Lewis Jones, being duly sworn, says that he is one of
the executors named in the will of John Doe, late of
the city of Troy, in said county, deceased, proceedings
for the proof of whose will are now pending in this
court: That Henry Jones residing in the city of Milwaukee, in the state of Wisconsin, is a necessary and
material witness in this proceeding in support of the
probate of said will as he is advised by James Lansing, Esq., his counsel in this proceeding, after stating
to him the facts which deponent expects to prove by
said Henry Jones, and deponent prays for a commission
to examine said Henry Jones accordingly.

LEWIS JONES.

Sworn before me this 5th day }
   of December, 1873. }

D. DUNN,
Com'r of Deeds, Troy, N. Y.

NOTICE.

(Title, *same as affidavit*).

Please take notice, that upon an affidavit of which
the annexed is a copy, a motion will be made in this
matter, before the surrogate of Rensselaer county at
his office in the Court House in the city of Troy, on

the 17th day of December 1873, at ten o'clock in the
forenoon of that day, for an order that a commission
issue out of and under the seal of this court, to be
directed to Robert N. Austin, Esq., residing in the city
of Milwaukee, in the state of Wisconsin, counselor at
law, authorizing him to examine Henry Jones, a witness residing in said city of Milwaukee, on oath, in
support of the proof of the will propounded in this proceeding, on interrogatories to be annexed to said commission.

Dated Troy, Dec. 5, 1873.

                                  Yours, etc.
To George Scott, Esq.   JAMES LANSING,
     William Low, Esq.   *Proctor, for Executor.*
     Dennis Miller jr., sp'l guardian.

ORDER.

At a Surrogate's Court held in and for the county
    of Rensselaer, at the Court House in the
    city of Troy, on the 17th day of Decem-
    ber, 1873.

        Present — Hon. Moses Warren, Surrogate.

In the matter of the application
    for probate of the will
            of
    John Doe, deceased.

On reading and filing the affidavit of Lewis Jones,
the executor named in the paper writing purporting to
be the last will and testament of John Doe, late of
Troy, deceased, and it appearing therefrom, that Henry
Jones, residing in the city of Milwaukee, in the state of
Wisconsin, is a material witness in this matter, and on
proof of due service of notice of this motion upon all

the parties who have appeared in this proceeding, and after hearing Mr. La Mott W. Rhodes, in opposition, ordered that a commission issue out of and under the seal of this court, directed to Robert N. Austin, Esq., counselor at law, in the said city of Milwaukee, authorizing him to take the testimony of the said Henry Jones, on oath, upon interrogatories to be annexed to said commission, and that the return thereon may be sent by mail, addressed to the surrogate of the county of Rensselaer.

Moses Warren,
Surrogate.

COMMISSION.

The people of the state of New York to Robert N. Austin, Esq., counselor at law, residing in the city of Milwaukee, in the state of Wisconsin.

Know, ye, that with full faith in your prudence [L. S.] and competency, we have appointed you a commissioner, and by these presents do authorize you to examine Henry Jones residing in the city of Milwaukee, aforesaid, as a witness, in the matter of the application for the probate of the will of John Doe, late of the city of Troy, deceased, upon the interrogatories annexed to this commission; to take and certify the depositions of the said witness and return the same according to the directions hereunto annexed.

Witness, Moses Warren, surrogate of our county of Rensselaer, at the city of Troy this seventeenth day of December in the year one thousand eight hundred and seventy-three.

Moses Warren,
Surrogate.

James Lansing,
Proctor.

INTERROGATORIES TO SUBSCRIBING WITNESS.

Interrogatories to be administered to Henry Jones, a witness to be produced, sworn and examined, before Robert N. Austin, Esq., commissioner, in the city of Milwaukee, in the state of Wisconsin, in the matter of the application for probate of the will of John Doe, deceased, now pending before the surrogate of the county of Rensselaer, under and in pursuance of the commission hereunto annexed.

First Interrogatory. What is your name, your age, your occupation or profession, and where do you reside?

Second Interrogatory. Did you know John Doe, late of the city of Troy, in the state of New York, in his lifetime? How long did you know him?

Third Interrogatory. Look at the instrument in writing hereunto annexed, dated Dec. 5, 1871, purporting to be the last will and testament of the said John Doe, and say whether you saw the said John Doe sign the same? State when he signed it, the place where, and who were present at the time?

Fourth Interrogatory. State whether at the time the said John Doe signed said instrument anything was said and by whom, as to what the instrument was? What was said on that subject?

Fifth Interrogatory. Did you sign the instrument? If yea, at whose request did you sign?

Sixth Interrogatory. Who else signed it beside yourself and at whose request? When did you and Sarah Williams sign?

Seventh Interrogatory. State whether, in your opinion at the time spoken of, the said John Doe was of sound mind, and whether you observed any indication that he was under restraint or subject to the influence of any person at that time?

Eighth Interrogatory. What was the age of the said John Doe at that time? Was he a citizen of the United States?

Ninth Interrogatory. Do you know any other matter or thing relating to the execution of the said paper and the condition of the mind of the said John Doe, at that time?

The interrogatories above settled are to be indorsed by the surrogate:

" Allowed Jan. 17, 1873,

Moses Warren,
Surrogate."

The directions in regard to the execution of the commission, are the same as in case of a commission issued out of the Supreme Court. The commission, returns, depositions and exhibits thereto annexed shall remain on file in the office of the surrogate to whom the same were addressed. (2 R. S., 395, § 22.)

When, however, the witnesses to the will are . produced before the surrogate and there is no contest, it is usual to take their depositions jointly.

DEPOSITION.

Surrogate's Court, Rensselaer county.

In the matter of proving the last
will and testament
of
John Doe, deceased.

Rensselaer county, ss :

Lewis Jones of the town of Nassau, and Grove P. Jenks, of the town of Schodack in said county, being each duly sworn, do each depose and say and each for himself says, that he is a subscribing witness to the last will and testament of John Doe late of the city of Troy, in said county, deceased, and that the said deceased did, on the ...... day of ...., 1869, in the presence of these deponents, subscribe his name at the end of the instrument which is now shown to these deponents and which purports to be the last will and testament of the said deceased, and which bears date on the day last aforesaid, and that the said deceased at the time of subscribing his name as aforesaid, declared said instrument to be his last will and testament and requested these deponents to subscribe the same as witnesses, and that these deponents did thereupon subscribe their names at the end of said will as witnesses.

And these deponents further say, that at the time of subscribing said instrument as aforesaid, the said John

Doe, was of sound mind and memory, above twenty-one years of age and not under any restraint, and was a citizen of the United States.

LEWIS JONES,
GROVE P. JENKS.

Subscribed and sworn before me, this }
    5th day of December, 1873.   }

MOSES WARREN,
Surrogate.

As to the evidence and proceedings in case the will is contested, see the next section.

If it shall appear, upon the proof so taken, that such will was duly executed; that the testator, at the time of executing the same, was in all respects competent to devise real estate and not under restraint, the said will and the proofs and examinations so taken, shall be recorded in a book to be provided by the surrogate, and the record thereof shall be signed by him (2 R. S., 58, § 14), and this section is made applicable to wills of personal estate. (S. L., 1837, chap. 460, § 18.) But notwithstanding this, the will of an alien or of an infant can be proved as a will of personal estate.

ORDER ADMITTING WILL TO PROBATE.

At a Surrogate's Court held in and for the county of .... at the surrogate's office in the city of .... on the 5th day of December, 1873.

Present — Hon. ...., Surrogate.

In the matter of proving the last
  will and testament
      of
...................., deceased.

On reading and filing due proof of the service of the citation issued in this matter, and upon due proof of the execution of the paper propounded as the last will and testament of ...., late of the .... of ...., in said county, deceased, bearing date the .... day of ...., 1870, A B, and C D, heirs-at-law and next of kin, appearing in person and A F, G H, and A R, infants, heirs at law and next of kin of said deceased, appearing by ...., their special guardian, and it appearing by such proof, that the said will was duly executed; that the testator at the time of executing the same, was of full age for making a will, was of sound mind and memory, and not under restraint, and in all respects competent to devise real estate.

It is ordered, adjudged, and declared, that the said paper purporting to be the last will and testament of the said ...., deceased, was duly executed to pass real and personal estate, and that the same with the proofs thereof be recorded and admitted to probate as a will of real and personal estate.

...................., *Surrogate.*

SECTION III.

Opinions of Witnesses.

Subscribing witnesses to the will, are the subject of an exception to the general rule, that witnesses must state facts and not opinions. They may give their opinion as to the soundness or unsoundness of the testator's mind when the will was executed. (*De Witt* v. *Barley,* 9 N. Y., 371.) For subscribing witnesses are called for the express purpose of observing and testifying as to this.

The history of judicial decisions in relation to the general question of the competency of unskilled witnesses to give their opinions, as to whether the testator was of sound mind or not, in this state, is interesting.

The courts in this state, seem to have held uniformly, that in cases requiring skill or science to form an opinion, non-experts could not give such opinions. (See cases in *De Witt* v. *Barley, sup.*) But in many cases, the rule as stated above, was relaxed, as the courts said, *ex necessitate*, but in the case before us, they held positively, that the question of the soundness or unsoundness of the testator's mind, was a question involving special skill and science, and, holding that medical men might give their opinions, they held as conclusively, that laymen, not having special or scientific knowledge, could not give their opinions. Judge Denio, relying upon the opinions of the judges of the Ecclesiastical Courts in England and the rule as held in other states of the Union, dissented from the prevailing opinions and the case was sent to a new trial and came again before the Court of Appeals. (See 19 N. Y., 340.)

The learned judge delivering the opinions of the court, on the reargument, proved, that in the Ecclesiastical courts in England, answering to our Probate Courts, in Vermont, Connecticut, Pennsylvania, Ohio, Maryland, North Carolina, Tennessee, Georgia, Alabama, and Indiana, and in the courts of the United States, such opinions are uniformly received, and he limits the decision of the court in the same case as formerly decided, to holding merely, that a non-professional witness cannot be asked the broad question whether he considered the party *non compos mentis*, or, which is the same thing, incapable of managing his affairs.

The will of De Witt was, in that case, in question, and was contested, not on the ground that he was a maniac, but that he was affected with mental imbecility, arising from old age, and the learned judge says : " To me it seems a plain proposition, that upon inquiries as to mental imbecility arising from age, it will be found impracticable, in many cases, to come to a satisfactory conclusion, without receiving, to some extent, the opinion of witnesses. How is it possible to describe in words, that combination of minute appearances, upon which the judgment, in such cases, is formed? The attempt to try such a question, would, in most cases, I am persuaded, prove entirely futile. Such an attempt was made in the present case, and the learned judge before whom it was tried, had, I presume, the decision of this court before him, and intended to conform to it; but, as I shall hereafter show, without success. A witness can scarcely convey any intelligible idea, upon such a question, without infusing into his testimony more or less of opinion. Mental imbecility is exhibited in part by attitude, by gesture, by the tones of the voice, and the expression of the eye and face. Can they be described in language, so as to convey, to one not an eye witness, an adequate conception of their force?"

Again he says (p. 350), in relation to the statement that the question of sanity or insanity, is one of science, and that only experts should be permitted to give their opinions : " Now, however true this reasoning may be of cases of the mere *derangement* of mental powers, otherwise vigorous, it has no application to cases of idiocy, or of imbecility from the natural decay of those powers. The latter class of cases depend upon indications which are equally patent to all; and a man of sound judgment and experience in life, can observe these indications and draw just inferences from them, as well without, as with a scientific education. But even in cases of insanity proper, if the derangement of the mind is general, science is hardly necessary to enable persons having opportunities for personal observation, to judge of its existence. It is only where the derangement is partial, involving only a portion of the mental powers, or where it consists in some single hallucinated idea, that much difficulty arises. It would be far better to make of these cases (cases of partial insanity), an exceptional class, than to adopt a general rule in reference to them, which would include a much larger class, to which such rule could have no just application."

The court here, puts imbecility in the same category as to opinions of witnesses, as intoxication, identity of persons, proof of hand-writing, and age of persons, being admitted *ex-necessitate*, because the impression is produced on the mind of the witness by facts and circumstances which cannot, by any possibility, be conveyed to another. The court held finally, that upon an issue in regard to

the mental imbecility of a grantor, the opinions of
unprofessional witnesses, founded upon personal
observation of his appearance and conduct, may be
given in evidence. The opinions received, however,
must be confined to facts alone, and must not em-
brace any matter of law. Such opinions are received *ex-necessitate*, as they are in the other cases
above referred to.   But in such cases, the witnesses
must state, so far as they are able, the facts and
reasons upon which their conclusions are founded,
that the jury, or court, may have all practicable
means of estimating the accuracy of their opinion.

The next case in point is *Clapp* v. *Fullerton*, (34
N. Y., 109.)   Here the will was contested on the
ground of the imbecility of the testator, and that he
had an insane delusion in regard to the illegiti-
macy of one of his children, who contested the
will. Non professional witnesses, not being subscribing witnesses, were permitted to state before the
surrogate, the facts on which their opinions were
based, and that in their opinion, the testator was
incapable of transacting business during the last
year of his life, his incapacity arising from imbecility induced by age.   It would seem that such
evidence, from these witnesses, was within the rule
established in *Dewitt* v. *Barley* (*sup.*)

The court held (p. 194), " When a layman is
examined as to facts within his own knowledge

and observation, tending to show the soundness or unsoundness of the testator's mind, he may characterize, as rational or irrational, the acts and declarations to which he testifies. It is legitimate to give them such additional weight as may be derived from the convictions they produced at the time. The party calling him, may require it, to fortify the force of the facts, and the adverse party may demand it, as a mode of proving the truth and good faith of the narration. But to render his opinions admissible, even to this extent, it must be limited to his conclusions from the specific facts he discloses. His position is that of an observer, and not of a professional expert. He may testify to the impressions produced by what he witnessed ; but he is not legally competent to express an opinion on the general question, whether the mind of the testator was sound or unsound." The court, holding this, professes to affirm the decision in *Dewitt* v. *Barley* (*sup.*)

But the profession have generally supposed that the cases are in conflict, and that *Clapp* v. *Fullerton*, overrules *Dewitt* v. *Barley*. It is difficult, and perhaps impossible, to reconcile them, while they both seem to be authority ; but it may be properly said, that upon the question of the imbecility of a testator, distinguishing imbecility from *dementia*, which is accompanied by derangement, unprofessional witnesses may give their opinions, with the facts upon which they are founded, as to the soundness or unsoundness of the mind of the testator.

The rules as to the admissibility of the opinions of witnesses in the common law courts, differ widely from the rule as above stated. Indeed it may be doubted whether the rules established in the common law courts can properly be applied in the Probate Courts. In the latter courts, the testimony is considered by the same officers who rule as to its admissibility, and appeals from them are in the nature of a re-hearing in equity, and the Appellate Court succeeds to the jurisdiction and authority of the old Court of Chancery (*Clapp* v. *Fullerton, sup.*) ; and it may be presumed that the rules of evidence of the latter court are to be observed, and that the cases are to be distinguished from the criminal trials in which insanity is set up as a defence.

We can conceive of no other supposition which will reconcile the cases above reviewed with later decisions upon review, of verdicts in criminal cases.

In the case, *O'Brien* v. *The People* (36 N. Y., 267), an unprofessional witness, a printer by trade, testified that he saw the prisoner about twelve or one o'clock of the day of the homicide; that he had a wild, vacant look about his eyes ; was fidgety and uneasy ; spoke in a husky tone of voice. The coun-

sel for the prisoner then proposed to prove him insane or delirious, by the opinion of the witness,
and asked, "was he, or not, in your opinion, insane
or delirious." The question was excluded and the
ruling was correct within *Clapp* v. *Fullerton*. The
witness could not testify generally as to the insanity of the prisoner, he could only give the impression which the acts and conversation which he
stated and narrated produced in his mind; this he
was not asked to do, counsel not seeming to conform to the decision in *Clapp* v. *Fullerton*.

So in *Reid* v. *The People* (42 N. Y., 270), the
prisoner being on trial for murder, witnesses were
asked: From what you saw that night, what impression did his acts and words make upon your
mind; what impression as to the state of his mind
did his words and conduct have upon your mind?"
It does not seem that they were called upon to
state the acts, conduct and conversation of the prisoner and then to give the impression which the
acts, conduct, and conversation which they detailed and related, produced upon their minds.
The court, affirming *Clapp* v. *Fullerton*, held the
questions improper, that the witnesses were not
competent to give an opinion as to whether the
facts testified to by them indicated mental unsoundness.

The Supreme Court in deciding case *Sisson* v.

Conger (1 N. Y. Sup. C. Rep., 564), seemed to have misapprehended the distinction taken by the Court of Appeals in the case of *Reid* v. *The People*. The action was brought to establish a lost or destroyed will made by Nathaniel Sisson, and it was defended, among other grounds, on the ground of the mental unsoundness of the testator, and several non-professional witnesses were asked : " From the acts and declaration of S. (the deceased), by you related and testified, and as you observed, what impression did it make on your mind, as to his mental condition?" The court held that the question was almost identical with those put to the witnesses in the case of *Reid* (42 N. Y., 270), and held it called for an opinion which the witnesses were not competent to give; that the incorporation into the question of the words, " by you related and testified," do not make the question competent.

We submit that the court missed the very distinction taken by the Court of Appeals, which must be considered as holding that the *impression* produced by acts and conversations related, is a different thing from an *opinion* as to the mental condition of the testator.

CHAPTER VI.

Of Mental Unsoundness.

" All persons, except idiots, persons of unsound mind, and infants, may devise real estate." (2 R. S., 56, § 1, as amended by S. L., 1849, 528.)

" Every male of the age of eighteen years, and every female of the age of sixteen years, of sound mind and memory, and no others, may bequeath personal estate." (2 R. S., 60, § 21, as amended as above.)

Unsoundness of mind may be considered under three divisions, idiocy, imbecility and lunacy.

Idiocy, is a congenital defect. An idiot is a person who has been without understanding from his nativity, and whom the law therefore presumes never likely to attain any. Idiocy implies either congenital defect, or some obstacle to the development of the faculties in infancy. It is an imbecility (congenital) or sterility of the mind, not a perversion of the understanding. (Bouvier's Law Dict., tit. idiocy, idiot.)

Idiocy is not always readily distinguished from imbecility. Where the former is caused, not by absolute congenital defect, but by an arrest of development, the line of distinction may be with difficulty traced. Thus, if development should be arrested at an early stage of infancy, at the age of a few months, the subject would be an idiot, not recognizing friends and showing scarcely more intelligence than the brute creation. But if development continue to the age of some years, and the infant shall have acquired some education in its affections and perceptions and then development be arrested, it may be very difficult to decide whether the subject is an idiot, an imbecile, or *compos mentis.*

The Court of Errors formerly held in *Stewart* v. *Lispenard* (26 Wend., 255), that, mere imbecility does not incapacitate. An imbecile, of however low degree of capacity, has the power of legal assent, or will, and the question in each such case is, whether that power was duly exercised.

This rule which in its application in the case before the court, declared a person of the very lowest grade of human intelligence, competent to make a valid will, never received the cordial assent of the courts, or the profession at large, although the courts felt compelled to follow it until the case of *Delafield* v. *Parish* (25 N. Y., 9), in which case the former was overruled.

The question in *Delafield* v. *Parish* was, whether, as a question of fact, the testator, Parish, after an apoplectic stroke, which resulted in permanent paralysis of the right side (*hemiplegia*), was degraded to a state of absolute *dementia*, or whether his mind became so active that he was *compos mentis*. The court, in deciding the case, took the view, from the conflicting evidence, that the testator, after the seizure, did not utter an intelligible word, and was *non compos mentis*, and states the rule thus. The only standard as to mental capacity, in all who are not idiots or lunatics, is found in the fact whether the testator was *compos mentis*, or *non compos mentis*, as these terms are used in their fixed legal meaning, and the question in every case, is, had the testator as *compos mentis*, capacity to make a will; not, had he capacity to make the will produced. If *compos mentis* he can make any will, however complicated; if *non compos mentis* he can make no will, not the simplest. (*Delafield* v. *Parish, sup.*)

The Supreme Court, in the case of *Forman* v. *Smith* (7 Lansing, 443), in a well considered opinion by Justice Miller, states the doctrine established in *Delafield* v. *Parish*, thus: " The doctrine is well settled, that to enable a person to dispose of his property by will, it is not enough that he should be found to be possessed of some degree of intelligence and mind. He must in addition, have sufficient mind to comprehend the nature and effect of

the act he was performing; the relation he held
to the various individuals who might naturally be
expected to become the objects of his bounty, and be
capable of making a rational selection among
them." This brings us back to the former decisions. Thus in *Clark* v. *Fisher* (1 Paige, 171), the
chancellor held that a testator must be of sound and
disposing mind and memory, so as to be capable
of making a testamentary disposition of his property with sense and judgment, in reference to the
situation and amount of such property, and to the
relative claims, of the different persons who are,
or might be the object of his bounty. In considering the question of capacity, it is proper to look
into the will proposed, and if it is unreasonable on
its face, when taken in connection with the amount
of property, and situation of relatives, this may be
considered, in judging of the state of the testator's
mind. (*Clark* v. *Fisher, sup.*)

But where the testator has mind and memory
to understand his relations to other persons, his
will must stand for the reason of the act, and it is
not sufficient to impeach his competency, that the
will is not such, in all respects, as might have been
expected. (*Watson* v. *Donnelly*, 28 Barb., 653.)

It would seem to us, that where the family relations of the testator were simple, and his property
was small in amount, and consisted of few items,

a will would be sustained with evidence of a lower grade of intellect than would be required in such a case as that of Parish, where the property was vast and widely distributed, and where the family relatives were collateral.

The terms *compos mentis,* and *non compos mentis* as used in *Delafield* vs. *Parish (sup.),* are simply equivalent to the terms in the statute, of *sound mind and memory,* and of its converse, *of unsound mind.*

The phrase then, persons *non compos mentis,* includes a designation of all those who may not make wills, except those incapacitated by nonage. The incapacity may proceed from idiocy or congenital defect, from imbecility, produced by disease or otherwise, to a degree which produces unsoundness; by sickness, inducing delirium or perverted affections or perceptions; by drunkenness, or by absolute mania.

As there are no two cases in which imbecility exists to the same extent, or with the same precise indications, each case must be judged by itself, with the light of the authorities above quoted.

A lunatic, in the former signification of the term, was defined as an insane person, who has lucid intervals, sometimes enjoying his senses, and sometimes not. (Burrill's Law Dict., tit. Lunatic.) But, the term lunacy has latterly come to be considered more as synonymous with insanity; (See Bouvier's Law Dict., tit. Insanity) except, perhaps, that the term *insanity* may be considered as broader than *lunacy* and to include the signification of the terms, *lunacy*, *idiocy*, and *unsoundness* of mind. This latter sense and use of the term insanity, and the consequent disuse of the term lunatic, has come about by reason of the discovery that the opinions formerly held as to the recurrence of lucid intervals, are in a great degree erroneous. For formerly, a lucid interval was supposed to be the result of a complete remission of the disease, or temporary complete restoration, while "in modern practice, the term lucid interval, signifies merely a remission of the disease, an abatement of the violence of the morbid action; a period of comparative calm; and the proof of its occurrence, is generally drawn from the character of the act in question. It is hardly necessary to say, that this is an unjustifiable use of the term, which should be confined to the genuine lucid interval that does occasionally occur." (Bouvier, *sup.*) Insanity then, when distinguished from idiocy, and as synonymous with lunacy, is defined by Bouvier as "the prolonged departure, without adequate cause, from the states of feeling and modes of thinking, usual to the individual in health." We are disposed to criticize this definition and amend it thus, " the prolonged departure, *through morbid action*, from the states of feeling and modes of thinking usual to the individual in health."

Lucid intervals, we have seen, are not so much favored as formerly, and do not occur so usually as formerly supposed, while it is admitted that they *may* and sometimes do occur; and during the occurrence of a lucid interval, the subject may make a valid will. (*Gombault* v. *Public administrator*, 4 Brad., 226.) Where the condition of insanity is established by proof, the burden of proving that the will was executed in a lucid interval falls upon the proponent (Id.), and it is no light burden. Some high authorities have declared that there are no such periods as lucid intervals, as distinguished from entire recovery (Ray's Med. Juris., § 382), and compare the condition of the subject of the disease in the apparent lucid interval, to the condition of one laboring under a quotidian fever, during the intermission of the disease. He may be better, but the disease still exists. (Id., § 377.) Dr. Reid (Essays on Hypochondriacal and other Nervous Affections 21st essay), says: "There are few cases of mania or melancholy, where the light of reason does not now and then shine out between the clouds. In fevers of the mind, as well as those of the body, there occur frequent intermissions. But the mere interruption of a disorder, is not to be mistaken for its cure, or its ultimate conclusion. Little stress ought to be laid upon those occasional and uncertain disentanglements of intellect, in which the patient, for a time only, is extricated from the labyrinth of his morbid hallucinations. Madmen may show, at starts, more sense than ordinary men." Dr. Combe (Observations on Mental Derangement, p. 241), says : " But however calm and rational the patient may appear to be, during the lucid intervals, as they are called, and while enjoying the quietude of domestic society. or the limited range of a well regulated asylum, it must never be supposed, that he is in perfect possession of his senses, as if he had never been ill."

But the Ecclesiastical Court in England, in the proof of wills, has gone very far in holding that lucid intervals exist, and in admitting to probate wills made in such supposed conditions; much further formerly than of late. Thus in *Cartwright* v. *Cartwright* (1 Phillimore 90, quoted in Ray's Med. Juris., § 390), a single woman in 1775, having been afflicted with the worst symptoms of insanity and so furious as to render it necessary to tie her hands, prevailed on her physician to liberate her that she might write, he remarking that it made no difference what she wrote, as she was not fit to make a proper use of them. She wrote on several

pieces of paper in succession, and tore them up and
threw them into the grate, walking up and down
the room in a wild and ferocious manner and
muttering to herself. After one or two hours
spent in this manner, she succeeded in writing a
will that suited her, occupying but a few lines.
It was decided that this was done in a lucid interval.
" For," said the court, " I think the strongest and
best proof that can arise as to a lucid interval, is
that which arises from the act itself; that I look
upon as the thing to be first examined, and if it
can be proved and established, that it is a rational
act, rationally done, the whole case is proved."
The court begged the whole question, and held it to
be a rational act because it was a proper and consistent will. The same court in *Groom* v. *Thomas* (2
Hagg., 433), denied probate where the evidence of
lucid interval was much stronger than in *Cartwright* v. *Cartwright.* In a more recent case
Chambers v. *The Queen's Proctor* (2 Curtis, 515),
probate was granted in case of a man who was admitted to have entertained insane delusions during
three days immediately preceding the execution
of the will and to have committed suicide the next
day after. (See cases in Ray, §§ 390, etc.)

Partial insanity, as it was formerly called, now
distinguished as *monomania*, does not necessarily
invalidate a will, where the provisions of the will

are entirely unconnected with the particular delusion ; but, otherwise, if the delusion relates to the subjects of his will and has perverted the testator's judgment so as to control the dispositions of the will. (*Stanton* v. *Wetherwax*, 16 Barb., 259.) But where the delusion has not only impaired but perverted the testator's judgment and understanding in relation to subjects connected with the provisions of the will, so as to exercise a controlling influence in the disposition of his property, the will is not the will of a person of sound mind ; the mind of the testator being unsound in relation to the very subject on which he is called to exercise its powers. (Id.) In this case, the testator was held to be more than a monomaniac.

To the same purport is the case of *Thompson* v. *Thompson* (21 Barb., 107), holding that absurd opinions on some subjects, do not show insanity in a person who continues in the possession of his faculties, discreetly conducting business, where the court is satisfied, as a matter of fact, in view of the above rule, that his false opinions did not incapacitate him. The testator Thompson, in this case had the most extravagant opinions about religion, the finding of treasures and the philosopher's stone, imaginable, in this age. The case is reported fully in 2 Bradford, at page 449, in which the doctrine that a reasonable will is evidence of a rational mind is carried to the extreme.

Drunkenness, does not necessarily invalidate a will. The mere fact that a man is an habitual drunkard, and *non compos* in his drunken fits, is not enough to invalidate a will executed by him. (*Gardner* v. *Gardner*, 22 Wend., 526.) But where intoxication has been indulged in to such extent as to produce imbecility, then the will will be invalidated, not because of the habitual intoxication but because of the consequent imbecility. (*Burritt* v. *Silliman*, 16 Barb., 198.) This last case was reversed in 13 N. Y., 93, but upon another ground than the above decision.

Undue influence will invalidate a will made through such influence.

Undue influence is presumed in a case where the will was drawn by a beneficiary. (*Campbell* v. *Dubois*, 4 Barb., 393.) By the civil law such presumption absolutely invalidated a will drawn by the beneficiary. But our law goes not to this extent, merely carefully inquiring into the circumstances, and demanding satisfactory proof that the party executing the will, clearly understood, and freely intended to make that disposition of his property which the instrument purports to direct. (Id., p. 398 ; see also *Vreeland* v. *McClelland*, 1 Brad., 393 ; *Wilson* v. *Moran*, 1 Id., 172.)

Whenever a person of weakened and imbecile mind is induced by fraud, imposition or undue influence to make a testamentary disposition of his property, differently from what he would if in the full possession of his faculties, the same will be set aside upon the same principle that a Court of Chancery sets aside a conveyance of property obtained under like circumstances. (*Clark* v. *Fisher*, 1 Paige, 171.)

So undue influence may be proved by circumstances and presumption from facts, unrebutted by the party charged therewith. (*Leaycraft* v. *Simmons*, 3 Brad., 35.)

But it was held in *Bleecker* v. *Lynch* (1 Brad., 458), that the dependence of the testatrix upon the principal beneficiary of the will, for the management of her pecuniary and domestic affairs, is not, of itself, ground for the imputation of fraud or undue influence.

In determining whether a will has been procured to be made by undue influence, it is proper to see if the testamentary provisions are in harmony with the decedent's dispositions and affections. (*Allen* v. *Public Administrator*, 1 Brad., 378.) This rule is to the same effect as that in cases of alleged unsoundness of mind, that the court will look into the will and family relations to see if it be a reasonable and consistent will. (*Clark* v. *Fisher*, 1

Paige, 171.)   But the testator's declaration that
he had been influenced to make will, in which he
had not done justice, was held not to be evidence
that it was induced by undue influence. (*Nelson*
v. *McGiffort*, 3 Barb., ch. 158.)   While in seeming
contradiction to the last principle, it has been held
that subsequent recognition of the will by the decedent, when in health, and in the undoubted full
possession of his faculties, are material facts in its
favor ; and repeated statements of testamentary
intentions made to acquaintances, may have weight
in ascertaining whether the will accorded with his
mind. (*Allen* v. *Public Administrator*, 1 Brad.,
378, and *O'Neil* v. *Murray*, 4 Brad., 311.)

But if the will proposed be the will of another,
to which the testator assented from mere habit,
produced by prostration of both body and mind, it
cannot be sustained as his will. (*Newhouse* v. *Godwin*, 17 Barb., 236.)

One has a right, by fair agreement, or persuasion,
to induce another to make a will and even to make
it in his own favor.   Influence without artifice or
fraud, does not avoid a will. (*Blanchard* v. *Nestle*,
3 Den., 37 ; *Tunison* v. *Tunison*, 4 Brad., 138.)
And although the mere fact that the mind of the
testator has been influenced by the arguments and
persuasions of the person principally benefitted,
however indecorous, indelicate or improper they

may be, will not ordinarily, in the absence of fraud, vitiate a will; still to be sustained, it must be the will of the testator, however induced. (*Newhouse* v. *Godwin, sup.*)

In nearly every case where undue influence is alleged it is complicated with imbecility, for it is hardly possible to conceive of the absolute substitution of the volition of one for that of another, except where the decedent was greatly enfeebled in mind and body, affected with congenital imbecility, or under the influence of, or degraded by, the effects of stimulants and drugs. In the last condition, it seems peculiarly to be the fact, that the opium eater, when under the influence of the drug, is almost incapable of resisting importunity, and in the execution of a will, as in any other act, if subjected to any influence however slight, would yield, whatever the consequences of the yielding, rather than exert the little force necessary to assert independence. This condition is the result of the stupifying influence of the drug, begetting the most absolute indifference to external objects and intensifying the wish which all men have, for self indulgence.

Senile imbecility is considered as one form of *dementia*, and in considering it the age of the decedent is not by any means the only question to be considered. For all are aware that by reason

of a hereditary tendency to long life, or by observing habits of temperance, some men are younger
at eighty years of age than others at sixty.

Senile imbecility proceeds generally from morbid
disturbance of the circulation, resulting in a deficiency of the supply of blood to the brain, and
defective stimulation of that organ. This disturbance
may proceed from several causes, prominent among
which are, lack of supply of blood from defective
digestion and assimilation of the food, or mechanical
obstruction to circulation, caused by ossification of
certain arteries.   In either case, the brain, lacking
the stimulus of a healthy and normal circulation,
the person is deficient in perception, and incapable
of reflection, and *dementia* is the result.

But such cases are clearly to be distinguished
from the slowness of intellect manifested even in
vigorous old age.   In the latter case, the brain
takes the impression from the perception more
slowly perhaps, and requires more time to arrive
at a conclusion, but its action is normal, and
its results reliable.   To compare the immaterial
with the material ; the machine, through reduced
supply of power, operates more slowly, but, time
being given, the appropriate product is achieved.
This phenomenon is observable in many persons,
even before advanced age is attained.

Still the same question is to be asked as to the

will of the old man as to the will of the young and vigorous testator; was the decedent *compos mentis*, or was he *non compos mentis ?*

The courts have been very tender of the wills of old persons, and inclined to go as far as possible in carrying them into effect; and in the opinions may be found a strain of sentiment unusual in judicial determinations.

Chancellor Kent, in *Van Alstyne* v. *Hunter* (5 Johns. Ch., 148), in a case where the decedent at the making of the proposed will was between ninety and one hundred years of age, and greatly debilitated says: " It is one of the painful conse- quences of extreme old age, that it ceases to excite interest, and is apt to be left solitary and neglected. The control which the law still gives to a man over the disposal of his property, is one of the most efficient means which he has in protracted life to command the attention due to his infirmities. The will of an aged man, ought to be regarded with great tenderness, when it appears not to have been procured by fraudulent acts, but contains those very dispositions which the circumstances of his situation and the course of the natural affections dictated." From this extract it will be perceived that the Chancellor felt moved with sympathy, and regarded the will with *tenderness*, but the question may be asked, with whom did he have this sym-

7

pathy, with the living or the dead? Manifestly, with the dead, who could not appreciate it.

Notwithstanding, it is not to be disguised, that the aged, with perceptions blunted and reflections dulled, readily falls into a state of dependence upon the persons surrounding him, and insensibly, the will of such person is substituted for the will of the decedent, and testamentary dispositions may be obtained which are to be looked upon with suspicion and not tenderness. Here the principle that the will is to be looked into to see if the testamentary disposition is in accordance with the natural claims of the objects of the testator's bounty, above referred to, is of great value, and if it appears, that the testator omitted to give suitable bequests to those whom he always had regarded with affection, it affords grave ground for suspicion of undue influence.

Delirium is a temporary insanity and during its continuance renders the subject of it incompetent to make a valid will, and is aptly defined by Wharton and Stillé (Med. Juris., § 235), as a "state of dreams, brought on, not by sleep but by disease." The perceptive powers of the subject are suspended, or their objects distorted and the patient reasons as he perceives, irrationally, and this is true of all forms of the disease, however caused.

Letters Testamentary and Complaint against Executor.

After the proof of a will of personal estate, letters issue of course thereon, to the parties named therein as executors, if there be no notice of objection to their issue, and the letters so issued are the warrant of the executors in the execution of their duties. The surrogate enters an order for the issue of letters, either in the following form, or he may include this order in the order for probate.

ORDER FOR ISSUE OF LETTERS.

At a Surrogate's Court held in and for the county of ...., at the surrogate's office in the .... of ...., on the ...... day of ...., 1874.

Present — ...., Surrogate.

| In the matter of the will |
| of |
| ...., deceased. |

The will of said deceased having been duly proved as a will of real and personal estate it is ordered that letters testamentary issue thereon to ...., executrix and ...., executor in said will named, upon their taking and filing the oath, prescribed by law.

.................., *Surrogate.*

The oath of office may be administered and certified by the surrogate, county judge, a commissioner of deeds, or the clerk appointed by the surrogate, or in King's county, by the clerks of the surrogate. (S. L., 1863, chap. 392, S. L., 1837, ch. 460, § 59.) The oath is as follows:

OATH OF EXECUTOR.

State of New York,   } ss.
.... county. }

    I, ..., do solemnly swear that I will honestly and faithfully discharge the duties of executor of the will of ...., deceased, according to law.

....

Sworn before me this 9th day }
    of December, 1873. }

..................., *Surrogate.*

At any time before the issue of the letters, any person intended as legatee, or creditor, may file an affidavit that he intends to interpose objections to the competency of an executor or the executors named, and on the filing of such affidavit, the surrogate shall stay the granting of letters for thirty days, unless the matter shall be sooner disposed of. (S. L., 1837, chap. 460, § 22.)

If the affidavit shows an intention to file objections against only one of several executors, the surrogate will suspend action as to all. (*McGregor* v. *Buel*, 24 N. Y., 166.)

If the objector shall swear positively that he is a creditor, it seems that the surrogate will not try the issue as to whether he is a creditor, but will entertain the objection. (*Estate of Horatio N. Ferris*, 1 Tucker, 15.)

AFFIDAVIT OF INTENTION TO FILE OBJECTIONS.

Surrogate's Court, Rensselaer county.

In the matter of letters testamentary upon the will
of
...., deceased.

Rensselaer county, ss:

A B, of the town of ...., in said county, being duly sworn, says: that he is a legatee named in the will of (or a creditor of),................., late of said town, deceased, which has been admitted to probate by the surrogate of said county, in which said will C D is named as an executor. That deponent intends in good faith to file with said surrogate, objections to the competency of said C D, to act as such executor, and he is advised and believes that there are just and substantial objections to his competency and to the granting of letters testamentary to the said C D.

                                                A B.

Sworn, etc.

Having filed his affidavit, the objector has thirty days in which to file his objections and prosecute them.

He will therefore prepare his objections. The following states all the legal objections to the issue of letters as is believed, and the pleader may use them all, or only use those upon which he intends to rely.

OBJECTIONS TO ISSUE OF LETTERS.

Surrogate's Court, Rensselaer county.

In the matter of letters testamentary upon the will
of
.... deceased.

To the Surrogate of the county of Rensselaer:

The undersigned, a legatee named in the will of (or a creditor of) the above named deceased, objects to the issue of letters testamentary to C D, an executor in said will named, for the following reasons:

First: That the said C D is incompetent to execute the duties of such trust as an executor, by reason of his improvidence.

Second: That the said C D is incompetent to discharge the duties of such trust, by reason of habitual intemperance in the use of alcoholic liquors.

Third: That the said C D is an alien, not being an inhabitant of this state.

Fourth: That the said C D has been convicted of an infamous crime, to wit, the crime of ....

Fifth : That the said C D's circumstances are so precarious as not to afford adequate security for his proper administration of the estate of the deceased.

Sixth : That the said C D is unable to read and write the English language.

Dated Dec. 9, 1873.   A B.

JAMES LANSING,
                Proctor.

These objections are framed upon the provisions of the revised statutes (2 R. S., 698, 70), and upon chap. 782, laws of 1867, §5.

The surrogate upon filing the objections will, on the application of the objector, order that a summons issue to the executor against whom the objections are made, to show cause why he should not be compelled to give bonds for the faithful performance of his trust.

ORDER FOR SUMMONS.

At a Surrogate's Court, held in and for the county of ....,at the surrogate's office in the ...... of ...., on the ...... day of ...., 1873.

Present — ...., Surrogate.

In the matter of letters testamentary upon the will

of

................., deceased.

The will of said deceased having been proved and A B having filed objections to the issue of letters testamentary to C D, an executor in said will named, now on motion of said A B : Ordered that a summons issue to the said C D, requiring him to show cause why he should not be required to give bonds as such executor upon the issue of such letters to him.

.. .., *Surrogate.*

The summons thereupon is issued under the seal of the surrogate which is usually made so as to allow for a service of six days prior to its return.

SUMMONS.

The people of the state of New York to C D
[L. S.]   Greeting.

You are hereby summoned to appear before our surrogate of our county of Rensselaer at his office in the city of Troy on the ...... day of ...., 1873, at ten o'clock in the forenoon then and there to attend the adjudication of our said surrogate upon certain objections filed to your competency to act as an executor of the will of ...., late of the town of ...., deceased, and to show cause, if required, why you should not be ordered to give bond for the faithful performance of your duties as such executor.

Witness Moses Warren, Surrogate of our said county and the seal of our said court this ...... day of ...., 1873.

................., *Surrogate.*

It would seem that if the objector does not prosecute his objections during the thirty days in which

the issue of letters is stayed, he will be deemed
to have abandoned them, and letters will issue to
the executor against whom the objections were filed.

On the return of the summons, the parties join
issue and it is suggested that the issue be framed
fully in writing.

ANSWER TO OBJECTIONS.

Surrogate's Court, Rensselaer county.

In the matter of letters testamentary on the will
        of
   ...., deceased.

C D, an executor named in the will of the above
named deceased, in answer to the objections filed by
A B in this matter, respectfully says:

That he, the said C D, is not incompetent to discharge the duties of executor as aforesaid by reason of
habitual intemperance in the use of alcoholic liquors.

And he prays the adjudication of the court upon such
objection.

                                        A B.

Dated, Dec. 11, 1873.
L. W. RHODES,
          Proctor.

The issue having been joined, the burden of proof
is upon the objector, to show that the executor is
incompetent, for incompetence, is not presumed,
more than unsoundness of mind.

The proof as to the objections, must necessarily vary as to each.

Upon the objection that the executor named has been convicted of an infamous crime, however guilty or base he may be, the record of conviction must be produced to sustain the objection or it will fail. (1 *Coope* v. *Lowerre*, Barb. Ch., 47 ; *Harrison* v. *McMahon*, 1 Brad., 289 ; *McMahon* v. *Harrison*, 6 N. Y., 443 ; *Emerson* v. *Bowers*, 14 N. Y., 449.)

A professional gambler is presumptively incompetent. (*McMahon* v. *Harrison, sup.*)

Where an executor had no property except an unliquidated demand, and was about to remove from the state he was required to give security. (*Wood* v. *Wood*, 4 Page, 299 ; *Holmes* v. *Cock*, 2 Barb. Ch., 426.)

But an executor should not be required to give security, merely because he does not own property to the full value of the estate of his testator, and where there is no ground for supposing that the trust fund is in danger. (*Mandeville* v. *Mandeville*, 8 Paige, 475.)

The hearing having been concluded, the surrogate either sustains or dismisses the objections. If he sustains the objections to the competency of the executor, he will enter an order in terms, " that the surrogate doth order and adjudge that the executor named in the will of said deceased is incompetent to execute the trust imposed upon him by reason of his being an alien, not an inhabitant of this state " (or, whatever the objection be). But if he fail to sustain the objections, he may, without further delay, enter an order for the issue of letters.

Ordinarily, unless required by the terms of the will appointing them, or unless required by the surrogate, executors are not required to give bonds.

§ 7. (2 R. S., 70.) If any person applying for letters testamentary, shall be a *non*-resident of the state such letters shall not be granted, until the applicant shall give the like bond (as is required of executor adjudged to be in circumstances inadequate to afford security for the estate). But (S. L., 1873, chap. 657), such non-resident executor may receive such letters without bond, if the testator, by words in his last testament, has requested that his executor be allowed to act without giving bond, and if such executor has his usual place of business within this state.

Executors may renounce.

§ 8. (2 R. S. 70.) Any person named as executor in a will, may renounce such appointment, by an instrument in writing under his hand, attested by two witnesses, and on the same being proved to the satisfaction of the surrogate, who took the proof of the will, it shall be filed and recorded by him.

The renunciation may be in the following form.

Surrogate's Court, ... county.

| In the matter of the will |
| of |
| .. .. deceased. |

I, C D, named as an executor in the will of the above named deceased, do hereby renounce the appointment as such executor.

(Signed)   C D.

Dated Troy, Dec. 30, 1874.

In presence of

E F.

G H.

The execution of this may be proved by one of the subscribing witnesses, or may be acknowledged by the executor, in the form in which deeds are required to be acknowledged, to entitle them to be recorded.

But such renunciation may be retracted at any time before letters are issued to others, or afterwards, when the letters first issued are revoked, or the person to whom they shall have been issued shall die. (*Robertson* v. *McGoech,* 11 Paige, 640; *Casey* v. *Gardiner,* 4 Brad., 13.)

But should some or one of the executors fail to appear, it would seem to be irregular to issue letters testamentary, without a renunciation of the remaining executors, or until they shall have been summoned as provided by law.

§ 9. (2 R. S., 70.) If any person named as executor, shall not appear to qualify and take upon himself the execution of a will, within thirty days after the same was proved, and shall not have renounced, the surrogate shall, on application of any other executor, or of the widow, or any of the next of kin, or any legatee, or creditor of the testator, issue a summons directed to such executor, requiring him to appear and qualify, within a certain time therein to be limited, or that, in default thereof, he will be deemed to have renounced the said appointment.

PETITION THAT THE EXECUTOR NAMED BE SUMMONED TO ACCEPT OR RENOUNCE.

Surrogate's Court, Rensselaer county.

In the matter of the goods and chattels of John Doe, deceased.

To the Surrogate of the county of Rensselaer:

The petition of A B, respectfully shows, that your petitioner is one of the legatees named in the will of John Doe, deceased (or, a creditor of the above named deceased), who died on or about the .... day of ...., 1872, as your petitioner is informed and believes, having first made his last will and testament, which was, on the ...... day of .... 1872, duly proved in this court. That one C D is named, as an executor in said will, and has not renounced, and has hitherto neglected to take the oath required by law, and receive letters testamentary, notwithstanding that more than thirty days have elapsed since said will was admitted to probate as aforesaid. Wherefore, your petitioner prays that a summons issue to said C D, requiring him according to law, to appear and qualify, as such executor, within a certain time in said summons limited, or that he be deemed to have renounced the appointment as executor in said will.

Dated Dec. 13, 1872.

A B.

Rensselaer county, ss:

A B, being duly sworn says that the foregoing petition by him subscribed is true.

A B.

Sworn before me this 13th }
    Dec., 1872.   }
        A R, *Notary Public.*

Upon this petition an order is entered for the issue of a summons according to the statute.

ORDER FOR A SUMMONS.

At a Surrogate's Court, held in the county of ...., at the surrogate's office in the .... of ...., on the ...... day of ...., 1874.

In the matter of the will
of
..................., deceased.

On reading and filing the petition of A B, one of the legatees named in the will of the above named deceased, showing that C D, an executor named in said will, has not renounced, and has hitherto neglected to take the oath required by law, notwithstanding more than thirty days have elapsed since said will was proved :

Ordered that a summons issue to said C D, requiring him to appear and qualify as such executor on or before the ...... day of ...., 1874.

.................., *Surrogate.*

§ 10. (2 R. S., 70.)   If the person to whom such summons is directed, reside within this state, it shall be served personally on him, at least fourteen days before the time limited therein for him to appear.   And if he reside, or be out of the state, or his residence be unknown, such summons may be served by publishing it in the state paper, for at least six weeks before the time therein specified for such person to appear.

§ 11. In case sickness, or other accident, or any reasonable cause, exist, to prevent the attendance of such person, upon the same being proved to the surrogate, he may, in his discretion, allow a further time for such person to appear and qualify.

§ 12. If any person so notified, shall not appear, according to the tenor of such summons, or within the time allowed by the order of the surrogate, and qualify as an executor, by taking an oath and giving a bond, if one shall have been required, he

shall be deemed to have renounced the appointment of executor, and the surrogate shall thereupon enter an order, reciting the said summons,
the proof of the service thereof, and such subsequent order allowing time, if any was made, and
the neglect of such person to appear and qualify,
and declaring and decreeing that such person has
renounced his appointment as such executor.

SUMMONS TO EXECUTOR.

The people of the state of New York:

   To C D, named as executor of the last will
 [Seal] and testament of .... deceased.
 Greeting:

You are hereby summoned, personally to be and
appear before our surrogate of our county of ....
on, or before the ...... day of .... 1874, at
ten o'clock in the forenoon, at the office of the surrogate in the .... of .... in said county,
to take the oath of office as executor of the last will
and testament of said deceased, and receive letters testamentary therein; or in default thereof, you will be
deemed to have renounced the appointment as such
executor.

   Witness .... surrogate, and the seal
    of said court this ...... day of ....,
   1874.

      ...., *Surrogate.*

Should the executor appear and qualify, letters
will issue, the other executor or executors having

already taken the oath; but should he not appear an order will be entered that he be deemed to have renounced.

ORDER THAT EXECUTOR BE DEEMED TO HAVE RENOUNCED.

At a Surrogate's Court, held in the county of ...., at the surrogate's office in the .... of ...., on the ...... day of ...., 1874.

Present—Hon. ...., Surrogate.

In the matter of the will
of
.................., deceased.

On filing the summons heretofore issued in this matter, upon the petition of ...., returnable here this day, and, due proof of the due service thereof, on A B, executor named in the will of said deceased, and the said A B having neglected to appear, and take the oath as required in said summons: It is ordered and adjudged, that the said A B, by reason of such neglect, has, and is to be deemed to have renounced the appointment as executor as aforesaid.

.................., *Surrogate.*

Letters testamentary upon a will of a testator domiciled without the state, at the time of his death, may also be issued by the surrogate of any county in which there may be any property or effects of the deceased. (S. L., 1863, 694.)

8

After letters testamentary shall have been issued, complaint may be made against an executor.

§ 18. (2 R. S., 72.) If, after letters testamentary shall have been granted to any person, named as executor in any will, complaint shall be made to the surrogate of the county, in which such letters were granted, by any person interested in the estate, that the person so appointed as executor, has become incompetent by law to serve as such, or that his circumstances are so precarious as not to afford adequate security for his due administration of the estate, or that he has removed or is about to remove from this state, the surrogate shall proceed to inquire into such complaint.

The complaint should undoubtedly be on oath, stating the cause of the complaint, and the facts which give the surrogate jurisdiction of the case.

COMPLAINT AGAINST EXECUTOR.

To Hon. ...., Surrogate of the county of ....

The petition of ...., a legatee named in the will of ...., deceased, respectfully shows :

That said ...., lately died, having first duly made and published his last will and testament, in which among other things, he bequeathed to your petitioner, a legacy of .... dollars, and appointed ...., executor in said will. That said will was duly proved in the Surrogate's Court of the said county of Rensselaer, and letters testamentary were thereupon issued to the said .... , by the surrogate of said county, on the ...... day of ...., 1862, as by the record thereof, will more fully appear, and said ...., has taken upon himself the administration of the estate of said deceased, and has possessed himself of the personal property of said deceased, to a very considerable amount, as your petitioner is informed and believes.

And your petitioner further says, that the said ...., is in such precarious circumstances as not to afford adequate security for his due administration of the said estate (or other cause of complaint).

Your petitioner therefore prays, that the said......... .... may be superseded ; or for such other relief in the premises as the nature of the case may require.

Dated December 13th, 1871.

(Signed), ...

Rensselaer county, ss :

.................., being duly sworn, says that the foregoing petition, by him subscribed, is true.

(Signed), ...

Sworn before me this ...... day ⎫
  of ...., 1871.   ⎬
        ...., *Notary Public.*

§19. (2 R. S., 72.) Such surrogate shall thereupon issue a citation to the person complained of, requiring him to appear before such surrogate, at a day and place therein to be specified, to show cause

why he should not be superseded; which citation
shall be personally served on the person to whom it
may be directed, at said six days before the return
thereof, if he be in the county; and if he shall have
absconded from such county, it may be served by
leaving it at his place of residence.

ORDER FOR CITATION TO EXECUTOR TO SHOW CAUSE WHY HE SHOULD NOT BE SUPERSEDED.

> At a Surrogate's Court, held in the county of
> ...., at the surrogate's office,
> in the .... of.............., on the ......
> day of ...., 1874.
> Present — Hon. ...., Surrogate.

In the matter of the application
of ...., for citation
against ...., executor,
etc.

       of

................., deceased.

On reading and filing the petition of ....,
duly verified, showing that (*giving cause*), and praying
that the said .... be superseded as such
executor :

Ordered that a citation issue to the said ....,
requiring him to appear in this court, on the ...... day
of ...., next, at ten o'clock in the forenoon,
to show cause why he should not be superseded, as
such executor; and to abide such order as shall be
made in the premises.

.................., *Surrogate,*

Where an executor has no property except an unliquidated demand, and was about to remove from the state, held, that he should be required to give security. (*Wood* v. *Wood*, 4 Paige, 299; *Holmes* v. *Cock*, 2 Barb. Ch., 426.)

An executor should not be required to give security, merely because he does not own property to the full value of the estate, and when there is no ground for supposing that the trust fund is in danger. (*Mandeville* v. *Mandeville*, 8 Paige, 475.)

The main point is, whether, the circumstances being considered, it is doubtful whether the trust fund is safe in his hands, to be administered as directed. (*Cottrell* v. *Brock*, 1 Brad., 148.)

§ 20. Upon due proof of the service of such citation, the surrogate shall proceed at the day appointed, or on such other day as he shall appoint, to hear the proofs and allegations of the parties; and if it shall appear that the circumstances of the person so appointed, are precarious as aforesaid, or that such person has removed, or is about to remove, from this state, he shall require such person to give bond, with sureties, like those required by law of administrtrators, within a reasonable time, not exceeding five days.

ORDER FOR SURETIES.

At a Surrogate's Court held in the county
of .... at the surrogate's office in
the .... of ...., on the ......
day of ...., 1873.
Present — Hon. ...., Surrogate.

In the matter of the state
of
..............., deceased.

A citation having been duly issued to ....,
the executor of the will of the above named deceased,
requiring him to show cause why he should not be
superseded, and said citation having been duly served
and the said .... having failed to appear (or
the said .... having appeared and the surrogate
having examined into the circumstances and being
satisfied that the circumstances of the said executor
have become so precarious as not to afford adequate
security for the due administration of the estate), it
is ordered that the said .... give a bond with
sureties, like that required by law of administrators, in
a penalty of .... thousand dollars, within ...... days.

.... , *Surrogate.*

There is no provision for the service of this order,
and if the executor appear in the proceeding, no
service will be necessary; but if he had not appeared, and is within the jurisdiction of the court,
he should be served.

§ 21. If such person neglect to give such bond, or if it appear that he is legally incompetent to serve as executor, the surrogate shall, by order, supersede the letters testamentary, so issued to such person, whose authority and rights as an executor shall thereupon cease ; and if there be no acting executor of such will, the surrogate shall grant letters of administration with the will annexed, of the assets of the deceased left unadministered, as provided in this title.

ORDER SUPERSEDING EXECUTOR.

At a Surrogate's Court, held in the county of ...., at the surrogate's office in the ...... of ...., on the .... day of ...., 187.
Present — Hon. ...., Surrogate.

In the matter of the application
of ...., for citation
against ...., executor,
etc.,

of

...., deceased.

On filing the citation heretofore issued in this matter, and due proof of the service thereof on .... and having heard the proofs and allegations of the petitioner and said .... and it appearing to the court that the said .... has become incompetent by law to serve as such executor, by reason of (*state reasons*) :

It is ordered and adjudged, that the letters testamentary, heretofore issued to the said ....,
on the last will and testament of ...., deceased, be, and are hereby superseded.

...., *Surrogate.*

The costs of the application should, if granted,
be charged against the estate of the deceased.
(*Holmes* v. *Cock*, 2 Barb. Ch., 426).

New Hearing of Proof within one Year.

The effect of the decree of the court establishing
the validity of a will is fixed by statute.

§ 29. (2 R. S., 61.) The probate of any will of
personal property, taken by a surrogate having
jurisdiction, shall be conclusive evidence of the
validity of such will, until such probate be reversed on appeal or revoked by the surrogate, as
herein directed, or the will be declared void by a
competent tribunal.

The word probate as used in this section, and in
our revised statutes generally, is synonymous or
nearly so, with the word *proof*, or, the proceedings
for *proof*. The word has an entirely different signification in the English statute, and reports. There
after a will has been proved, a copy is engrossed
upon parchment and to it is affixed a certificate of

the Probate Court that the will so engrossed has been proved in the court, and this parchment is called *probate*, and it is synonymous with the letters testamentary with us, and it is said that *probate* is granted to an executor, as we say, that letters testamentary are issued to an executor.

§ 30. (2 R. S., 61.) Notwithstanding a will of personal property may have been admitted to probate, any of the next of kin to the testator, may, at any time, within one year after such probate, contest the same, or the validity of such will, in the manner herein provided.

These proceedings are not confined to cases of wills bequeathing or affecting personal property only; but may be taken as to wills affecting both real and personal estate. (*Matter of will of John Kellum*, 50 N. Y., 298, reversing same case, 6 Lans., 1.)

§ 31. For that purpose, such relative shall file in the office of the surrogate by whom the will has been proved, his allegations in writing, against the validity of such will, or against the competency of the proof thereof.

ALLEGATIONS TO CONTEST PROBATE, WITHIN
ONE YEAR.

Surrogate's Court.

In the matter of the will
of
John Doe, deceased.

To the Surrogate of the county of Rensselaer:

A B, one of the next of kin of John Doe, late of the
town of Nassau, in said county, deceased, alleges that
heretofore, on or about the ...... day of ....
1871, and within one year from the exhibiting hereof,
a certain instrument in writing was admitted to probate by the surrogate of the county of Rensselaer, as
and for the last will and testament of said John Doe,
deceased, and letters testamentary thereon, were afterwards issued by said surrogate to D J B, executrix,
named in said supposed will. And that A B, C D,
E F, are named as legatees in said will and reside in
the state of New York.

And the said A B further alleges

First. That the said John Doe did not sign said supposed will.

Second. That the witnesses to said supposed will, did
not sign the same.

Third. That the said will was not published as by
law required, nor did the said John Doe request the
witnesses thereto to sign the same as witnesses.

Fourth. That at the time of the execution of the said
supposed will, the said John Doe was not of sound
mind and memory, but of unsound mind and memory,
and was incapable of making a valid will.

Fifth. That the proof heretofore presented to said surrogate, was uncertain and not competent to establish the due execution thereof, and the competency of the said John Doe.

The said A B therefore prays that a citation may be issued to the said D J B, executrix, and the said (legatees resident in this state), requiring them to appear before the surrogate at a time and place to be therein fixed, to show cause why the probate of the said supposed will should not be revoked.

Dated Dec. 20, 1872.

(Signed),   A B.

X Y, *Proctor* for said A B.

It does not seem that the allegations require to be verified.

§ 32. Upon the filing of such allegations, the surrogate shall issue a citation to the executors who shall have taken upon them the execution of such will, or to the administrators with such will annexed, and to all the legatees named in such will, residing in this state, or to their guardians, if any of them be minors, or to their personal representatives, if any of them be dead, requiring them to appear before him on some day to be therein specified, not less than thirty and not more than sixty days from the date thereof at his office, to show cause why the probate of such will should not be revoked.

For the purpose of ascertaining who are the legatees named in the will, residing in the state, reference may be had to the petition for proof filed
when the will was originally offered, and without
doubt the surrogate may take such proof as he
deems proper, as to whether they are still alive, or,
if deceased, who are their personal representatives,
and who are the guardians for minors, and he
thereupon orders that a citation issue.

ORDER FOR CITATION ON FILING ALLEGATIONS.

> At a Surrogate's Court, held in the county of
> ...., at the surrogate's office
> in the ...... of ...., on the ......
> day of ...., 187 .
> Present — Hon. ...., Surrogate.

In the matter of the will
of
John Doe, deceased.

On reading and filing the allegations of A B, claiming that (setting forth the main allegations).

Ordered, that a citation issue to C D, executor of
the will of said deceased, and to ....,
legatees named therein, resident in this state, requiring them to appear in this court, on the ...... day
of ...., 1872, to show cause why the probate
of said will should not be revoked.

..................., *Surrogate.*

§ 33. After the service of the citation, such executor or administrator shall suspend all proceedings in relation to the estate of the testator, except the collection and recovery of moneys and the payment of debts, until a decision shall be had on such allegations.

§ 34. At the time appointed for showing cause, and at such other times thereafter as the surrogate may appoint, upon due proof being made of the personal service of such citation, upon every person named therein, at least fourteen days before the time appointed for showing cause, the surrogate shall proceed to hear the proofs of the parties. If any legatees named in the will so contested, shall be minors, and have no guardians, he shall appoint guardians to take care of their interests in the controversy.

The proceedings upon the hearing are the same as if no proofs had been taken on the former hearing, and such party may produce and examine witnesses, and by section 36, the depositions of the witnesses taken on the first proof of the will, who may be dead, insane, or out of the state, may be received in evidence.

§ 35. If, upon hearing the proofs of the parties, the surrogate shall decide that such will is for any reason invalid, or that it is not sufficiently proved to have been the last will and testament of the testator, he shall annul and revoke the probate thereof; if otherwise, he shall confirm such probate. Appeals from such decision may be made in the manner, within the time and with the effect, prescribed by law.

ORDER FOR REVOCATION OF PROBATE.

At a Surrogate's Court held in the county of .... at the surrogate's office in the .... of .... on the ...... day of ...., 187.

Present — Hon. ...., Surrogate.

In the matter of the paper purporting to be the will

of

John Doe, deceased.

A B having heretofore filed allegations against the probate of the above mentioned paper, and a citation having been issued to the executor and legatees named therein, and proofs having been offered in the matter, and the surrogate having deliberated thereon, and it appearing that the said John Doe, deceased, at the time of the making of the instrument in writing, admitted to probate in this court, on the .... day of ...., 1871, as the last will and testament of the said deceased, was not of sound mind (or that said will was not duly executed) :

It is ordered, adjudged and decreed, that the probate heretofore granted by this court, on the said instrument as, and for the last will and testament of the said John Doe, deceased, be and the same is, hereby annulled and revoked.

It is further ordered that notice of this order be served on ...., executor, and be published for three weeks successively, in a newspaper printed in the said county of Rensselaer.

.................., *Surrogate.*

§37. Whenever any surrogate shall annul and revoke the probate of any will of personal property, as herein provided, he shall enter such revocation in his record, and attest the same ; and shall cause notice thereof to be immediately served on the executor therein named, or upon the administrators with such will annexed, and to be published for three weeks in a newspaper printed in his county, if there be one, the expense of which publication shall be taxed as part of the costs of the proceedings.

§ 38. Upon such notice being served upon such executor or administrator, his powers and authority shall cease, and he shall account to the representatives of the deceased person, whose alleged will was contested, for all moneys and effects received ; but such executor or administrator shall not be liable for any act done in good faith, previous to the service of the citation, nor for any act so done in the collection of moneys, or the payment of debts, after the service of the citation and previous to the service of the notice of revocation.

It is further provided that costs may be adjudged against a party resisting the revocation, in case the probate shall be revoked; and payment thereof may be enforced by attachment.

CHAPTER VI.

ADMINISTRATION.

Administration is the legal right to settle and control the estate of deceased persons, and also, the exercise of that right. Letters of administration, are the warrant under the seal of the court giving the legal right.

Letters of administration are of three kinds; first, upon the goods, chattels and credits of a person who shall have died intestate; that is, without having made his last will and testament; second, special letters of administration authorizing the administrator to collect and preserve the estate, either of a testator, in certain cases; or, of an intestate; and third, letters of administration authorizing the person appointed to execute the powers given by the will of the deceased, called letters of administration with the will annexed, or *cum testamento annexo.*

The jurisdiction of the court and the rights of parties interested, are controlled by the statute.

§ 23. The surrogate of each county shall have sole and exclusive power, within the county for which he may be appointed, to grant letters of administration of the goods, chattels and credits of persons dying intestate, in the following cases:

9

" 1. Where an intestate at, or immediately previous to his death, was an inhabitant of the county of such surrogate, in whatever place such death may have happened ;

" 2. Where an intestate, not being an inhabitant of this state, shall die in the county of such surrogate, leaving assets therein ;

" 3. Where an intestate, not being an inhabitant of this state, shall die out of the state, leaving assets in the county of such surrogate and in no other county;

" 4. Where an intestate, not being an inhabitant of this state, shall die out of the state, not leaving assets therein, but assets of such intestate shall thereafter come into the county of such surrogate." (2 R. S., 73.)

" § 24. Whenever an intestate, not being an inhabitant of this state, shall die out of the state, leaving assets in several counties, or assets of such intestate shall, after his death, come into several counties, the surrogate of any county in which such assets shall be, shall have the power to grant letters of administration on the estate of such intestate; but the surrogate who shall first grant letters of administration on such estate, shall be deemed thereby to have acquired sole and exclusive jurisdiction over such estate, and shall be vested with all the powers incidental thereto." (Id.)

" § 25. The persons appointed administrators by the surrogate who shall have first granted letters of administration in the cases specified in the last section, shall have sole and exclusive authority as such, and shall be entitled to demand and recover from every person subsequently appointed administrator of the same estate, the assets of the deceased in his hands. But all acts in good faith, of such subsequent administrator, done before notice of such previous letters, shall be valid; and all suits commenced by him, may be continued by and in the name of the first administrator." (Id., 74.)

It does not seem that section 23, providing as above, for the cases in which the surrogate of a particular county may grant letters, includes the case where a person, not an inhabitant of the state, dies within the county of the surrogate, leaving no assets in such county, but leaving assets in another county. Nor does it provide for the case where a non-inhabitant shall die in the county of the surrogate not leaving assets therein, but assets shall thereafter come into the county. But in these cases, it has been held by Surrogate Bradford, in a well considered opinion (*Kohler* v. *Knapp*, 1 Brad., 241), that this, although an omission to regulate the power of the surrogate, does not restrict or limit his power to grant administration in the cases prescribed and conferred by statute. He accordingly held that if assets of the deceased non-inhabitant have come into the county of the surrogate since his death, or were there at the time of his death, he has jurisdiction to grant administration.

The rights of persons interested in the estate of an intestate, to general administration, are also regulated by the statute as follows:

"§27. Administration, in cases of intestacy, shall be granted to the relatives of the deceased, who would be entitled to succeed to his personal estate, if they, or any of them, will accept the same, in the following order:

First. To the widow;

Second. To the children;

Third. To the father;

Fourth. To the mother;

Fifth. To the brothers;

Sixth. To the sisters;

Seventh. To the grand-children;

Eighth. To any other of the next of kin who would be entitled to share in the distribution of the estate.

"If any of the persons so entitled be minors, administration shall be granted to their guardians; if none of the said relatives or guardians will accept the same, then to the creditors of the deceased, and the creditor first applying, if otherwise

competent, will be entitled to a preference; if no
creditor apply, then to any other person or persons
legally competent. But in the city of New York,
the public administrator shall have preference, after
the next of kin, over creditors and all other persons; and in the other counties, the county trea-
surer shall have preference next *after* creditors,
over all other persons. And in the case of a married
woman, dying intestate, her husband shall be entitled to administration in preference to all other
persons. * * * This section shall not be construed
to authorize the granting of letters to any relative
not entitled to succeed to the personal estate of the
deceased as his next of kin, at the time of his decease." (2 R. S., 74, as amended by chap. 782,
Laws of 1867.)

Letters of administration issue upon the estate
of an illegitimate in the following order : *First*, to
the widow; *Second*, to the children or other descendants; *Third*, to the mother; and, *Fourth*,
to the relatives on the part of the mother in the
order of their nearness of kindred to him through
the mother. (S. L., 1845, chap. 236.)

" § 28. Where there shall be several persons of
the same degree of kindred to the intestate, entitled to administration, they shall be preferred in
the following order: First, males to females ; second, relatives of the whole blood, to those of the

half blood ; Third, unmarried women to such as
are married; and where there are several persons
equally entitled to administration, the surrogate
may in his discretion, grant letters to one or more
of such persons." (2 R. S., 74.)

" § 29. A husband, as such, if otherwise competent according to law, shall be solely entitled to
administration on the estate of his wife and shall
give bonds as other persons, but shall be liable, as
administrator, for the debts of his wife, only to the
extent of the assets received by him * * * *."
(Id., 75.)

" § 31. In all cases, where persons, not inhabit-
ants of this state, shall die, leaving assets in this
state, if no application for letters of administration
be made by a relative entitled thereto and legally
competent, and it shall appear that letters of administration on the same estate, or letters testamentary have been granted by competent authority,
in any other state of the United States, then the
person so appointed, on producing such letters,
shall be entitled to letters of administration in
preference to creditors, or any other persons except
the public administrator in the city of New York."
(Id.)

" § 32. No letters of administration shall be
granted to any person convicted of an infamous
crime, nor to any one incapable by law of making

a contract, nor to any person not a citizen of the United States (unless such person reside within this state), nor to any one who is under twenty-one years of age, nor to any person who shall be judged incompetent by the surrogate, to execute the duties of such trust by reason of drunkenness, improvidence, or want of understanding * * * *. (Id. as amended by chap. 782, S. L., 1867.)

Any surrogate may also, in his discretion, refuse the application for administration, of any person unable to read and write the English language. (§ 5, S. L., 1867, chap. 782.)

"§ 33. If any person, who would otherwise' be entitled to letters of administration as next of kin, or to letters of administration with the will annexed, as residuary or specific legatee, shall be a minor, such letters shall be granted to his guardian, being in all respects competent, in preference to creditors or other persons. (2 R. S., 75.)

"§ 34. Administration may be granted to one or more competent persons not entitled to the same, with the consent of the person entitled to be joined with such person; which consent shall be in writing, and be filed in the office of the surrogate." (Id.) This consent, once acted on and letters issued in accordance with it, cannot be revoked. (*Estate of Williams*, 1 Tuck., 8.)

"§ 26. Before any letters of administration shall

be granted on the estate of any person who shall
have died intestate, the fact of such person's dying
intestate shall be proved to the satisfaction of the
surrogate; who shall examine the persons applying
for such letters, on oath, touching the time, place
and manner of the death, and whether or not the
party dying left any will; and he may also, in like
manner, examine any other person, and may compel such person to attend as a witness for that
purpose." (2 R. S., 74.)

The provisions in the last above quoted section
of the statute, are usually complied with by em-
bodying the facts in a sworn petition, for presentation to the surrogate.

This is the only petition, in proceedings in this
court, which must necessarily be verified before
the surrogate personally; for in this case, the surrogate must "examine the persons applying for
such letters, on oath," and it would seem to be irregular, ordinarily, to issue letters, except upon the
personal attendance of the petitioner.

There is no provision in the statute, as to objections to the issue of letters to any person otherwise entitled, as there is in the case of an executor,
and usually, if the applicant for letters is entitled
in his own right, or is one of a class entitled, letters
would immediately issue to him on his filing the
proper bond, notwithstanding that he might bei n-

competent, or might be found incompetent on a hearing before the surrogate. But it is believed that the surrogate would entertain objections from any person interested in the estate as one of the next of kin, or as a creditor, and that an affidavit of intention to file objections might be filed with the same effect, and to be followed by the same proceedings, as in the case of objections to an executor, and reference is made to the consideration of that subject. (See *ante.*)

But the surrogate cannot exclude a person, otherwise entitled to letters of administration, except for the causes specified in the statute. (*Coope* v. *Lowerre*, 1 Barb. Ch., 45.)

PETITION FOR ADMINISTRATION.

Surrogate's Court, Rensselaer county.

In the matter of the personal
estate
of
...., deceased.

To Moses Warren, Esq.,
　　　　Surrogate of the county of Rensselaer :

The petition of ...., of the city of Troy in said county, respectfully shows :

That ...., late of said city, died from disease, on or about the 15th day of December, 1873, at the city of Troy, aforesaid, without leaving any last will and testament ; that said deceased at the time of his death, was possessed of certain personal property within the state of New York, the value whereof does not exceed the sum of .... dollars, as your petitioner is informed and verily believes; and that your petitioner is a creditor of the said deceased. Your petitioner further shows that the said deceased left him surviving his widow .... (or your petitioner), and his children, ... and .... of Troy aforesaid (naming all who are interested in the personal estate as entitled to share therein), his only next of kin, and that he was at, or immediately previous to his death an inhabitant of the county of Rensselaer.

Your petitioner prays that administration upon the estate of the said deceased may be granted to your petitioner, jointly with ...., of the city of Troy.

Dated Troy, Dec. 18, 1873.

....

State of New York,   } ss.
    Rensselaer county.   }

................., being duly sworn, says : that the foregoing petition by him subscribed is true.

Sworn before me this 18th day }
    of December, 1873.   }

                MOSES WARREN,
                  Surrogate.

CONSENT OF PERSON TO BE JOINED TO BE ENDORSED UPON PETITION.

I, ..., named in the within petition, consent that administration upon the goods, etc., of ...., deceased, be granted to me jointly with .... as asked for in said petition.

Dated Dec. 18, 1873.

....

In reference to the issue of letters upon petition, see *Farley* v. *McConnells*, (52 N. Y., 630.)

"§ 35. When any person shall apply for administration, either with the will annexed, or in cases of intestacy, and there shall be any other person having prior right to such administration, the applicant shall produce, prove and file with the surrogate, a written renunciation of the persons having such prior right. If he fail to do so, before any such letters shall be granted, a citation shall be issued to all persons having such prior right, to show cause, at a day therein to be specified, why administration should not be granted to such applicant." (2 R. S., 76.)

RENUNCIATION.

Surrogate's Court, Rensselaer county.

In the matter of the goods, etc.,
of
James Murphy, dec'd.

I, ..., of the city of Troy, in the county of Rensselaer, widow (or, one of the next of kin), of James Murphy, late of said city, dec'd, intestate, do hereby renounce my right to administration of the goods, chattels and credits of said intestate.

Dated, Troy, Dec. 18th, 1873.

Signed in presence of
Wm. Lord,
Dennis Miller jr.

Rensselaer county, ss :

William Lord of the town of Brunswick, in said county, being duly sworn, says that he knows ...., above named, and that he saw the said . ... sign the foregoing instrument, and that he thereupon became a subscribing witness thereto.

WM. LORD.

Sworn before me, this 18th }
    day of Dec., 1873.   }

DENNIS MILLER, Jr.,
Com'r of Deeds, Troy, N. Y.

But if a citation is necessary it is issued upon the order of the surrogate.

ORDER FOR CITATION.

At a Surrogate's Court held in and for the county of ...., at the surrogate's office in the city of ...., on the ...... day of ...., 1873.

Present — ...., Surrogate.

In the matter of the goods, etc.,
    of
................., deceased.

On reading and filing the petition of ...., a creditor of the above named deceased for administration upon the estate of said deceased, and it appearing that said deceased left him surviving .... his widow and .... and ...., his next of kin. Ordered that a citation issue to said widow and next of kin of said deceased, requiring them personally to appear in this court on the ...... day of ......

next, at ten o'clock in the forenoon, to show cause why administration of all and singular the goods, chattels and credits of the said deceased, should not be granted to the said petitioner.

.................., *Surrogate.*

CITATION.

The people of the state of New York. To ...., widow and ....

[L. S.] ...., next of kin of ....,
late of the city of Troy, dec'd, intestate,
Greeting:

You and each of you are hereby cited personally to be and appear before our surrogate of the county of Rensselaer at his office, in the city of Troy, on the ...... day of ...., next at ten o'clock in the forenoon of that day to show cause why administration of the goods, chattels and credits of the said intestate should not be granted to ...., a creditor of said intestate.

Witness, Moses Warren, Surrogate, and the seal of said court this .... day of ...., 1873.

MOSES WARREN,
Surrogate.

The time for the return of the citation is necessarily governed by the time to be taken for the service.

"§ 36. If any person to whom such citation shall be directed, shall reside within the county of such surrogate, such citation shall be served personally, or by leaving a copy at the residence of such person, at least six days before the return day thereof. If any such person reside out of such county, but within the state, and such residence can be ascertained, service shall be made in the same manner, at least forty days before the return day of the citation, if any such person reside out of the state, or his residence cannot be ascertained, such citation may be personally served without the state, forty days before its return, or may be published once in each week, for six weeks successively, in the state paper." (2 R. S., 76.)

In all cases of publication, a copy of the citation must be mailed to such of the parties to be served whose place of residence can be ascertained, at least thirty days before the return day of the citation. (S. L., 1863, chap. 362, § 1.)

"§ 37. In all cases of application for letters of administration in cases of intestacy, a citation to show cause as aforesaid, shall be issued to, and served on, the attorney general, at least twenty days before the return day thereof, previous to granting such letters, unless it shall be shown to the surrogate by the affidavit of the applicant, or other written proof, that the intestate left kindred entitled to his estate, specifying the names of such kindred and their places of residence, as far as the same can be ascertained." (2 R. S., 76.)

The parties cited may come into court, even before the return day of the citation, and petition
for the issue of letters to themselves, and if the
petitioners have the prior right, or produce the
renunciation of those entitled to letters in preference to them, letters will undoubtedly issue forthwith upon the filing of the proper bond and oath
of office.

But, upon the return day of the citation, if there
shall be no legal objections made to the person
applying for letters, and no one having a prior
right shall apply, the surrogate will order the issue
of letters to the applicant.

And, notwithstanding parties entitled, may have
renounced, they may retract such renunciation at
any time before letters shall actually be issued to
another. (*Casey* v. *Gardnier*, 4 Brad., 13.)

There may be a case, in which several parties
equally entitled, shall apply for letters, and there
is no provision in the statute as to which shall
be preferred, except males to females, relatives of
the whole blood to those of the half blood, etc.
(*Sup.*, § 28.) If, therefore, several sons of the
intestate should apply, it would seem that the surrogate may exercise his discretion as to whom he
will issue the letters (*Taylor* v. *Delancey*, Caines'
cases, 149), and he would undoubtedly be governed
in the exercise of his discretion, by the wishes of

the parties interested in the distribution as next
of kin, who for the purpose of expressing their preference might either unite in the petition of one,
or petition independently for the appointment of
any one.

It is error, to grant letters unless all the persons
having right to them in preference to the applicant,
shall have renounced, or shall have been deemed
to have renounced after citation.   Thus it was held,
that where one died intestate, leaving a father and
brothers, it was error to grant letters to a creditor,
upon the renunciation of the father only.   (*Lathrop*
v. *Smith*, 35 Barb., 64, and 24 N. Y., 417.)

The question as to priority having been disposed of, the surrogate enters an order for the issue
of the letters.

ORDER FOR LETTERS.

At a Surrogate's Court, held in and for the
county of ...., at the surrogate's
office in the .... of ...., on
the ...... of ...., 1873.
Present — Hon. ...., Surrogate.

In the matter of the goods, etc.,

of

.... , deceased.

On reading and filing proof of the due service of the
citation in this matter on .... and ....
and on motion of ...., who has petitioned for

the issue of letters of administration of the goods, chattels and credits of the above named deceased intestate, no one opposing :

Ordered that letters of administration of the goods, chattels and credits of the said deceased, issue to the said ...., upon his filing the oath of office as such administrator, and a bond as required by law in the penalty of (ten thousand) dollars with two or more sureties approved by the surrogate.

.................., *Surrogate.*

The oath of administrator, may be taken before any officer authorized to administer oaths.

OATH OF ADMINISTRATOR.

State of New York, ... county, ss :

I, ..., do solemnly swear, that I will honestly and faithfully discharge the duties of administrator of the goods, chattels and credits of ...., deceased, according to law.

....

Sworn before me, this 24th }
   day of Dec., 1873.   }

.................,
      Justice of the Peace.

" § 42. Every person appointed administrator, shall, before receiving letters, execute a bond to the people of this state, with two or more competent

10

sureties, to be approved by the surrogate, and to be jointly and severally bound. The penalty in such bond shall not be less than .twice the value of the personal estate of which the deceased died possessed, which value shall be ascertained by the surrogate, by the examination on oath of the party applying, and of every other person he may think proper to examine. The bond shall be conditioned, that such administrator shall faithfully execute the trust reposed in him as such, and also that he shall obey all orders of such surrogate, touching the administration of the estate committed to him." (2 R. S., 77.)

When there are several administrators, the statute requiring the surrogate to take from every administrator a bond with sureties, as above provided, is complied with by taking one joint and several bond from all the administrators, with competent approved sureties. (*Kirby* v. *Turner*, Hopk., 309.)

BOND OF ADMINISTRATOR.

Know all men by these presents: that we, John Doe, Richard Roe and Thomas Nokes, of the city of Troy, are held and firmly bound unto the people of the state of New York, in the sum of two thousand dollars, lawful money of the United States, to be paid to the said people, to which payment, well and truly to be made, we bind ourselves, our and each of our, heirs, executors and administrators, jointly and severally, firmly by these presents.

Sealed with our seals, and dated this 22d day of February, 1862.

The condition of this obligation is such, that if the above bounden John Doe, administrator of all and singular the goods, chattels, and credits of Richard Roe, late of the city of Troy, deceased, shall faithfully execute the trust reposed in him as such, and also, that he obey all orders of the surrogate of the county of Rensselaer, touching the administration of the estate committed to him, then this obligation to be void, otherwise to remain in full force.

(Signed),   JOHN DOE.   [L. S.]

RICHARD ROE.   [L. S.]

THOMAS NOKES.   [L. S.]

Sealed and delivered in }
     the presence of   }

MOSES WARREN.

State of New York,   }
     Rensselaer county, } ss.

On this 22d day of February, 1862, before me personally appeared John Doe, Richard Roe, and Thomas Nokes, to me known to be the same persons described in and who executed the foregoing bond and severally acknowledged that they executed the same for the uses and purposes therein mentioned.

GEO. SCOTT,
Com'r of Deeds, Troy, N. Y.

Rensselaer county, ss:

Richard Roe and Thomas Nokes of the city of Troy, duly sworn, do each depose and say that he is worth

the sum of two thousand dollars over and above all
debts he owes, or liabilities incurred by him.

RICHARD ROE,
THOS. NOKES.

Sworn before me this 22d day }
   of February, 1873.   }

GEO. SCOTT,
Com'r of Deeds, Troy, N. Y.

The justification of the sureties is not necessary,
unless exacted by the surrogate as a condition of
his approval of them. His approval may either
be endorsed at the time of filing, or it would seem,
that when the surrogate himself files the bond, his
approval would be presumed. If a question should
be raised, the surrogate might at any time endorse
his approval, *nunc pro tunc.*

The letters of administration issued under the
seal of the Surrogate's Court are *prima facie* evidence of the appointment. (*Belden* v. *Meeker,* 47
N. Y., 307.) And such letters cannot be attacked
collaterally, nor in any proceeding except one
specially instituted to revoke them. (*Flinn* v.
Chase, 3 Den., 84.)

Administration de bonis non.

Administration of the goods, chattels and credits
of an intestate, not administered upon by a former
administrator, issue of course, when the office of

such former administrator becomes vacant, by death, or revocation of his letters, for any cause specified in the statute.

The rules as to priority are the same as in the first issue and the same proceedings would be taken in regard to citation of all persons having such prior right to letters.

The petition for such letters should however state the fact of the issue of such former letters, and the death of the former administrator, or revocation of the former letters, and that such former administrator " left unadministered, certain assets and personal property of the intestate, of the value of about $, as the petitioner is informed and verily believes."

In such case also the petitioner could have any proper person joined with him in the administration, as in the case of the first issue.

The bond would be the same, and the administrator should in all respects pursue the same course as if appointed in the first instance.

Administration with the Will Annexed.

Administration with the will annexed is granted, when there are no persons named as executors in the will ; when all the executors named shall have renounced, or, after summons, shall be deemed to have renounced, or shall be legally incompetent ;

or after letters testamentary shall have been superseded or revoked (2 R. S., 71, § 14 ; Id., 72, § 21 ; Id., 81, § 19), " then letters testamentary shall issue and administration with the will annexed be granted, as if no executors were named in such will, to the residuary legatees, or some or one of them if there be any ;

" If there be none that will accept, then to any principal or specific legatee, if there be any ;

" If there be none that will accept, then to the widow and next of kin of the testator, or to any creditor of the testator in the same manner and under the like regulations and restrictions, as letters of administration in case of intestacy." (2 R. S., 71, § 14.)

But a guardian of an infant, who is not a residuary or specific legatee, is not entitled to letters with the will annexed, in preference to the widow of the testator. (*Cluett* v. *Mattice*, 43 Barb., 417.)

" § 20. Such letters of administration, or letters testamentary, shall supersede all former letters, and shall deprive the former executor or administrator of all power, authority and control over the personal estate of the deceased, and shall entitle the person appointed, by such letters, to take, demand, and receive the goods, chattels and effects of the deceased wherever the same may be found." (2 R. S., 85.)

pointment as trustee to execute a power of sale, and that when appointed, he would execute the power solely as trustee.

Special Letters of Collection.

These are issued in the discretion of the surrogate, in the cases provided by law.

" § 38. In case of a contest relative to the proof of a will, or relative to granting letters testamentary or of administration with the will annexed, or of administration in cases of intestacy, or when, by reason of absence from this state of any executor named in a will, or for any other cause, a delay is necessarily produced in granting such letters, the surrogate authorized to grant the same, may, in his discretion, issue special letters of administration, authorizing the preservation and collection of the goods of the deceased." (Chap. 460, S. L., 1837.)

" § 43. Every collector appointed by special letters, shall execute a bond with sureties, to be approved by the surrogate, in the same penalty as in case of an administrator, and the same proceedings shall be had to ascertain such penalty. The condition of such bond shall be, that he will make a true and perfect inventory of such of the assets of the deceased as shall come into his possession or knowledge, and return the same, within three months, to the office of the surrogate granting such letters; that he will faithfully and truly account for all property, money and things in action, received by him as such collector, whenever required by the said surrogate, or any other court of competent authority, and will faithfully deliver up the same to the person or persons who shall be appointed executors or administrators of the deceased, or to such other person as shall be authorized to receive the same by the surrogate." (2 R. S., 77.)

When appointed he will take the oath of office as other administrators.

The petition should show the death of the testator or intestate, his residence in the county of the surrogate, or other facts to give the surrogate jurisdiction, the amount of the personal property of the deceased, the delay in issue of letters in chief, and the cause, and the reasons rendering it desirable that special letters should issue, and a prayer for their issue.

Inasmuch as their issue is in the discretion of the surrogate, no citation need be issued.

But by chap. 71, Laws of 1871, the special administrator shall be appointed only after notice of two days, in writing, shall have been given to the attorneys of the parties who have appeared in the case, of the names of the persons who are proposed as sureties of the special administrator, and the time and place of their justification. On the day fixed, the sureties may be fully examined, and if they shall not appear to be worth, collectively, double the penalty of the bond, no letters shall issue.

Like notice of ten days shall be given of the application for a special administrator before the application shall be made.

No sale or transfer of personal property shall be made by the special administrator, except on the order of the surrogate, made on notice to all parties who have appeared by attorney.

The time of the notice shall be ten days, and shall be served on the attorneys in the manner provided by law, for service of notice of motions in civil actions. The time, when service is by mail, will require to be twenty days.

By the same chapter, every special administrator shall, within ten days, after receipt of moneys as such, deposit them with some person who shall give adequate security by a bond in a penalty to be fixed by the surrogate with two sufficient sureties to be approved by him, or with such banking association as the surrogate shall direct. In the county of New York, he shall deposit such moneys, in an incorporated trust company. These moneys shall not be withdrawn, except upon the order of the surrogate, to be presented to the depository, and no order shall be made for such withdrawal, except upon notice to the attorneys of all parties who have appeared in the estate.

The special administrator, is, by the same act, made liable to account for all interest received by him, in the same manner as for principal.

The condition of the bond of the special administrator expresses fully his liability, and his duties extend only to the collection and preservation of the estate. He may collect the goods, chattels, personal estate and debts of the deceased, and secure them at such reasonable expense as the surrogate shall allow.

For these purposes, he may maintain actions, as administrator.

When the necessity for the special administration shall have ceased, he may be compelled to account and to deliver the assets to his successor, by citation to him, or may ask for a settlement of his account. When decree has been made against him, obedience to it may be enforced by attachment, as in other cases of administration.

In regard to the liability of his sureties, it was held that they are liable for moneys in his hands received before his appointment as special administrator. (*Gottsberger* v. *Taylor*, 19 N. Y., 150.)

CHAPTER VII.

GENERAL PROVISIONS IN REGARD TO LETTERS TESTA-
MENTARY AND OF ADMINISTRATION. FOR WHAT REA-
SONS LETTERS ARE REVOKED, ETC.

§ 44. (2 R. S., 78.) In case any one of several executors or administrators, to whom letters testamentary or of administration shall have been granted, shall die, become lunatic, convict of an infamous offense, or otherwise become incapable of executing the trust reposed in him; or in case that letters testamentary or of administration shall be revoked or annulled according to law, with respect to any one executor or administrator, the remaining executors or administrators shall proceed and complete the execution of the will or the administration, according to law.

§ 45. If all such executors or administrators shall die, or became incapable, as aforesaid, or the power and authority of all of them shall be revoked, according to law, the surrogate having authority to grant letters originally, shall issue letters of administration upon the goods, chattels, credits and effects of the deceased left unadministered, with the will annexed, or otherwise, as the case may be, to the widow, or next of kin, or creditors of the deceased, or others, in the same manner as hereinbefore directed, in relation to original letters of administration; which administrator shall give bonds in the like penalty, with like sureties and conditions, as hereinbefore required of administrators, and shall have the like power and authority. And such letters shall supersede all former and other letters testamentary, and of administration upon the same estate.

§ 46. If, after granting any letters of administration on the ground of intestacy, any will shall be subsequently proved, and letters testamentary or of administration, with the will annexed, be thereupon issued, a revocation of such letters of administration shall be made by the surrogate; and until the same be made and served on such administrator, his acts done in good faith shall be valid; and the executors, to whom letters testamentary shall be issued, shall be entitled to demand, collect, and sue for, the goods, chattels and effects remaining unadministered.

§ 47. All sales made in good faith, and all lawful acts done, either by administrators before notice of a will, or by executors or administrators, who may be removed or superseded, or who may become incapable, shall remain valid, and shall not be impeached, on any will afterwards appearing, or by any subsequent revocation or superseding of the authority of such executors or administrators.

§ 25. (S. L., 1837, 460, S. L., 1862, 229.) When any person interested in the estate of the deceased shall discover that the sureties of any executor or administrator are becoming insolvent, that they have removed or that for any other cause they are insufficient (by § 35, when the estate is discovered to be larger than at first supposed), such person may make application to the surrogate who granted the letters testamentary or of administration for relief.

The application is in the usual form of petition.

PETITION WHERE SURETIES ARE INSUFFICIENT.

To Hon ...., Surrogate of.............. county.

The petition of .... , one of the next of kin of ...., late of the town of ...., in the county of ...., respectfully shows:

That heretofore, in the Surrogate's Court of said county, administration upon the goods, chattels and credits of the said deceased were duly granted and issued to .... of the town of .... and A B and C D were the sureties for the said .... upon the bond filed by him prior to the issue of such letters.

And your petitioner further shows:

That he has discovered that the said C D, one of said sureties, is becoming insolvent (or is about to remove, or has removed from the state).

Wherefore your petitioner prays that the said ...., administrator as aforesaid, may be cited to give further sureties, or be superseded in the administration, or for such other or further relief as may be proper in the premises.

Dated, Dec. 31, 1874.

(Signed), ...

.... County, ss:

................., being duly sworn, says that the foregoing petition by him subscribed is true.

(Signed), ...

Sworn before me this ...... }
    day of ...., 1874. }

....

Commissioner of Deeds.

§ 26. If the surrogate shall receive satisfactory evidence that the matter requires investigation, he shall issue a citation to such executor or administrator, requiring him to appear before such surrogate, at a time and place to be therein specified, to show cause why he should not give further sureties, or be superseded in the administration; which citation shall be served personally on the executor or administrator, at least six days before the return day thereof; or if he shall have absconded, or cannot be found, it may be served by leaving a copy at his last place of residence.

The executor or administrator cited to show cause why he should not be superseded, may also be enjoined by the surrogate from further action, until the matter in controversy shall be settled. (S. L., 1837, 535.)

ORDER FOR CITATION.

At a Surrogate's Court held in the county of .... at the surrogate's office in the ...... of ...., on the ...... day of ...., 187....

Present—Hon. ...., Surrogate.

In the matter of the estate
of
.................., deceased.

R F, one of the next of kin of the above named deceased, having presented his petition under oath, alleging that C D, one of the sureties of .... , the administrator of all and singular the goods, chattels and credits of the above named deceased, is about to remove from the estate, on praying for relief:

Ordered that a citation issue to ...., said administrator, to appear before the surrogate at his office in the .. .. of ...., on the .... day of ...., 1874, at ten o'clock in the forenoon, to show cause why he should not be required to give further sureties or be superseded in the administration.

.................., *Surrogate.*

Upon the return day, the administrator may demur to the sufficiency of the petition, or deny the allegations of it, on oath, and if he do deny them, the burden of proof rests on the petitioner. (*Cottrell* v. *Brock*, 1 Brad., 148.)

§ 27. On the return of such citation, or such other time as the surrogate shall appoint, he shall proceed to hear the proofs and allegations of the parties; and if it shall satisfactorily appear that the sureties are, for any cause, insufficient, the surrogate shall make an order requiring such administrator to give further sureties, in the usual form, within a reasonable time, not exceeding five days.

ORDER REQUIRING FURTHER SURETIES.

At a Surrogate's Court, held in the county of ...., at the surrogate's office in the ...... of ...., on the .... day of ...., 187....

Present, Hon. ...., Surrogate.

In the matter of the estate

of

...................., deceased.

R F having heretofore presented his petition praying that ...., the administrator of the estate of the above named deceased, be required to give further sureties, and a citation having been duly issued therein, and the same having been returned with proof of the due service thereof, and the said ...., having appeared, and the surrogate having heard the proofs

PETITION OF SURETY FOR RELIEF.

To Hon. ...., Surrogate of the county of ....

The petition of ...., of the town of ....,
in said county, respectfully shows,

That your petitioner is one of the sureties of ....
to whom administration on the goods, chattels and
credits of ...., late of the town of ....,
were on the ...... day of ...., last, granted out
of this court; and your petitioner desires to be released
from responsibility on account of the future acts or
defaults of such administrator.

Your petitioner therefore prays that the said ....
may be required to give new sureties.

Dated, December, ... 1874.

(Signed), ...

.... county, ss :

..............., being duly sworn, says that the foregoing
petition by him subscribed is true.

(Signed), ...

Sworn before me this ...... }
day of ...., 1874. }

...................,

Notary Public.

§ 30. The surrogate shall thereupon issue a citation to such executor or administrator, requiring
him to appear before such surrogate, at a time and
place therein to be specified, and give new sureties
in the usual form, for the discharge of his duties;

which citation shall be served in the manner prescribed by the 26th section of this act (personally
at least six days, or by leaving a copy thereof at
his residence if he shall have absconded, or cannot
be found).

ORDER FOR CITATION ON APPLICATION OF SURETY.

At a Surrogate's Court, held in the county of
.................., at the surrogate's office in
the .... of ...., on the......
day of ...., 1874.
Present — Hon. ...., Surrogate.

In the matter of the estate
of
.................., deceased.

A B, one of the sureties for C D, the administrator
of the goods, chattels and credits of the above named
deceased, having presented his petition, praying to
be released from further responsibility for the future
acts or defaults of the said administrator :

Ordered that a citation issue to said C D, to appear
in this court, on or before the ...... day of ....,
1874, at ten o'clock in the forenoon, to give new sureties in the usual form, in place of said A B.

.................., *Surrogate.*

§ 31. If such executor or administrator shall give
new sureties to the satisfaction of the surrogate, the
surrogate may thereupon make an order, that the

surety or sureties who applied for relief, in the premises, shall not be liable on their bond, for any subsequent act, default or misconduct of such executor or administrator.

ORDER RELEASING SURETY.

At a Surrogate's Court, held in the county of
.................., at the surrogate's office in
...... of ...., on the ...... day of
...., 1874.
Present — Hon. ...., Surrogate.

In the matter of the estate
of
.................., deceased.

A B, one of the sureties of C D, the administrator of the goods, chattels and credits of the above named deceased, having applied to this court for relief, and an order having been made that said administrator give further sureties in place of said A B, and the said C D having given further sureties to the satisfaction of the surrogate, which said bond is filed this day:

Ordered, that the said A B, shall not be liable on the bond signed by him as surety for the said C D, for any subsequent act, default or misconduct of said C D.
.................., *Surrogate.*

§ 32. If such executor or administrator neglect to give new sureties to the satisfaction of the surrogate, on the return of the citation, or within such reasonable time as the surrogate shall allow, not exceeding five days, the surrogate shall, by order, revoke the letters testamentary or of administration issued to such executor or administrator, whose authority and rights as an executor or administrator shall thereupon cease.

ORDER REVOKING LETTERS.

At a Surrogate's Court, held in the county of ...., at the surrogate's office in the ...... of ...., on the .... day of ...., 1874.

Present—Hon. ...., Surrogate.

In the matter of the estate
of
................., deceased.

C D, the administrator of the goods, chattels and credits of the above named deceased, having been ordered by the court to give a bond in the usual form with new sureties in place of A B, one of his sureties, who petitioned for relief, and having neglected to give such bond, and the time limited therefor having expired:

Ordered that the letters of administration granted in this court to said C D, on the ...... day of ...., 1873, on the estate of the above named deceased, be and they are revoked and annulled, and the authority and rights of said C D, as such administrator shall cease.

...., *Surrogate.*

It is further provided by section 33, of the same chapter which we have been considering, that in all cases in which letters testamentary or of administration shall have been granted to more than one person, and the surrogate granting such letters shall have revoked them as to part only of such executors or administrators, the person or persons whose letters shall not have been revoked shall have the further administration of the respective estates, subsequent to such revocation. Any suit brought previous to such revocation, may be continued the same as if no revocation had taken place. In all other cases of revocation, as aforesaid, the surrogate shall grant administration of the goods, chattels and credits not administered, in the manner prescribed by law.

Letters granted on false Representations may be revoked.

§ 34. (S. L., 1837, chap. 460.) Whenever it shall appear to the surrogate, that letters of administration, or letters of guardianship have been granted on, or by reason of false representations, made by the person to whom the same were granted ; and also, whenever it shall appear that an administrator or guardian has become incompetent by law to act as such, by reason of drunkenness, improvidence, or want of understanding, the surrogate shall have power to revoke such letters.

The revocation may be made when issued on false representations, even when they were made, not fraudulently, but by mistake. (*Paley* v. *Sands*, 3 Edwd. Ch., 325; *Proctor* v. *Wanamaker*, 1 Barb. Ch., 302; *Kerr* v. *Kerr*, 41 N. Y., 272.)

Independently of this statute, the surrogate has power to revoke letters granted upon a false suggestion of a matter of fact, and without due citation to the party having prior right to such letters. (*Proctor* v. *Wanamaker, sup.*)

The proceedings under this provision would be conducted upon a petition of some person interested, showing the false representations, upon which a citation would issue to the administrator or guardian to show cause why the letters should not be revoked. The forms given heretofore, may be conveniently adapted to these proceedings.

Under chap. 288, of Laws of 1846, whenever an absent or non-resident executor or administrator shall have been duly served with a citation to account, and shall without reasonable cause, neglect or refuse to appear in pursuance thereof, the surrogate may, in his discretion, revoke the letters to such executor or administrator.

The surrogate of the county of New York, may revoke the letters of an executor, administrator or collector, or of a testamentary trustee, or guardian, upon his own application, for good cause shown, and on notice to the persons interested ; and may make such terms and conditions for the security of the estate, as in his judgment are required. After such revocation, the surrogate may issue letters of administration, letters with the will annexed, or of collection, or appoint a successor to such trustee or guardian. (Chap. 359, Laws of 1870.)

CHAPTER VIII.

Discovery and Recovery of Assets.

The legislature by chap. 394, of Laws of 1870, have provided for a summary process, to discover assets belonging to a deceased person, or to which he was entitled at the time of his decease, when they are improperly concealed or withheld by any person, by a subpœna, and an examination of persons designated, by the executor or administrator.

The statutory provisions are as follows :

"§ 1. Whenever any executor or administrator, to whom letters testamentary, or of administration, shall have been issued by any Surrogate's Court, in this state, shall have reasonable grounds to believe that any goods, chattels, credits or effects of the deceased, or of which he had possession at the time of his death, or within two years prior thereto, shall not have been delivered to such executor or administrator, nor accounted for satisfactorily, by the persons who were about the person prior to his decease, or in whose hands the effects of the deceased, or any of them, may be supposed at any time to have fallen, such executor or administrator may institute an inquiry concerning the same, and upon satisfying the surrogate of the county in which said letters shall theretofore have been issued, by affidavit, that there are reasonable grounds for suspecting that any such effects are concealed or withheld, such executor or administrator shall be entitled to a subpœna, to be issued by such surrogate under his seal of office to such persons as may be designated by said executor, or administrator, requiring them to appear before such surrogate, at the time and place therein to be specified, for the purpose of being examined touching the estate and effects of the deceased.

" § 2. If the surrogate be absent, such application for a subpœna may be made to any justice of the Supreme Court, to the county judge, and in the county of New York to any judge of the Court of Common Pleas, or to the mayor or recorder of any city, either of whom is authorized to issue such subpœna under his hand and seal in the same manner as the surrogate.

" § 3. Such subpœna, shall be served in the same manner as in civil actions, and if any person shall refuse or neglect to obey the same, or shall refuse to answer touching the matters hereinafter specified, such person shall be attached and committed to prison by the said surrogate, or other officer so issuing such subpœna, in the same manner as for disobedience of any citation or subpœna issued by a surrogate in any other case within his jurisdiction."

The proof to be produced to the surrogate or other officer is to be by affidavit, and it must appear to the satisfaction of such officer, that there are reasonable grounds for believing that the effects sought to be recovered are concealed or withheld.   In analogy to the practice in the Supreme Court, in warranting an order for arrest, it is presumed that the circumstances, from which a reasonable presumption may be drawn, that such effects are concealed or withheld, should be verified by the affidavit or affidavits used.   It will not be sufficient to move upon papers simply declaring that there are reasonable grounds for the belief that the effects are concealed or withheld.

The following is suggested as a form for the principal affidavit, to be made by the executor or administrator.

AFFIDAVIT.

Surrogate's Court, Rensselaer county.

In the matter of the goods, etc., of J....... D...... , dec'd.

Rensselaer county, ss:

A B, of the town of ...., in said county, being duly sworn, says: that he is the executor of the

The subpœna, is the ordinary subpœna of the court.

§ 4. Upon the appearance of any person so subpœnaed before such surrogate or other officer, such person shall be sworn truly to answer all questions concerning the estate and effects of the deceased, and shall be examined fully and at large in relation to said effects.

§ 5. If, upon the inquiry, it shall appear to the officer conducting the same, that any effects of the deceased are concealed or withheld, and the person having possession of such property shall not give the security in the next section specified for the delivery of the same, such officer shall issue his warrant, directed to the sheriff, marshals and constables of the city or county where such effects may be, commanding them to search for and seize the said effects, and for that purpose, if necessary, to break open any house in the day time, and to deliver the said property so seized, to the executor or administrator of the deceased ; which warrant shall be obeyed by the officers to whom the same shall be directed and delivered, in the same manner as the process of a court of record.

If it shall appear to the surrogate from the testimony, that effects of the deceased are concealed, or withheld, and are in the possession of certain persons, it is presumed that he will make an alterna-

12

tive order for the delivery of them, or that sureties be given within a reasonable time.

ORDER.

At a Surrogate's Court held in and for the county of Rensselaer at the surrogate's office in the city of Troy, on the ...... day of .... , 1874.
Present Hon. Moses Warren, Surrogate.

In the matter of the goods, etc.,

of

J......... D.........., deceased.

It appearing from the testimony in this matter, that certain effects of the above named deceased, to wit: one bay horse, one gold watch (naming and describing the articles), are concealed (or withheld) by G B, of the town of Nassau, in said county: Ordered, if the said G B shall not, within five days after the service of the copy of this order on him, give a bond to J D, executor of the will of the said deceased, in the penalty of $2,000, with two or more sureties to be approved by the surrogate, conditioned that the obligors will account for and pay to said executor the full value of such property to wit, one bay horse, one gold watch (enumerating the articles), whenever it shall be determined in any suit to be brought by said executor that said property belongs to the estate of said deceased, that a warrant issue to the sheriff, and constables of the county, to search for and seize such property according to law.

Moses Warren,

Surrogate.

It would seem that a copy of such order should be served upon the person in whose possession such property is supposed to be, and if he shall not give such bond, approved by the surrogate, the warrant will issue.

"§ 6. But such warrant shall not be issued to seize any property of the person in whose possession such property may be, if he or any one in his behalf, shall execute a bond, with such sureties and in such penalty as shall be approved by the surrogate or the officer acting in his place, to the executor or administrator of deceased, conditioned that such obligors will account for, and pay to, the said executor or administrator, the full value of the property so claimed and withheld, and which shall be enumerated in the said condition, whenever it shall be determined, in any suit to be brought by said executor or administrator, that said property belongs to the estate of such deceased person."

WARRANT.

The People of the state of New York to the
[SEAL.]   sheriff of the county of Rensselaer or any
constable of said county, Greeting:

We command you, that upon the receipt hereof, you do forthwith search for and seize, one bay horse, one gold watch (enumerating the articles) supposed to be in the possession of G B, in your bailiwick, and for that purpose, if necessary, to break open any house in

the day time, and that you deliver said property to J.
D, the executor of the will of A B, deceased, and that
you make return thereof with this writ, to our surrogate of the county of Rensselaer.

Witness, Moses Warren, Surrogate of our county
of Rensselaer and the seal of our said
court this ...... day of ...., 1874.

MOSES WARREN,
Surrogate.

CHAPTER IX.

Appointment of Appraisers and the Inventory.

The duty of taking an inventory is too often neglected, while in fact the omission to make and file it, according to the statute, is a strong circumstance in support of the charge of improper conduct in an administrator. (*Hart* v. *Ten Eyck,* 2 Johns' Ch., 80.)

"Upon the application of any executor or administrator, the surrogate who granted letters testamentary or of administration, shall by writing, appoint two disinterested appraisers, as often as occasion may require, to estimate and appraise the property of the deceased person ; and such appraisers shall be entitled to receive a reasonable compensation for their services, to be allowed by the surrogate, but not exceeding five dollars for each day actually employed in making an appraisement or inventory, in addition to his actual expenses necessarily incurred; the number of days services so rendered, and the amount of such expenses to be verified by the affidavit of the appraisers performing such services, to be made and delivered to the executor or administrator before payment of such fees, and to be adjusted by the surrogate. And no clerk or employee in a surrogate's office shall act as appraiser in any matter before such surrogate." (2 R. S., 82, § 1, as amended by chap. 225, Laws of 1873.)

This act would seem to require a warrant of appointment of the appraisers, and such, in fact, is the practice, to issue the warrant upon the order of the court.

ORDER FOR APPRAISERS.

At a Surrogate's Court, held in and for the county of .... at the surrogate's office in the .... of ...., on the ...... day of ...., 1874.
Present — Hon. ...., Surrogate.

In the matter of the estate
of
..............., deceased.

On the application of ...., executor of the last will and testament of ...., deceased :

Ordered that ...., of the city of ...., and ...., of the town of .... be appointed appraisers of the personal estate of the said deceased, and that their appointment issue under the seal of this court.

..............., *Surrogate.*

WARRANT OF APPOINTMENT

[L. S.] The people of the state of New York, by the grace of God free and independent, to .... and ...., of the town of ...., in the county of ...., send greeting:

Whereas ...., the executor of the will of ...., late of ...., in said county, deceased, has this day applied to the surrogate of the county of ...., for the appointment of two disinterested appraisers of the personal estate of said deceased, with a view of making an inventory thereof; now, therefore, said surrogate hath appointed, and by these presents does appoint you, the said ...., and ...., to estimate and appraise the personal property of the deceased, and to aid the said executor in making a true and perfect inventory of the goods, chattels and credits of the said deceased.

Witness ...., surrogate and the seal of this court this ...... day of ...., 1874.

....................,
Surrogate.

The duty of the appraisers being, to fix a value to charge the executor or administrator as between him and the next of kin, legatees etc., it would seem to be a very proper rule to appoint only such as could act as jurors in a trial at law, in which any of these parties might be interested.

" § 2. The executors and administrators of any testator or intestate, within a reasonable time after

It is not required, but it is believed to be good practice, to annex to the inventory when filed, proof by affidavit, of the service and posting of the notice of the appraisement.

" § 4. Before proceeding to the execution of this duty, the appraisers shall take and subscribe an oath to be inserted in the inventory made by them, before any officer authorized to administer oaths, that they will truly, honestly, and impartially appraise the personal property which shall be exhibited to them, according to the best of their knowledge and ability."

" § 5. The appraisers shall, in the presence of such of the next of kin, legatees or creditors of the testator or intestate as shall attend, proceed to estimate and appraise the property which shall be exhibited to them, and shall set down each article separately, with the value thereof, in dollars and cents distinctly in figures, opposite to the articles respectively." (Id.)

INVENTORY.

We, whose names are hereunder assigned, appraisers, appointed by the surrogate of the county of Rensselaer, having first taken and subscribed the oath hereinafter inserted, do certify that we have estimated and appraised the property in the annexed inventory contained, exhibited to us, according to the best of our knowledge and ability, and we have signed duplicate inventories thereof.

Dated this ...... day of ....

.... } *Appraisers.*
....

State of New York, } ss.
  Rensselaer county,

I, ... do solemnly swear that I will truly, honestly and impartially appraise the personal property of ...., deceased, which shall be exhibited to me, according to the best of my knowledge and ability.

....

Subscribed and sworn, this ......
  day of .... 18 ......, before me. }

....

State of New York, }
  Rensselaer county,

I, ... do solemnly swear that I will truly, honestly and impartially appraise the personal property of ...., deceased, which shall be exhibited to me according to the best of my knowledge and ability.

....

Subscribed and sworn, this ......
  day of .... 18 ......, before me. }

....

A true and perfect inventory, of all and singular, the goods, chattels and credits of ...., deceased, made by ...., etc., of the deceased, with the aid of ...., Appraisers, appointed by the surrogate of the county of Rensselaer, duly qualified, and after service of notice, as the law directs, on the . .... day of ...., one thousand eight hundred and seventy.. ....

The following articles are stated but not appraised, being set apart, according to law, for the widow (and minor children), to wit:

One spinning wheel.
One weaving loom.
One knitting machine.
One sewing machine.
Three stoves kept for use of the family.
[And so on to property exempt from appraisal.]

The following articles are appraised and set apart for the use of the widow (and minor children), in addition to those enumerated above, in pursuance of the statute, to wit:

One mahogany bureau, ...	$15.00
One bay mare, ...	75.00
One half barrel flour, ...	5.00
One cord wood split for use, . . .	5.00
Cash, ... ,	50.00
	150.00

The following are enumerated as assets in addition to the above:

Forty sheep, ...	$100.00
1 sorrel horse, ...	60.00
1 black horse, ...	75.00

[And thus through like articles.]

The following accounts and notes are considered good and collectable.

Note John Myers, dated Feby. 10, 186?, for $100, interest endorsed for two years now worth, ... $100.00
Account against James Jones, . . . 15.00
[And thus through the good items.]

The following are considered doubtful.

Note Thomas Nokes, dated Aug. 1, 1872, no
    endorsement, ...   16.00
    [And so through the doubtful.]

The following are considered bad.
[State items in detail.]
Dated June 5, 1874.
        (Signed),
                .... } *Appraisers.*
                ....

The inventory is made in duplicate, one copy for
filing, and one to be preserved by the executors or
administrators.

"§ 6. The following property shall be deemed
assets and shall go to the executors or administrators, to be applied and distributed as part of the
personal estate of their testator or intestate, and
shall be included in the inventory thereof :"

"1. Leases for years ; lands held by the deceased
from year to year, and estates held by him for the
life of another person." (*Reynolds* v. *Collier*, 3 Hill,
441.)

"2. The interest which may remain in the deceased at the time of his death, in a term for years,
after the expiration of any estate for years therein,
granted by him or any other person.

3. The interest in lands devised to an executor,
for a term of years, for the payment of debts.

4. Things annexed to the freehold, or to any building for the purpose of trade or manufacture, and not fixed into the wall of a house so as to be essential to its support."

Hop poles used on the land are a part of the realty. (*Bishop* v. *Bishop*, 11 N. Y., 123.)

Cotton machinery is personal property. (*Van Derpoel* v. *Van Allen*, 10 Barb., 157.)

Looms in a woolen mill are personal estate (*Murdock* v. *Gifford*, 18 N. Y., 28), while the water wheel, gearing, millstones and bolting apparatus are part of the realty. (*Murdock* v. *Gifford, sup.*, and *House* v. *House*, 10 Paige, 158.)

Manure, the produce of a farm, passes with the realty. (*Middlebrook* v. *Corwin*, 15 Wend., 169 ; *Goodrich* v. *Jones*, 2 Hill, 142 ; see also *Foy* v. *Muzzey*, 13 Gray (Mass., 53.) On the other hand, by parity of reasoning and without doubt, the accumulations of a livery stable or scavenger, are personal property.

" 5. The crops growing on the land of the deceased, at the time of his death."

Meaning, as qualified in the next subdivision, crops which are produced annually, by cultivation.

" 6. Every kind of produce, raised annually by labor and cultivation, excepting grass growing and fruits not gathered.

" 7. Rent reserved to the deceased, which had accrued at the time of his death."

Rents accrued and collected after the decease of the testator or intestate, go to the heir, as incident to the reversion, and the executor is not responsible for it, and can maintain no action to recover it. (*Kohler* v. *Knapp*, 1 Brad., 241; *Fay* v. *Halloran*, 35, Barb. 295.)

Where a lease ended in April, and the tenant had the privilege to gather winter crops, and to pay the rent in wheat in August, and the landlord died in June, *held* that the rent due in August went to the executors. (*Wadsworth* v. *Alcott*, 6 N. Y., 64.)

Where a tenant for life, having demised premises, dies, on or after the day the rent becomes due, his executors or administrators may recover the rent. But if he dies before the rent becomes due, the rent shall be apportioned between the executors or administrators and the reversioners. (2, R. S., 747, § 22.)

" 8. Debts secured by mortgage, bonds, notes, or bills, accounts, money and bank bills, or other circulating medium, things in action and stock in any company, whether incorporated or not.

"9. Goods, wares, merchandise, utensils, furniture, cattle, provisions and every other species of personal property and effects, not hereinafter excepted."

The inventory must include all the personal property of the decedent wherever situated, whether in this state, or in some other state, which has come to the hand, or knowledge of the executor or administrator. (*Matter of Butler*, 38 N. Y., 397.) In this case, the executor was ordered to make an inventory of assets in the state of Louisiana.

Some difficulty has been experienced in inventorying the interest of the decedent in a partnership, but it seems to be well settled now by the opinion of Mr. Surrogate Bradford in *Thompson* v *Thompson* (1 Brad., 24). He there holds, that inasmuch as the surviving partner is a trustee as to the interest of the decedent, the assets are not to be inventoried. That as the executor or administrator is only entitled to a balance on an accounting, it is sufficient as to the partnership interest, to state it in the inventory, as an interest in an unascertained balance.

" § 7. Things annexed to the freehold, or to any building, shall not go to the executor, but shall descend with the freehold, to the heirs or devisees, except such fixtures as are mentioned in the fourth subdivision of the last section.

§ 8. The right of an heir to any property not enumerated in the preceding sixth section, which by the common law would descend to him, shall

not be impaired by the terms of that section."
(Id.)

Fixtures have been well defined to be " chattels
so annexed to the land that the owner of the
chattels has no right to remove them, as a general
rule, except when he is the owner of the land."
(Bingham on Real Estate, 453.   See also *Tifft* vs.
Horton, 53 N. Y., 377.)

" § 9. (As amended chap. 782, Laws of 1867,
and Laws of 1874.) When a man having a family,
shall die leaving a widow, or a minor child or
children, or a widow shall die leaving a minor child
or children, the following articles shall not be
deemed assets (*for the purpose of distribution, the
payment of debts or legacies*), but shall be included
and stated in the inventory of the estate without
being appraised.

I. All spinning wheels, weaving looms, one knitting
machine, one sewing machine and stoves put up or
kept for use by his family.

II. The family Bible, family pictures and school
books used by or in the family of such deceased person, and 'books not exceeding in value fifty dollars,
which were kept and used as part of the family library
before the decease of such person.

III. All sheep to the number of ten, with their
fleeces, and the yarn and cloth manufactured from the
same ; one cow, two swine, and the pork of such swine,
and necessary food for such swine, sheep or cow for

sixty days; and all necessary provisions and fuel for such widow, or child, or children, for sixty days after the death of such deceased person.

IV. All necessary wearing apparel, beds, bedsteads and bedding; necessary cooking utensils; the clothing of the family; the clothes of the widow, and her ornaments proper for her station; one table, six chairs, twelve knives and forks, twelve plates, twelve teacups and saucers, one sugar dish, one milk pot, one teapot and twelve spoons, and also other household furniture which shall not exceed one hundred and fifty dollars in value.

§ 13. (S. L., 1867, chap. 782.) * * * * All articles and property set apart, in accordance with law for the benefit of a widow and a minor or minors, shall be and remain the sole personal property of such widow, after such minor or minors shall have arrived at age.

But notwithstanding, the widow is not entitled to the possession of these articles, until they are inventoried and set apart by the appraisers. (*Volckner* v. *Hudson*, 1 Sandf., 215.) These provisions for the widow and minor child or children, apply whether the decedent was a householder or not, and even if the deceased, or his widow or children, are non-residents. (*Knapp* v. *Public Administrator*, 1 Brad., 258.)

The provision that the articles set apart shall remain in the possession of the widow, is explained

13

in *Scofield* v. *Scofield* (6 Hill, 642), to mean that she is entitled to hold the articles during the minority of the children, notwithstanding their voluntarily leaving her, without her fault.

A husband cannot divest his widow of these articles by his will. (*Vedder* v. *Saxton*, 46 Barb., 188.)

§ 2. (S. L., 1842, chap. 157, as amended chap. 782, of Laws of 1867). Where a man having a family shall die, leaving a widow or minor child or children; or a widow shall die leaving a minor child or children. there shall be inventoried and set apart for the use of the widow, or for the use of such widow and child or children, or for the use of such child or children, in the manner now prescribed by the ninth section, necessary household furniture, provisions or other personal property, in the discretion of said appraisers, to the value of not exceeding one hundred and fifty dollars, in addition to the personal property now exempt from appraisal by said section.

Thus it seems that the appraisers shall use their discretion as to what articles they shall set apart, not as to whether they shall set apart any or not, for it has been held (*Scofield* v. *Scofield*, 6 *Hill*, 642), that where the articles reserved by the statute for the use of the widow are not set apart as required by the statute, in the inventory, the surrogate may cite the executor or administrator, and cause him to have the inventory corrected. Or the error may be corrected on the accounting of the executor or administrator. (*Clayton* v. *Wardell*, 2 Brad., 1.)

But if the executor or administrator so omitting, sell the whole personal property, the widow may affirm the sale, and on the accounting claim her $150, and the surrogate may, on cause shown, decree the payment of the avails to her. (*Sheldon* v. *Bliss*, 8 N. Y., 31.)

But the appraisers' estimate of value, is not judicial as to articles set apart, and errors may be corrected by the surrogate. (*Applegate* v. *Cameron*, 2 Brad., 119.) If the appraisers' memorandum of articles set apart shows that they exceed $150 in value, the allotment is void. (Id.)

§ 11. (2 R. S., 84.) The inventory shall contain a particular statement of all bonds, mortgages, notes or other securities for the payment of money, belonging to the deceased, which are known to such executor or administrator, specifying the names of the debtor in such security, the date, the sum originally payable, the endorsements thereon, if any, with their dates, and the sum which in the judgment of the appraisers, may be collectable on such security.

§ 12. The inventory shall also contain an account of all moneys, whether in specie or bank bills, or other circulating medium, belonging to the deceased, which shall have come into the hands of the executor or administrator ; and if none shall have come into his hands, the fact shall be so stated in such inventory.

It may oftentimes occur that, before the appraisal, the executor or administrator may have paid out some of the moneys which came into his hands, for funeral expenses, or other necessary charges ; notwithstanding, he should state in the inventory the amount which came originally into his possession, and charge in his account, what he shall have paid out.

§ 13. The naming of any person executor in a will, shall not operate as a discharge or bequest of any just claims which the testator had against such executor, but such claims shall be included among the credits and effects of the deceased, in the inventory, and such executor shall be liable for the same, or for so much money in his hands, at the time such debt or demand becomes due ; and he shall apply and distribute the same in the payment of debts and legacies, and among the next of kin as part of the personal estate of the deceased. (See also *Decker* v. *Miller*, 2 Paige, 149.)

Notwithstanding the duty of the executor to state a claim of the deceased against himself in the inventory, on the hearing on final settlement, it is competent to show any legal defense which he may have to the claim. (*Everts* v. *Everts*, 62 Barb., 677.)

§ 14. The discharge or bequest in a will, of any debt or demand of the testator against any executor named in his will, or against any other person, shall not be valid as against the creditors of the deceased; but shall be construed only as a specific bequest of such debt or demand, and the amount thereof shall be included in the inventory of the credits and effects of the deceased, and shall, if necessary, be applied in the payment of his debts; and if not necessary for that purpose, shall be paid in the same manner and proportions as other specific legacies.

§ 15. Upon the completion of the inventory, duplicates thereof shall be made and signed by the appraisers; one of which shall be retained by the executor or administrator, and the other shall be returned to the surrogate within three months from the date of such letters.

§ 16. Upon returning such inventory the executor or administrator shall take and subscribe an oath, * * * * stating that such inventory is in all respects just and true, that it contains a true statement

of all the personal property of the deceased which
has come to the knowledge of such executor or administrator, and particularly of all money, bank
bills and other circulating medium, belonging to
the deceased, and of all just claims of the deceased
against such executor or administrator, according
to the best of his knowledge.   Such oath shall be
endorsed upon or annexed to the inventory.

OATH TO INVENTORY.

Surrogate's Court,
State of New York, Rensselaer county, } ss.

.............., of ...., deceased, being duly
sworn, does depose and say that the annexed inventory
is in all respects just and true; that it contains a true
statement of all the personal property of the said deceased which has come to the knowledge of this deponent, and particularly of all money, bank bills, and
other circulating medium belonging to the said deceased, and of all just claims of the said deceased against
this deponent.

....
Subscribed and sworn this ...... day of }
.................., 187–, before me. }

....

Return of Inventory.—How Compelled.

It will have been observed, that one copy of the
inventory, verified by the oath of the executor or
administrator shall be filed with the surrogate
within three months from the issue of letters testa-

mentary, or of administration. (See § 15, *supra*.)
But the time for the filing of the inventory may be
extended for cause shown, by the surrogate, not exceeding four months longer. This extension should
be granted by order, upon a petition stating the
reasons fully why the inventory cannot be com-
pleted within the three months time allowed by
the statute, and if the application, which is made
ex parte, shall seem reasonable, the surrogate will
grant an order, thus :

ORDER EXTENDING TIME FOR FILING INVENTORY.

At a Surrogate's Court held in and for the
county of Rensselaer, at the surro-
gate's office in the city of Troy, on the ......
day of ...., 1874.
Present — Hon. ...., Surrogate.

In the matter of the estate
of
.................., dec'd.

On reading and filing the petition of ....,
the executor of the will of the above named dec'd,
praying for further time in which to file the inventory
of the personal estate of said deceased, and said application seeming reasonable :

Ordered, that said executor have until the ...... day
of ...., next to make and file such inventory.

.................., *Surrogate.*

§ 19. (2 R. S., 85.) If any executor or administrator shall neglect or refuse to return such inventory within the time aforesaid, or within such further time, not exceeding four months, as the surrogate shall for reasonable cause allow; the surrogate shall issue a summons requiring such executor or administrator, at a short day, therein to be appointed, to appear before him and return an inventory according to law, or show cause why an attachment should not be issued against him.

PETITION FOR SUMMONS.

Surrogate's Court, Rensselaer county :

In the matter of the estate of ...., deceased.

To the Surrogate of the county of Rensselaer :

The petition of C D, of the town of ...., in said county, respectfully shows : That your petitioner is a creditor (or one of the next of kin of, or a legatee named in the will), of the above named deceased. That letters testamentary upon the will (or letters of administration upon the estate) of the above named deceased were, on the first day of June, 1874, duly granted and issued to J D, of the town of Brunswick, and that notwithstanding more than three months have elapsed since the issue of such letters, the said J D has not filed an inventory of the personal estate of the said deceased, in the office of said surrogate, as he was by law required to do.

Wherefore your petitioner prays that a summons issue to the said J D, requiring him to appear before said surrogate, and return an inventory according to law, or show cause why an attachment should not issue against him.

Dated September 23, 1874.

C D.

Rensselaer county, ss :

C D, being duly sworn, says that the foregoing petition by him subscribed is true.

C D.

Subscribed and sworn, etc.

The surrogate thereupon enters an order for the issue of the summons and fixing the time for the return thereof. It would seem that ordinarily the summons should give at least five days to the executor or administrator, to enable him to serve notices for the taking of the inventory, and make the same.

ORDER FOR SUMMONS.

At a Surrogate's Court, held in and for the county of ...., at the surrogate's office in the city of ...., on the ...... of ...., 1874.

Present — Hon. ...., Surrogate.

In the matter of the estate

of

...., deceased.

On reading and filing the petition of C D, showing that he is a creditor of ...., late of the town

of ...., in said county, deceased, that J D is
the executor of the will of said deceased and that more
than three months have elapsed since the granting of
letters to the said J D, and that he has hitherto neglected to file an inventory of the personal estate of the
said deceased:

Ordered that a summons issue to the said J D, requiring him to appear before the surrogate at his office
in the city of Troy, on the ...... day of ....
next, then and there to return an inventory of the
personal property, goods, chattels and credits of the
said deceased, according to law, or show cause why an
attachment should not issue against him.

................, *Surrogate.*

SUMMONS TO RETURN INVENTORY.

The people of the state of New York to J D,
executor of the last will and testament

[L. S.]   of ...., late of the town of
................, in the county of ....,
deceased.

You are hereby summoned and required to appear
before the surrogate of the county of ...., at
his office in the city of ...., on the ...... day
of ...., 1874, at ten o'clock in the forenoon,
then and there to return an inventory of the goods,
chattels and credits of the said ...., deceased,
according to law, or show cause why an attachment
should not issue against you.

Witness ...., surrogate, and the seal
of our said court, this ......, day of
................, 1874.

................, *Surrogate.*

It would seem that the proper manner of serving the summons, is by delivering to the executor or administrator a copy thereof, at the same time showing to him the original with the seal attached.

§ 18. (2 R. S., 85.) If after personal service of such summons, such executor or administrator shall not, by the day appointed, return such inventory on oath, or obtain further time to return the same, the surrogate shall issue an attachment against him, and commit him to the common jail of the county, there to remain until he shall return such inventory.

The attachment may be executed in any county where the executor or administrator may be. (*People* v. *Pelham,* 14 Wend., 485.)   It is issued upon an order as follows:

ORDER FOR ATTACHMENT.

At a Surrogate's Court held in and for the county of ...., at the surrogate's office in the city of Troy, on the ......, day of ...., 1874.

Present — Hon. ...., Surrogate.

In the matter of the estate
of
.................., deceased.

A summons having been issued out of this court returnable this day, to J D, executor of the will of the above named deceased, requiring him to appear and file an inventory of the goods, chattels and credits of the said deceased or show cause why an attachment should not issue against him, and said summons having been duly and personally served, and the said J D, not having appeared (or, having appeared and not filing an inventory as required), and no cause being shown why an attachment should not issue against him:

It is ordered and adjudged, that an attachment issue against the said J D, directed to the sheriff of the county of ...., and that he be committed to the common jail of the county of ...., there to remain until he shall return such inventory, or be thence discharged according to law; and that said sheriff make return of such attachment on the ...... day of ...., next.

................., *Surrogate.*

And thereupon issues the

ATTACHMENT.

The people of the state of New York to the [SEAL.] sheriff of the county of ...., Greeting:

Whereas on the ...... day of ...., 1874, by a certain order made in our Surrogate's Court of the county of ...., before our surrogate of said county, at the surrogate's office in the village of ...., in said county, in a certain proceeding pending in our said court in the matter of the estate of ...., deceased, it was ordered that an attachment issue against J D, executor of the will of said deceased, and that he be committed to the common jail of the county of ...., until he shall return to our Surrogate's Court of said county, an inventory of the goods, chattels and credits of the said deceased, or be thence discharged according to law, as by the said order remaining of record in our said Surrogate's Court more fully appears, the said J D having refused (or neglected) to return such inventory, balthough required so to do by an order and summons of our said court :

Now therefore we, command you, that you take the body of the said J D, if he shall be found in your bailiwick, and him safely keep in your custody, until he shall return such inventory, or until he shall be thence discharged by due course of law ; and you are to make and return to our Surrogate's Court, on the ...... day of ...., 1874, a certificate under your hand, of the manner in which you shall have executed this writ, and have you then and there this writ.

> In testimony whereof we have caused this writ to be subscribed by our said surrogate and the seal of the court to be affixed this ......day of ...., 1874.
>
> ...., Surrogate.

Endorsed.

Title, ...

Attachment against J D, executor, etc., of ...., deceased, for not returning an inventory of the goods etc., of said deceased.

..................., Surrogate.

§ 22. (2 R. S., 86.) Every executor or administrator committed to prison, as aforesaid, may be discharged by the surrogate or a justice of the Supreme Court, on his delivering upon oath, all the property of the deceased under his control, to such person as shall be authorized by the surrogate to receive the same.

§ 19. (2 R. S., 85.) If such summons cannot be served personally, by reason of such executor or administrator absconding or concealing himself, or, if after being committed to prison, such executor or administrator shall neglect for thirty days to make and return such inventory, the surrogate may thereupon issue under his seal of office, a revocation of the letters testamentary, or letters of administration, before granted to such executor or administrator, reciting therein the cause of such revocation, and shall grant letters of administration of the goods, chattels and effects of the deceased, unadministered, to the person entitled thereto (other than such executor or administrator), in the same manner as original letters of administration, or letters testamentary.

This revocation issues upon an

ORDER FOR REVOCATION.

At a Surrogate's Court, held in and for the county of ...., at the surrogate's office in the ...... of ...., on the ...... day of ...., 1874.

Present Hon. ...., Surrogate.

In the matter of the estate

of

................., deceased.

An attachment having been heretofore issued against C D, executor of the will of the above named deceased, committing him to the common jail of the county of ...., until he should return an inventory of the goods, chattels and credits of said deceased; and it appearing by the certificate of the sheriff of said county, endorsed upon said attachment that more than thirty days have elapsed since the said C D was committed to his custody, and the said C D, having still neglected to return such inventory:

[Or, It appearing to the surrogate by affidavit that the summons heretofore issued to C D, the executor of the will of the above named deceased, cannot be served personally on the said C D, by reason of his absconding, or concealing himself:]

Ordered that the letters testamentary heretofore issued to the said C D, as executor of the last will and testament of the above named deceased, be revoked, and that a revocation under the seal of this court, forthwith issue.

.. .., *Surrogate.*

REVOCATION.

[SEAL.] To C D, as executor of the last will and testament of A B, late of the .... of ...., deceased, and all others whom it may concern, Greeting :

Whereas, on the ...... day of ...., 1870, letters testamentary were duly issued to the said C D, as executor of the last will and testament of A B, late of the ...... of ...., deceased, by the surrogate of the county of .... : And whereas the said C D, neglected to return an inventory of the goods, chattels and credits of said deceased within the time required by law, and a summons was issued thereupon by said surrogate, on the application of ...., a creditor of the said deceased, requiring the said C D to appear before said surrogate and return such inventory, on a day now past, or show cause why an attachment should not issue against him : And whereas it clearly appears to our said surrogate, that the said summons could not be served personally upon the said C D by reason of his absconding (or concealing himself), or, and whereas the said summons was duly served on the said C D personally, and the said C D omitted to return such inventory, by the day therein appointed, and such proceedings were thereupon had, that an attachment for not returning such inventory was duly issued against the said C D, to the sheriff of the county of ...., by virtue of which, the said C D, has been imprisoned for thirty days and upwards in the common jail of said county, during all of which time he has neglected and still neglects to return such inventory :)

Now, therefore, be it known, that in pursuance of an order of our said Surrogate's Court, and of the

statute in such case made and provided, we have revoked and do revoke the letters testamentary issued
as aforesaid to said C D; and do command the said
C D, to desist and refrain from any further intermeddling with the estate of the said deceased.

> Witness, ..., surrogate of our said
> county, and the seal of said court this ......
> day of ...., 1874.
>   ...., *Surrogate.*

§ 23. (2 R. S., 86.) Any one or more of the executors or administrators named in any letters, on
the neglect of the others, may return an inventory;
and those neglecting shall not thereafter interfere
with the administration, or have any power over
the personal estate of the deceased; but the executor or administrator so returning an inventory,
shall have the whole administration, until the delinquent return and verify an inventory, agreeably
to the provisions of this article.

After an inventory shall have been made it may
often happen that new assets are discovered and
then it becomes the duty of the executor or administrator to make a supplementary inventory.

§ 24. (2 R. S., 86.) Whenever personal property
or assets of any kind, not mentioned in any inventory that shall have been made, shall come to the
possession or knowledge of an executor, or adminis-

14

trator, he shall cause the same to be appraised in manner aforesaid, and an inventory thereof to be returned, within two months after the discovery thereof; and the making of such inventory and return may be enforced in the same manner as in the case of the first inventory.

The petition of any person interested, in case of default showing discovery of the property, former inventory and neglect to return inventory of the property discovered, will be ground for the entry of an order for summons and for proceedings as above detailed. The forms before given can be readily adapted to the case here presented.

CHAPTER X.

Of the Collection and Care of the Estate; Compromising Debts due the Estate, and Advertising for Claims.

Several co-executors or co-administrators are in law, but one person, and the act of one, in reference to the sale, delivery, release or gift of the decedent's goods, is deemed the act of all. (*Gardner* v. *Miller*, 19 Johns., 188.) One, without the concurrence of his co-executors, or administrators, may release a portion of mortgaged premises from the lien, or give a satisfaction piece (*Stuyvesant* v. *Hall*, 2 Barb. Ch., 151), and either executor or administrator, as against his associates, may retain possession of the assets. (*Burt* v. *Burt*, 41 N. Y., 46.)

So, two executors, against the will of a third, may compromise and release a mortgage, or other debt of the estate. (*Murray* v. *Blatchford*, 1 Wend., 583.) One executor also, may assign a note, as security for a judgment against the estate. (*Wheeler* v. *Wheeler*, 9 Cow., 34.)

Where two executors take an obligation to themselves, jointly as representatives of a testator, for a debt belonging to the estate, one of them can receive payment, and lawfully discharge the obligation ; and the obligation in this case being a bond and mortgage, it was held, that one could execute a proper satisfaction piece.

So, a *bona fide* purchaser from one executor, of a bond and mortgage given to two executors, for the purchase money on their sale of lands, under a power in the will, will be protected in his purchase, even though the executor divert and waste the purchase money. (*Bogert* v. *Hertell*, 4 Hill, 492.)

They should keep the estate funds separate from other funds; if they mingle them with their own, they are liable for losses (*Kellett* v. *Rathbone*, 4 Paige, 102) ; and they may be required by the surrogate to deposit the funds of the estate with a savings bank, or trust company, so as to be earning interest, while the estate is in process of settlement. (*Lockhart* v. *Public Administrator*, 4 Brad., 21.)

Letters testamentary, or of administration, are local in their character, and the authority given by them is co-extensive only with the limits of the state where issued. (2 Kent Com., 430, note.) But an executor who has obtained probate and letters in another state, can (without action), dispose of his testator's personal property in this state, without taking out ancillary letters here.   For the title of an executor arises from the will, and not the probate, or letters, and consequently the executor is vested with all the personal estate of his testator wherever situated. (*Middlebrook* v. *Merchant's Bank*, 27 How., 474; *Peterson* v. *Chemical Bank*, 29 How., 240.)

The duty of the executor, or administrator in regard to collections and investment of the estate, is clear, and he must proceed to convert the property which may not be producing interest into money, and deposit it, so as that the moneys may draw interest. He must also collect the money loaned on personal security, for if he neglect to do so and a loss accrue through his neglect, which would have been avoided by an early collection he will be chargeable for the loss. (Williams on Ex'rs, 15, 43.)

He is amply empowered in making collections, and may bring suit in all the courts of this state.

It is the duty of an executor or administrator to treat all transfers made by his testator or intestate in fraud of the rights of creditors, as void, and he may recover of any person who shall have received the property of the deceased, the full value thereof. (S. L., 1858, chap. 314.)

"§ 2. (2 R. S., 113.) Actions of account, and all other actions upon contract, may be maintained by and against executors in all cases, in which the same may have been maintained against their respective testators * * *."

"§ 3. Administrators shall have actions to demand and recover the debts due to their intestate, and the personal property and effects of their intestate; and shall answer and be accountable to others, to whom the intestate was holden, or bound, in the same manner as executors."

§ 4. Executors and administrators shall have actions of trespass against any person who shall have wasted, destroyed, taken or carried away, or converted to his own use, the goods of their testator or intestate, in his lifetime. They may also maintain actions for trespass committed on the real estate of the deceased, in his lifetime.

§ 5. Any person, or his personal representatives, shall have actions of trespass against the executor or administrator of any testator or intestate, who, in his lifetime, shall have wasted, destroyed, taken or carried away, or converted to his own use, the goods or chattels of any such person, or committed any trespass on the real estate of any such person.

§ 6. The executors and administrators of every person, who as executor, either of right, or in his own wrong, or as administrator, shall have wasted or converted to his own use any goods, chattels or estate of any deceased person, shall be chargeable in the same manner as their testator or intestate would have been if living."

§ 1. (2 R. S., 447.) For wrongs due to the property, rights or interest of another, for which an action might be maintained against the wrongdoer, such action may be brought by the person injured, or, after his death, by his executor or administrator against such wrongdoer; and, after his death, against his executors or administrators, in the same manner, and with the like effect, in all respects, as actions founded upon contracts.

§ 2. But the preceding section shall not extend to actions for slander, for libel, or to actions of assault and battery, or false imprisonment, nor to actions on the case, for injuries to the person of the plaintiff, or to the person of the testator or intestate of any executor or administrator.

§ 1. (S. L., 1847, chap. 450, as amended 1849, chap. 256.) Whenever the death of a person shall be caused by wrongful act, neglect, or default, and the act, neglect, or default is such as would (if death had not ensued), have entitled the party injured to maintain an action and recover damages in respect thereof; then, and in any such case, the person, who, or the corporation which, would have been liable, if death had not ensued, shall be liable to an action for damages, notwithstanding the death of the person injured; and although the death shall have been caused under such circumstances as amount in law to felony.

§ 2. Every such action shall be brought by and in the names of the personal representatives of such deceased person; and the amount recovered in every such action shall be for the exclusive benefit of the widow and next of kin of such deceased person, and shall be distributed to such widow and next of kin in the proportion provided by law in relation to the distribution of personal property left by persons dying intestate; and in every such action, the jury may give such damages as they shall deem a fair and just compensation, not exceeding five thousand dollars, with reference to the pecuniary injuries resulting from such death, to the wife and next of kin of such deceased person, provided that every such action shall be commenced within two years after the death of such person. * * * *"

§ 102. (Code.) If a person entitled to bring an action die before the expiration of the time limited for the commencement thereof, and the cause of action survive, an action may be commenced by his representatives, after the expiration of the time, and within one year from his death.

§ 104. (Code.) If an action shall be commenced within the time prescribed therefor, and a judgment therein for the plaintiff be reversed on appeal, the plaintiff, or, if he die and the cause of action survive, his heirs or representatives may commence a new action within one year after the reversal.

§ 14. (Code.) No action shall abate by the death, marriage or other disability of a party, or by the transfer of any interest therein, if the cause of action survive or continue. In case of death, marriage, or other disability of a party, the court, on motion, at any time within one year thereafter, or afterwards, on a supplemental complaint, may allow the action to be continued by or against his representative or successor's interest.

So also the Revised Statutes provide :

§ 14. (2 R. S., 115.) No suit that may have been commenced by any executors or administrators who shall die, be removed or superseded, or who shall become incapable of acting, shall be abated thereby, but may be continued by the co-executor or administrator, if there be any ; and if there be none, by and in the name of the person who shall succeed the executor or administrator so dying, removed, superseded, or becoming incapable, in the administration of the same estate.

But the successor cannot be compelled to continue an action brought by his predecessor. (*Bain* v. *Pine*, 1 Hill, 615; *Campbell* v. *Bowne*, 5 Paige, 34.)

§ 13. (2 R. S., 449.) Any subsequent executors or administrators, shall have execution upon any judgment that may have been recovered by any person who preceded them in the administration of the same estate, within one year from the time of docketing of such judgment, without reviving the same by *scire facias*, and without any other proceeding to give notice to the defendant in such judgment.

The statute also protects creditors of deceased persons, and enables them in suits by executors or administrators to set up their demands against the deceased.

§ 23. In suits brought by executors and administrators, demands existing against their testators or intestates, and belonging to the defendant, at the time of their death, may be set off by the defendant in the same manner as if the action had been brought by and in the name of the deceased.

But in a suit, by an administrator, upon a cause of action which arose after the death of the intestate, the defendant cannot set off a debt due to him from the intestate. (*Fry* v. *Evans*, 8 Wend., 530; *Hills* v. *Tallman's adm'rs*, 21 Wend., 674; *Mercein* v. *Smith's adm'rs*, 2 Hill, 201; *Merritt* v. *Seaman*, 6 Barb., 330.)

In pleading by an executor or administrator, the complaint should set forth the cause of action, then allege the death of the testator, or intestate, and that on a certain day letters testamentary or of administration were issued by a certain surrogate. (*Beach* v. *King*, 17 Wend., 197; *Sheldon* v. *Hoy*, 11 How., 11; *White* v. *Joy*, 13 N. Y., 83.)

They are bound to endeavor to make collections from solvent persons in other states, and, if necessary, to procure some proper person to be appointed administrator there, and where such debt is lost by reason of their neglect, they are liable. (*Shultz* v. *Pulver*, 11 Wend., 361.)

But they are liable only for gross or collusive negligence in making collections. (*Ruggles* v. *Sherman*, 14 Johns., 446.)

They may collect of a legatee or distributee for a debt due the estate, by retaining a legacy or distributive share in whole or in part. The legatee or distributee is not entitled to his share, so long as he retains in his own hands a part of the funds out of which payment is to be made. (*Smith* v. *Kearney*, 2 Barb. Ch. R., 533.)

But an executor or administrator cannot sue his co-executor or co-administrator, to recover a debt due to the estate; but on the final settlement, the executor or administrator, debtor to the estate, may be charged with his indectedness. (*Decker* v. *Miller*, 2 Paige, 149.) Or his indebtedness may be settled in the Surrogate's Court, or a Court of Equity, on the application of his co-executor or co-administrator, and such disposition of the fund as justice and equity may require, may be directed

by the court. (*Smith* v. *Lawrence*, 11 Paige, 206;
11 Barb., 546.)

The statute gives one year extension of the
statute of limitations, in favor of the estate of a
deceased person, against debtors, or seven years in
all, upon simple contract debts which were not
barred at the decedent's death; while the time is
extended eighteen months, and the time which
elapses between the death of the testator or intestate, and the granting of letters, in favor of creditors and against the estate.

S. L., 1868, chap. 594, provides as follows: "But
the statute of limitations shall not be made available as a defense to such debt or claim (against
decedent), provided the same shall be presented at
the first accounting, and provided the same was
not barred by the statute, at the time of the death
of the testator or intestate. (See also *Scovill* v.
Scovill, 45 Barb., 517.)

In regard to the disposition of the assets of the
estate the following statutory provision is to be
noted.

" § 25. If any executor or administrator shall
discover that the debts against any deceased person,
and the legacies bequeathed by him, cannot be paid
and satisfied without a sale of the personal property
of the deceased, the same, so far as may be necessary for the payment of such debts and legacies,

shall be sold. The sale may be public or private, and, except in the city of New York, may be on credit, not exceeding one year with approved secu rity. Such executor, or administrator shall not be responsible for any loss happening by such sale, when made in good faith and with ordinary prudence."

"§ 26. In making such sales, such articles as are not necessary for the support and subsistence of the family of the deceased, or as are not specifically bequeathed, shall be first sold, and articles so bequeathed, shall not be sold, until the residue of the personal estate has been applied to the payment of debts." (2 R. S., 87.)

Notwithstanding the apparent restriction of the power to sell in sec. 25, as above quoted, it was held (*Sherman* vs. *Willett*, 42 N. Y., 146), that executors and administrators have the right to sell the personal property of the deceased, and that right is not limited by that section, which provides that they may sell *if necessary*. They have the right to sell for the payment of debts and legacies, and for the purpose of distribution ; and to sustain a sale, it need not be proved that the sale was necessary for the payment of debts, etc. (See also *Nichols* v. *Chapman*, 9 Wend., 452.)

The title of a purchaser in good faith from an executor, of personal property belonging to the estate of his decedent, *e. g.* bank stock, is not affected by the fact that the sale was made by the executor, in violation of his duty. (*Seitch* v. *Wells*, 48 N. Y., 585.)

In *King* v. *King* (3 Johns. Ch., 552), it was held that when an administrator sold leasehold property on credit, without security, whereby purchase money was lost, he was liable to the next of kin. But if the sale is made in good faith and with ordinary prudence as to security, he would not be responsible for any loss that might happen. (*Orcutt* v. *Arms*, 3 Paige, 459.)

In regard to a partnership, of which the deceased was a member, the executor of the deceased partner may insist, that the stock on hand be sold for cash, so as to pay the debts of the partnership, and close the business as soon as possible. (*Evans* v. *Evans*, 9 Paige, 178.)

In making sales of property of his decedent, the executor or administrator is a trustee for the parties interested in the estate, and as such, he cannot be allowed, either openly, or by means of another person, to become the purchaser of any part of the assets. If he make such purchase, he may be held to account for the utmost value of the articles so purchased, without regard to the price paid for them. (Williams on Ex'rs, 801; *Campbell* v. *Johnson*, 1 Sand. Ch., 148; *Van Epps* v. *Van Epps*,

9 Paige, 237 ; *Ames* v. *Downing*, 1 Brad., 34 ; 4 Kent Com., 438.)

Of Investments.

An executor or administrator, pending the final settlement of his accounts, should not suffer any considerable balances to lie unproductive. When real securities are not to be had, he should obtain the approval of the surrogate as to the investment. Pending the final settlement, he may be required by the surrogate, to deposit the funds with a trust company, so as to be earning interest. (*Lockhart* v. *Public Administrators*, 4 Brad., 21.)

This being the case, it follows, that on a representation by petition, that the executor or administrator, is allowing considerable sums to lie unproductive, the surrogate will issue a citation to him, to show in what manner he has the estate invested, and, if the case seem a proper one, he will order investment in a trust company or a savings bank.

The executor should always exercise the care which a prudent man would use about his own affairs, as to title, when real estate is in question, or as to the security offered by a bank if a deposit is made of the fund. (*Bogart* v. *Van Velsor*, 4 Edwd. Ch., 722.)

In making permanent investments as trustees, executors can only loan on real estate or on state or United States bonds. (*King* v. *Talbot*, 40 N. Y., 76.) And the rule is established in equity, that if the executor make a loan on personal security and a loss accrue, he shall bear the loss. (*Bogart* v. *Van Velsor, sup.*)

If trustees, exercising a general power to make investments, go beyond the limits prescribed by law in selecting a mode of investment, neither good faith, nor care, nor diligence will protect them in the event of an actual loss. In such cases, they assume the risk, and are responsible accordingly. (*Ackerman* v. *Emott*, 4 Barb., 620.) In this case, it was held that a trustee would not be protected against loss arising from the depreciation of trust funds invested by him, except when the loan was made on real security, or in some fund approved by the court. Accordingly, when the executor invested the legacy of an infant in stock of a bank which, at the time of settlement, had greatly depreciated in value, he was held liable to account to the infant, on her arriving at age, for the whole legacy and interest.

In collecting moneys loaned by the decedent, or themselves on mortgage security, executors or administrators, may be obliged to foreclose, and if bidders do not appear to run up the property to a sufficient amount to pay the debts, and the property seems to be about to sell below its actual value, it becomes their duty to purchase for the estate which they represent. They will take a deed to themselves, in their representative capacity, and hold the estate until they can sell at a fair price. And where the property remains in their hands unsold, at the time of accounting, the surrogate may direct a sale thereof and a distribution of the proceeds, as a part of the estate. (*Clark* v. *Clark*, 8 Paige, 152; *Bogart* v. *Van Velsor*, *sup.*)

While it is the undoubted duty of the executor to collect what of the estate may have have been loaned by his testator on personal security, as we have heretofore seen, still it was held, (*McRae* v. *McRae*, 3 Brad., 199), that a fall in the market value of certain rail road stocks purchased by the decedent, is not, of itself, enough to charge the executor with the loss occasioned by the depreciation; but to have that effect, the circumstances should show affirmatively, that he acted unreasonably in retaining the stock, and that the failure to sell was unjustifiable.

CHAPTER XI.

ADVERTISING FOR CLAIMS AND REFERENCE OF DISPUTED CLAIMS.

The statutory provisions in regard to the publication of notice to present claim against the decedent, are as follows :

§ 34. (2 R S., 88.) Any executor or administrator, at any time, at least six months after the granting of the letters testamentary, or of administration, may insert a notice once in each week for six months, in a newspaper printed in the county, and in such other newspapers, as the surrogate may deem most likely to give notice to the creditors of the deceased, requiring all persons having claims against the deceased, to exhibit the same with the vouchers thereof, to such executor or administrator, at the place of his residence or transaction of business, to be specified in such notice, at or before the day therein named, which shall be at least six months from the day of the first publication of such notice.

The paper or papers in which the notice is to be published must be designated by the surrogate,

which he does in an order made on the application
of the executor or administrator, thus :

ORDER TO ADVERTISE FOR CLAIMS.

At a Surrogate's Court held in the county
of ...., at the surrogate's office
in the .... of ...., on the
......, day of ...., 1874.
Present Hon. ...., Surrogate.

In the matter of the estate

of

A .... B ...., deceased.

It appearing that more than six months have elapsed
since the issue of letters of administration upon the
goods, chattels and credits of A B, late of the ....
of ...., deceased.

Now on the application of C D, administrator :

Ordered, that said administrator publish a notice
once a week, for six months, in the ...., requiring
all persons having claims against said deceased, to
present the same, with the vouchers thereof, to the
said administrator, on or before the ...... day of
..............., next.

.................., *Surrogate.*

NOTICE.

In pursuance of an order of ...., Esq.,
surrogate of the county of ...., notice is
hereby given, to all persons having claims against A
B, late of the .... of ...., deceased,
that they are required to exhibit the same with the
vouchers thereof, to the subscriber, executor of the

will of said deceased, at his residence in the town
of ...., on or before the 15th day of May next.
    Dated Nov. 11, 1874.

                    (Signed),   A D, *Executor.*

The notice to present claims must be to the executor or administrator personally, not to an
attorney, for the power to accept or reject cannot
be delegated. (*Hardy* v. *Ames*, 47 Barb., 413.)

A publication in one newspaper printed in the
county, pursuant to the order of the surrogate, is
sufficient, unless he directs a publication in some
other paper also.   (*Dolbeer* v. *Casey*, 19 Barb., 149.)

The executors may select a place for presentation of claims, and their designation of it in the
notice, makes it their place of business or residence
for the purpose of the statute.   (*Hoyt* v. *Bennett*,
58 Barb., 529 ; *Whitlock's Estate*, 1 Tuck., 491.)

But *Murray* v. *Smith*, decided in special term of
the Superior Court (9 Bosw., 689), holds to the
contrary of *Hoyt* v. *Bennett*. It is also held in
Hoyt v. *Bennett*, that claims not yet due may be
presented under this notice.

But where executors or administrators are substituted for a deceased defendant in a pending
action, they are not entitled to a presentation of
the claim in suit, nor are they to be exempted from
costs if the plaintiff recovers judgment.   The repre-

sentatives in such case come into the place of the decedent and the action must proceed against them, as it would have done against him. (*Tindall* v. *Jones*, 11 Abb., 258, and 19 How., 469.)

§ 35. (2 R. S., 88.) Upon any claim being presented against the estate of any deceased person, the executor or administrator may require satisfactory vouchers in support thereof, and also the affidavit of the claimant that such claim is justly due, that no payments have been made thereon, and that there are no offsets against the same to the knowledge of such claimants, which oath may be taken before any justice of the peace, or other officer authorized to administer oaths.

The affidavit may be in the following form.

AFFIDAVIT TO CLAIM.

Rensselaer county, ss :

A B, of the city of ...., being duly sworn, doth depose and say, that the foregoing claim against the estate of ...., deceased, is justly due and owing to this deponent; that no payments have been made thereon (other than those stated therein), and that there are no offsets against the same to the knowledge of deponent.

(Signed),   A B.

Sworn before me this ...... day ⎰
   of ...., 1874. ⎱
C D,
Notary Public.

The claims may be presented by letter, or in any way which deals fairly with the executor or administrator, and the estate which he represents, and the claimant need not produce vouchers, or make an affidavit unless requested. (*Gansevoort* v. *Nelson*, 6 Hill, 389.)

So also, where a claim has been virtually presented and acknowledged by the executor or administrator, before notice to creditors to present claims, it is not necessary to present it again for allowance under the statute. And where the executor, or administrator admits the validity of the claim, by paying interest on it from time to time, it is tantamount to a formal admission of its justice upon presentation under notice. (*Johnson* v. *Corbett*, 11 Paige, 265.)

In respect to creditors of the estate, the executor or administrator, is a trustee, and not a creditor. And like all trustees, where the names of the *cestui que trusts* are not given in the deed, he is bound to exercise the utmost care, before he accepts a claim as entitled to payment, and the law will afford him all reasonable means of so doing. He cannot be coerced to pay debts short of a year from the time of granting letters. The remedies of the creditor, in the meantime, however, are not absolutely suspended; he may prosecute an action, but he must do so at his own cost and expense, and not at the

cost and expense of the estate, unless he can show
that the executor or administrator has been guilty
of some *laches*, or illegal act in regard to the adjustment of the claim (*Buckhurst* v. *Hunt*, 16
How., 407.)

The statute provides for a summary method of
determining claims against the estate of a decedent
by a reference.

§ 36. (2 R. S., 88, amended chap. 261, Laws
of 1859.) If the executor or administrator doubt
the justice of any claim so presented, he may enter
into an agreement, in writing with the claimant,
to refer the matter in controversy, to one or three
disinterested persons to be approved by the surrogate, and on filing such agreement and approval
in the office of the clerk of the Supreme Court * * *
a rule shall be entered by such clerk, either in va-
cation or in term, referring the matter in controversy to the person or persons selected.

The rejection of the claim should be made upon
the ground that it, or some part of it, is not legally
due. (*Kidd* v. *Chapman*, 2 Barb. Ch., 414.) To
protect the executor or administrator from costs,
he should accompany his rejection with an offer
to refer it. But the offer to refer need not be in
writing. (*Lansing* v. *Swartz*, 9 How., 434.)

In one case (*Gorham* v. *Ripley*, 16 How., 313),
where a creditor's demand having been rejected,

he offered to refer to referees to be approved by
the surrogate, not naming them. The executors
instead of accepting this offer, offered to refer to three
referees named by themselves, to be approved by the
surrogate; it was held at Special Term, that this
was a refusal by the executors to refer, which rendered them liable for costs in an action on the demand.

AGREEMENT TO REFER CLAIM.

Whereas A B, has lately presented a claim to the
executor of the will of C D, late of ...., deceased,
for $ ...., a copy whereof is attached hereto, the
justice of which claim is doubted by the said executor;
it is thereupon agreed that the matter in controversy
be referred to .... a referee to hear and determine the same.

Dated Nov. 14, 1874.

> (Signed),   A B,
> C D, *Executor.*

I hereby approve of the referee named in the foregoing agreement.

Dated Nov. 14, 1874.

> E F, *Surrogate.*

ORDER ENDORSED.

On reading and filing the within agreement and approval of the surrogate of Rensselaer county : Ordered
that ...., Esq., be and he is appointed referee

to hear and determine the matter in controversy mentioned in said agreement.

Dated Nov. 16, 1874.

WM. LAPE.
Clerk of Supreme Court.

It is not essential that the agreement and approval be so formal. In *Bucklin* v. *Chapin* (53 Barb., 488, and 35 How., 155), an order was signed by the surrogate, reciting the presentation of the claim, and that the parties had agreed to a reference, and a consent to the order signed by the attorneys, on behalf of the parties, was held to amount to an agreement in writing to refer, which is sufficient under the statute. To confer jurisdiction under the statute, a substantial compliance with its terms is enough. The naming of the referees in the order of the surrogate, is sufficient evidence, also, that they were approved by him.

The order of reference must be entered. When the agreement to refer is not filed, and no order entered, the Supreme Court does not get jurisdiction of the cause. (*Comstock* v. *Olmsted,* 6 How., 77.)

Nearly every class of claims, both legal and equitable, may be so presented and referred. (*White* v. *Story,* 43 Barb., 124.) Unliquidated claims by surviving parties against the decedent, may be so

referred. (*Francisco* v. *Fitch,* 25 Barb., 130.)   A
claim for a tort committed by the decedent also is
referable.   (*Brockett* v. *Buck,* 18 Abb., 337.)   But
a claim against the deceased as an executor, for
assets held by him as such, is not so to be treated.
The statute cannot be applied to trust moneys or
property in the hands of an executor at the time
of his death.   It contemplates an ordinary debt,
for which the deceased was liable in his lifetime,
upon a promise, express or implied ; a debt which
may be supported by the oath of the creditor,
which is justly due, which may be the subject of
an offset, and which was cognizable by the common law courts.   (*Sands* v. *Craft,* 10 Abb., 216
and 18 How., 438.)

The powers and duties of the referees are regulated by the same statute.

§ 37. (2 R. S., 89.) The referees shall thereupon
proceed to hear and determine the matter, and
make their report thereon to the court in which
the rule for their appointment shall have been entered.   The same proceedings shall be had in all
respects, the referees shall have the same powers,
be entitled to the same compensation, and subject
to the same control, as if the reference had been
made in an action in which such court might, by
law, direct a reference; and the court may set
aside the report of the referees, or appoint others

in their place, and may confirm such report, and adjudge costs, as in actions against executors ; and the judgment of the court thereupon shall be valid and effectual, in all respects, as if the same had been rendered in a suit commenced by the ordinary process.

Short Statute of Limitations as to rejected Claims.

§ 38. (2 R. S., 89.) If a claim against the estate of any deceased person be exhibited to the executor or administrator, and be disputed or rejected by him, and the same shall not have been referred, the claimant shall within six months afte such dispute or rejection, if the debt or any part thereof shall be then due, or within six months after some part thereof shall have become due, commence a suit for the recovery thereof, or be forever barred from maintaining any action thereon : and no action shall be maintained thereon, after the said period by any other person deriving title thereto from such claimant, and any executor or administrator may, on the trial of any action founded upon such demand, give in evidence in bar thereof, under a notice annexed to the general issue, the facts of such refusal and neglect to commence suit.

The particular method of pleading, is changed of course by the case. The facts must now be pleaded, by way of answer.

The rejection of the claim may be waived. Thus, where the executor, when the claim was presented, rejected it, but afterwards entertained negotiations in reference to a settlement, it was held that his previous rejection was waived, and the statutory bar to an action could not be interposed. (*Calanan* v. *McClure*, 47 Barb., 206.)

CHAPTER XII.

Funeral Expenses.

Reasonable funeral expenses are to be paid in preference to any debts, and are charged as expenses of administration. But in such case, the question arises, what are reasonable funeral expenses.

The erection of a headstone at the decedent's own grave, may be considered a part of his funeral expenses, where the rights of creditors cannot be defeated thereby. (*Wood* v. *Vandenburgh*, 6 Paige, 277.)

Tombstones were allowed as part of the funeral expenses, in Connecticut, even where the estate was insolvent. (*Fairman's Appeal*, 30 Conn., 205.) But a charge for a monument was not allowed to executors in *Springsteed* v. *Samson* (32 N. Y., 703).

When the decedent dies away from home, the necessary expense of notifying his family and removing his body to his late home, are proper funeral expenses. (*Hasler* v. *Hasler*, 1 Brad., 248.)

And moderate expenses for mourning for the widow and family, may be allowed as part of the funeral expenses. (*Wood's Estate*, 1 Ashmead, 314.)

The rule that an executor, if he have sufficient assets, is liable to a third person who, as an act of duty or necessity, has provided for the interment of the deceased, applies equally in the case of an administrator; and a person who defrays the necessary funeral expenses of an intestate, though before letters of administration are granted, is entitled to be reimbursed out of the assets which come into the hands of the administrator. (*Rappelyea* v. *Russell*, 1 Daly, 214.) Accordingly, an undertaker, who superintends the funeral of an intestate, having no friends or relations in the city, may recover the charges therefor, from the administrator who afterward took out letters, and having in his hands sufficient assets, refused to pay the bill.

It may be remarked, that an executor contracting for funeral expenses or other services for the benefit of the estate of his intestate, binds himself but not the estate. He cannot create a liability for the estate. (*Austin* v. *Munro*, 47 N. Y., 360.)

The question as to who is liable for obligations contracted by the executor or administrator, was settled in *Ferris* v. *Myrick* (41 N. Y., 315). A judgment for such contracts must be *de bonis propriis;* and not against the estate in his hands, and such causes of action cannot be joined in the same complaint, with a cause of action arising upon the contracts of the deceased.

An executor cannot bind himself to pay the debts of his testator unless the agreement therefor or some memorandum or note thereof be in writing, and signed by the executor or by some other person by him thereunto specially authorized. (2 R. S., 113.) His promise, except in the manner required by this statute is void, and he cannot bind his decedents estate by such a void promise.

Compromise of Claims.

At common law, executors or administrators could compromise claims due to the estate, and could, in a proper case, take less than the full amount of the claims. They might be held responsible for any serious error in so doing. Consequently the act, chap. 80, Laws of 1847, was passed, which enables them to obtain the sanction of the judgment of the surrogate, in addition to their own. (*Chouteau* v. *Suydam*, 21 N. Y., 179.)

The act is as follows:

§ 1. Executors and administrators may be authorized by the surrogate, or the officer authorized to perform the duties of surrogate, in the county where their letters testamentary, or of administration were issued, on application, and good and sufficient cause shown therefor, and on such terms

as said surrogate, or officer shall approve, to compromise or compound any debt or claim, belonging
to the estate of their testator or intestate.

§ 2. Nothing in this act contained, shall prevent
any party, interested in the final settlement of said
estate, from showing, on the final settlement of the
accounts of said executor or administrator, that
such debt or claim, was fraudulently or negligently
compromised or compounded.

For the purpose of procuring the judgment of
the surrogate the facts are to be embodied in a
petition, fortified, if possible, by affidavits, and upon
them, the surrogate will make an order, undoubtedly *ex parte*.

PETITION.

To Hon. ...., Surrogate of Rensselaer county.

The petition of A B, of the town of ...., in
said county respectfully shows:

That your petitioner is the executor of the will of
C D, late of Troy, in said county, deceased, and that
letters testamentary have been duly issued to him.

That among the assets comprising the estate of the
said deceased is a claim against E F, of the town
of ...., amounting to the sum of $148. That
your petitioner presented said claim to the appraisers
duly appointed to appraise the estate of said deceased
and they did inventory and appraise the same as good
(or bad, or doubtful). That since such appraisal your
petitioner has made efforts to collect the said claim

and has (state what efforts, if suit has been brought, state result), but has been unable to collect the same, or any part thereof.

That your petitioner has learned and verily believes that the said E F is insolvent, and that there are numerous judgments against him, and that execution upon them, or some of them, have been returned wholly unsatisfied.

That the said E F has offered to pay to your petitioner   per cent of said claim, and for a release thereupon, and your petitioner verily believes no more can be collected than is so offered.

Whereupon your petitioner prays that he may be authorized to make a settlement and compromise, or compound the claim against the said E F, on the terms above stated.

Dated Troy, Nov. 11, 1874.

A B.

Rensselaer county, ss :

A B being duly sworn, says that the foregoing petition by him subscribed is true.

A B.

Sworn before me this ⎱
  11th Nov., 1874. ⎰

M W, Surrogate.

If the surrogate shall be satisfied that the compromise offered is favorable to the estate, and that the amount to be realized, is probably as much as would be obtained upon a sale of the claim under his order, he will make an order authorizing the

compromise.   The following   may be used as a
precedent.

At a Surrogate's Court held in and for the county
of ...., at the surrogate's office in
the .... of ....

Present — Hon. ...., Surrogate.

> In the matter of the estate
>
> of
>
> C .... D.........:, deceased.

On reading and filing the petition of A B, executor
of the will of the above named deceased (and the affidavits annexed to said petition.)

And it appearing to the surrogate thereupon, that
the terms stated in said petition as proposed for the
compromise of the claim held by said executor against
C D, are favorable to the estate of said deceased :

Ordered that said executor may compromise the said
claim, amounting to $148, and may accept in settlement
the sum of $100.

(Signed), ...,......, Surrogate.

Payment of Debts and how Enforced.

At the expiration of one year from the issuing
of letters, the executor or administrator, is presumed to know, not only the assets in hand, but,
having advertised for claims, also the liabilities of
the estate, and he may proceed to pay debts and
legacies, and distribute to the next of kin.

Debts are preferred to legacies, or the claims of the next of kin as such, and as has been seen, the executors or administrators are trustees for the creditors.

§ 27. (2 R. S., 87.) Every executor or administrator shall proceed with diligence to pay the debts of the deceased, and shall pay the same according to the following order of classes :

1. Debts entitled to a preference under the laws of the United States ;

2. Taxes assessed upon the estate of the deceased, previous to his death ;

3. Judgments docketed, and decrees enrolled against the deceased, according to the priority thereof respectively ;

4. All recognizances, bonds, sealed instruments, notes, bills and unliquidated demands and accounts.

Each class above stated, is entitled to payment in full, before any payments can be made upon a debt of a subsequent class.

§ 28. (2 R. S., 84.) No preference shall be given in the payment of any debt, over other debts of the same class, except those specified in the third class ; nor shall a debt due and payable be entitled to preference over debts not due ; nor shall the commencement of a suit for the recovery of any debt, or the obtaining a judgment thereon against the executor or administrator, entitle such debt to any preference over others of the same class. (*Mount* v. *Mitchell*, 31 N. Y., 356. See also 1 Tucker, 126.)

§ 29. Debts not due may be paid by an executor or administrator, according to the class to which they belong, after deducting a rebate of legal interest upon the sum paid, for the time unexpired.

§ 30. Preference may be given by the surrogate to rents due, or accruing, upon leases held by the testator or intestate at the time of his death, over debts of the fourth class, whenever it shall be made to appear to his satisfaction that such preference will benefit the estate of such testator or intestate. (*Hovey* v. *Smith*, 1 Barb., 372.)

Taxes, assessed upon the real estate of the deceased in his lifetime, have priority of all other debts, except those entitled to a preference under the law of the United States, the only noticeable example of which, is the bond given for payment of duties. But taxes assessed on real estate subsequently to the death of decedent, are not to be paid by the executor or administrator. (*Wilcox* v. *Smith*, 26 Barb., 316.)

So also an assessment, confirmed at the time of the testator's decease, although a lien upon the real estate, is also a debt to be paid out of the personal estate, but in the fourth class. (*Seabury* v. *Bower*, 3 Brad., 207.)

The judgments docketed and decree enrolled, which are to be paid in the third class before simple contract debts, according to the priority in point of time of docketing or enrolling, and without reference to any supposed lien of the judgment or decree upon real estate. (*Ainslee* v. *Radcliffe*, 7 Paige.) It was accordingly held, in the case last cited, that some of the judgments having been docketed more than ten years and some less, they were all to be paid according to the priority of their being docketed.

So a judgment of a Justices Court, or of the marine or other inferior court, when it has been docketed, becomes entitled to this preference.

But this preference does not extend to the judgments of courts in other states, or of foreign countries. Neither at common law, nor under the statutes of this state, have judgments recovered in another state, any title to priority of payment over simple contract debts. Creditors claiming on such judgments, must come in with the creditors of the deceased, described in the fourth class. (*Brown* v. *Public Administrator*, 3 Brad., 212.)

Mortgages, which would come under the fourth class, cannot be paid out of the personal estate, unless such payment is provided for in the will. (*Waldron* v. *Waldron*, 4 Brad., 114.) Where a creditor has additional security, he should be compelled to exhaust that security, and only come in against the personal estate for the deficiency. (*Halsey* v. *Reed*, 9 Paige, 446.)

But where the real and personal estate are thrown into one fund, in which the same parties are interested equally, the executor may, for the benefit of the estate, apply personal property to pay a mortgage on the realty. (*Hepburn* v. *Hepburn*, 2 Brad., 47.) Without dissenting from the opinion of Mr. Surrogate Bradford, we would remark, that only in a very special case, would the executor be authorized to apply the personal property in such a way. It would be an interference with the rights of the devisee which would not be sanctioned, under ordinary circumstances. His right is to have the estate as it is devised to him, the personal as such and the real as the executor finds it as near as may be, and if he shall choose to pay mortgages, very well.

Creditors of an insolvent co-partnership, in case of the death of one of the co-partners, cannot collect their debts against the separate estate of the decedent, until his individual liabilities shall have been paid in full. (*Wilder* v. *Keeler*, 3 Paige, 167 ; *Payne* v. *Matthews*, 6 Id., 19.)

A voluntary bond of the testator, given in his lifetime, payable, at or immediately after his death, is a valid debt, has preference over legacies, but is postponed to debts for valuable considerations. (*Isenhart* v. *Brown*, 2 Edwd., 341.)

The claim of a son who had acted as agent for his aged mother, presented against her estate, upon a contract with her for board and on her promissory note in his favor, is presumptively invalid, on account of the confidential relation ; and cannot be claimed unless there is actual proof rebutting the presumption. (*Comstock* v. *Comstock*, 57 Barb., 453.)

The executor or administrator will not be protected in paying a debt or claim barred by the statute of limitations, nor will his promise revive such a claim. (*Bloodgood* v. *Bruen*, 8 N. Y., 362.) A provision in the will, for the payment of *all just debts*, does not revive a debt barred by the statute (3 Wend., 503), and the statute of limitations may be interposed by an executor, or any person interested. (*Warren* v. *Poff*, 4 Brad., 260.)

In regard to leases held by the decedent, it is the duty of the executor to collect the rents on such leases, and pay them to the landlord, not to put them with the assets of the estate. The executor is personally liable to the landlord to the extent of the rents received by him as for money had and received. *Prima facie*, the rents received, are sufficient to pay the landlord. If they are not, it is a matter of defense. (*Miller* v. *Knox*, 48 N. Y., 232.)

§ 31. (2 R. S., 88.) In any suit against an executor or administrator, the defendant may show, under a notice for that purpose, given with his plea, that there are debts of a prior class unsatisfied, or that there are unpaid debts of the same class with that on which the suit is brought, and judgment shall be rendered only for such part of the assets in his hands, as shall remain after satisfying debts of the prior class, and as shall be a just proportion to the other debts of the same class, with that on which the suit is brought. But the plaintiff may, as in other cases, take a judgment for the whole or part of his debt, to be levied of future assets.

§ 24. (2 R. S., 355.) Whenever a set-off is established in a suit brought by executors or administrators, the judgment shall be against them in their representative character, and shall be evidence of a debt established, to be paid in the course of administration ; but execution shall not issue thereon, until directed by the surrogate who granted letters testamentary or of administration.

§ 32. (2 R. S., 88.) No execution shall issue upon a judgment against an executor or administrator, until an account of his administration shall have been rendered and settled, or unless on an order of the surrogate who appointed him. And if an account has been rendered to the surrogate, by such executor or administrator, execution shall issue only for the sum that shall have appeared on the settlement of such account to have been a just proportion of the assets applicable to the judgment.

Practically, it will scarcely ever be necessary to proceed under this section, for, as will appear, a better method of proceeding against the executor or administrator, will be to proceed upon the decree upon the accounting, and either docket it in the office of the clerk of the county, and thus make it a lien upon real estate ; or, proceed against the executor or administrator, as for a contempt in not paying.

§19. (2 R. S., 116.) Where a creditor shall have obtained a judgment against an executor or administrator, after a trial at law upon the merits, he may at any time thereafter, apply to the surrogate, having jurisdiction, for an order against such executor or administrator, to show cause why an execution on such judgment should not be issued.

§ 20. The surrogate to whom such application may be made, shall issue a citation, requiring the executor or administrator complained of, at a certain time and place therein to be named, to appear before him, and if, upon such accounting, it shall appear that there are assets in the hands of such executor or administrator, properly applicable, under the provisions of this chapter, to the payment, in whole or in part, of the judgment so obtained, the surrogate shall make an order, that execution be issued for the amount so applicable. (*St. John* v. *Voorhees*, 19 Abb., 53.)

This section and these provisions, must be construed together with section 31, above quoted, and the amount for which the execution shall be ordered is to be ascertained by the order on accounting. The statute proceeds :

§ 21. Every such order shall be conclusive evidence that there are sufficient assets in the hands of such executor or administrator, to satisfy the amount for which the execution is directed to be levied; and no appeal shall be made from any such order, unless the person making the same shall execute to the plaintiff in such execution, a bond with sufficient sureties, to be approved by the surrogate, conditioned for the payment of the full amount so directed to be levied, with interest thereon, and the costs of defending the appeal, in case the order appealed from shall be affirmed.

§ 22. If the whole sum for which judgment may have been obtained, shall not be collected on the execution so directed to be issued, and assets shall thereafter come into the hands of such executor or administrator, the surrogate shall make a further order for issuing execution, upon the application of the creditor, his personal representatives or assignees, and shall proceed in the same manner, from time to time, whenever assets shall come to the hands of the executor or administrator, until such judgment be satisfied.

The statute provides also, especially for set-offs in action against executors and others in a representative capacity.

§ 25. (2 R. S., 355.) In actions against executors or administrators, and against trustees and others sued in their representative character, the defendants may set off demands belonging to their testators or intestates, or those whom they represent, in the same manner as the person represented would have been entitled to set off the same, in an action against them.

In regard to the collection of judgments entered against the decedent in his lifetime, by execution, provision is made by the statute.

§ 27. (2 R. S., 368.) If any party dies after judgment rendered against him, but before execution issued thereon, the remedy on such judgments shall not be suspended by reason of the non-age of any heir of such party; but no execution shall issue on any such judgment, until the expiration of one year after the death of the party against whom the same was rendered.

§ 1. (S. L., 1850, chap. 295.) Notwithstanding the death of a party after judgment, execution thereon against any property, lands, tenements, real estate, or chattels real upon which such judgment shall be a lien, either at law or in equity, may be issued and executed in the same manner, and with the same effect as if he were still living, except that such execution cannot be issued within a year after the death of the defendant, nor in any case, unless upon permission granted by the surrogate of the county who has jurisdiction to grant administration, or letters testamentary on the estate of the deceased judgment debtor, which surrogate may, on sufficient cause shown, make an order granting permission to issue such execution, as aforesaid.

When the surrogate after hearing, grants an order that an execution issue, an appeal lies from the order. (*Mount* v. *Mitchell*, 31 N. Y., 356.)

This proceeding being against heirs at law, or devisees, the notice of it or citation to show cause must run to them, and, as such a judgment is a preferred debt and might be paid by the executor or administrator, if letters have been issued, he also should be included in the citation. The proceeding would be upon petition as other cases.

PETITION FOR LEAVE TO ISSUE EXECUTION.

To Hon. ...., Surrogate of the county of .... :

Your petitioner A R of the town of ...., in said county, respectively shows :

That heretofore your petitioner recovered a judgment against C D, late of the town of ...., in said county, in his life time, in the Supreme Court, for the sum of $ ...., damages and costs, which said judgment was entered in said county on the ...... day of ...., 1872.

That afterwards, and on or about the ...... day of ...., 1873, and more than one year since, said C D, died, leaving him surviving E F (and others, naming them), his heirs at law (or having made his will which was duly proved in this court in which E F is named devisee of the real estate of said deceased). That letters of administration of the goods, chattels and credits of the said deceased were granted by this court to G H, of the town of ...., in said county.

Your petitioner further shows that the said deceased was seized in his life time and at the time of his death of certain real estate, upon which the aforesaid judgment is a lien.

Wherefore your petitioner prays that a citation issue to the aforesaid administrator and said heirs at law (or devisees), requiring them to appear in this court on a day to be named therein, to show cause why an execution should not issue upon said judgment, or for such other or further relief, as the court shall deem proper in the premises.

Dated Nov. 23, 1874.

(Signed), A B.

Rensselaer county, ss:

A B, being duly sworn, says that he has heard the foregoing petition by him subscribed read, and that the same is true.

(Signed),   A B.

Sworn before me, this ...... day $\big\}$
    of ...., 1874. $\big\}$
              A B, *Com'r of Deeds, Troy, N. Y.*

Upon this petition the surrogate enters an order for the issue of a citation, and issues the citation which, in analogy to other proceedings and to motions in other courts, should be served at least eight days before the return day of it.

If five years have elapsed since the entry of the judgment, leave of the court in which the judgment was ordered may also be necessary, under sec. 284, of the code of procedure.

The code, also in sections 376 to 381, inclusive, provides a manner for the collection of like judgments.

In case of the death of a judgment debtor after judgment, his personal representatives may, at any time within one year after his appointment, be summoned to show cause why the judgment should not be enforced against the estate of the judgment debtor in their hands. The summons shall be subscribed by the judgment creditor, his representatives or attorney, shall describe the judgment, and require the person summoned to show cause within twenty days after the service of the summons ; and shall be served in like manner as an original summons.

The summons shall be accompanied by an affidavit of the person subscribing it, that the judgment has not been satisfied, to his knowledge, information or belief, and shall specify the amount due thereon.

Upon such summons, the party summoned may answer within the time specified therein, denying the judgment, or setting up any defense which may have arisen subsequently.

The party issuing the summons may demur or reply to the answer, and the party summoned may demur to the reply, and the issues may be tried and judgment may be given in the same manner as in an action, and be enforced by execution, or the application of the property charged, to the payment of the judgment, may be compelled by attachment, if necessary.

The answer and reply shall be verified in the like cases and manner, and be subject to the same rules, as the answer and reply in an action.

Payment of a Debt due to the Executor or Administrator.

An executor or administrator, creditor of the estate of his decedent, may not settle his own claim and pay it, he must have it allowed, on due proof by the surrogate.

§ 33. (2 R. S., 88.) No part of the property of the deceased shall be retained by an executor or administrator in satisfaction of his own debt or claim, until it shall have been proved to, and allowed by, the surrogate ; and such debt or claim shall not be entitled to any preference over others of the same class.

§ 37. (Chap. 460, Laws of 1837, as amended by chap. 594, Laws of 1858.)   The proof of the debt or claim of any executor or administrator required by the thirty-third section of title three, chapter six, of the second part of the Revised Statutes, may be made on the service and return of a citation for that purpose, directed to the proper persons, or on the final account of any such executor or administrator, pursuant to the third article of the third title of chapter six of the second part of the Revised Statutes.   But the statute of limitations shall not be available as a defense to such debt or claim, provided the same shall be presented and claimed at the first accounting, and provided the same was not barred by statute at the time of the death of the testator or intestate.

An executor or administrator, who makes a claim against the estate, must support it by a sworn voucher, such as he may require from others under § 35, of the statute, and it is error for the surrogate to allow it, whatever the force of the proof, unless so verified. However strong the proof may be it is the duty of the surrogate to exact an oath that there have been no payments, and that there are no offsets. (*Clark* v. *Clark*, 8 Paige, 152; *Terry* v. *Dayton*, 31 Barb., 519.)

We are aware that the decision *In the Matter of Cunningham*, 1 Hun., 214, is adverse to the law as above stated, but notwithstanding it is the most recent, the older authorities were not examined or referred to, and it cannot be considered as authority overruling the well considered cases quoted above. The facts were briefly as follows:

The executor included in his account as executor on final settlement, an account for sums paid out by him for clothing, nursing and medical attendance on testator, and other matters, in his lifetime, and it does not appear that there was any affidavit such as is required of a creditor, or other equivalent testimony from the executor. But the claim was proved.

17

The surrogate, upon the report of an auditor, disallowed the claim. On appeal, the decision was modified and the claim allowed. He cannot retain moneys for a debt due to himself, barred by the statute of limitations, in the lifetime of his testator. (*Rogers* v. *Rogers,* 3 Wend., 503.) And on the hearing, any person interested may set up the statute. (*Vreat* v. *Fortune,* 2 Brad., 116.)

The proof of the claim before the surrogate, whether on return of the citation presently to be noticed, or upon final settlement, must be such as would warrant a verdict, if the trial were before a jury.

If the executor or administrator purpose to have a citation to the proper persons and prove his debt before the final settlement, under section 37, as above quoted, although the practice is not indicated with precision, it is presumed he may safely act under the section. The citation is to be issued to all persons interested in the estate, and if creditors are interested by reason of a lack of sufficient assets to pay them in full, they must be cited. The number of days service for the citation is not prescribed, but the surrogate must see that a reasonable notice is given, and it is presumed for resident parties eight days would be considered reasonable.

The following may indicate the practice.

PETITION FOR PROOF OF DEBT, DUE TO AN EXECUTOR OR ADMINISTRATOR.

To the Surrogate of the county of .... :

The petition of ...., of the ....
of ...., in said county, respectfully shows :

That your petitioner is one of the executors named in the last will and testament of ...., late of ...., in said county, deceased ; that said will was duly proved, and letters testamentary issued to your petitioner on the ...... day of .... last, and your petitioner has made and returned an inventory of the personal estate of the said deceased, by which it appears that said personal estate, applicable to the payment of debts, legacies and expenses amounts to about .... dollars. That at the time of the death of said ...., he was indebted to your petitioner in the sum of .... dollars, arising out of the following facts : that on the ..... day of .... , 1869, the said ...., made his promissory note in writing, dated on that day, whereby, for value received, he promised to pay your petitioner, or order, the sum of .... dollars, on the ...... day of ...., 1869, with interest; and delivered the same to your petitioner, but said note was not paid at maturity, and still remains wholly unpaid, and there is due thereon, to your petitioner, the sum of .... dollars, with interest from the ...... day of ...., 1869. That no payment has been made on said note, nor are there any offsets against the same, or any other defense thereto, to the knowledge and belief of your petitioner.

Your petitioner further shows, that he has advertised, pursuant to law, for claims against said estate, and none have been exhibited (or, claims have been exhibited to the amount of about .... dollars). That C D, of ...., is co-executor with your petitioner, and .... is the widow, and .... and ...., are the children and legatees named in the will of said deceased, and all reside in the .... of ....

Your petitioner, therefore, prays that the debt due to your petitioner may be proved in this court, and that he may be permitted to retain the amount thereof out of the assets in his hands, and he prays that a citation issue, pursuant to the statute, directed to the persons above named, requiring them to attend the proof of said debt, at a time and place therein to be stated.

Dated, December 1, 1872.

(Signed), ...

Rensselaer county, ss:

..............., being duly sworn, says that the foregoing petition, by him subscribed, is true of his own knowledge, except as to the matters which are therein stated on information and belief, and as to those matters he believes it to be true.

(Signed), ...

Sworn, etc.

ORDER FOR CITATION.

At a Surrogate's Court held for the county
of .... at the surrogate's office in
the .... of ...., on the ......
of ...., 1874.

Present — Hon..............., Surrogate.

In the matter of the estate

of

..............., deceased.

On reading and filing the petition of ....,
as executor of the will of said deceased, showing that
he has a claim against the estate of the said deceased,
and praying that the same be proved before said surrogate :

Ordered, that a citation issue to the executor of the
will of said ...., deceased, and to the legatees
named in said will requiring them to appear in the
court on the ...... day of ...., next, as prayed
for in said petition.

..................., *Surrogate.*

An executor or administrator may be compelled,
under certain circumstances, to pay a debt of his
decedent, before the expiration of the time before
final settlement.

§ 18. (2 R. S., 116.) The surrogate having
jurisdiction, shall have power to decree the payment of debts, * * * * against the executor or ad-

ministrator of a deceased person in the following cases :

1. Upon the application of a creditor, the payment of any debt or proportional part thereof, may be so decreed, at any time after six months shall have elapsed from the granting of letters testamentary, or of administration.

The proceeding is upon petition of the creditor, whereupon a citation will issue to the executor or administrator to show cause why he should not be ordered to pay the claim.   Upon the return of the citation, the executor or administrator may absolutely reject the claim, which will compel the creditor to bring suit in the common law courts ; or, he may deny sufficiency of assets, and if it appear that the estate is involved to such a degree that it would be imprudent to pay the claim in full, or difficult to ascertain the proper percentage, it is presumed that the order for payment would be denied.

But the surrogate's order denying a creditor's application for payment of his claim, does not prevent the creditor from maintaining his action in any other proper court. (*Fitzpatrick* v. *Brady*, 6 Hill, 581; *Flagg* v. *Ruder*, 1 Brad., 192; see also, 18 Wend., 666, and 6 Barb., 152.)

PETITION BY A CREDITOR FOR PAYMENT OF A DEBT.

To the Surrogate of the county of .... :

The petition of ...., of the ....
of ...., respectfully shows:

That your petitioner is a creditor of said deceased,
upon a claim for .... dollars, as follows:

That your petitioner sold and delivered to said deceased, in his lifetime, goods, wares and merchandise
to the value of .... dollars, which sum the
said deceased, in his lifetime, promised to pay at the
expiration of .... months; that said ....
did not pay the same in his lifetime, nor have any payments been made thereon since, and there are no
effects against the same, to the knowledge of your petitioner, and there is due to your petitioner the sum
of .... dollars, with interest thereon, from
the ...... day of ...., 1869.

That on or about the ...... day of ...., 1871,
the last will and testament of said deceased was duly
proved in this court, and letters testamentary were
issued to ...., executor named therein, who
has duly returned an inventory of the personal estate
of said deceased. That said executor advertised for
the presentation of claims against the estate of said
deceased, and your petitioner duly presented his claim,
which was not disputed, and your petitioner, after the
expiration of one year from the granting of such letters,
demanded payment of his said claim from the said
executor who has hitherto neglected and refused to
pay the same, or any part thereof. Wherefore, your
petitioner prays that an order be made for the payment

of said claim, or for such other order as shall be agreeable to law and equity.

Dated, Dec. 6, 1872.

(Signed), ...

Rensselaer county, ss :

.... being duly sworn, says, that the foregoing petition, by him subscribed, is true of his own knowledge, except as to the matters which are therein stated on information and belief, and as to those matters he believes it to be true.

(Signed), ...

Sworn, etc.

ORDER FOR CITATION TO ADMINISTRATOR.

At a Surrogate's Court, held for the county of ...., at the surrogate's office in the .... of ...., on the ...... day of ...., 1874.

Present — Hon. ...., Surrogate.

In the matter of the estate

of

...., deceased.

On reading and filing the petition of ...., showing that he is a creditor of said deceased ; that he has presented his claim to ...., administrator, etc., of said deceased ; that said claim was not disputed, and that more than one year has elapsed since letters of administration were issued to the said ....

Ordered, that a citation issue to the said ...., administrator, requiring him to show cause why he should not be ordered to pay the claim of the said petitioner.

................., *Surrogate.*

If, upon the return day, no cause be shown to the contrary, the surrogate will order the payment of the debt, and the payment may be enforced by attachment, or by suit upon the bond given by the executor or administrator.

Payment of a Debt may be enforced after a Trial upon the Merits and Judgment.

§ 19. (2 R. S., 116.) Where a creditor shall have obtained a judgment against any executor or administrator, after a trial at law upon the merits, he may, at any time thereafter, apply to the surrogate having jurisdiction, for an order against such executor or administrator, to show cause why an execution on such judgment should not be issued.

§ 20. The surrogate to whom such application may be made, shall issue a citation, requiring the executor or administrator complained of at a certain time and place therein to be named, to appear and account before him; and if upon such accounting it shall appear that there are assets in the hands of such executor or administrator, properly applicable, under the provisions of this chapter, to the payment, in whole or in part, of the judgment so obtained, the surrogate shall make an order, that execution be issued for the amount so applicable.

PETITION.

To Hon. ...., Surrogate of the county
of ....

Your petitioner, A B, of the town of ....,
in said county, respectfully shows :

That C D, late of said town, was a creditor of your
petitioner, and that he having died, letters testamentary
upon his will have been duly issued from the Surrogate's Court of this county, to E F, an executor named
in said will :

That your petitioner brought an action upon his claim
against said E F, as executor as aforesaid, in the
Supreme Court, and the same having been at issue, a
trial of said action was had upon the merits, and your
petitioner obtained judgment against said executor, for
the sum of .... dollars and ... cents, damages and
costs, on the ...... day of ...., 1874, as will
appear by a transcript of said judgment, made by the
county clerk of the county of ...., annexed
hereto.

That said executor has not paid said judgment, or
any part thereof, but that the whole amount, with
interest from the day in which the same was entered
as aforesaid, is due to your petitioner.

Wherefore your petitioner prays that a citation issue
to said E F, as executor as aforesaid, requiring him to
appear before your honor at a time and place therein
to be named, and account before you, and that your
petitioner may be permitted to issue an execution for
the amount so due as aforesaid, upon said judgment.

Dated................., Nov. 26, 1874.

(Signed),   A B.

Rensselaer county, ss :

A B, being duly sworn, says that the foregoing petition by him subscribed, is true of his own knowledge,
except as to the matters which are therein stated on information and belief, and as to those matters he believes
it to be true.

(Signed),   A B.

Sworn before me this ...... ⎫
    day of ...., 1874. ⎭

....

Commissioner of Deeds, Troy, N. Y.

ORDER FOR CITATION.

At a Surrogate's Court, held in the county
of .... at the surrogate's office in
........, of .... on the ...... day
of ...., 1874.
Present — Hon. ...., Surrogate.

In the matter of the estate
       of
C...... D......, deceased. ⎬

On reading and filing the petition of A B, duly verified, from which it appears, that the said A B has recovered a judgment in the Supreme Court against E F,
as executor of the last will and testament of the above
named C D, deceased, upon a claim against said deceased, after a trial upon the merits :

Ordered that a citation issue to the said E F, as such
executor, requiring him to appear in this court on
the ...... day of ...., 1874, at ten o'clock A.M.

(not less than eight days), to account, as such executor, and to show cause why an execution should not be permitted upon such judgment.

...................., *Surrogate.*

The citation is so familiar that no form is desirable. The terms of it follow the order.

Before an order can be entered the executor must render an account, which will not differ generally from an account rendered on final settlement of his accounts, but it must appear also, that there are no debts of a prior class unpaid, or that there are enough assets to pay them all, and it must also show how much the debts of the same class as the judgment, amount to, and the amount in hand applicable to the payment thereof.

These facts could not be ascertained, until after publication of notice to creditors to present claims had been made.

The statute proceeds as follows;

§ 21. Every such order shall be conclusive evidence, that there are sufficient assets in the hands of such executor or administrator, to satisfy the amount for which the execution is directed to be levied; and no appeal shall be made from any such order, unless the person making the same shall execute to the plaintiff in such execution, a bond with sufficient sureties, to be approved by the surrogate, conditioned for the payment of the full amount so directed to be levied, with interest thereon, and the costs of defending the appeal, in case the order appealed from shall be affirmed.

§ 22. (Page 117.) If the whole sum for which a judgment may have been obtained, shall not be collected on the execution so directed to be issued, and assets shall thereafter come into the hands of such executors or administrators; the surrogate shall make a further order for issuing execution, upon the application of the creditor, his personal representatives or assignees, and shall proceed in the same manner, from time to time, whenever assets shall come to the hands of the executor or administrator, until such judgment be satisfied.

After publication for claims, the executor or administrator may pay, or ratably pay, the claims presented, and if there be a surplus, may distribute such surplus according to the will or among the next of kin.

§ 39. (2 R. S., 89.) In case any suit shall be brought upon a claim which shall not have been presented to the executor or administrator of a deceased person, within six months from the first publication of such notice, as hereinbefore directed, such executor or administrator shall not be chargeable for any assets or money that he may have paid in satisfaction of any claims of an inferior degree, or of any legacies, or in making distribution to the next of kin, before such suit was commenced, but may prove such notice published by him as aforesaid, and such payment and distribution, in support of his plea of having administered the estate of the deceased.

§ 40. In such action the plaintiff shall be entitled to recover only to the amount of such assets as shall have been in the hands of such executor or administrator, at the time of the commencement of the suit; or he may take judgment for the amount of his claim, or any part thereof, to be levied and collected of assets which shall thereafter come into the hands of such executor or administrator.

§ 41. (Page 89.) In such suit no costs shall be recovered against the defendants. * * * *

§ 42. But any creditor who may have neglected to present his claims as aforesaid, may, notwithstanding, recover the same in the manner prescribed by law, of the next of kin and legatees of the deceased to whom any assets shall have been paid or distributed.

CHAPTER XIV.

LEGACIES, AND DISTRIBUTIVE SHARES AND PAYMENT THEREOF.

A legacy, in general terms, is a gift by will of some property other than real estate.

Legacies are general and specific.

A legacy is general, when it is bequeathed in terms not pointing out a particular item of the estate from which it shall be paid. It is specific, when the thing is bequeathed and pointed out.

To illustrate: A legacy of one thousand dollars, is general; a legacy of a certain bond and mortgage is specific.

A legacy is said to be *demonstrative*, when the fund or portion of the estate is designated, as the source from which payment is to be made. If the testator say, I give to A, one of my horses, the legacy is demonstrative as to the class of property from which it is to be paid. The delivery of *any* horse satisfies the legacy.

Legacies are said to be *vested*, when they are to be paid in the future, contingent when they may fail, being dependent on some contingency or survivorship.

They are also absolute and conditional, and all classes of legacies may lapse by failure of a proper person to take, or to be adeemed by the destruction of the subject matter, in the lifetime of the testator.

Inasmuch as most general legacies are subject to abatement, while specific legacies are not, the courts generally incline to consider legacies general, rather than specific.

Where a legacy is given to a widow in lieu of dower, or to a creditor in lieu of the debt owed to him, the legatee may, within a suitable time, elect which shall be accepted.

But certain legacies do not lapse.

§ 52. (2 R. S., 66.) Whenever any estate, real or personal shall be devised or bequeathed to a child or other descendant of the testator, and such legatee or devisee shall die during the lifetime of the testator, leaving a child or other descendant who shall survive such testator, such devise or legacy shall not lapse, but the property so devised or bequeathed, shall vest in the surviving child or other descendant of the legatee or devisee, as if such legatee or devisee had survived the testator and had died intestate.

The surrogate has power to enforce the payment and delivery of legacies. (2 R. S., 90.)

*Payment of Legacies and Distributive Shares, and
how Enforced.*

The Supreme and the Surrogate's Courts, have
concurrent jurisdiction to compel the payment of
legacies, after they shall become due by the terms
of the will creating them; but the Surrogate's
Court, as will be seen, can, in a proper case, compel
such payment before they become due.

§ 18. (2 R. S., 116.) The surrogate, having
jurisdiction, shall have power to decree the payment of debts, legacies and distributive shares,
against the executor or administrator of a deceased
person, in the following cases :

* * * * * *

2. Upon the application of a legatee or relative
entitled to a distributive share, payment of such
legacy or distributive share, or its just proportional part, may be so decreed at any time, after
one year shall have elapsed from the granting of
such letters.

This section should be considered in connection
with the following sections.

§ 43. (2 R. S., 90.) No legacy shall be paid by
an executor or administrator, until after the expiration of one year from the time of granting letters
testamentary or of administration, unless the same
are directed by the will to be sooner paid.

18

§ 44. In case a legacy is directed to be sooner paid, the executor or administrator may require a bond, with two sufficient sureties, conditioned that if any debts against the deceased shall duly appear, and which there shall be no other assets to pay, and there shall be no other assets to pay other legacies, or not sufficient, that then the legatee shall refund the legacy so paid, or such ratable proportion thereof with the other legatees, as may be necessary for the payment of said debts and the proportional parts of such other legacies, if there be any, and the costs and damages incurred by reason of the payment to such legatee ; and that if the probate of the will, under which such legacy is paid, shall be revoked, or the will declared void, then, that such legatee shall refund the whole of such legacy with interest, to the executor or administrator entitled thereto.

BOND ON PAYMENT OF LEGACY BEFORE EXPIRATION OF YEAR.

Know all men by these presents, that we, A B, as principal, and C D and E F, of the city of Troy, in the county of Rensselaer, and state of New York, are held, and firmly bound unto J D, as executor of the will of John Doe, late of the town of Brunswick, deceased, in the sum of .... dollars, for which payment, well and truly to be made, we bind our and each of our heirs, executors and administrators jointly and severally, firmly by these presents.

Sealed with our seals, and dated this }
 14th day of December, A.D. 1872. }

Whereas, in and by the will of said John Doe, deceased, dated the ...... day of ...., 1870, a legacy was bequeathed to the said A B, of one hundred dollars, payable by the terms of said will, in ...., after the decease of said John Doe, and before the expiration of one year from the granting of letters testamentary to the said J D, executor named therein, and the said J D has, at the request of the said A B, paid said legacy: Now the condition of this obligation is such that, if any debts against the deceased shall duly appear, and which there shall be no other assets to pay, and there shall be no other assets to pay other legacies, or not sufficient, then the said A B shall refund the legacy so paid, or such ratable proportion thereof, with the other legatees, as may be necessary for the payment of said debts, and the proportional parts of such other legacies, and the costs and charges incurred by reason of the payment to such legatee; and that if the probate of the said will shall be revoked, or the will declared void, then the said A B shall refund the whole of such legacy with interest to the said J D, or the administrator entitled thereto, then this obligation to be void, otherwise to remain in full force and effect.

A B. [L. s.]
C D. [L. s.]
E F. [L. s.]

Add acknowledgment.

§ 45. After the expiration of one year from the granting of any letters testamentary or of administration, the executors or administrators shall discharge the specific legacies bequeathed by any will, and pay the general legacies, if there be assets, and if there be not sufficient assets, then abatement of the general legacies shall be made in equal proportions. Such payments may be enforced by the surrogate, in the same manner as the return of an inventory, as hereinbefore provided, and also by a suit, on the bond of such executor or administrator, whenever directed by the surrogate.

Payment may be enforced by petition, order and attachment in the Surrogate's Court, or an action may be commenced in the Supreme Court.

Specific legacies are not subject to abatement, unless the testator clearly expresses his intention that they shall be so. (1 P. Williams, 540.)

The rule as to abatement of general legacies, applies only to such as are mere gratuities. Where the legacy is given for a debt, owing to the legatee, or for the relinquishment of any right, or interest, as of her dower by a widow, such legacy will be entitled to a preference of payment over the general legacies, which are mere bounties. (1 P. Williams, 127; 6 Paige, 298; 1 Russ's Ch. R., 543; 1 Edwards Ch., 411.) A legacy of piety, as for headstones at a parent's grave, will not be subject to abatement.   (6 Paige, 278.)

PETITION FOR ORDER TO ACCOUNT AND FOR PAYMENT OF LEGACY.

The petition of C D, of the town of ...., in the county of ...., to Hon. ...., Surrogate of said county, respectfully shows:

That your petitioner is a legatee named in the last will and testament of A B, late of the town of ....,...., in said county, deceased:

That said will was submitted to probate, by said surrogate, and letters testamentary were thereon issued to J D, an executor named therein, on the first day of ...., 1872, and more than one year has elapsed since the issue of such letters.

That in and by said will, a legacy of .... dollars was bequeathed to your petitioner, payable in one year after the decease of the testator.

That said testator left a large personal estate amounting to .... dollars, as by the inventory thereof on file in the office of said surrogate, will fully appear, and that such personal estate was amply sufficient, as your petitioner is informed and believes, to pay all the funeral expenses, and debts of the testator, the expenses of administration, and the legacies bequeathed in said will.

Your petitioner has, since the expiration of one year from the issue of letters as aforesaid, applied to said executor and ·requested him to pay the legacy so bequeathed to your petitioner, but he has not paid the same.

Wherefore your petitioner prays that said executor may be required to account according to law for his proceedings as such executor, that he may be ordered to pay said legacy to your petitioner and that such other or further proceedings may be had as may be requisite to enforce the payment of such legacy as shall be just and equitable.

(Signed),   C D.

Rensselaer county, ss:

C D, being duly sworn, says that the foregoing petition by him subscribed is true, of his own knowledge, except as to the matters which are therein stated on information and belief, and as to those matters he believes it to be true.

(Signed),   C D.

Sworn before me this ...... day ⎫
   of ...., 1874. ⎬

....................,
Notary Public.

ORDER FOR CITATION.

At a Surrogate's Court held in the county of
..................., at the surrogate's office
in the .... of ...., on the
...... day of ...., 1874.
Present. — Hon. ...., Surrogate.

In the matter of the estate
of
A B, deceased.

On reading and filing the petition of C D, one of the legatees named in the will of the above named deceased, and it appearing that more than one year has elapsed since the issue of letters testamentary to E F, executor named in said will, and that the legacy to said C D, has not been paid :

Ordered that a citation issue to said executor requiring him to be and appear before said surrogate on the ..... day of ...., 1874, at his office in the village of ...., at ten o'clock in the forenoon, to render his account as such executor, and show cause why he should not be ordered to pay the legacy bequeathed in said will to said C D.

..................., *Surrogate.*

For disobedience to the citation, or to the order for payment, the executor or administrator may be attached, or a suit may be brought on his bond.

The account rendered, will necessarily be a full one, of all receipts and disbursements, and will not differ from the account on final settlement, more fully treated of hereafter.

But the executor may, doubtless, admit a sufficiency of assets, and thus render an account unnecessary.

In all cases on payment of a legacy, the executor should take a receipt for it.

RECEIPT FOR LEGACY.

Whereas, James Richards, late of the town of Schodack, in the county of Rensselaer, deceased, lately made his last will and testament, dated the ...... day ...., 1862, in which he gave and bequeathed to me the sum of (five hundred dollars): Now, therefore, I hereby acknowledge the receipt of said sum so bequeathed to me, of John Richards, executor named in said will.

Dated, Schodack, March 1, 1862.

(Signed),   MARY WILLIAMS.

Payment of a legacy or a distributive share, or a part thereof, may be obtained in certain cases against any executor or administrator, except the public administrator of the city of New York, under the following sections:

§ 82. (2 R. S., 98.) Any person entitled to any legacy, or to a distributive share of the estate of a deceased person, at any time previous to the expiration of one year from the granting of letters testamentary or of administration, may apply to the surrogate, either in person or by his guardian, after giving reasonable notice to the executor or administrator, to be allowed to receive such portion of such legacy or share, as may be necessary for his support.

§ 83. If it appear to the surrogate that there is at least one third more of assets in the hands of such executor or administrator, than will be sufficient to pay all debts, legacies and claims against the estate, then known, he may, in his discretion, allow such portion of the legacy or distributive share to be advanced as may be necessary for the support of the person entitled thereto, upon satisfactory bonds being executed for the return of such portion with interest, whenever required.

The forms for proceeding under these provisions may readily be had, by adopting the forms already given for enforcing the payment of legacies after one year has elapsed which see (p. 277).

The following are the statutory provisions in regard to the payment of legacies to minors:

§ 46. (2 R. S., 91.) In case any legatee be a minor, his legacy, if under the value of fifty dollars, may be paid to his father, to the use and for the benefit of such minor.

§ 47. If the legacy be of the value of fifty dollars or more, the same may, under the direction of the surrogate, be paid to the general guardian of a minor, who shall be required to give security to the minor, to be approved by the surrogate, for the faithful application and accounting for such legacy.

The security required in this section, is in addition to the security given on the appointment of the general guardian, obviously, for the reason that a legacy given after the appointment, made no part of the estate of the minor, on which the amount of the former security was based.

The bond may run as follows :

BOND ON PAYMENT OF LEGACY.

Know all men by these presents, that we, John Dean, Samuel Stiles and John Doe, of the city of Troy, in the county of Rensselaer and state of New York, are held and firmly bound unto James Dean, of the city of Troy, aforesaid, a minor, in the sum of two thousand dollars, to be paid to the said James Dean, his certain attorney, executors, administrators and assigns, to which payment, well and truly to be made, we bind ourselves, our and each of our heirs, executors and administrators, jointly and severally firmly by these presents :

Sealed with our seals and dated this 26th day of November, 1874.

The condition of this obligation is such, that if the above bounden John Dean, shall render a just and true account of the sum of one thousand dollars, received by him as guardian of the above named James Dean, from A R, the executor of the will of D F, late of the city of Troy, deceased, and being a legacy bequeathed to the said James Dean by the will of said deceased, and of the application thereof to any court having cognizance thereof, when thereunto required, and shall pay to said James Dean, his executors, administrators or assigns, such sum as such court shall direct said John Dean to pay, then this obligation to be void, otherwise to remain in full force and virtue.

(Signed),   JOHN DEAN.   [L. S.]

SAMUEL STILES.   [L. S.]

JOHN DOE.   [L. S.]

As to Justification of Sureties and Acknowledgment of Execution.

§ 48. (2 R. S., 91.) If there be no such guardian, or the surrogate do not direct such payment, the legacy shall be invested in permanent securities, under the direction of the surrogate, in the name and for the benefit of such minor, upon annual interest; and the interest may be applied, under the direction of the surrogate, to the support and education of such minor.

§ 49. It shall be the duty of the surrogate, where there is no guardian of such minor, to keep in his office the securities so taken, and to collect, receive and apply the interest; and when necessary, to collect the principal and reinvest the same, and also to reinvest any interest that may not be necessarily expended, as aforesaid.

§ 50. On such minor coming of age, he shall be entitled to receive the securities so taken, and the interest or other moneys that may have been received; and the surrogate and his sureties shall be liable to account for the same.

§ 51. In case of the death of such minor before coming of age, the said securities and moneys shall go to his executors or administrators, to be applied and distributed according to law; and the surrogate and his sureties shall, in like manner, be liable to account to such executor or administrator.

There is also a provision in regard to an action to be brought against an executor or administrator, by a legatee as one of the next of kin for a legacy or distributive share.

§ 9. (2 R. S., 114.) If, after the expiration of one year from the granting of letters testamentary or administration, there be more than sufficient assets to pay the debts of the testator or intestate, and, if after reasonable demand made, and the offer of a bond with sufficient sureties, as in the next section prescribed, by any legatee or by any of the next of kin entitled to share in the distribution of the estate, such executor or administrator shall refuse to pay the legacy bequeathed by the will to such legatee, or the share of any person entitled to distribution, he shall be liable to an action at the suit of such legatee or next of kin or their personal representatives.

§ 10. Previous to the commencement of the action, a bond to the executor or administrator shall be filed with the county clerk, with such sureties as the court or any judge thereof shall approve in double the sum of such share or legacy, conditioned that if any debt owing by the testator or intestate shall afterward be recovered or duly made to appear, for the payment of which there shall be no assets other than the said share or legacy, that then such person shall refund the legacy or share that may be recovered in such action, or such ratable part or proportion thereof with the other legatees or representatives of the deceased, as may be necessary for the payment of the said debts and the costs and charges incurred by a recovery against such executor or administrator in any suit therefor.

§ 11. When given by a legatee, the bond shall be further conditioned, that if no sufficient assets shall thereafter remain to pay any other legacy which may be due, that then such person shall refund such ratable part or proportion thereof, with the other legatees or representatives of the deceased, as may be necessary for the payment of the proportional part of such other legacy.

§ 12. A minor may bring such action by his guardian or next friend, as in other cases; but not until such guardian or next friend shall have filed, with the clerk of the court, a bond to the minor, in such sum, and with such sureties as the court shall approve, conditioned that such guardian or next friend shall duly account to such minor, when of full age, or to his personal representatives, in case of his death, for all moneys which may be recovered in such suit.

§ 13. In any such suit brought by a legatee, if it appear that there are not assets sufficient to pay all the legacies that may have been given, then an abatement shall be made in proportion to the

legacies so given, and such legatee shall recover
only a proportionate part.

The following are the provisions in relation to
the trial of the actions provided for in these sections.

§ 19. (2 R. S. 450.)   Whenever an action shall
be brought by any legatee against an executor or
administrator, and the want of assets to pay all
the debts of the deceased, and all the legacies bequeathed by him, or any of them, shall be pleaded,
the cause shall be referred to referees, to examine
the accounts of the defendants, and to hear and
report upon the allegations and proofs of the parties
in respect to such plea.

§ 20. Such referees shall proceed in the manner
provided by law in respect to references of actions
in which there is a long account; and all the provisions of law in relation to such references shall
apply to referees appointed pursuant to the last
section, and to their proceedings and the judgment
thereon.

§ 21. In such cases, the costs of the action, or of
either party, shall be paid as the court may direct,
out of the estate of the deceased, or by the defendants personally, if their refusal to pay such legacy
or their defense of the action shall appear to have
been unreasonable.

§ 22. If the plaintiff in such suit shall recover
only part of his demand, for the want of assets

in the hands of the defendants, and assets shall afterwards come to their hands, he shall have a new action for the recovery thereof, or of the proportionate share thereof to which he may be entitled ; and the same proceedings, in all respects, shall be had in such action.

CHAPTER XV.

Costs against Executors or Administrators.

The liability of executors and administrators for costs, either as against themselves, or against the estate which they represent, is regulated by statute.

The code provides for costs to the plaintiff or defendant generally, in §§ 304 and 305, and further provides as to executors and administrators.

§ 317. In an action prosecuted or defended by an executor, administrator, trustee of an express trust, or a person expressly authorized by statute, costs shall be recovered, as in an action by and against a person prosecuting or defending in his own right; but such costs shall be chargeable only upon, or collected of, the estate, fund, or party represented, unless the court shall direct the same to be paid by the plaintiff or defendant personally, for mismanagement or bad faith in such action or defense; but this section shall not be construed to allow costs against executors or administrators, when they are now exempted therefrom by section 41, of tit. 3, chapter 6, of the second part of the Revised Statutes; and whenever any claim against a deceased person, shall be referred pursuant to the provisions of the Revised Statutes, the prevailing party shall be entitled to recover the fees of referees and witnesses and other necessary disbursements, to be taxed according to law. And the court may, in its discretion, in the cases mentioned in this section, require the plaintiff to give security for costs.

The part of section 41 (2 R. S., 80), referred to in the foregoing section of the code, is as follows :

§ 41. * * *; nor shall any costs be recovered in any suit at law against any executors or administrators, to be levied of their property, or of the property of the deceased, unless it appear that the demand on which the action was founded was presented within the time aforesaid (the six months of publication), and its payment was unreasonably resisted or neglected, or that the defendant refused to refer the same pursuant to the preceding provisions; in which case, the court may direct such costs to be levied of the property of the defendants, or of the deceased, as shall be just, having reference to the facts that appeared on the trial. If the action be brought in the Supreme Court, such facts shall be certified by the judge before whom the trial shall have been had. The costs when paid, shall be chargeable upon the estate of the deceased, unless for mismanagement or bad faith in the action the court shall charge the executor or administra-

CHAPTER XVI.

ACCOUNTING AND FINAL SETTLEMENT.

Executors or Administrators may be ordered to Account, and may have Final Settlement.

The rights of creditors and next of kin, are to some extent suspended, during eighteen months from the time of granting letters. They may indeed sue, but the creditor obtains no priority, and he pays his own costs, unless he can show that the executor or administrator refused to refer, or unreasonably resisted the payment of the claim, as we have seen (p. 289.) But eighteen months having elapsed, a creditor, legatee, or one of the next of kin may exact an accounting, and the creditor may obtain payment of his claim or its *pro rata* dividend if it has been established upon a trial or admitted by the executor or administrator ; for the executor or administrator admits the justice of a claim if he does not dispute it.

§ 52. (2 R. S., 92, as amended by chap. 261, Laws of 1859.) An executor or administrator, after the expiration of eighteen months from the time of his appointment, may be required to render an account of his proceedings, by an order of the surrogate, to be granted upon application from some person having a demand against the personal estate of the deceased, either as creditor, legatee, or next of kin ; or of some person on behalf of any minor having such claim, or without such application, and in the case of an administrator, upon the application of any person who is, or has been his bail, or of the legal representatives of such person.

An heir at law, cannot, as such, petition for an accounting (*Shumway* v. *Cooper*, 16 Barb., 556), and it is a curious fact, that a widow of an intestate, although entitled to one-third of the whole surplus of the estate on settlement, is not strictly within the terms of the statute, entitled to compel an accounting. " She is, however," remarks Mr. Dayton (Dayton's Sur., 3d ed., 487), " clearly within the equity and spirit of the section, and beyond all doubt, an account may be decreed upon her application." Unquestionably, the surrogate might order such an account, if an application were made to him by a widow, as if made without the application of any person, and upon his own motion, under the above section. So also, it is probably the duty of the surrogate, where infants only are concerned, to call executors or administrators to an account, after a reasonable time has elapsed, beyond the eighteen months allowed by law, without the application of any one, if he has reason to apprehend that the interests of the infants require his action. (*Smith* v. *Lawrence*, 11 Paige, 211.)

The following petition for a legatee, may be readily adapted to the case of a creditor or one of the next of kin.

PETITION FOR AN ORDER THAT EXECUTOR ACCOUNT.

To the Surrogate of the county of Rensselaer :

The petition of C D, of the town of ...., in said county, respectfully shows :

That your petitioner is a legatee, named in the will of A B, late of the town of ...., in said county, deceased (or is a creditor of the above deceased).

That said will was admitted to probate, by said surrogate, and letters testamentary were thereon issued to J D, an executor named therein, on the first day of September, 1872, and more than eighteen months have elapsed since the issue of said letters.

That in and by said will, a legacy of .... dollars was bequeathed to your petitioner payable in one year from the decease of the testator.

That said testator left a large personal estate amounting to .... dollars, as by inventory thereof on file in the office of said surrogate will fully appear, and that such personal estate was amply sufficient, as your petitioner is informed and believes, to pay all the funeral expenses, and debts of the said testator, the expenses of administration and the legacies bequeathed in said will.

Your petitioner has, since the expiration of eighteen months from the issue of letters as aforesaid, applied to said executor and requested him to account and pay the legacy so bequeathed to your petitioner, but notwithstanding, such executor has not accounted nor paid said legacy.

Wherefore, your petitioner prays that said executor may be required to pay the aforesaid legacy to your petitioner, and that he may be required to account according to law, for his proceedings as such executor, and that such further or other proceedings may be had as may be requisite to enforce the payment of your petitioner's legacy, and as shall be just and equitable.

(Signed),   C D.

Rensselaer county, ss:

C D, being duly sworn, says that the foregoing petition, by him subscribed, is true.   C D.

Sworn before me, etc.

    GEO. SCOTT, *Notary Public.*

    Rensselaer county, N. Y.

ORDER THAT EXECUTOR ACCOUNT.

At a Surrogate's Court, held in the county of ...., at the surrogate's office in ...... of ...., on the ...... day of ...., 1874.

Present — Hon. ...., Surrogate.

In the matter of the estate
of
................., deceased.

On reading and filing the petition of ....,
one of the legatees named in the will of ....,
late of the town of ...., deceased:

Ordered, that ...., the executor of the said will, personally, be and appear before the surrogate of the county of ...., at his office in the .... of ...., on the ..... day of .... next, at ten o'clock in the forenoon, to render an account of his proceedings, as such executor, or show cause why an attachment should not issue against him.

................., *Surrogate.*

§ 76. (S. L., 1837, chap. 460.) When a surrogate shall make an order under the above fifty-second section, requiring an executor or administrator to render an account of his proceedings, the same shall be served upon such executor or administrator by showing him the original, and at the same time delivering him a copy thereof, or in case of his absence from home, by leaving a copy thereof with his wife, or some suitable person, at the place of his residence, thirty days before the day of hearing. But if such executor or administrator shall not reside within this state, the order shall be served, by publishing it once in each week, for three months before the return day thereof, in the state paper, and also in the county paper where the surrogate resides who issued the order, if any such paper there is published in said county, and if not, in the county paper of some adjoining county, unless the order be personally served on any such executor or administrator residing out of the state at the time of service, such service shall be made at least sixty days before the return day thereof.

§ 53. (2 R. S., 92.) Obedience to such order may be enforced in the manner hereinbefore directed, to compel the return of an inventory ; and in case of disobedience, the same proceedings may be had to attach the party so disobeying, and to discharge him. And the like revocation of the letters granted to him may be made, in case parties absconding or concealing himself so that the order cannot be personally served, or of his neglecting to render an account within thirty days after being committed ; and new letters shall be granted with like effect as in those cases.

These provisions have been fully treated of in a former part of this work, in relation to the inventory. (See *ante*.)

§ 1. (S. L., 1846, chap. 288.) Whenever an absent or non-resident executor or administrator shall have been duly cited to appear and account before the surrogate, in pursuance of the above fifty-second section, and the citation shall have been duly served in the manner prescribed by law, and such executor or administrator shall, without showing reasonable cause, neglect or refuse to appear, in pursuance of said citation, the surrogate issuing such citation, may, in his discretion, thereupon make an order revoking the letters testamentary, or of administration, before granted to such executor or administrator, reciting therein the cause of such revocation ; and shall grant letters testamentary or of administration of the goods, chattels and effects of the deceased, unadministered, to the person entitled thereto (other than such executor or administrator), in the same manner as original letters of administration, or letters testamentary, with the like effect as is provided in the twentieth and twenty-first sections of title third, chapter six, part second, of the Revised Statutes, where an executor or administrator has neglected or refused to return an inventory.

The costs of the proceeding, may, in the discretion of the surrogate, be charged upon the executor or administrator personally. (S. L., 1867, chap. 782, § 8.)

The applicant should be careful to ask for the relief, the payment of the debt or legacy, or of a distributive share, which he thinks himself entitled to, as well as demand an account, for it has been held that, where the payment is not asked for, the executor or administrator may render an account and thus fully comply with the prayer of the petion, and the jurisdiction of the surrogate under the same, except for the purpose of examining the executor or administrator, under oath, according to the statute, will be exhausted. The party can have no further relief under that petition. No settlement of the account can properly be made in such case, without presenting a new petition to the surrogate for the settlement and adjustment of the account and the payment of the claims of the petitioner. (*Westervelt* v. *Gregg*, 1 Barb. Ch., 478; *Smith* v. *Van Keuren*, 2 id., 473; *Campbell* v. *Bruen*, 1 Brad., 224 ; *Guild* v. *Peck*, 11 Paige, 475.)

When the executor, on being cited to account, alleged that the petitioner had assigned his interest in the estate, it was held that the surrogate could not try the question whether the assignment was valid, and the executor was ordered to account. (*Bonfanti* v. *Deguerre*, 3 Brad., 429.)

A mere appearance of interest in the applicant, for an order to require an inventory and account, is sufficient to authorize such order. (*Thomson* v. *Thomson*, 1 Brad., 24.)

As a general rule, if the creditor swears positively to a debt due to him from the estate, he will be entitled to an order for an inventory and account. (*Gratacap* v. *Phyfe*, 1 Barb. Ch., 485.)

If the surrogate, on hearing the proofs, is satisfied that the petitioner is not interested, he will dismiss the application with costs; but if he finds that the petitioner is interested, he will order that the accounting proceed.

The executor or administrator, however, instead of contesting the right of the petitioner to an account, or, if after contest he is ordered to account, may apply for a final settlement. He may make this application, at any time after the expiration of one year from this appointment, the time formerly being eighteen months.

§ 60. (2 R. S., 93.) If, upon being required by any surrogate to render an account, an executor or administrator desires to have the same finally settled, he may apply to the surrogate for a citation, which such surrogate shall issue, requiring the creditors and next of kin of the deceased, and the legatees, if there be any, to appear before him on some day therein to be specified, and to attend the settlement of such account.

§ 61. The citation shall be served personally on all those to whom it shall be directed, living in the county of the surrogate, at least fifteen days before the return thereof; and upon those living out of the county, or who, or whose residence may be unknown, either personally fifteen days previously, or by publishing the same in a newspaper printed in the county, at least four weeks before the return thereof, and in such newspapers printed in any other counties, where any creditors or other persons interested in the estate of the deceased may reside, as the surrogate, upon due inquiry into the facts, shall direct.

§ 62. " If there be any such creditors, or other persons interested residing in any other state of the United States, or in either of the provinces of Canada, the citation shall be published once in each week for three months, in the state paper, unless such citation be personally served on such creditors or other persons interested at least forty days before the return thereof; and if there be any such creditors, or other persons interested, residing out of the United States and out of the province of Canada, the citation shall be published as aforesaid, six months."

In case of the publication of the citation, a copy of it should also be mailed to each party to be served at his place of residence or post office address, at least thirty days before the return day thereof. (S. L., 1863, chap. 362.)

In all cases requiring the publication of the citation in the state paper, heretofore, the same shall be published for the same period in some paper in the county, to be designated by the surrogate, and the publication of the same in the state paper is optional with the surrogate, and if the surrogate shall certify that the estate is less than two thousand dollars in value, no charge for such publication in the state paper shall be made. (Chap. 437, S. L., 1874.)

The citation shall be served on minors in the same manner as citations to attend probate (S. L., 1874, chap. 156) that is, by delivering a copy to such minor personally, if resident in the county, and also a copy to his father, mother or guardian, or if there be none in the county, then by delivering a copy to the minor and one to the persons having the care or control of such minor, or with whom he shall reside, or in whose service he shall be employed. (See *ante*, p. 47.)

The proof of the service should be by affidavit, and an admission of service of the parties of full age, signed by them, is undoubtedly sufficient, on proving the signatures by affidavit.

§ 70. (2 R. S., 95, as amended S. L., 1867, chap. 782, § 14.) An executor or administrator, after the expiration of one year from the granting of letters testamentary or of administration, may render a final account of his proceedings to the surrogate who appointed him, though not cited to do so, and may obtain a citation to all persons interested in the estate to attend a final settlement of his accounts; which citation shall be served and published in the manner prescribed in the preceding sections of this title, and thereupon the same proceedings shall be had for a final settlement, and with the like effect, in all respects, as in the case of a settlement at the instance of a creditor.

In either case provided for by these sections, whether compelled to account, at the instance of a claimant, and, desiring to account finally, or rendering a final account voluntarily, the executor or administrator petitions for the proper process of the court.

The following is a form for a petition, and it is noticeable that it is the only written petition in practice, not verified. We presume the verification was omitted originally, for the reason that every fact stated is a matter of record in the court.

PETITION FOR FINAL SETTLEMENT.

In Surrogate's Court, county of Rensselaer :

To Moses Warren, Esq., Surrogate of Rensselaer county :

The petition of (Richard Roe), of the town of Brunswick, in the county of Rensselaer aforesaid, respectfully shows : that your petitioner was duly apppointed and qualified, by the surrogate of the county of Rensselaer, as the executor of the last will' and testament (or as administrator of all and singular the goods, chattels and credits), of Henry Jones, late of said town of Brunswick, deceased, and that more than one year has elapsed since letters testamentary (or of administration), were issued to your petitioner by the surrogate aforesaid ; that your petitioner has returned to the surrogate of said county, an inventory of the personal estate of said deceased (and has advertised for claims, in pursuance of the order of said surrogate).

Your petitioner is now desirous of rendering an account of his proceedings as such executor (administrator) as aforesaid, and, therefore, prays that a citation may issue out of, and under the seal of this court, to be directed to the creditors, legatees (next of kin), and all persons interested in the estate of the said deceased, requiring them to appear as in said citation directed, and attend the final settlement of the accounts of your petitioner as such executor (administrator) as aforesaid.

Dated, this 30th day of April, 1862.

(Signed),   RICHARD ROE.

ORDER FOR CITATION TO ATTEND FINAL SETTLEMENT.

> At a Surrogate's Court, held in the county of ...., at the surrogate's office in the ...... of ...., on the ...... day of ...., 1874.
>
> Present—Hon. ...., Surrogate.

In the matter of the estate

of

.................., deceased.

Richard Roe, the executor of the last will and testament of ...., late of ...., deceased, having filed his petition, praying for a final settlement of his accounts as such executor, and more than one year having elapsed since the issue of letters to him :

Ordered, that a citation issue to the creditor, legatees, and all persons interested in the estate of said deceased, requiring them to appear on the ...... day of ...., next, at ten o'clock in the forenoon, to attend such final settlement.

.................., *Surrogate.*

Upon the return day of the citation, and on proof of the due service and publication thereof being filed, if it shall appear that any of the parties cited are minors, the surrogate will appoint a special guardian for them for the sole purpose of appearing for them and caring for their interests, and no proceeding shall be had on the accounting until he shall appear.

The executor or administrator then files his account.

ACCOUNT OF EXECUTOR OR ADMINISTRATOR.

[This form may be adapted to any estate or any amounts.]

A B, Executor or (Administrator), in account with the Estate of C D, deceased.

1862.   DR.

To amount of inventory on
   file, ... $550 00
Jan. 2. To received, savings bank
   deposit not inventoried,...   15 50
To received, interest from
   E F, not included in inventory, ...   6 10
                  ———— $571 60

1860.   CONTRA.   CR.

July 1. By paid surrogate, letters
   · testamentary, &c.,......... $15 00
By expenses to and at Troy
   to obtain letters, ...   3 10
By paid C D, witness to will,   2 00
          20

By paid E F, witness to wills,............................	1 50		
9. By paid J H, and E R, appraisers, ...	6 00		
By paid surrogate on filing inventory,.....................	50		
July 20. By paid funeral charges, ...	40 50		
29. By paid support of widow			
1861. and family for 40 days,...	10 50		
Jan. 3. By paid, surrogate's order to advertise for claims, &c.,	75		
By paid, printing same,.....	5 50		
		$85 25	
By loss on sale of inventoried articles,..............	16 00		
By expenses to Troy three times, ...	4 50		
		20 50	
		$108 75	
Showing balance for commissions, debts and distributions of,..............		462 25	

The inventory herein was filed on the ...... day of ...., 1869.

Notice to creditors to present claims was first published on the ...... day of ...., 1870.

The following claims have been presented under the notice and allowed.

Edward Murphy,.. $150 00
James Jones,.. 16 00

The following claims were presented and disputed :

S. Foster, ... $60.00
Irving Hayner, ... 500.00

Actions have been commenced against the executor and judgments obtained against him for the following sums :

In favor of S. Foster,........................... $95.00
"   "   " Irving Hayner,..................... 610.50

The following affidavit is to be included in, or annexed to the account.

Rensselaer county, ss :

A B, of the town of ...., in the county of Rensselaer, being duly sworn, says : That he is executor of the last will and testament of (or administrator of all and singular the goods, chattels and credits of) C D, late of said town of ...., deceased, and that the foregoing (or annexed) account, is in all respects just and true; that the same, according to the best of his knowledge and belief, contains a full and true account of all his receipts and disbursements, on account of the estate of said deceased, and of all sums of money and property belonging to the estate of the said deceased, which have come into his hands as such administrator, or which have been received by any other person, by his order or authority, for his use; and that he does not know of any error or omission in the said account, to the prejudice of any of the parties interested in the estate of the said deceased.

And he further says, that the sums under twenty dollars, charged in said account, for which no vouchers or other evidence of payment are herewith filed, or for which he has not been able to produce vouchers or

other evidences of payment, have actually been paid
and disbursed by him as charged.

(Signed),   A B.

Sworn before me, this ...... }
   day of ...., 1862. }

The verification was fixed by the Court of Chancery and its terms settled in *Gardner* v. *Purdy* (7
Paige, 112).

The account must state, as part of the executor's
proceedings, when the inventory was filed, when
the advertisement for claims was published, what
claims were allowed, what disputed, and what rejected by the executor, and the time and manner
in which they were disputed or rejected; what
suits, if any, have been commenced thereon, and
which are pending and the amount claimed. Also
what claims have been presented and allowed
since the expiration of the advertisement for claims.
If no such claims have been rejected or disputed,
and no suits have been commenced, it must be so
stated. It is material also that the character of
the debts paid, allowed or presented, should be
stated; that is, whether they are judgments docketed, or debts of an inferior class. (*Matter of Jones*,
1 Redf., 263.)

The executor must charge himself with the
amount of the inventory and the increase, or state
that there is no increase. The first credit is for

articles perished or lost. The cause of loss must be stated. He must credit himself with the decrease, and with the debts due and not collected, and the facts justifying the credit must be stated. Stating that they are not collectable, will not justify a decree that they were not collectable. He must then credit himself with the funeral charges, expenses of administration, moneys paid to creditors, naming them, and other payments to legatees and next of kin. If any are minors, the fact must be so stated, and whether they have any guardians, and if so, their names and residences, and how appointed. Any other fact which has occurred as part of his proceedings, which may affect the estate or the rights of any distributee, or his own rights, he must state. He must also produce vouchers. (*Matter of Jones, sup.* See also *Willcox* v. *Smith*, 26 Barb., 316.)

§ 54. (2 R. S., 92.) In rendering such account, every executor or administrator shall produce vouchers for all debts and legacies paid, and for all funeral charges and just necessary expenses, which vouchers shall be deposited and remain with the surrogate; and such executor or administrator may be examined on oath, touching such payments, and also touching any property or effects of the deceased which have come into his hands, and the disposition thereof.

The statute requiring vouchers is imperative; and if an account can be allowed in any case, without vouchers and without proof, other than the oath of the executor or administrator, it is only where creditors refused to give vouchers, or where they have been lost or destroyed. (*Willcox* v. *Smith*, 26 Barb., 316.)

§ 63. (2 R. S., 94.) Any creditors, legatees, or other persons interested in the estate of deceased, as next of kin or otherwise, may attend the settlement of such account, and contest the same; and they and the executor or administrator shall have process, to be issued by such surrogate, to compel the attendance of witnesses.

ALLEGATIONS ON CONTEST OF ACCOUNT.

Surrogate's Court, ... county.

In the matter of the estate
of
...................., deceased.

A B, C D, and E F, next of kin of the above named deceased (or legatees named in the will of said deceased), contesting the account filed by A B, administrator of the estate of said deceased, alleged that the said account is erroneous, and that the same should be surcharged by the following items:

First. That it does not include an item of .... dollars, a claim against the said executor, for a debt owing to the deceased in his life time.

Second. That it does not include the proper sum received or chargeable against said executor, for interest.

That the said account is further erroneous in the following particulars :

First. That the item of .... dollars, for funeral expenses is extravagant, and not according to the station of the deceased.

Second. That the item of .... paid to ....
in that the pretended claim was not due, and was barred by the statute of limitations.

(And so in detail).

Dated, Dec. 1, 1872.

JAMES LANSING,
for said Contestants.

§ 64. (2 R. S., 94.) The hearing of the allegations and proofs of the respective parties may be adjourned from time to time ; as shall be necessary. And the surrogate may appoint one or more auditors to examine the accounts presented to him, and to make report therein, subject to his confirmation ; and he may make a reasonable allowance to such auditors, not exceeding two dollars per day, to be paid out of the estate of the deceased.

In the Surrogate's Court of the city and county of New York, the surrogate may appoint a referee, to take testimony, examine the account, to hear and determine all disputed claims, and make report subject to the confirmation of the surrogate. The referee shall have the same power and compensation, as referees appointed by the Supreme Court. (S. L., 1870, chap. 355, § 6.)

ORDER REFERENCE.

At a Surrogate's Court held in the county of
.... at the surrogate's office in
the ...... of ...., on the ...... day
of ...., 1874.
Present—Hon. ...., Surrogate.

In the matter of the estate

of

..................., deceased.

A B, the executor of the last will and testament of the above named deceased, having filed his account for final settlement, and sundry persons interested having filed objections to said account, (and sundry creditors having presented their claims against the estate of the said deceased which are disputed):

Ordered, that said account, objections (and claims) be referred to C D, Esq., as auditor (referee) to examine the same and to make report thereon to this court (to take testimony, examine the account, to hear and determine all disputed claims and make report thereon to this court).

..................., *Surrogate.*

Upon the trial of the objections, where the affidavit annexed to the account of the executor or administrator is full and clear as to payments, and the items of disbursments, under twenty dollars, do not exceed in the aggregate, five hundred dollars, and the payments of sums over that amount are supported by vouchers, it is for the party who objects to the account to falsify and surcharge it, on the form of distinct and specific allegations with proof thereof. (*Metzger* v. *Metzger*, 1 Brad., 265; *Marre* v. *Ginochio*, 2 Brad., 165; *Westervelt* v. *Gregg*, 1 Barb. Ch., 465; *Bainbridge* v. *McCullough*, 1 How., 488; *Gardner* v. *Gardner*, 7 Paige 112.)

But the inventory is not conclusive against the executor, of what the assets consist of, and their value, although it is *prima facie* evidence against him, on the accounting before the surrogate. (*Hasbrouck* v. *Hasbrouck*, 24 How., 24; *Matter of Saltus*, 3 Keyes, 590.)

In the matter of interest, where the executor or administrator mixes up the trust fund with his own, or neglects to keep regular accounts of investments, and of the interest received on such funds, he is chargeable with interest, as if the trust fund had been kept invested upon interest, payable periodically. (*Spear* v. *Tinkham*, 2 Barb. Ch., 211; *Jacot* v. *Emmett*, 11 Paige, 142.)

In case items of the account are disputed by a contestant, it is sufficient if the executor produces vouchers for such items. The voucher is not to be rejected for want of an affidavit of the claimant to whom payment was made. It is doubtless the prudent course for the executor, in every case, to demand such an affidavit, but it is entirely optional with him to do so or not, as will be seen by reference to the statute already quoted. (2 R. S., 88.)

If the contestant object that there are assets not accounted for, beyond these stated in the inventory, the burden is with him, to show that such assets exist, and bring proof of the knowledge of their existence to the executor. (*Marre* v. *Ginochio*, 2 Brad., 165.) The legatees can adduce evidence to charge the executor with more assets than he acknowledges, and it is competent for him to show that the assets were his own property, or the property of a third party, and not part of the testator's estate. (*Merchant* v. *Merchant*, 2 Brad., 432.)

The executor is bound to protect the estate from all improper claims, and only in so doing can he protect himself. He is therefore bound to interpose the defense of the statute of limitations, in a proper case for such defense, and a direction in the will to pay *all just debts* will not be construed to revive a claim barred by the statute, nor will a direction in the will to sell real estate to pay debts, prevent the statute from running. (*Martin* v. *Gage*, 9 N. Y., 398.)

But it seems that the statute is in some cases suspended. Where a valid claim against the decedent, against which the statute had not run at

the time of his death, has been presented to the
executor or administrator, and has been recognized
and allowed by him within the seven years and a
half from the time the debt accrued, and the proceedings for the accounting of the executor or
administrator have taken place within six years
from the time of such presentation and allowance
of the claim, neither the executor or administrator,
nor legatees or next of kin, can successfully interpose the statute of limitations to defeat the claim
on the accounting before the surrogate. (*Willcox*
v. *Smith*, 26 Barb., 316.)

It has now been definitely settled, that the statute does not confer upon the surrogate the power
of deciding upon the validity of a claim against an
estate, where such claim is disputed, and the right
of the surrogate to make such determination, is also
denied. Though he may decree the payment of a
debt which has been established, as by the admission of the executor or administrator, or by the
recovery of a judgment, he has not jurisdiction to
try or to establish a disputed claim, under any circumstances. (*Tucker* v. *Tucker*, 4 Abb. Ct. App.
Dec. & 4 Keyes, 136.)

So also the executor may present his own claim
on the final settlement, and the surrogate has jurisdiction to allow or disallow it. If the statute of
limitations has not passed upon it in the life-time

of the decedent it can not successfully be interposed against it, if presented on the first hearing.
(See *ante*.)   On the hearing, he must not only
verify it by his own affidavit, like any other creditor, but he must support it by legal evidence
(*Williams* v. *Purdy*, 6 Paige 166; *Clark* v. *Clark*,
8 Id., 132.)

§ 56. (2 R. S., 92.)   The surrogate may make
allowance to any executor or administrator for
property of the deceased perished or lost, without
the fault of such executor or administrator.

§ 57. No profit shall be made by executors or
administrators by the increase, nor shall they sustain any loss by the decrease, without their fault,
of any part of the estate; but they shall account
for such increase, and be allowed for such decrease,
on the settlement of their accounts.

Upon this settlement, we see the benefit of having
made an inventory, and thus having secured the
judgment of appraisers as to the accounts due to
the decedent.   For when a contestant would charge
an executor with claims inventoried as bad or
doubtful, he must show that the executor had become aware they were good or collectable.   But
where no inventory was made, the whole estate is
presumed to be good and collectable, and the executor or administrator, charging any of the claims
as bad, must prove them so, if objection is made.

In adjusting the accounts of executors and administrators, the Surrogate's Court is governed by principles of equity as well as of law, and it is at all times competent for them, unimpeded by technical rules, to show the fairness of their dealings, the real nature of their transactions, and the amount for which they should be held liable. (*Upson* v. *Badeau*, 3 Brad., 13.)

On the closing of the proof, or on the coming in of the report of the auditor or referee, the surrogate decrees the amount of the commissions upon the estate, which are computed upon the aggregate sum received by all the executors or administrators. (*Valentine* v. *Valentine*, 2 Barb. Ch., 430.)

Commissions, etc.

At common law, executors, administrators and trustees were not entitled to any compensation whatever for services rendered in the execution of their several trusts. Unless, therefore, the instrument creating them fixed their compensation, they were without remedy and their services were gratuitous. (*Manning* v. *Manning*, 1 Johns. Ch., 527.)

The legislature in 1817, authorized the Court of Chancery to fix the proper allowance to be made for commissions, and the court fixed the rate.

Afterward the rate so fixed by the court was incorporated in the Revised Statutes and remained

unchanged until 1849 when it was amended, and
again amended in 1863.   The section is in full as
follows :

§ 58. On the settlement of the account of an
executor or administrator, the surrogate shall allow
to him for his services, and if there be more than
one, shall apportion among them, according to the
services rendered by them respectively, over and
above his or their expenses :

For receiving and paying out all sums of money
not exceeding one thousand dollars, at the rate of
five dollars, *per cent.*

For receiving and paying out any sums exceeding one thousand dollars and not amounting to ten
thousand dollars, at the rate of two dollars and
fifty cents, *per cent.*

For all sums of above ten thousand dollars at
the rate of one dollar *per cent.*   And, in all cases,
such allowance shall be made for their actual and
necessary expenses as shall appear just and reasonable.   But if the personal estate of the testator
or intestate shall amount in value to not less than
one hundred thousand dollars, over and above all
debts and liabilities of the testator or intestate,
and there shall be more than one executor or administrator, then, instead of apportioning the compensation hereinbefore mentioned, among such
executors or administrators, each and every of

such executors or administrators shall be entitled to, and shall be allowed the full amount of compensation to which he would have been entitled, by the provisions of this act, if he had been sole executor or administrator ; provided, however, that the whole amount of the compensation of such executors or administrator shall not exceed, what would be, by the provisions hereof, paid to three executors or three administrators ; and that if there shall be more than three executors or administrators, then, what would be the compensation of three executors or administrators, shall be divided among them, all the executors or administrators, in equal shares, and there shall also be allowed on each settlement such sum for counsel fee thereon, and preparing therefor, as to said surrogate shall seem reasonable, not exceeding the sum of ten dollars for each day engaged therein.

Executors cannot claim extra compensation from the estate, for such services as they are not personally bound to render as executors, but for which they might properly employ and pay other persons. Accordingly it was held, that where one co-executor rendered professional services specially useful to the estate, and if rendered by another person, of great value, he could not recover any extra compensation for such services, notwithstanding they were rendered upon an express retainer and promise to pay therefor on the part of his co-executor. (*Collier* v. *Munn*, 41 N. Y., 198.)

These rates must be adhered to and the court cannot make any special allowances. (*Mc Whorter* v. *Benson*, Hopk., 28 ; *Vanderheyden* v. *Vanderheyden*, 2 Paige, 287.)

When there are several executors the commissions should be computed on the aggregate sum received and paid out by all, collectively, and not on the amount received and paid out by each individually. (*Valentine* v. *Valentine*, 2 Barb. Ch., 430.)

Commissions are not allowed on articles specifically bequeathed (*Burtis* v. *Dodge*, 1 Barb. Ch., 77) ; but when the executor or administrator transfers stocks, notes, or bonds and mortgages, or other property to a legatee, or one of the next of kin, in payment of a general legacy or distributive share, he may be allowed commissions on the amount of them as money. (*Cairns* v. *Chaubert*, 9 Paige, 160.)

Commissions are not chargeable on legacies, unless indirectly by way of abatement, when the general estate is insufficient to pay them. On a general accounting, the whole amount of receipts and disbursements forms the basis of charging commissions, which are deducted, and the legacies are then paid out of the surplus remaining after payment of the debts and expenses of administration. (*Westervelt* v. *Westervelt*, 1 Brad., 198.)

Where an executor holds funds, as such, upon a trust which is inseparable from the executorship, he can charge commissions only in one capacity; and where he invested a legacy, pursuant to the provisions of the will, and paid the interest annually to the legatee, it was held that he could retain but one *per cent* upon the interest. (*Drake* v. *Price*, 5 N. Y., 430.)

But in such a case, where he is required to invest a portion of the estate, he is entitled to full commission on the whole estate on the final settlement. (*Mann* v. *Lawrence*, 3 Brad., 424.)

But where the will provides that extra compensation shall be given to the executor the court will allow it (*Clinch* v. *Eckford*, 8 Paige, 412); and where the will provides that a reasonable compensation shall be given to the executor beyond the commission, without fixing the amount, the court will allow a fair amount according to the services rendered.

The right to the commissions is an absolute one, and does not rest in the discretion of the surrogate at all. He cannot withhold them, nor state a balance excluding them. (*Halsey* v. *Van Amringe*, 6 Paige, 12, and *Dakin* v. *Demming*, Id., 95.)

§ 59. (2 R. S., 93.) Where any provision shall be made by any will for specific compensation to an executor, the same shall be deemed a full satisfaction for his services, in lieu of the allowance aforesaid, or his share thereof, unless such executor shall, by a written instrument, to be filed with the surrogate, renounce all claim to such specific legacy.

But this statute cannot be held to apply when it is plain that the testator intended the specific compensation to be in addition to the commission. And undoubtedly, the executor before determining whether he will accept a legacy or commission, is entitled to wait until it is determined whether the estate can pay the legacy, for it may prove to be embarrassed, and the legacies may be used up in the payment of debts. It would seem, that he need not decide until the final settlement, when payment of either the legacy, or the commissions must be decreed. (See Dayton's Sur., 3d ed., p. 539.)

The same section, which provides for the commissions and the rate of the allowance, provides for such an " allowance for their actual and necessary expenses as shall appear just and reasonable." (See ante.) Where the items in the aggregate do not exceed five hundred dollars, and no one item exceeds twenty dollars in amount, the oath of the executor or administrator as to the payment makes his case, until it shall be impeached. This impeachment must, from necessity, be founded upon the examination of the executor or administrator on oath, as to the payments. The examination is in the nature of a cross-examination and may be made very close, as to each item. There has been a good deal of discussion on this point in the reported cases.

While it is the duty of the executor to attend to collections himself, and give his personal attention to the business of the estate, there may be circumstances in which he would be justified in the employment of an agent, if a provident person would so do in his own matter. In such a case the expense is a proper charge, whether the will gives a special authority for it or not. (*McWhorter* v. *Benson*, Hopk., 28; *Vanderheyden* v. *Vanderheyden*, 2 Paige, 287; *Cairns* v. *Chaubert*, 9 Id., 160.)

The traveling expenses of an executor or administrator necessarily incurred, in the business of the estate, are always a proper charge, unless he has been in some default. (*Hasler* v. *Hasler*, 1 Brad., 250.) But it is very doubtful if he could properly charge for the hire of his own horse and carriage. He certainly ought not 'to make any profit on it, or be under the temptation of endeavoring to make such a profit. (See Dayton's Sur., 540.)

Counsel fees may necessarily be incurred, and may be proper charges against the estate, but should not be allowed when incurred in defending the executor in an unreasonable course, against the legatees or next of kin (see Dayton's, *sup.*).

Where it was considered that the executors acted in good faith, in bringing suit in the name of a third person, and the defense of usury having been set up, and the substitutes defeated with costs, so that they paid costs of both plaintiff and defendant, it was held right to allow them for the payment of such costs, although they might have avoided being mulcted in costs if they had sued as executors. For where an executor in such a case, acts in good faith, under the advice of counsel, and apparently for the interest of the estate he represents, he ought not to be subjected to a personal loss, because the result of his exertions was not quite as beneficial to the estate, as a different course of proceeding might have been. (*Collins* v. *Hoxie*, 9 Paige, 87.) But where the executor employed a person not authorized to practice law, to foreclose a mortgage, and through his mismanagement a portion of the mortgage debt was lost, it was held that the executor must make good the loss. (*Wakeman* v. *Hazleton*, 3 Barb., 148.)

It may appear on final settlment, that some of the personal estate is, for good cause, not collected, but remains still invested. The statute makes provisions for the distribution of them *in specie*, as well as for the payment of debts not yet due.

§ 71. (2 R. S., 95.) Whenever an account shall be rendered and finally settled under any of the preceding sections in this article, except the sixty-eighth, and sixty-ninth (which relate to an accounting of one whose letters shall have been revoked), if it shall appear to the surrogate that any part of the estate remains to be paid or distributed, he shall make a decree for the payment and distribution of what shall so remain, to and among the creditors, legatees, widow and next of kin of the deceased, according to their respective rights; and in such decree shall settle and determine all questions concerning any debt, claim, legacy, bequest or distributive share; to whom the same shall be payable; and the sum to be paid to each person.

But we have seen, that notwithstanding this provision as to debts, the surrogate cannot adjudicate upon a claim disputed, and in a case in which his jurisdiction is denied. (See *ante.*)

§ 72. In such order the surrogate may, upon the consent in writing of the parties who shall have appeared, direct the delivery of any personal property, which shall not have been sold, and the assignment of any mortgages, bonds, notes or other

demands not yet due, among those entitled to payment or distribution, in lieu of so much money, as
such property or securities may be worth, to be ascertained by the appraisement and oath of such
persons as the surrogate shall appoint, for that purpose.

§ 73. Every person to whom any such securities
may be assigned, may sue and recover the same,
at his own costs and charges, in the name of the
executor or administrator making such assignment,
or otherwise, in the same manner as such executor
or administrator might have done.

This section is practically abrogated by the provisions of the code, requiring every action to be
brought in the name of the real party in interest.

§ 74. If, upon the representation of an executor
or administrator, or otherwise, it shall appear to
the surrogate, that any claim exists against the
estate of the deceased, which is not then due, or
upon which a suit is then pending, he shall allow
a sum sufficient to satisfy such claim, or the proportion to which it may be entitled, to be retained
for the purpose of being applied to the payment
of such claim when due, or when recovered, or of
being distributed according to law. The sum so
retained, may be left in the hands of the executor
or administrator, or may be directed by the sur-

rogate, to be deposited in some safe bank, to be drawn only on the order of the surrogate.

We will now consider the question of the interest to be allowed upon legacies, by the decree.

Generally, it may be said, that legacies draw interest only from the time when by law, or by the will they are payable (*Lupton* v. *Lupton*, 2 Johns. Ch., 614), and the time fixed by statute is as follows :

§ 43. (2 R. S., 90.) No legacies shall be paid by any executor or administrator, until after the expiration of one year from the time of granting letters testamentary, or of administration, unless the same are directed by the will to be sooner paid. (And see *Bradner* v. *Faulkner*, 12 N. Y., 472 : and *Burtis* v. *Dodge*, 1 Barb. Ch., 77.)

This statutory provision, is in affirmance of the common law rule and has not changed the time when interest begins to run, on general legacies. (*Cooke* v. *Meeker*, 36 N. Y.)

But there are exceptions as to this rule, beside the case where the will provides for the particular time of payment. Thus, a bequest of a life estate to a child, or to a widow, in lieu of dower, draws interest from the testator's death. (*Hepburn* v. *Hepburn*, 2 Brad., 74 ; *Seymour* v. *Butler*, 3 Id., 192 ; *Williamson* v. *Williamson*, 6 Paige, 298.) But when the provision for the widow is not expressed to be in lieu of dower, and the legacies are to children otherwise provided for by the testator, and were directed to be paid as soon as convenient, they were held to draw interest only after the lapse of a year. (*Matter of Williams,* 5 N. Y. Leg. Obs., 179, and *Williamson* v. *Williamson, sup.*)

Where no provision was made for minor children, other than the income from the legacies bequeathed to them, such legacies draw interest from the testator's death. (*King* v. *Talbot,* 40 N. Y., 76.)

The executor is not excused from paying interest on a legacy, after the lapse of a year, by the fact that the legatee was not in condition to receive it, or omitted to demand it. (*Marsh* v. *Hayne,* 1 Edw., 174.)

A specific legacy draws no interest. (*Isenhart* v. *Brown,* 2 Edw., 341.)

In making the final settlement, the advancement which may have been made by a parent deceased, is to be taken into account.

§ 76. (2 R. S., 97.) If any child of such deceased person shall have been advanced by the deceased, by settlement or portion of real or personal estate, the value thereof shall be reckoned with that part of the surplus of the personal estate which shall remain to be distributed among the children ; and if such advancement be equal or superior to the amount which, according to the preceding rules, would be distributed to such child, as his share of such surplus and advancement, then such child and his descendants shall be excluded from any share in the distribution of such surplus.

§ 77. But if such advancement be not equal to such amount, such child. or his descendants, shall be entitled to receive so much only, as shall be sufficient to make all the shares of all the children, in said surplus and advancement, to be equal, as near as can be estimated.

Under a Massachusetts statute, similar to ours, it has been held in two cases (*Quarles* v. *Quarles*, 4 Mass., 680, and *Kenny* v. *Tucker*, 8 Mass., 143), that a release to the father of claims on distributive share in expectancy, given in consideration of an advancement, operates as a release, and is a bar to claim on final settlement; even when the amount received for such release is less than the distributive share would be.

§ 78. The maintaining, or educating, or the giving of money to a child, without a view to a portion or settlement in life, shall not be deemed an advancement, within the meaning of the last two sections ; nor shall those sections apply in any case, where there shall be any real estate of the intestate, to descend to the heirs.

There are also, further statutory provisions in regard to the descent of real estate and the allowance of advancements.   (1 R. S., 754.)

§ 23. If any child of an intestate shall have been advanced by him, by settlement or portion of real or personal estate, or of both of them, the value thereof shall be reckoned, for the purposes of this section only, as a part of the real and personal estate of such intestate, descendible to his heirs, and to be distributed to his next of kin, according to law; and if such advancement be equal or superior to the amount of the share which such child would be entitled to receive of the real and personal estate of the deceased, as above reckoned, then such child and his descendants shall be excluded from any share, in the real and personal estate of the intestate.

§ 24. But if such advancement be not equal to such share, such child and his descendants shall be entitled to receive so much only of the personal estate, and to inherit so much only of the real estate of the intestate, as shall be sufficient to make all the shares of the children in such real and personal estate and advancement, to be equal, as near as can be estimated.

§ 25. The value of any real or personal estate so advanced, shall be deemed to be that, if any, which was acknowledged by the child, by an instrument in writing; otherwise such value shall be estimated according to the worth of the property, when given.

§ 26. The maintaining or educating, or the giving of money to a child, without a view to a portion or settlement in life, shall not be deemed an advancement.

The manner of estimating an advancement, and of determining the distributive share would seem to be as follows:

Ascertain the amount which has come to the hands of the administrator, and deduct therefrom the expenses of administration, the debts and funeral expenses paid and the commissions, which will give as a result the amount for distribution in the hands of the administrator : To this result, add the various advancements made to the children of the intestate, and the sum divided by the number of distributees, will show the share of each.   If the share so found of any one, is less than the sum advanced, then he will be excluded; if more, he will be entitled to distribution.

To illustrate : the estate of A, after deducting expenses of administration, funeral expenses and debts paid, is $9500, and is to be divided between four children, B, C, D and E.   C and E have received advancements from their father, C of $3200, and E of $1600 state the problem thus:

Estate for distribution, ...	$9,500.00
C's advancement, ...	3,200.00
E's "	1,600.00
Divide sum by four children, ... 4)	14,300.00
Share of each child is, ...	$3,575.00
Deduct advancement of C, ...	3,200.00
Distribution to C, ...	$ 375.00
" " E, ... $1,975.00	
" " B, & D, each, .. 3,575.00	

Distribution.

The statute of distribution in case of intestacy, is as follows:

§ 75. (2 R. S., 96.)   Where the deceased shall have died intestate, the surplus of his personal estate remaining after payment of debts; and where the deceased left a will, the surplus remaining after the payment of debts and legacies, if not bequeathed, shall be distributed to the widow, children or next of kin of the deceased in the manner following:

1. One-third part thereof to the widow, and all the residue by equal portions, among the children, and such persons as legally represent such children, if any of them shall have died before the deceased.

2. If there be no children, nor any legal representatives of them, then one moiety (that is, one-half) of the whole surplus, shall be allotted to the widow,

and the other moiety shall be distributed to the next of kin of the deceased, entitled under the provisions of this section.

3. If the deceased leave a widow, and no descendant, parent, brother or sister, nephew or niece, the widow shall be entitled to the whole surplus; but if there be a brother or sister, nephew or niece, and no descendant or parent, the widow shall be entitled to a moiety of the surplus, as above provided, and to the whole of the residue, where it does not exceed two thousand dollars; if the residue exceed that sum, she shall receive in addition to her moiety two thousand dollars, and the remainder shall be distributed to the brothers and sisters and their representatives.

4. If there be no widow, then the whole surplus shall be distributed equally to and among the children, and such as legally represent them.

5. In case there be no widow and no children, and no representatives of a child, then the whole surplus shall be distributed to the next of kin, in equal degree to the deceased, and the legal representatives.

6. If the deceased shall leave no children, and no representatives of them, and no father, and shall leave a widow and a mother, the moiety not distributed to the widow, shall be distributed in equal shares to his mother and brothers and sisters, or

the representatives of such brothers and sisters; and if there be no widow, the whole surplus shall be distributed in like manner to the mother and to the brothers and sisters, or the representatives of such brothers and sisters.

7. If the deceased leave a father, and no child or descendant, the father shall take a moiety, if there be a widow, and the whole if there be no widow.

8. If the deceased leave a mother, and no child, descendant, father, brother, sister, or representatives of a brother or sister, the mother, if there be a widow, shall take a moiety, and the whole if there be no widow. And if the deceased shall have been illegitimate, and have left a mother, and no child or descendant or widow, such mother shall take the whole, and shall be entitled to letters of administration, in exclusion of all other persons, in pursuance of the provisions of this chapter. And if the mother of such deceased be dead, the relatives of the deceased on the part of the mother shall take in the same manner as if the deceased had been legitimate, and be entitled to letters of administration in the same order.

9. Where the descendants or next of kin of the deceased, entitled to share in his estate, shall be all in equal degree to the deceased, their shares shall be equal.

10. When such descendants, or next of kin shall be of unequal degrees of kindred, the surplus shall be apportioned among those entitled thereto, according to their respective stocks; so that those who take in their own right, shall receive equal shares, and those who take by representation shall receive the shares to which the parent whom they represent, if living, would have been entitled.

11. No representation shall be admitted among collaterals after brothers' and sisters' children.

12. Relatives of the half blood, shall take equally with those of the whole blood in the same degree, and representatives of such relatives shall take in the same manner as the representatives of the whole blood.

13. Descendants and next of kin of the deceased begotten before his death, but born thereafter, shall take in the same manner as if they had been born in the lifetime of the deceased, and had survived.

§ 1. (S. L., 1855, ch. 547.) Illegitimate children, in default of lawful issue, may inherit real and personal estate from their mother, as if legitimate ; but nothing in this act shall affect any right or title, in, or to, any real or personal property already vested in the lawful heirs of any person heretofore deceased.

We will here consider the doctrine of representation referred to in the foregoing eleventh subdivision.

As the statute of distributions says that no representatives shall be admitted among collaterals, after brothers and sisters' children, it was held in *Pett* v. *Pett* (1 Salk. Rep., 250; 1 P. Wms., 25), that a brother's grandchildren, could not share with another brother's children, and therefore, if the intestate's brother A, be dead, leaving only grandchildren; and his brother B, be dead, leaving children, and his brother C, be living, the grandchildren of A will have no share, and cannot take. One half of the personal estate will go to the children of B, and the other half to C. But if all the brothers and sisters and their children be dead, leaving children, those children cannot take *by representation*, for it does not extend as far, but they are all *next of kin*, and in that character, would take *per capita*. Representation in the descending lineal line, proceeds on *ad infinitum*. It has also been decided, that if the intestate leave no wife, or child, brother or sister, but his next of kin are an uncle, by his mother's side, and a son of a deceased aunt, the uncle takes the whole, and the representation is not carried down to the representatives of the aunt. (2 Kent. Com., 424, 425.)

Distribution is made *per capita*, when the distributees take equally, in their own right, or *per stirpes*, when they take by way of representation. Thus, if the brothers and sisters of the deceased, are all dead, all leaving children, entitled to his estate, notwithstanding the families may be unequal in numbers, they will divide the estate equally among them, or *per capita*. But if one brother remain alive, and others have died, leaving children, such children take *per stirpes*, or what their parent would have been entitled to if living. (William on Exrs., 1299.)

So that next of kin take *per stirpes*, or by representation, only when they stand in unequal degrees of kindred to the deceased. Where they stand in equal degrees, as all brothers, all children, all grandchildren, they take each an equal share. (See also *Matter of Burr*, 2 Barb. Ch. R., 208.)

§ 79. (2 R. S., 98, as amended chap. 782, Laws of 1867.) The preceding provisions respecting the distribution of estates, shall apply to the personal estates of married women leaving descendants them surviving; and the husband of any such deceased married woman, shall be entitled to the same distributive share in the personal estate of his wife, to which a widow is entitled in the personal estate of her husband, by the provisions of this chapter, and no more.

The common law rule in regard to the estates of married women was, that the whole estate belonged to the husband, from the time of marriage,

22

and of course upon the death of the wife, the rule was applied; and the Revised Statutes provided that the provisions of the statutes of distribution should not apply to the estates of married women, but that their husbands surviving, might demand, recover and enjoy the same, as they were entitled by the rules of the common law. (2 R. S., 98, § 79.) The legislature on amending this statute as above, also repealed § 30, 2 R. S., 75, which provided that if letters of administration on the estate of a married woman, shall be granted to any other person, other than her husband, by reason of his neglect, refusal, or incompetency to take the same, such administrator shall account for, and pay over the assets remaining in his hands, after the payment of debts, to such husband, or his personal representatives.

Soon after the amendment of section seventy-nine the Supreme Court held (*Barnes* v. *Underwood*, 3 Lansing, 526), that the repeal of section thirty, above referred to, deprived the husband of all claims to the estate of his wife, except where she leaves descendants, in which case he will take one-third. But the Court of Appeals overruling this case, held that the common law rule obtains as to the estate of a married woman, unless she leaves descendants.

§ 80. (2 R. S., 98.) Where a distributive share

is to be paid to a minor, the surrogate may direct the same to be paid to the general guardian of such minor, and to be applied to his support and education ; or he may direct the same to be invested in permanent securities, as hereinbefore provided in respect to legacies to minors, with the like authority to apply the interest, and subject to the same obligations.

§ 81. When administration is granted to any person not the widow of, or next of kin to a deceased person, and no one shall appear to claim the personal estate of the deceased, within two years after such letters were granted, the surplus of such estate, which would be distributed as aforesaid, shall be paid into the treasury of this state, for the benefit of those who may thereafter appear to be entitled to the same.

Having thus considered the rules governing the first settlement, and the statutes in regard to the distribution of the estates of intestates and the payment of legacies, we now proceed to the decree.

§ 2. (S. L., 1837, chap. 360.) The surrogate shall file the accounts of administrators, executors and guardians rendered before him, and shall record with his decree, a summary statement of the same, as the same shall be finally settled and allowed by him, which shall be referred to and taken as a part of the final decree.

DECREE ON FINAL SETTLEMENT.

At a Surrogate's Court, held in and for the county of ...., at the surrogate's office, in the ...... of ...., on the day of ...., 1872.

Present — Hon. ...., Surrogate.

In the matter of the estate of ...., deceased.

Upon the application of ...., executor named in the will of ...., late of the ...., of ...., in said county, deceased, the surrogate on the ...... day of ...., last past, issued a citation to the creditors, legatees, and all persons interested in the estate of said deceased, requiring them to appear before him on the .... day of ...., then next, to attend the final settlement of the account of said executor; and on the said last mentioned day, the said executor appeared in person, and, by James Lansing, his counsel, and filed due proof of the publication of said citation in the state paper for three months, and in the ...., a newspaper, printed in said county for four weeks, and of personal service of the same, on ...., and ...., and of service by mail on ...., and ...., and it appearing that said ...., is an infant, the surrogate appointed ...., of the city of Troy, special guardian for said ...., to appear and take care of his interest in this matter, and the said ...., appeared as such special guardian.

The said ...., executor, as aforesaid, filed his account as such, duly verified, and the above named

................., appearing in person, and by ....,
his counsel, objected to said account, and sundry items
in the same, and further claimed that said account
should be surcharged by the sum of ....
dollars, received by said executor as interest, and the
issue being so joined, the surrogate proceeded to examine the same, and take testimony thereon, and the
matter was adjourned from time to time, to this day.

And now having heard the proofs and allegations of
the parties, and maturely considered the same, the surrogate proceeded to settle the said account according
to a summary statement hereto annexed, forming a
part of this decree, and to be recorded therewith.

It is therefore ordered, adjudged and decreed, that
the said ...., as executor, be charged as
stated in his account with the sum of fifteen hundred
dollars, and with the further sum of two hundred dollars interest, not stated in his account, in all the sum
of seventeen hundred dollars.

That he be credited with the sum of three hundred
and fifty dollars paid by him for debts of his testator,
and for expenses of administration ; with the sum of
sixty-seven dollars and fifty cents commissions, and
with ten dollars expenses of this proceeding.

It is further ordered, that he pay to ....,
counsel for him in this proceeding, the sum of twenty
dollars, and to ...., counsel for the said
..................., twenty dollars, and that he distribute
the balance remaining in his hands, to wit, the sum of
twelve hundred and thirty-two dollars and fifty cents,
as follows :

That he pay to ...., for his legacy, six
hundred dollars, and to ...., for his legacy,
six hundred dollars, and the remainder, two hundred

and thirty-two dollars to ...., residuary legatee named in said will.

And it is further ordered, that, it appearing that
.................., above named, is an infant, the said executor may pay the above legacy to said ....,
to ...., the general guardian of said..............,
on ·receiving proof, that the said ...., has
given bonds approved by the surrogate, for the faithful
application of the same.

        In testimony whereof, we have caused the seal
           of our said court to be hereunto affixed,
[SEAL.]   and the same to be subscribed by our
           surrogate.

        Witness, ..., surrogate, the day and
        year first above written.

                ...., *Surrogate.*

SUMMARY STATEMENT REFERRED TO, IN THE FOREGOING DECREE.

The executor .... is charged by his account with,...............................			$1500 00
His account shall be surcharged by the sum of interest received by him,..................			200 00
			$1700 00
He is credited with debts and expenses of administration paid,.....	350 00		
With commissions,.:......................	67 50		
With his expenses on this accounting, ...	10 00		
He shall pay .... his counsel,	20 00		
He shall pay.............,.. counsel for ....,	20 00	467 50	
Showing for distribution the sum of		$1232 50	

              ...., *Surrogate.*

These provisions as to accounting and final settlement, are applicable to testamentary trustees and testamentary guardians, as well as to executors and administrators.

§ 66. (2 R. S., 95, as amended chap. 272, Laws of 1850.) Any trustee created by any last will or testament, or appointed by any competent authority to execute any trust created by any such last will or testament, or any executor or administrator with the will annexed, authorized to execute any such trust, may from time to time render and finally settle his accounts before the surrogate of the county in which such last will and testament was proved, in the manner provided by law for the final settlement of the account of executors and administrators, and may for that purpose, obtain and serve, in the same manner, the necessary citations requiring all persons interested to attend such final settlement, and the decree of the surrogate on such final settlement, may be appealed from, in the manner provided for an appeal from the decree of a surrogate on the final settlement of the accounts of an executor or administrator, and the like proceedings shall be had on such appeal. The final decree of the surrogate on the final settlement of an account provided for in this section, as the final determination, decree or judgment of the appellate tribunal, in case of an appeal, shall have the same force and effect, as the decree or judgment of any other court of competent jurisdiction, on the final settlement of such accounts, and of the matters relating to such trust, which shall have been embraced in such accounts, or litigated or determined on such settlement thereof.

§ 1. (S. L., 1867, chap. 782.) The surrogate shall have power and jurisdiction, to compel testamentary trustees and guardians, to render account of their proceedings, in the same manner as executors, administrators and guardians appointed by such surrogate, are now required to account.

The above sixty-sixth section, was further amended by chap. 115, of Laws of 1866, that, on all such accountings of such trustees, the surrogate before whom such accounting may be had, shall allow to the trustee or trustees the same compensation for his or their services, by way of commissions, as are allowed by law to executors and administrators, and also such allowance for expenses as shall be just and reasonable, and if there be more than one trustee, and the estate be insufficient to give full commissions to each trustee, said surrogate shall apportion such compensation and allowance among said trustees according to the services rendered by them respectively.

So, also, an executor or administrator whose letters have been revoked, may be required to render an account.

§ 36. (S. L., 1837, chap. 460, amended by chap. 229, Laws of 1862.) The surrogate shall have the same jurisdiction in requiring any executor or administrator, whose letters have been revoked, as hereinbefore provided, to render an account of his proceedings, as is conferred by the third article, of title three, chapter six, of the second part of the Revised Statutes. The new executor or administrator shall, within a reasonable time, or in case of his neglect, the other person mentioned in such article, may make application for such account, and such application may be made at any time after the revocation of the letters aforesaid.

The proceedings referred to in the section, are the proceedings for compelling an account which we have just treated of, and the person who may apply for the account thereunder, is any person interested as creditor, legatee or next of kin.

CHAPTER XVII.

The Effect of the Decree of the Surrogate, and how it may be Enforced.

The decree of the surrogate is conclusive, as to the matters specified in the statute.

§ 65. (2 R. S., 84.) The final settlement of such account, and the allowance thereof by the surrogate, or upon appeal, shall be deemed conclusive evidence against all creditors, legatees, next of kin of the deceased, and all other persons in any way interested in the estate, upon whom the said citation shall have been served, either personally or by publication, as herein directed, of the following facts, and of no others.

1. " That the charges made in such account for moneys paid to creditors, to legatees, to the next of kin and for necessary expenses, are correct.

2. " That such executor or administrator has been charged all the interest for moneys received by him, and embraced in his account, for which he was legally accountable.

3. " That the moneys stated in such account as collected, were all that were collectable on the debts

stated in the account, at the time of the settlement thereof.

4. " That the allowances in such account for the decrease in the value of any assets, and the charges therein for the increase in such value, were correctly made."

The decree is conclusive *only*, as to the points stated in the statute, and *only* upon those persons properly served with the citation. The executor or administrator, may, notwithstanding the settlement, be charged with assets received by him and not stated in the account; with debts collected by him and not stated in the account, and with interest on such items. He may also be charged with assets, discovered for the first time, after the settlement, as to which his duties are unaltered by the previous final settlement. (*Bank of Poughkeepsie* v. *Hasbrouck*, 6 N. Y., 216.)

And a decree does not bar the claim of a creditor of the estate, which was not presented by the creditor, or by any one in his behalf. (Id.)

And a final accounting by co-executors, is no bar to an action by one against the other, for a debt due by the latter to the estate, and which did not enter into the accounting. (*Wurtz* v. *Jenkins*, 11 Barb., 546.)

The term final accounting does not mean the last accounting, but, a conclusive one, as to the matters embraced therein. There may be several final accountings. (*Glover* v. *Holley*, 2 Brad., 291.)

The decree may be vacated or opened, for cause shown. Where a decree was taken by default, in consequence of mistake or accident, by which one of the parties has been deprived of any hearing, the surrogate ought to open the default and the decree. This power is essential to the due administration of justice. (*Pero* v. *Hastings*, 1 Barb. Ch., 452; *Harrison* v. *McMahon*, 1 Brad., 283.)

He can and ought to set aside an order entered by him, which he had no power to make. (*Vreedenburgh* v. *Calf*, 9 Paige, 128.)

He has power to open a decree made by him on a final accounting of an administrator, and to require a further account in respect to an error in the account as allowed by the decree, after a lapse of four years from the entering of the decree, where there was nothing to show but that it was made promptly upon discovery of the error. (*Cipperly* v. *Baucus*, 24 N. Y., 46.)

He has power, of necessity, in the administration of justice, to undo what he has been induced to do through fraud, or on a mistaken supposition of jurisdiction; and may open decrees taken by default or correct mistakes, the result of oversight or accident. (*Bricks' Estate*, 15 Abb., 12.)

The practice in proceedings to open the decree or order, is to prepare a petition stating the proceeding sought to be opened, the error, and asking for a correction. A citation would thereupon issue to the parties interested, and the court on coming in of the parties, will make the order which seems to be just.

PETITION TO OPEN A DECREE.

To the Surrogate of the county of.................. :

The petition of A B, one of the legatees named in the will of C D, late of the town of..................., in said county, deceased, respectfully shows :

That your petitioner is one of the legatees named in the will of said deceased, and that letters testamentary on said will, were heretofore issued to E. F., an executor named therein :

That in due time, the said E F, had a final settlement of his accounts as such executor, and filed and rendered his account, and such proceedings were thereupon had, that on the ...... day of .... , last, a decree was entered in this court allowing said account and decreeing the distribution of the moneys appearing to be due thereby, to the legatees named in said will.

And your petitioner further shows : That the account so rendered by the said executor and the decree so entered in this court was erroneous in a sum amounting to ninety-nine dollars, which error arose, as your petition verily believes, from mistake as follows :

The said executor charged himself with the sum of one dollar, being the value of a certain claim not inventoried, which in fact was worth and should have been charged against the said executor, at one hundred dollars, the error arising from the improper location of the figures. That your petitioner has but just discovered said error, and he prays that the same may be corrected.

Dated ......, Dec. 9, 1874.

(Signed), A B.

County of ...., ss :

A B, being duly sworn, says that the foregoing petition by him subscribed, is true of his own knowledge, except as to the matters which are therein stated on information and belief, and as to those matters, he believes it to be true.

Sworn before me, this 9th }   A B.
    day of Dec., 1874.   }
              ...., *Surrogate.*

Whereupon an order is made for a citation to the proper parties, who in a proceeding to open a decree of final settlement, are the executors or administrators, and all other persons cited on the first accounting.

ORDER.

   At a Surrogate's Court, held in the county
     of ...., at the surrogate's office
     in the ...... of ...., on the ......
     day of ...., 1874.
     Present Hon. ...., Surrogate.

In the matter of the estate
of
C......... D ...., deceased.

It appearing by the petition of A B, that upon the final settlement of the account of E F, executor of the

will of the above named deceased and in the decree of
this court entered on the ...... day of ....,
last, that there was an error :

Ordered that a citation issue to said E F, one of the
creditors of said deceased, and the legatees named in
said will, requiring them to appear in this court on the
..... day of ...., next, at ten o'clock in the
forenoon, to show cause why said decree should not be
opened and said error corrected.

.................., *Surrogate.*

It would seem that the citation should be served
at least eight days before the return day.

The opening of the decree, or the vacating of an
order erroneously made, is the only method in
which some mistakes can be corrected or parties
heard.

Very many of the orders of this court are made
ex parte and without notice to the parties interested
as creditors, legatees or next of kin, and unless the
power to vacate the order is used, in some cases
great wrong might result.

To illustrate : an executor asks for the appointment of appraisers, and nominates C D who appears
to be unexceptionable to the surrogate, and he is
appointed.   It is a fact that C D is a near relative
of the executor, and the legatees think that his
affinity would induce him to make an improper
inventory in favor of the executor.   The surrogate,

on presentation of the facts, would revoke the appointment.

Enforcing the Decree.

A decree for the payment of money, made in the Surrogate's Court may be enforced in three ways:

1. By execution as on a judgment.

2d. By attachment, as for a contempt; and 3d. By suit on the bond given by the executor or administrator.

We will consider the first and third methods together.

§ 63. (Chap. 460, Laws of 1837.) After any decree is made by a surrogate, for the payment of money by an executor, administrator or guardian, on application, 'he shall make out a certificate, stating the names of the parties against and in favor of whom the decree is made, with the trade, profession or occupation of the parties respectively, and their places of residence, in which he shall state the amount of debt and costs, directed to be paid by such decree.

§ 64. On such certificate being filed with any clerk of the Supreme Court, the same shall be entered on the docket of the court, and shall thenceforth be a lien on all the lands, tenements and real estate of every person against whom such decree shall be entered, and execution shall be issued thereon, in the same manner as though the same was a judgment obtained in said court.

§ 65. If such execution be issued, and returned unsatisfied, the surrogate shall, on application, assign the bond given by such executor, administrator or guardian, to the person in whose favor such decree is made for the purpose of being prosecuted.

CERTIFICATE OF DECREE TO BE DOCKETED.

Otsego county, Surrogate's Court.

| In the matter of the estate |
| of |
| ...., deceased. |

I, E. G. Card, surrogate of the county of Otsego, do hereby certify that on the ...... day of... ...., 187..., a decree was made by me in this matter in favor of ...., residing in the town of ...., in said county, by occupation a " seamstress," a creditor of ...., late of the town of ...., in said county, deceased, against ...., residing in the town of................., in said county, by occupation a rail road employee, as administrator of the goods, chattels and credits of said................, deceased, directing the payment of the said..............., of the said................., administrator, as aforesaid, to the said ...., of the sum of .... dollars and .... cents for the debt, due to the said .... from the said ...., deceased,

23

and the sum of twenty-five dollars for her costs and disbursements, making in the whole the sum of .... dollars and .... cents.

Witness my hand and seal of office, at the village of [L. S.]   ...., this ...... day of ...., 1872.

(Signed), ..., *Surrogate.*

EXECUTION ON DECREE DOCKETED.

To the sheriff of the county of ....:....... Greeting;

Whereas, on the .... day of ...., 187...,
.... surrogate of the county of .... and the surrogate's court of said county, of............, duly made a decree for, and directing the payment by ...., residing in .... in said county, by occupation a rail road employee, the administrator of the goods, chattels and credits of .... , deceased, to ...., of the town of ...., in said county, by occupation a seamstress, of the sum of .... dollars and ...... cents for a debt due to the said ...., from the said deceased, and the sum of .... dollars and ...... cents, for her costs and expenses in the proceeding before said surrogate, making in the whole the sum of .... dollars and ...... cents; and after such decree was made by said surrogate, to wit on the ...... day of ...., 187..., he made out a certificate stating the names of the parties against and in favor of whom the decree was made and their respective occupations and places of residence in which he stated the amount of such debt and costs, directed to be paid by such decree; and whereas on said ...... day of ...., such certificate was filed with the clerk of the county of ...., and the same was, on said .... day of ...., 187..., entered and docketed in the

book required by law for the docketing of judgments;
and whereas, there is now actually due on said decree,
the sum of .... dollars and ....
cents, with interest thereon from the ...... day of 187....
You, are therefore commanded and required to make
said sum of .... dollars, and ....
cents, out of the goods, chattels and personal property
of the said ...., in your county, and if sufficient thereof cannot be found in your county, then out
of the real property in your county of which the said
.... was seized and belonging to him on the
said .... day of ...., 187..., the day on
which the said decree was docketed in your county, or
at any time thereafter in whose hands soever the same
may be, and that you return this execution with your
proceedings thereon to the clerk of the county of
Otsego, in sixty days after the receipt of the same.

Dated, ...

(Signed), ..., *Attorney.*

Endorsement on above.

....
against
....

Execution to Otsego county,
...., attorney.

Levy and collect .... dollars with interest
from the ...... day of ...., 187.., besides your
fees and poundage and return this execution in sixty
days after its receipt by you to the clerk of the county
of ....

(Signed), ..., *Attorney.*

PETITION FOR ASSIGNMENT OF BOND OF ADMINISTRATOR.

Surrogate's Court, county of .... :

In the matter of the estate
of
................., deceased.

 The petition of ...., of the town of ....,
in said county of ...., respectfully shows :
 That heretofore a decree was made in this court, on
the ...... day of ...., 187.., in favor of your
petitioner against ...., administrator of the
goods, chattels and credits of ...., late of
the town of ...., in said county, deceased,
requiring and directing the said .... to pay
to your petitioner the sum of .... dollars,
and .... cents, for the debt due from said
deceased to your petitioner, and the further sum of
.... dollars, and .... cents, for her
costs of the proceedings, and thereupon the surrogate
duly made a certificate of said decree, as required by
law, and the same certificate was duly filed in the
office of the clerk of the county of ...., and
was docketed in the book required by law to be kept
for the docketing of judgments, on the ...... day of
..................., 187.. ; and thereupon an execution was
duly issued upon such decree certified as aforesaid, to
the sheriff of the county of ...., which execution has been duly returned by said sheriff, wholly
unsatisfied.

Your petitioner begs leave to refer to such certificate and execution, certified copies whereof are hereto annexed.

Your petitioner, therefore, prays, that the bond given by the said ...., upon the granting to him of letters of administration of the goods, chattels and credits of said ...., deceased, may be assigned by said surrogate to your petitioner, to the end, that your petitioner's claims against the said ...., may be enforced and collected.

      And your petitioner will ever pray, etc.

Dated, ...

         (Signed), ...

Rensselaer county, ss :

    ...., being duly sworn, says, that she is the petitioner named in the foregoing petition, and that she has read the same, and knows the contents thereof, and that the same is true, of her own knowledge, except as to the matters which are therein stated on information and belief, and as to those matters, she believes it to be true.

         (Signed), ...

Sworn before me, this ...... }
   day of ...., 187... }

        ....

Thereupon the order for the assignment of the bond is made. The effect of the order, is to authorize an action by the creditor in whose favor it is made, but the bond itself should remain in the custody of the surrogate; for other creditors may seek the same remedy.

ORDER ASSIGNING BOND OF ADMINISTRATOR.

At a Surrogate's Court, held in and for the
county of ...., at the surrogate's
office in the .... of ...., on
the .... day of ...., 187....
Present—Hon. ...., Surrogate.

In the matter of the estate

of

................., deceased.

On reading and filing the petition of ....,
showing that heretofore a decree was made in her
favor, on the .... day of ...., 187..., in
this court directing ...., administrator of
the goods, chattels and credits of ...., deceased, to pay to the said ...., the sum of
.... dollars and .... cents, and
the further sum of .... dollars and ....
cents, costs of the proceedings; that a certificate of
said decree, was on the .... day of ....,
187..., duly docketed in the office of the county clerk,
of the county of ...., and that an execution
was duly issued thereon to the sheriff of the county of
................., which said execution has been returned
by said sheriff, wholly unsatisfied. Now, on motion
of ...., Esq., of counsel for the petitioner, it
is ordered, that the bond, given by the said ....,
as principal, with ...., and ...., as
sureties, upon the appointment of the said ....,
as administrator of the goods, chattels and credits of
................., deceased, dated and filed in the office
of the surrogate of this county, on the .... day of

..............., 186..., be, and the same is hereby assigned to the said ...., petitioner.

(Signed),

..............., *Surrogate*.

Attachment may Issue.

§ 66. (Chap. 460, Laws of 1837.)   Process of
attachment or other compulsory process authorized
by law, to enforce the order, process or decrees of
the Surrogate's Courts, may be issued by the
surrogate of one county, to the officers required
by law to serve such process in any other
county of the state, where it may be necessary to
serve the same; and the officer receiving the same,
shall have power and authority to arrest the person
or persons against whom said process may be issued,
and to convey the person or persons so arrested to
the county and place where this writ may be returnable.

§ 67. All attachments and other compulsory
process which may be issued by any surrogate,
shall be made returnable to the county where the
same may issue; and the tenth, twelfth and thirteenth sections, and section sixteenth to thirty-
second, title thirteenth of chapter eight, of the
third part of the Revised Statutes inclusive, shall
apply to attachments issued by surrogates.

These sections referred to, relate to proceedings to punish contempts, and we would refer the practitioner to the details regulated by these sections.

For the purpose of obtaining the attachment, a demand of payment must first be made upon the executor or administrator personally, accompanied by the service of a copy of the decree or order verified by the surrogate ; should payment not be then made, the surrogate, upon proof by verified petition, of the neglect or refusal to pay, will issue an attachment under his seal, directed to the sheriff of the county in which the delinquent resides, commanding him to attach the person of the delinquent and bring him before his court.   On the return, the surrogate, if no satisfactory reason be rendered for the non-payment, may commit the delinquent executor or administrator to the common jail to remain until discharged by the order of the same surrogate. (*Seaman* v. *Duryea,* 11 N. Y., 324 ; *Est. of John Woodhead,* 1 Tucker, 92.) But it was held at special term (*In the Matter of Abram E. Watson,* 3 Lans., 408), that the Surrogate's Court, not being a Court of Record, cannot punish as for a criminal contempt, except for interruptions to business during judicial proceedings. On appeal in the same case (5 Lans., 466), the Supreme Court decided that the Surrogate's Court could imprison (p. 471), for non-payment of a sum decreed to be paid, by means of a writ, in the nature of a *capias ad satisfaciendum*. (See also *People* v. *Cowles*, 4 Keyes, 46, and *Brush* v. *Lee*, 6 Abb. N. S., 56.)

The following may be used as forms in the proceeding.

PETITION FOR ATTACHMENT.

To Hon. ....,
 Surrogate of the county of..................

Your petitioner A B, of the town of .... in said county, respectfully shows:

That he is a legatee named in the will of C D, late of the town of ...., in said county, deceased.

That in certain proceedings in this court the account of E F, was finally settled, and on the ...... day of ...., last, a decree was made, whereby the said E F, was directed to pay to your petitioner the sum of $......... which, by the terms of said decree, became due and payable upon demand:

That after the entry of said decree, your petitioner procured a certified copy thereof, and by power of attorney under his hand, authorized A G to make demand of said E F, of said sum of $......... in behalf of your petitioner.

And he further shows, that as he is informed and believes, said demand was made, as appears by the affidavit hereunto annexed and said E F did not pay said sum, nor has he since paid said sum to your petitioner, or any one in his behalf.

Wherefore your petitioner prays, that a precept issue out of and under the seal of this court directed to the sheriff of the county of ...., commanding him to take the body of the said E F, if he shall be found in his bailiwick, and commit him to the common jail of said county of .... and· to keep and detain him therein under his custody, until he shall pay said sum of $........., as required by said decree, and such further sum as the court shall allow for costs and expenses and the fees of said sheriff, or for such other or further relief as the court shall see fit to grant.

Dated, Dec. 11th, 1874.

(Signed),   A B,

County of ...., ss :

A B, being duly sworn, says that the foregoing petition by him subscribed is true of his own knowledge except as to the matters which are therein stated on information and belief, and as to those matters he believes it to be true.

(Signed),   A B.

Sworn before me this ...... day ⎞
     of ...., 1874.   ⎠
           ...., *Notary Public.*

AFFIDAVIT OF SERVICE OF COPY OF DECREE AND DEMAND.

County of ...., ss :

A G, of etc., being duly sworn, says that on the ...... day of ......, 1874, he served a copy of the decree hereto annexed on E F, in said decree named, by delivering the same to, and leaving the same with the said E F, in said county at his residence in the town of ...., and that the copy he so served was duly certified as a copy, by certificate under the seal of the Surrogate's Court of said county of ....

And deponent further says that at the time of the service of said copy of said decree as aforesaid, he personally, on behalf of A B, in said decree named, demanded of the said E F, payment of the sum of $.................., by said decree to be paid to said A B ; but that said E F neglected and refused to pay the same or any part thereof.

And deponent further says, that such demand was made on behalf of the said A B, and that deponent was duly authorized to make such demand as appears by the power of attorney annexed hereto, and that at the time deponent made his demand as aforesaid, he stated to the said E F, the nature of his authority, and showed him the said power of attorney.

(Signed),   A G.

Sworn before me, this ...... day ⎰
    of ...., 1874.   ⎱

....

Annex Copy Decree and Power of Attorney.

ORDER FOR ATTACHMENT.

At a Surrogate's Court, held in the county of ...., at the surrogate's office in the ...... of ...., on the .... of ...., 1874.

Present—Hon. ...., Surrogate.

In the matter of the estate
of
C .... D........., deceased.

On reading and filing the petition of A B, dated this day and the affidavit therein referred to, showing due personal service on E F, the executor of the will of the above named deceased, of a copy of the decree of this court made in this matter on the ...... day of .... , 1874, and also showing a demand on the said E F, personally for the payment of the sum of $ .... as in said decree required, and of his neglect and refusal to pay the same or any part thereof, and the costs of this proceeding to compel such payment having been fixed by the court at $......... :

Now on motion of ...., of counsel for petitioner, it is ordered that a precept be issued out of and under the seal of this court, directed to the sheriff of the county of ...., commanding him to take the body of the said E F, if he shall be found in his bailiwick and commit him to the common jail of said county of ...., and to keep and detain him therein, under his custody, until he shall pay the sum of .... dollars as required by said decree, and the further sum of .... dollars for the costs and expenses of the proceeding to compel such payment, together with the sheriff's fees on such precept.

................., *Surrogate.*

ATTACHMENT.

The people of the state of New York to the
[SEAL.]   sheriff of the county of ....,
Greeting:

Whereas, on the ...... day of ...., 1874, by a certain decree made in our Surrogate's Court for the county of ...., in a certain proceeding in relation to the final settlement of the accounts of E F, an executor of the last will and testament of C D, deceased, it was ordered and adjudged that the said E F pay to A B, the sum of .... dollars, as a legacy bequeathed in said will:

And whereas, we have been informed in our said court, that, although the said sum of .... dollars has been personally demanded of the said E F, by or on behalf of the said A B, yet the said E F has hitherto neglected and refused, and still neglects and refuses to pay the same or any part thereof, and whereas the costs and expenses of the proceeding on the part of the said A B to compel payment thereof, amount to .... dollars.

Now therefore we command you to take the body of the said E F, if he shall be found in your bailiwick, and commit him to the common jail of the county of ...., and keep and detain him therein under your custody, until he shall pay the said sum of .... dollars, for the said moneys ordered to be paid by said decree; and also the sum of .... dollars for the costs and expenses of the proceeding to compel payment of the same, together with your fees on this writ.

And you are to make and return to said Surrogate's Court on the ...... day of ...., next, at the surrogate's office in the city of ...., a certificate under your hand of the manner in which you have executed this writ, and have you then and there this writ.

Witness, ..., surrogate at the city of . ..., on the ...... day of ...., 1874.

.................., *Surrogate.*

After the decree shall have been entered, and even after it had been docketed, it may be discharged.

§ 9. (S. L., 1867, chap. 782.) Any decree or order of a surrogate for the payment of moneys, may be discharged by filing with him a release of the amount executed by the person to whom such money is directed to be paid, and acknowledged, or proved, as is now required, as to a conveyance of real estate; and such surrogate, on filing such release, shall endorse such discharge on the margin of the record of such decree or order. When the decree has been docketed in the office of any county clerk, by the filing of the certificate of the surrogate, as to the decree, then on filing with the same clerk, a certificate of the surrogate, of the discharge, the clerk shall enter the discharge upon his docket.

RELEASE FOR DISCHARGE OF DECREE.

Surrogate's Court, county .... :

In the matter of the estate
of
.................., deceased.

Whereas, by a decree of the surrogate of the county of .. .., in this matter, entered on the ...... day of ...., 1873, ..., executor of the will of the above named deceased, was ordered and directed to pay to the undersigned, a legatee named in said will, the sum of .... dollars, now I do hereby acknowledge the receipt of the said sum from said ...., and release him from all claims therefor, and request the surrogate of said county, to enter this as a discharge of said decree.

Witness my hand, this ...... day of ...., 1873
(Signed), ...

Rensselaer county, ss:

On this ...... day of ...., 1873, before me personally came ...., to me known to be the same person described in, and who executed the foregoing instrument and acknowledged that he executed the same for the uses and purposes therein mentioned.
(Signed), ...
Justice of the Peace.

CHAPTER XVIII.

OF THE MORTGAGE, LEASE, OR SALE OF REAL ESTATE, ON APPLICATION OF EXECUTOR OR ADMINISTRATOR.

The real estate of a testator or intestate, remains subject to his debts, and may be applied to the payment of them, by raising money on it by way of mortgage or lease, or by a sale thereof, and the executor or administrator on discovering that the personal estate is insufficient to pay debts, becomes a trustee for the creditors as to the real estate.

§ 1. (2 R S., 100, amended chap. 320, Laws of 1830.) After the executors or administrators of a deceased person shall have made and filed an inventory according to law, if they shall discover the personal estate of their testator or intestate to be insufficient to pay his debts, they may at any time, within three years after the granting of their letters testamentary or of administration, apply to the surrogate for authority to mortgage, lease, or sell as much of the real estate of their testator or intestate as shall be necessary to pay such debts.

The fact that the debts are not yet due is no obstacle to the application, if the personal estate shall be found to be insufficient. (*Moers* v. *White*, 6 Johns. Ch., 360.) Nor is it a bar that the creditor has neglected to report the claims to the executor. (*Wood* v. *Byington*, 2 Barb. Ch., 387.)

But the debts to pay which the application is made, must be debts of the decedent, not costs awarded against the executor since the testator's decease (*Sanford* v. *Granger*, 12 Barb., 392), nor a claim of a mother for the support of her infant children (*Woodruff* v. *Cook*, 2 Edwd., 259), nor expenses of administration (*Cornwallis's Estate*, 1 Tuck., 250), and the claims must not be barred by the statute of limitations. (*Gilchrist* v. *Rea*, 9 Paige, 66.)

The representation of the executor or administrator that there is a deficiency of assets, with the account of debts and assets, confers jurisdiction on the surrogate. In deciding whether the assets are insufficient, he acts judicially, and his error, if any, cannot affect his jurisdiction. (*Atkins* v. *Kinnan*, 20 Wend., 241 and cases cited.) And an account which in stating the personal property, does so in general terms, referring to the inventory for details is sufficient. (*Sheldon* v. *Wright*, 7 Barb., 39.) But an account and an account of debts is not required under the Revised Statutes. (*Fisher* v. *Halsay*, 26 N. Y., 53.)

§ 20. (Laws of 1837, chap. 460, amended 1874, chap. 267.) Executors or administrators may apply to the surrogate, pursuant to the fourth title of chapter six of the second part of the Revised Statutes (*above quoted*), for authority to mortgage, lease, or sell the real estate of such testator or intestate, and for the sale of the interest of such testator or intestate, in any land held under a contract for the purchase thereof, whenever they shall discover that the personal estate of the testator or intestate is insufficient to pay his debts and funeral expenses, subject to the provisions of the first section of said title, as the same has been amended.

§ 2. (2 R.S., 100.) The petition shall set forth :

1. The amount of personal property which has come to the hands of the executor or administrator.

2. The application thereof.

3. The debts outstanding against the testator or intestate, as far as the same can be ascertained.

4. A description of all the real estate of which the testator or intestate died siezed, with the value of the respective portions or lots, and whether occupied, or not, and if occupied, the names of the occupants; and

5. The names and ages of the devisees, if any, and of the heirs of the deceased.

And such petition shall be verified by the oath of the party presenting the same.

The following is a form of a petition :

PETITION FOR MORTGAGE, LEASE OR SALE OF REAL ESTATE.

Surrogate's Court, Rensselaer county :

> In the matter of the estate
> of
> A......... B........., deceased.

To Moses Warren, Esq., Surrogate of the county of Rensselaer :

The petition of C D, executor (or administrator) of the will of (or of the goods, etc., of) A B, late of the town of Brunswick, in the county of Rensselaer, deceased, shows, that your petitioner has made and filed an inventory of the personal property of the said A B, deceased, according to law and has discovered the same to be insufficient to pay the debts of the deceased.

That the amount of the personal property which has come to the hands of your petitioner amounts to the sum of $578.00.

That the outstanding debts of the deceased, which remain unpaid and which are justly due and owing, and which are not secured by judgment or mortgage, or expressly charged on the real estate of the deceased, as near as the same can be ascertained, amount to the sum of $1,050.00.

And your petitioner verily believes and states the fact to be, that he has proceeded with reasonable diligence in converting the personal property of said deceased into money, and applying the same to the payment of debts,

That the deceased died seized of the following real estate, situated in the county of Rensselaer aforesaid, valued at the sum respectively affixed to each lot or parcel, and occupied or not occupied as stated in respect to each of the several lots or parcels, that is to say, all (*stating fully metes and bounds*).

And your petition further shows, that S B, is the widow, and A B, C B, and E B, of the town of Brunswick, are children and heirs at law of the said A B, deceased, of the age of twenty-one years and upwards, and J B, and K B, are minors of the age of fourteen years and upwards, and L B and M B, are minors, and are also children and heirs at law of the deceased, and under fourteen years of age.

Your petitioner therefore prays that authority may be granted to him by the said surrogate (pursuant to the statutes of the state of New York in such case made and provided), to mortgage, lease or sell, so much of the real estate of the deceased as shall be necessary to pay the debts of the deceased.

And your petitioner will ever pray, etc.

(Signed),   C D.

State of New York,   }
   Rensselaer county, } ss:

C D, being duly sworn, deposes and says that the above petition, by him subscribed, is true, to the best of the knowledge, information or belief of the deponent.

Subscribed and sworn this .... }
   day of ...., 1862, before me. }

M. WARREN, *Surrogate.*

All the executors or administrators should join in the application. An order for sale will be erroneous in allowing the petitioning executors to make a sale without the consent of all, especially when no reason is stated in the petition for not making the one, or those not joining in the petition a party or parties to the proceeding. (*Fitch* v. *Whitbeck*, 2 Barb. Ch., 161.)

By the presentation of the petition in due form and time, the surrogate obtains jurisdiction as against all parties regularly brought into court (*Schneider* v. *McFarland*, 4 Barb., 139), and the subsequent exercise of the jurisdiction cannot, generally, be questioned collaterally for error or irregularity, but only on appeal. (*Farrington* v. *King*, 1 Brad., 182.)

The earlier authorities, (*Small* v. *Brownell*, Hill and Den. Sup., 154), held, that an account was absolutely necessary to confer jurisdiction, but it is now settled (*Forbes* v. *Halsey*, 26 N. Y., 62), that the Revised Statutes do not require, as the revised laws did, that the petition should be accompanied with an account of the personal estate of the intestate, or an account of his debts ; nor does either require an account of the names of the creditors, or of the consideration of the debts against him. Neither do the Revised Statutes require, that the petition should contain an account of the personal estate of the intestate, or of the debts against him, or of the names of his creditors, or the consideration of the debts due by him.

A petition which states " that the amount of the personal property which actually came to the executor's hands, as appraised by the inventory is," etc., sufficiently states the amount of personal property which actually came into his hands. And a statement of the amount received and that it is still in his hands unpaid and unapplied, sufficiently shows " the application " of the money received. (*Richmond* v. *Foote*, 3 Lans., 244.)

And a sworn statement in the petition for sale, that the decedent left no personal estate, was held to answer the purpose of an inventory. (*Butler* v. *Emmett*, 8 Paige, 12.)

§ 5. (2 R. S., 101.) If, upon such application to the surrogate, it shall appear, that all the personal estate of the deceased, applicable to the payment of his debts, has been applied to that purpose, and that there remained debts unpaid, for the satisfaction of which a sale may be made under the provisions of this title, he shall make an order, directing all persons interested in the estate to appear before him, at a time and place therein to be specified, not less than six weeks, and not more than ten weeks, from the time of making such order, to show cause why authority should not be given to the executors or administrators applying therefor, to mortgage, lease or sell so much of the real estate of their testator or intestate, as shall be necessary to pay such debts.

§ 41. (S. L., 1837, chap. 460.) The surrogate, may, in his discretion, order such mortgage, lease or sale to be made, although the whole of the personal property of the deceased which has come to the hands of the executor or administrator has not been applied to the payment of debts. But the surrogate before making any such order, shall have satisfactory evidence that the executor or administrator has proceeded with reasonable diligence in converting the personal property of the deceased into money and applying the same to the payment of debts.

ORDER TO SHOW CAUSE WHY REAL ESTATE
SHOULD NOT BE SOLD.

At a Surrogate's Court, held in the county of ...., on the ...... day of ...., 187..., at the surrogate's office in the ...... of ....

Present, Hon. ...., Surrogate.

In the matter of the real estate
of
A .... B........ , deceased.

On reading and filing the petition of C D, the executor of the last will and testament of A B, late of the

town of ...., deceased, praying that authority
may be given him by said surrogate, to mortgage,
lease or sell so much of the real estate of the said deceased, as shall be necessary to pay his debts; ordered,
that all persons interested in the said estate appear before the surrogate of the county of ...., at
his office in the ...... of ...., on the ...... day
of .... next, at ten o'clock in the forenoon,
to show cause why authority should not be given to
said executor to mortgage, lease or sell so much of the
real estate of the said deceased, as shall be necessary to
pay his debts; and it is further ordered that all persons
having claims against the said deceased, may exhibit
and prove the same before said surrogate, at the time
and place aforesaid.

.... , *Surrogate.*

§ 6. Every such order to show cause shall be
published for four weeks in a newspaper printed in
the county, and a copy thereof shall be served personally, on every person in the occupation of the
premises of which a sale is desired, wherever the
same may be situated, and on the widow and heirs
and devisees of the deceased, residing in the county
of the surrogate, at least fourteen days before the
day therein appointed for showing cause.

§ 7. If such personal service cannot be made, or
if such widow, heirs or devisees, do not reside in
such county, but reside in the state, then a copy
of such order may be served personally, forty days

before the day of showing cause, or by publishing the same once in each week for four weeks in succession, in the state paper. If such heirs or devisees do not reside within this state, or cannot be found therein, the order shall be published, once in each week, for six weeks successively, in the state paper, or a copy thereof may be personally served on them, at least forty days before the time appointed therein for showing cause.

§ 6. (S. L., 1863, chap. 362.) In proceedings to mortgage, lease or sell the real estate of deceased persons, under title four, chapter six, part two of the Revised Statutes, minors shall be served with the order to show cause, and special guardians appointed for them, in the same manner as citations are required to be served, and special guardians appointed, on the proof of wills, instead of in the manner special guardians are now required to be appointed for minors and service of the order to show cause to be made on them or said minors * * * *. That is, the service shall be made upon the minors personally, and if the minors be under fourteen years of age, then a copy shall also be delivered to the parent, or guardian of the minors, or to the person in whose care the minor shall be. (See *ante.*)

To give jurisdiction to further proceedings, it must appear that the order to show cause was properly served and properly published, and if it does not affirmatively appear that it was so served and published jurisdiction is not made out. (*Corwin* v. *Merritt*, 3 Barb., 341; *Bloom* v. *Burdick*, 1 Hill, 130; *Schneider* v. *McFarland*, 2 N. Y., 459.)

If there is an infant heir or devisee, a guardian must be appointed for such infant by the surrogate, even though it does not appear by the petition that such infant is an heir or devisee. No one can be divested of his rights by being ignored. He has a right to a day in court before that power can rightfully be exerted. (*Ackley* v. *Dygert*, 23 Barb., 177.)

When the general guardian of infants, being also administrator or executor, applies in the latter capacity for an order to mortgage, lease or sell, the appointment of a special guardian for the infants, is essential to give the surrogate jurisdiction. (*Havens* v. *Sherman*, 42 Barb., 636.)

On filing proof by affidavit of the due service and publication of the order to show cause, the surrogate will, under the last preceding section quoted, appoint a special guardian for the minors interested, who shall appear before any further step shall be taken. (For forms consent and appointment see *ante*, in relation to proof of wills.)

§ 8. (2 R. S., 101.) The surrogate, at the time and place appointed in the order, and at such other times and places, as the hearing shall be adjourned to, upon due proof of the service and publication above required, shall proceed to hear and examine the allegations and proofs of the executors or administrators applying for such authority, and of all persons interested in the estate, who shall think proper to oppose the application.

§ 9. The executors or administrators may be examined on oath, and witnesses may be produced and examined by either party; and process to compel their attendance and testimony, may be issued by the surrogate, in the same manner, and with like effect, as in cases of proving wills before him.

§ 10. On such hearing, it shall be competent to any heir or devisee of the real estate in question, and to any person claiming under them, to show that the whole of the personal estate of the deceased, has not been duly applied by the executors or administrators, to the payment of his debts; to contest the validity and legality of any debts, demands or claims, which may be represented as existing against the testator or intestate; and to set up the statute of limitations in bar to such claims; and the admission of any such claims so barred, by any executor or administrator, shall not be deemed to revive the same, so as in any way to affect the real estate of the deceased.

There seems to be no class of claims, legal or equitable, which may not be presented, proved and adjusted before the surrogate on the hearing. (*Renwick* v. *Renwick*, 1 Brad., 234.)

It may, and often does occur, that the executor or administrator, in ignorance of the extent of claims against the estate, has paid to some creditors in full, or more than their *pro rata* share from the personal estate. In such case, he is to be regarded as the equitable assignee of the claims which he has so paid, and to have them satisfied out of the proceeds of the real estate, in the same manner as the creditors would have been paid. (*Ball* v. *Miller*, 17 How., 300.)

§ 11. (2 R. S., 102.) If upon such hearing any question of fact shall arise, which, in the opinion of the surrogate, cannot be satisfactorily determined without a trial of jury, he shall have authority to award a feigned issue, to be made up in such form as to present the question in dispute, and to order the same to be tried at the next Circuit Court to be held in such county. New trials may be granted therein by the Supreme Court, as in personal actions pending in that court.

The final determination of such issue shall be conclusive as to the facts therein controverted, in the proceedings before the surrogate.

§ 12. The costs of such issue shall be paid by the party failing, on the order of the surrogate, and such payment may be enforced in the same manner as other orders and decrees.

§ 13. The demands which the surrogate shall, upon such hearing, adjudge valid and subsisting against the estate of the deceased, or which shall have been determined to be valid, on the trial of such issue, or which shall have been recovered against the executors or administrators, by the judgment of a court of law upon a trial of the merits, shall be by him entered in the book of his proceedings, fully and at large, and the vouchers supporting the same shall be filed in his office.

ENTRY OF DEMANDS ADJUDGED VALID.

At a Surrogate's Court, held in the county of ...., at the surrogate's office in the .... of ...., on the......, day of ...., 1874.
Present Hon. ...., Surrogate.

In the matter of the real estate
of
A.........B,......... deceased.

On hearing, at the time and place appointed, in the order to show cause, entered in this matter on the ...... day of ...., last, and at the times and places to which such hearing was adjourned, the said surrogate adjudged the demands of the following persons to be valid and subsisting against the said A B, deceased, in the amounts as stated as to each demand, that is to say:

A B, ... $519.00
C D, ... 642.00
E F, ... 350.00

(Signed), ..., *Surrogate.*

§ 14. (2 R. S., 102.) The surrogate shall make no order for the mortgaging, leasing or sale of the real property of the deceased, until, upon due examination, he shall be satisfied:

1. That the executors or administrators have fully complied with the preceding provisions of this title;

2. That the debts, for the purpose of satisfying which the application is made, are justly due and owing, and that they are not secured by judgment or mortgage upon, or expressly charged on the real estate of the deceased; or, if such debts be secured by a mortgage or charge on a portion of such estate, then, that the remedies of the creditor by virtue of such mortgage or charge have been exhausted;

3. That the personal estate of the deceased is insufficient for the payment of such debts, and that the whole of such estate, which could have been applied to the payment of the debts of the deceased, has been duly applied for that purpose.

Notwithstanding this third sub-division of this section, by comparison of section 41, of chap. 460 of Laws of 1837, above quoted in full, it will be seen that the order to mortgage, lease or sell may be made, although the whole of the personal property of the deceased which has come to the hands of the executor or administrator, has not been applied to the payment of debts. But the surrogate, before making any such order, shall have a satisfactory evidence that the executor or administrator, has proceeded with reasonable diligence, in converting the personal property of the deceased into money, and applying the same to the payment of debts.

§ 15. (2 R. S., 102.) The surrogate, when so satisfied, shall, in the first place inquire and ascertain whether sufficient moneys for the payment of such debts can be raised by mortgaging or leasing the real property of the deceased, or any part thereof; and if it shall appear that such moneys can be so raised, advantageously to the interest of such estate, he shall direct such mortgage or lease to be made for that purpose.

§ 16. No such lease shall be for a longer time, than until the youngest person interested in the real estate leased, shall become twenty-one years of age.

§ 17. A lease or mortgage, executed under the authority of the surrogate as aforesaid, shall be as valid and effectual, and of the same effect, as if executed by the testator or intestate, immediately previous to his death.

The surrogate's order giving leave to dispose of the real estate of a decedent for the payment of his debts, is conclusive upon the parties as to the question of the sufficiency of assets; and where the administratrix, by virtue of such order mortgaged the estate and subsequently became the purchaser of the mortgage, *Held*, that the heir, or devisee, or those claiming under them could not resist foreclosure, by proving that she concealed assets belonging to the estate, and purchased the mortgage with them. (*Graham* v. *Lindsey*, 50 N. Y., 547.)

§ 18. (2 R. S., 103.) If it shall appear to the surrogate that the moneys required can not be raised by mortgage or lease, advantageously to the estate, he shall, from time to time, order a sale of so much of the real estate, whereof the testator or intestate died seized, as shall be sufficient to pay the debts which the surrogate shall have entered in his books, as valid and subsisting.

§ 19. If such real estate consist of houses or lots, or of a farm, so situated that a part thereof can not be sold without manifest prejudice to the heirs or devisees, then the whole or a part thereof, although more than may be necessary to pay such debts, may be ordered to be sold, and if a sale of the whole real estate shall appear necessary to pay such debts, it may be ordered, accordingly.

§ 20. The order shall specify the lands to be sold, and the surrogate may therein direct the order in which several tracts, lots or pieces, shall be sold. If it appears, that any part of such real estate has been devised, and not charged in such devise with the payment of debts, the surrogate shall order that the part descended to heirs be sold before that so devised; and if it appear that any lands devised or descended, have been sold by the heirs or devisees, then the lands remaining in their hands unsold, shall be ordered to be first sold; and in no case shall land devised expressly charged with the payment of debts, be sold under any order of a surrogate.

§ 21. Before granting any order for the mortgaging or leasing any real estate, the surrogate shall require from the executor or administrator applying for the same, a bond to the people of this state, with sufficient sureties, to be approved by the surrogate, in a penalty double the amount to be raised by such mortgage or lease, conditioned for the faithful application of the moneys arising from such mortgage or lease, to the payment of the debts established before the surrogate, on granting the order, and for the accounting for such moneys,

25

whenever required by such surrogate, or by any court of competent authority.

BOND ON ORDER TO MORTGAGE.

Know all men by these presents : That we, John Doe, executor of the will of ...., late of the city of ...., deceased, A B, and C D, of the city of ...., in the county of Rensselaer, are held and firmly bound unto the people of the state of New York, in the sum of (*double the sum to be raised*) lawful money of the United States, to be paid to the said people; to the which payment, well and truly to be made, we bind ourselves, our and each of our heirs, executors and administrators, jointly and severally, firmly by these presents.

Sealed with our seal and dated this ⎫
    15th day of December, 1874.   ⎭

Whereas an application for authority to mortgage, lease or sell the real estate of the said ...., deceased to pay his debts, is now pending before the surrogate of the county of .... , on the petition of the above bounden John Doe, as executor of the will of said deceased, now therefore the condition of this obligation is such, that if the said John Doe, in case the said surrogate shall grant an order to mortgage said real estate, or any part thereof, shall faithfully apply the moneys arising on such mortgage, to the payment of the debts established before said surrogate, on granting such order, and shall account for such moneys whenever required by such surrogate, or by

any court of competent authority then this obligation
to be void, otherwise to remain in full force and virtue.

(Signed),   JOHN DOE.   [SEAL.]
                   A B.   [SEAL.]
                   C D.   [SEAL.]

Add acknowledgment and justification of sureties.

APPROVAL OF SURROGATE (*to be endorsed.*)

I approve of the within bond as to form, manner of
execution and the sufficiency of the sureties therein.
Dated Dec. 15, 1874.

................., *Surrogate.*

ORDER FOR MORTGAGE.

At a Surrogate's Court, held in the county
of .... at the surrogate's office in
.... of .... on the ...... day
of ...., 1874.
Present — Hon. ...., Surrogate.

In the matter of the real estate

of

..............., deceased.

C D, the executor of the last will and testament
of ...., late of the town of ...., deceased, having lately presented his petition to the surrogate of the county of ...., for authority to
mortgage, lease or sell so much of the real estate of the
said deceased, as shall be necessary to pay the debts
of the deceased, and such proceedings having been
thereupon had that the surrogate is satisfied that the
said executor has fully complied with the several pro-

visions of the statutes, that the debts outstanding
against the deceased, as far as the same can be ascertained, and which are valid and subsisting, and are not
secured by judgment, mortgage, or other lien, on the
real estate of the said deceased, amount to the sum
of .... dollars, that the personal estate of
the said deceased is insufficient to pay his debts, and
that the whole of said personal estate, which could
.have been applied to the payment of the debts of the
deceased has been applied to that purpose : and
whereas it has been made to appear that sufficient
moneys for the payment of such debts can be raised
advantageously to the interests of the estate, and the
said executor having, with two sureties executed a
bond, in the manner required by law which is duly
approved, acknowledged and filed : It is ordered and
adjudged that the said executor execute in due form
for record, a mortgage upon the following described
premises (describe premises), and it is further ordered
that said mortgage be made for the sum of ....
dollars, and be made payable in ...... year from the
date thereof, with semi-annual interest, and be secured
by an assignment of the policy or policies of insurance
against fire, procured upon the buildings on said premises.

..................., *Surrogate.*

The money received on the mortgage, is received
by the executor or administrator, and by him applied to the debts, proved before the surrogate, and
the mortgagee is not bound to see to it, that the
executor properly applies the money received on
the mortgage. (*Jackson* v. *Irwin*, 10 Wend., 441.)

§ 22. (2 R. S., 104.) Before granting any order for the sale of any real estate, the surrogate shall require a bond in like manner, and with sureties as above directed, in a penalty double the value of the real estate ordered to be sold, conditioned that such executors or administrators will pay all the moneys arising from such sale, after deducting the expenses thereof, and will deliver all securities taken by them on such sale, to the surrogate, within twenty days after the same shall have been received and taken by them.

Where the value of the real estate is great, and the proceeds expected large, security to a limited amount beyond the fund is sufficient. (*Holmes* v. *Cock*, 2 Barb. Ch., 426.)

BOND ON SALE OF REAL ESTATE.

Know all men by these presents : That we, John Doe, executor of the will of ...., deceased, A B and C D, of the city of Troy, in the county of Rensselaer, are held and firmly bound unto the people of the state of New York, in the sum of (double the value of the real estate to be sold), lawful money of the United States, to be paid to the said people ; to the which payment, well and truly to be made, we bind ourselves, our and each of our heirs, executors and administrators, jointly and severally, firmly by these presents.

Sealed with our seals, and dated this } tenth day of September, A.D. 1872. }

Whereas an application for authority to sell the real estate of ...., deceased, to pay his debts, is now pending before the surrogate of the county of Rensselaer, on the petition of the above bounden John Doe, as executor of the will of said deceased, now, Therefore, the condition of this obligation is such, that if the said John Doe, in case the said surrogate shall grant an order of sale of said real estate, or any part thereof, shall pay all the money arising from such sale, after deducting the expenses thereof, and shall deliver all securities taken by him on such sale to the said surrogate, within twenty days after the same shall have been received and taken by him, then this obligation to be void, otherwise to remain in full force and virtue.

(Signed),   JOHN DOE. [L.S.]

A B.   [L.S.]

C D.   [L.S.]

And acknowledgment and justification of sureties.

ORDER FOR SALE OF REAL ESTATE.

At a Surrogate's Court held for the county of .... at the surrogate's office in the .... of ...., on the ...... of ...., 1874.

Present — Hon............., Surrogate.

In the matter of the real estate

of

............., deceased.

C D, the executor of the last will and testament of ...., of ...., deceased, having lately presented his petition to the surrogate of the county

of .... for authority to mortgage, lease or
sell so much of the real estate of the said deceased as
shall be necessary to pay the debts of the deceased,
and such proceedings having been therefore had,
that the surrogate is satisfied that the said executor
has fully complied with the several provisions of the
statutes, that the debts outstanding against the deceased as far as the same can be ascertained, and which
are valid and subsisting, and are not secured by judgment, mortgage or other lien on the real estate of the
said deceased, amount to the sum of .... dollars;
that the personal estate of the said deceased, is insufficient to pay his debts, and that the whole of said personal estate which could have been applied has been applied to that purpose; and whereas it has been made
to appear to said surrogate, that the moneys required
to be raised, cannot be raised by mortgage or lease
advantageously to the said estate, and the said executor
having, with two sureties executed a bond in the manner required by law which is duly acknowledged, approved and filed: It is ordered and adjudged that the
said executor sell at public vendue, the following described real estate of the said deceased, to wit; (*Describe
the several parcels.*)

It is further ordered that the several parcels be sold
in the order in which they are above described, and
that on such sale, the executor be authorized to give
such length of credit, not exceeding three years, for
not more than three-fourths of the purchase money
as shall seem best calculated to procure the highest
price, and shall secure the moneys for which credit
shall be so given by a bond of the purchaser, and a
mortgage upon the premises sold. And it is further
ordered that before any deed or deeds of the premises
sold shall be executed, the said executor make return

of the proceedings had on this order, to the said surrogate, to the end that the said surrogate may examine
said proceedings and the fairness and the legality of
the said sale.

.................., *Surrogate*.

§ 23. (2 R. S., 104.) In case of the refusal or
neglect of the executors or administrators applying
for such order, to execute, within a reasonable time,
any bond required by the last two sections, the
surrogate shall appoint a disinterested freeholder to
execute such mortgage or lease, or to make such
sales, who shall execute a bond similar in all
respects to that required of the executors or administrators, in whose place he shall be appointed;
and, in making such appointment, he shall give
preference to any person who shall have been
nominated by the creditors of the deceased.

ORDER APPOINTING FREEHOLDER.

At a Surrogate's Court held in the county of
.................., at the surrogate's office
in the .... of ...., on the
...... day of ...., 1874.
Present. — Hon. ...., Surrogate.

In the matter of the real estate
of
A .... B ...., deceased.

The surrogate having heretofore made an order in
this matter, that all persons interested in the estate of

the above named deceased, appear on a day and at a place in said order fixed, and show cause why the real estate of the above named deceased should not be sold for the payment of his debts, which said order was dated on the ...... day of ...., last, and the surrogate having heard the proofs and allegations of the parties, and having determined that a sale of said real estate was necessary for the purpose aforesaid, and having given notice to the said executor applying for such disposition of said real estate, and having requested him to execute and file in this court, the bond required by law previous to making such order of sale, and a reasonable time having elapsed, and the said C D, having neglected to make and file such bond :

It is ordered that E F, of the town of ...., a disinterested freeholder nominated by the creditors of the said deceased, be and he is hereby appointed in place of said C D, to make sale of said real estate upon his executing and filing with the surrogate a bond in the penalty of .... dollars with the condition required by the statute in such case made and provided.

.................., *Surrogate.*

§ 24. (2 R. S., 104.) Upon executing and filing with the surrogate such bond, the surrogate shall order the mortgage, lease or sale to be made by the person so appointed, who shall possess all the power and authority by this title conferred on executors and administrators, in relation to the mortgaging, leasing or sale of the real estate of deceased, mentioned in the order of the surrogate, and shall, in like manner, be compelled to satisfy debts, to pay over moneys, and to deliver securities.

§ 25. (2 R. S., 104.) Whenever a sale is ordered, notice of the time and place of holding the same, shall be posted for six weeks, at three of the most public places in the town or ward where the sale shall be had, and shall be published in a newspaper, if there be one printed in the same county, and if there be none, then in the state paper for six weeks successively; in which notice the lands and tenements to be sold, shall be described with common certainty, by setting forth the number of the lots, and the name or number of the townships or towns in which they are situated; if the premises cannot be so described, they shall be described in some other appropriate manner, and in all cases, the improvements thereon, if any, shall be stated.

The executor or administrator may sell the real estate in separate parcels, if he deems it beneficial to the estate, although the order for sale described the property as a single parcel. (*Delaplaine* v. *Lawrence*, 3 N. Y., 301.)

The Surrogate's Court has no power to compel a purchaser to take his deed, and therefore there should be a reasonable percentage of the purchase money paid on the sale, sufficient at least, to pay the expenses of a new sale, in case the purchaser should fail to fulfil the terms, and a new sale should be necessary.

§ 26. (2 R. S., 104.) Such sales shall be in the county where the premises are situated, at public vendue, between the hour of nine in the morning, and the setting of the sun of the same day.

§ 27. The executors or administrators making the sale, and the guardians of any minor heirs, of the deceased, shall not directly or indirectly purchase, or be interested in the purchase of any part of the real estate so sold. All sales made contrary to the provisions of this section, shall be void; but this section shall not prohibit any such purchase by a guardian for the benefit of his ward.

The authorities adjudicating upon the last section above quoted, are *Moore* v. *Moore*, 5 N. Y., 256; *Boerman* v. *Schenk*, 41 Id., 132; and *Terwilliger* v. *Brown*, 44 Id., 237.

NOTICE OF SALE.

Executor's sale of Real Estate.

In pursuance of an order of the surrogate of the county of Rensselaer, the undersigned, the executor of the last will and testament of ...., late of the .... of ...., deceased, will sell at public vendue on the ...... day of ...., at the front door of the court house in the ...... day of ...., at ten o'clock in the forenoon of that day, the follow-

ing described real estate, to wit (describe the parcels);
upon said premises are a farm house, and the ordinary
farm buildings.

Dated, Dec. 1, 1872.

A B, Executor.

§ 28. (2 R. S., 105.) On such sales, the executors or administrators may give such length of
credit not exceeding three years, for not more than
three-fourths of the purchase money, as shall seem
best calculated to produce the highest price, and
shall have been directed, or shall be approved by
the surrogate; and shall secure the moneys for
which credit is given, by a bond of the purchaser,
and by a mortgage of the premises sold.

If it is desirable to sell upon credit, it would
seem to be the better practice to obtain authority
from the surrogate to give credit; but the statute
seems to be worded expressly to permit a sale upon
credit and the subsequent approval by the surrogate, providing for such credit, when it shall have
been directed, or *shall be approved by the surrogate.*

§ 29. (2 R. S., 105.) The executors or administrators shall immediately make a return of their
proceedings upon such order of sale, to the surrogate granting the same, who shall examine the
proceedings, and may also examine such executors
or administrators, or any other person on oath

touching the same ; and if he shall be of opinion that the proceedings were unfair, or that the sum bid is disproportionate to the value, and that a sum exceeding such bid at least ten per cent, exclusive of the expenses of a new sale, may be obtained, he shall vacate such sale and direct that another be had ; of which notice shall be given, and the sale shall be in all respects conducted as the sale on the first order.

REPORT OF SALE.

Surrogate's Court, Rensselaer county :

In the matter of the real estate
of
A B, late of the .... of
...., deceased.

In pursuance of a decretal order of the surrogate of the county of Rensselaer, bearing date the ....
day of ...., 1872, I, the subscriber, executor of the last will and testament of John Doe, late of the .... of ...., in said county, did on the .... of ...., 1872, at the front door of the court house, in the city of Troy, in said county, at 10 o'clock, in the forenoon, sell at public vendue, the whole of the premises in said order described, to ...., for the sum of .... dollars, which was the highest sum bid for the same.

And I further report, that before the said sale, I caused notice of the time and place thereof, to be regularly published, once a week, for six weeks, successively in ...., a newspaper printed in said county, and like notices to be posted for six weeks in ...., thereof, the most public places in the town of ...., and further, that said sale, was legally made, and fairly conducted, and that a greater sum could not be obtained for said premises.

Dated, Nov. 20, 1872.

(Signed), A B, *Executor.*

Rensselaer county, ss :

A B, being duly sworn, says that the foregoing report by him subscribed is true.

A B.

Sworn before me this 18th }
Dec., 1874. }

X Y, *Commissioner of Deeds.*

Upon the hearing upon the report, it is competent for the surrogate to confirm the sale as to some of the parcels sold, and to vacate it as to others. (*Delaplaine* v. *Lawrence*, 3 N. Y., 301.)

It is evident that the legislature contemplated that there might be litigation before the surrogate upon the coming in of the report of sale ; but strangely enough, made no provision for a notification to the parties, or the public, as to when the report would be presented, and a motion made for the confirmation of the sale. It was therefore suggested (*Delaplaine* v. *Lawrence*, 10 Paige, 604), that where any person interested wishes to have notice of the presentation of the report, he should file a *caveat* with the surrogate, with a request that he be notified of the time and place of hearing. It was held in the same case, that a purchaser on the sale, had such an interest in the proceeding, as to entitle him to appeal from the order of the surrogate, vacating the sale to him. The sale may be impeached, first, because it was unfair, which we take to mean that the premises were not fairly exposed, that the sale was not fairly continued so as to secure the bidding of those in attendance, or that it was unfairly struck off to some person, or if any fraud was practiced; or, second, that the sum bid is disproportionate to the value of the premises, *and* that a sum exceeding such bid, at least ten per cent, exclusive of the expenses of a new sale, may be obtained. These two requisites must exist together. In *Kain* v. *Masterton* (16 N. Y., 174), a new sale was denied, notwithstanding it appeared clearly, that on such sale the required advance could be obtained, but the denial was supported, on the ground that so long an interval had elapsed, and the rise after the first sale belonged to the purchaser, rather than to the estate. If the property was not sold at a sacrifice, but commanded a fair and adequate price at the time of the sale, the law has performed its office, and right and justice are maintained between vendor and purchaser.

But it was held in a case where there was no complication arising from delay, or other cause, that if, in the opinion of the surrogate, any parcel was sold at a price disproportionate to its value, and will produce ten per cent more on a resale, it is his duty to order a resale. (*Delaplaine* v. *Lawrence*, 3 N. Y., 301.)

It would seem that the surrogate should be assured that the premises would produce the required advance on a resale, and would, with some hesitation, suggest that a responsible purchaser be found, by the party desiring to impeach the sale, and that he enter into a contract with the executor under seal, that in case the sale made be vacated and a new sale be ordered, he will on such sale bid the sum so bid before and ten per cent in advance, exclusive of the expenses of a resale. This agreement should be filed with the surrogate and would, we think, be valid. The practice has been suggested, of filing with the surrogate a bond of the proposed purchaser, running to the people of the state, conditioned that he will bid the advance required. It may be objected to such a bond that it is not authorized by any statute and that it is void.

§ 30. (2 R. S., 105.) If it shall appear to the surrogate, that such sale was legally made and fairly conducted, and that the sum bid was not disproportionate to the value of the property sold, or, if disproportionate, that a greater sum, as above specified, cannot be obtained, he shall make an order confirming such sale, and directing conveyances to be executed.

ORDER CONFIRMING SALE.

At a Surrogate's Court, held in the county of ...., at the surrogate's office in the .... of ...., on the ...... day of ...., 1872.

Present — Hon. ...., Surrogate.

In the matter of the real estate of
..............., deceased.

On reading and filing the return of ...., executor of the will of ...., late of the........... of ...., deceased, and the proofs accompany· ing the same, and it appearing therefrom that the said executor, did, on the ...... day of ...., 1872, in obedience to the former order of this court, in this matter, bearing date the ...... day of...............; last, and in pursuance of the statute in such case, made and provided, sell at public vendue, to one...... ...., for the sum of .... dollars, the lands and

26

tenements in the said order mentioned, upon the terms
and conditions particularly mentioned in said return;
and it appearing to the surrogate, that the said sale
was legally made, and fairly conducted, and that a
greater sum cannot be obtained for said premises, than
was bid at said sale, it is therefore ordered, that the
sale be, and it is hereby confirmed; and it is further
ordered, that a conveyance of the premises so sold, be
made and executed by the said executor, to the said
.................., upon his complying with the terms of
sale, on his part to be performed.

.................., *Surrogate.*

§ 31. (2 R. S., 105.) Such conveyances shall
thereupon be executed to the purchaser by the executors or administrators, or by the person so appointed by the surrogate to make the sale. They
shall contain and set forth at large, the original
order authorizing a sale, and the order confirming
the same and directing the conveyance; and they
shall be deemed to convey all the estate, right and
interest in the premises of the testator or intestate
at the time of his death, free and discharged from
all claims for dower of the widow of such testator
or intestate.

The purchaser will hold the crops growing on
the land when sold, although they were sown by
the heir or his tenant. (*Jewett* v. *Keenholtz*, 16 Barb.,
193.)

Although the heir may sell or mortgage before the expiration of three years, the purchaser or mortgagee from the heir, though taking in good faith, takes the land subject to its liability to be sold to pay the decedent's debts, under the statute. This liability is a statutory lien, running with the land for three years. (*Hyde* v. *Tanner*, 1 Barb., 75; *Jewett* v. *Keenholtz*, *sup*.)

A sale in partition between the heirs, would not preclude a subsequent sale by order of the surrogate under the act, and the latter would over-reach the former. (*Hall* v. *Partridge*, 10 How., 188; *Richardson* v. *Judah*, 2 Brad., 157.)

The deed should contain the order, authorizing and confirming the sale, *at large*, and if the deed show a defect in form or purpose, and it appear on the face of it, the deed is void in law and in equity. (*Waldron* v. *McComb*, 1 Hill, 111.)

Under the revised laws, with the same requirement, it was held in the same way. (*Atkins* v. *Kinnan*, 20 Wend., 241.)

But if there be a mistake in reciting the order of sale in the deed, it will not vitiate it, where other parts of the deed furnish of themselves, obvious means of correcting the error. (*Sheldon* v. *Wright*, 5 N. Y., 497.)

DEED ON SALE.

This indenture, made this ...... day of ....,
one thousand eight hundred and seventy ......, between.................., as executor of the last will and
testament of ...., late of the ...... of ....,
in the county of ...., deceased, party of the
first part and ...., of the ....
of ...., in the county of ...., party
of the second part; whereas, at a surrogate's court, held
in and for the county of ...., at the surrogate's office in the ...., of .... on
the .... day of ...., one thousand eight
hundred and seventy ......, before ...., surrrogate of said county, a certain decretal order was made
for the sale of the real estate of the said deceased, and
which said order is in the words and figures following,
to wit: (insert order at length).

And, whereas, in obedience to said order, the said
party of the first part did, on the .... day of
.................., 187..., sell at public vendue the whole
of the premises in said order mentioned, to the said
party of the second part for the sum of ....
dollars, and did thereupon make return of his proceedings in the premises to the surrogate of said county of
.................., and there was thereupon made an order
in the words and figures following, to wit: (insert order
confirming sale).

And, whereas, the said party of the second part, has
in all things, complied with the terms of the said sale,
on his part to be performed. Now, therefore, this indenture witnesses, that the said party of the first part,
as executor as aforesaid, for and in consideration of
the sum of .... dollars, to him in hand paid

by the party of the second part, has granted, bargained
and sold, and by these presents does grant, bargain
and sell unto the said party of the second part, his
heirs and assigns forever, the lands and tenements in
said order mentioned, described as follows : (description) together with all and singular the hereditaments
and appurtenances thereunto belonging, or in any way
appertaining, and the reversion and reversions, remainder and remainders, rents, issues and profits
thereof; and also, all the estate, right, title, interest,
claim and demand which the said deceased had, at the
time of his death of, in and to the said premises; to
have and to hold the same to the said party of the
second part, his heirs and assigns forever, to the sole
and only proper use, benefit and behoof of the said
party of the second part, his heirs and assigns forever.

In witness whereof, the said party of the first
part, as executor as aforesaid, has hereunto set his hand and seal, the day in
this indenture first above written.

(Signed), ..., *Executor*.   [L.S.]

Rensselaer county, ss :

On this ...... day of ...., 187.., before me
personally came ...., to me known to be the
executor of the last will and testament of ....,
deceased, and the person described in and who executed the foregoing conveyance, and acknowledged that
he executed the same, as such executor, for the uses
and purposes therein mentioned.

A B,
Justice of the Peace.

§ 32. (2 R. S., 105.) Every sale and conveyance made pursuant to the provisions of this title, shall be subject to all charges by judgment, mortgage or otherwise, upon the lands so sold, existing at the time of the death of the testator or intestate.

§ 1. (Chap. 81, Laws of 1850.) Every sale heretofore made, or hereafter to be made, under any of the provisions of the fourth title, of chapter six, second part of the Revised Statutes, and of the acts amending the same, or in addition thereto, shall be deemed and held to be as valid and effectual, as if made by order of a court having original general jurisdiction, and the title of any purchaser, at any such sale made in good faith, shall not be impeached, or invalidated, by reason of any omission, error, defect, or irregularity, in the proceedings before the surrogate, or by any allegation of want of jurisdiction, on the part of such surrogate, except in the manner and for the causes, that the same could be impeached or invalidated, in case such sale had been made pursuant to the order of the court of original general jurisdiction.

§ 2. No such sale, under any of the provisions of the fourth title, of chapter six, of part second, of the Revised Statutes, and of the acts amending the same shall be invalidated, nor in any wise impeached, for any omission or defect in any petition of any executor or administrator, under the provisions of such title and acts amending the same, provided such petition shall substantially show that an inventory has been filed, and that there are debts, or is a debt, which the personal estate is insufficient to discharge, and that recourse is necessary to the real estate (or some of it) whereof the deceased died, seized.

§ 3. (As amended by chap. 260, of Laws of 1869, and chap. 92 of Laws of 1872.) Nor shall any such sale be invalidated, nor in any wise impeached, by reason that any such petition was or shall be presented, by less than the whole number of executors or administrators ; nor by reason, that after the filing of any such petition, any bond required by law, has been, or shall be given, by less than the whole number of the executors or administrators, petitioning ; nor by reason that any further proceeding, notice, sale, deed or return, has been or shall be had, or made by less than the whole number of executors or administrators, petitioning ; nor by reason of any omission to serve upon any minor, heir or devisee, personally, or by publication, a copy of the order to show cause required by the fifth section of the fourth title of chapter six, part second of the Revised Statutes ; provided such order shall have been duly served on the general guardian of the minor, or the guardian appointed in such proceeding ; nor by reason of any irregularity in any matter or proceeding, after the presenting of any petition, and the giving notice of the order to show cause why the authority or direction applied for, should not be granted, and before the order confirming such sale; nor after a lapse of five years from the time of such sale, where the notice of such sale has been published for six weeks successively before the day of such sale, although such publication may not have been for the full period of forty-two days; and in all cases where the records of the office of the surrogate, before whom such proceedings were taken, have been removed from the house, office, or other building in which such proceedings were taken, to another house, office or other building, after such proceedings were taken, and the full period of twenty-five years has elapsed since said sale, it shall be presumed that guardians have been duly appointed for all minor devisees of the real estate sought to be sold in such proceedings, such presumption to be rebutted only by record evidence in such office showing affirmatively that such guardian or guardians were not appointed; provided, that nothing in this act contained shall be construed to affect in any manner any suit or proceeding already commenced for the recovery of any lands or the proceeds thereof, sold under or by virtue of any order of a Surrogate's Court.

§ 4. This act shall not be construed as authorizing any surrogate, or officer performing the duties of the office of surrogate, to make any order for the sale of the real property of a deceased person, or to confirm such sale, unless, upon due examination, he shall be satisfied, that the provisions of said title have been complied with, as if this act had not been passed.

This act throws upon the party seeking to impeach a sale of real estate, under the order of a surrogate, the whole burden of proof; and if he fails to show a want of jurisdiction in the surrogate, to make the order, the law presumes that it was properly made. (*Wood* v. *McChesney*, 40 Barb., 417.)

According to the condition of the bond made by the executor or administrator before sale, they shall, immediately, within twenty days after receiving such moneys or securities, pay to the surrogate any moneys received on such sale, and any securities taken by them shall be delivered in like manner to him, to be collected and applied; and the surrogate may compel such payment and delivery in the same manner, by attachment and suit on the bond filed, as if such real estate had been originally personal estate in the hands of such executors or administrators.

The proceedings shall not abate by reason of the death, removal or other disqualification of the executor or administrator ordered to mortgage, lease or sell the real estate for payment of debts.

§ 1. (S. L., 1850, ch. 162.) Whenever an order has been or shall be made by a surrogate for the mortgage, lease or sale of the real estate, of any deceased person, and the executor or administrator, or other persons named therein shall die or be removed, or shall be otherwise disqualified from executing the same while the same order remains unexecuted in whole or in part, the proceedings in relation thereto shall be in no wise affected by such death, removal or disqualification; and it shall be lawful for the surrogate of the county, by whom said order was made, to authorize the administrator, to whom letters of administration shall have been issued, on the goods, chattels and credits unadministered of said deceased, with the will annexed, or otherwise, or a disinterested freeholder, as in the case of an original order, to execute said order in the same manner and with the like effect as if the said order had been executed by the executor, administrator or other person originally named therein; provided that the administrator or other person so to be authorized shall, before receiving such authority, give the like security as would be required on the granting for an original order for the mortgage, lease or sale of any real estate.

No executor or other person authorized to sell any real estate by order of any surrogate, shall be allowed any commission for receiving or paying to the surrogate the proceeds of such sale; but shall be allowed their expenses in conducting such sale, including two dollars for every deed prepared and executed by them thereon, and a compensation not exceeding two dollars a day for the time necessarily occupied in such sale. (S. L., 1844, ch. 300.) The claim for the expenses and for the *per diem* allowance should properly be put in to the surrogate, in items and on the oath of the executor or administrator. The state contemplates a *per diem* allowance only for the days necessarily and actually employed about the sale. It does not warrant the idea that the executor or administrator is upon a salary from the commencement to the conclusion of the business. (*Higbie* v. *Westlake*, 14 N. Y., 281.)

In regard to the expenses proper to be allowed, the statute seems to suppose that these proceedings shall be conducted wholly by the executors or administrators with the aid of the surrogate. Notwithstanding, so necessary and proper are the services of a skilled attorney in conducting the proceedings, which affect the title to real estate, that the court will make a liberal interpretation of the statutory claim as to expenses, and will allow a reasonable sum for professional advice and assistance. But where there is no contest, charges such as were allowed by the chancery fee bills for services in litigated cases, would be excessive. (*Higbie* v. *Westlake, sup.*)

§ 36. (2 R. S., 106, amended, chap. 400, Laws, 1863.) The surrogate shall, in the first place, pay out of the said moneys, the charges and expenses of the sale. He shall next satisfy any claim of dower which the widow of the testator or intestate may have upon the lands so sold, by the payment of such sum, in gross, as shall be deemed, upon the principle of law applicable to annuities, a reasonable satisfaction of such claim, if the widow shall consent to accept such sum in lieu of her dower, by an instrument under seal, duly acknowledged or proved, in the same manner as deeds entitled to be recorded, and then, from the residue he shall pay any sum which may have been found due to the executors or administrators upon the settlement of their accounts, after applying thereon the proceeds of the personal estate of the testator or intestate.

§ 37. If, after reasonable notice for that purpose, no such consent be given, then the surrogate shall set apart one-third of the purchase money to satisfy such claim, and shall cause the same to be invested in permanent securities, on annual interest, in his name of office, which interest shall be paid to such claimant during life.

He shall set apart one-third of the whole purchase money, without first deducting the expenses of sale. (*Higbie* v. *Westlake*, 14 N. Y., 281.)

And the rule as to the securities in which the surrogate may invest, is, undoubtedly the same governing executors and administrators in making investments and that they should invest only in United States, or state bonds or in bonds and mortgages.

NOTICE TO WIDOW TO ELECT.

In the matter of the real estate
of
.................., deceased.

To ...., widow of said deceased :

You are hereby notified and required to elect, whether you will accept such sum in gross, as shall be deemed upon the principles of law, applicable to annuities, a reasonable satisfaction of your claim for dower in the lands of the above deceased, in lieu of your dower; and you are notified, so to elect before the surrogate of the county of Rensselaer, at his office in Troy, on the ..... day of ...., 1872 (the day for distribution of proceeds).

Dated, November 20, 1872.

A B,
Executor of the will of said deceased.

CONSENT OF WIDOW TO ACCEPT A SUM IN GROSS.

In the matter of the real estate

of

................., deceased.

Whereas, certain lands and tenements of the above named deceased, in which the undersigned is entitled to dower, as the widow of said deceased, have been recently sold by virtue of an order of the surrogate of .... county, in this matter, and which said lands and tenements are bounded and described as follows : (description as in order for sale).

And whereas, the moneys arising from the said sale have been brought into the said Surrogate's Court for distribution : now, therefore, Know all men by these presents, that I, A B, the widow of the said deceased, do by these presents consent to accept in lieu of my dower, in the lands and tenements aforesaid, such sum in gross, as shall be deemed, upon the principles of law applicable to annuities, a reasonable satisfaction, for my said dower.

> In witness whereof, I have hereto set my hand and seal, this ...... day of ...., 187...

A B. [L.S.]

Rensselaer county, ss :

On this ...... day of ...., 187.., before me personally came A B, to me known to be the same

person described in and who executed the foregoing
instrument, and acknowledged that she executed the
said instrument for the uses and purposes therein
mentioned.

L. W. RHODES,
Commissioner of Deeds, Troy, N. Y.

ANNUITY TABLE AND RULE.

Age.	No. of years purchase.	Age.	No. of years purchase.	Age.	No. of years purchase.	Age.	No. of years purchase.
1,	10,107	25,	12,063	49,	9,563	73,	4,781
2,	11,724	26,	11,992	50,	9,417	74,	4,565
3,	12,348	27,	11,917	51,	9,273	75,	4,354
4,	12,769	28,	11,841	52,	9,129	76,	4,154
5,	12,962	29,	11,763	53,	8,980	77,	3,952
6,	13,156	30,	11,682	54,	8,827	78,	3,742
7,	13,275	31,	11,598	55,	8,670	79,	3,514
8,	13,337	32,	11,512	56,	8,509	80,	3,281
9,	13,335	33,	11,423	57,	8,343	81,	3,156
10,	13,285	34,	11,331	58,	8,173	82,	2,926
11,	13,212	35,	11,236	59,	7,999	83,	2,713
12,	13,130	36,	11,137	60,	7,820	84,	2,551
13,	13,044	37,	11,035	61,	7,637	85,	2,402
14,	12,953	38,	10,929	62,	7,449	86,	2,266
15,	12,857	39,	10,819	63,	7,253	87,	2,138
16,	12,755	40,	10,705	64,	7,052	88,	2,031
17,	12,655	41,	10,589	65,	6,841	89,	1,882
18,	12,562	42,	10,473	66,	6,625	90,	1,689
19,	12,477	43,	10,356	67,	6,405	91,	1,422
20,	12,398	44,	10,235	68,	6,179	92,	1,136
21,	12,329	45,	10,110	69,	5,949	93,	,806
22,	12,265	46,	9,980	70,	5,716	94,	,518
23,	12,200	47,	9,846	71,	5,479		
24,	12,132	48,	9,707	72,	5,241		

Rule for Computation.

Calculate the interest, at six per cent, for one year, upon the sum to the income of which the person is entitled, and multiply this interest by the number of years purchase set opposite the person's age in the table, and the product is the gross value of the life estate of such person.

EXAMPLE.

Suppose a widow's age is forty, and she is entitled to dower in real estate worth $1500; one-third of this is $500; interest on $500, one year, at six per cent, is $30; multiply this by 10,705, the number of years purchase set opposite her age, and you have $321.15 as the gross value of her dower right.

§ 38. (2 R. S., 106). If, after the deduction aforesaid, from the proceeds of such sale, there shall not be sufficient remaining to pay all the debts of the testator or intestate, then the balance of such proceeds shall be divided by the surrogate, among the creditors, in proportion to their respective debts, without giving any preference to bonds or other specialties, or to any demands on account of any suit being brought thereon.

§ 39. Every person to whom the deceased shall have been indebted, on a valuable consideration,

for any sum of money not due at the time of distribution, shall receive his proportion with other creditors, after deducting a rebate of legal interest upon
the sum distributed, for the time unexpired of such
credit.

§ 40. (2 R. S., 107.) Before any such distribution shall be made, notice of the time and place of
making the same, shall be published for six weeks
successively, in a newspaper printed in the county
where the surrogate resides.   He may also publish
such notice in such other newspaper as he may
deem most likely to give notice to the creditors.

The notice is published pursuant to an order.

ORDER FOR NOTICE OF DISTRIBUTION.

At a Surrogate's Court, held in the county of
............., at the surrogate's office in
the .... of ...., on the ......
day of ....:., 1874.
Present — Hon. ...., Surrogate.

In the matter of the real estate
of
A .... B ...., deceased.

The proceeds of the real estate of the above named
deceased, sold for the payment of his debts, having
been brought into court :

27

Ordered the same to be distributed in this court on the ...... day of ...., next, at ten o'clock in the forenoon, and that notice thereof be published for six weeks successively in the ...., a newspaper printed in the city of ....

..................., *Surrogate.*

NOTICE OF DISTRIBUTION.

Rensselaer county, ss:

To all persons interested in the estate of A B, late of the town of ...., in said county.

Notice is hereby given that the surrogate of said county will proceed to distribute the proceeds of the real estate, of the above named deceased, sold for payment of his debts, at his office in the city of Troy, on the ...... day of ...., next, at ten o'clock in the forenoon, of that day. All persons interested in the same may attend on that day, and creditors who have not proved their claims, may attend and prove them before said surrogate.

Dated, Troy, Dec. 19, 1874.

.. .., *Surrogate.*

§ 41. At the time and place appointed, and at such other times and places as the surrogate shall appoint, for that purpose, he shall proceed to ascertain the valid and subsisting debts against the testator or intestate, and shall hear the allegations and proofs of the claimants of such debts, and of the executors, administrators, heirs, devisees, or any other persons interested in the estate of the deceased, or in the application of the proceeds of such sale.

§ 42. Any debts, which shall have been established by the surrogate, on the application for the sale, shall not again be controverted, unless upon the discovery of some new evidence to impeach the same, and then only upon due notice given to the claimant. Any other debts or demands which shall be presented, and which were not so established, shall be proved to the satisfaction of the surrogate; and the same proceedings may be had to ascertain the same as are hereinbefore prescribed upon the hearing, on the application of any executors or administrators for authority to sell the real estate.

The remarks which have been heretofore made in relation to the character of the claims which may be presented, the rules of adjudicating upon them, the defenses which may be interposed and who may defend, are referred to, in regard to claims presented under the notice of distribution. (See *ante.*)

ORDER ESTABLISHING CLAIMS AND DECREEING DISTRIBUTION.

> At a Surrogate's Court, held in the county of
> ...., at the surrogate's office in
> the ...... of ...., on the ...... day
> of ...., 1874.
> Present—Hon. ...., Surrogate.

In the matter of the real estate

of

A.......... B.........., deceased.

The proceeds of the real estate of A B, late of the town of ...., deceased, sold under the order of this court for the payment of his debts, having been paid into court to the amount of ten thousand dollars, and the surrogate having caused a notice to be published for six weeks, that distribution would be made of such proceeds according to law and due proof of such publications having been filed and sundry creditors having attended and proved their claims to the satisfaction of the surrogate; and C B, widow of said deceased, having filed her consent to accept a sum in lieu of her dower in the premises sold, which consent is executed and acknowledged by the said C B, in the manner required as to deeds to entitle them to be recorded, and X Y, the executor of the will of said deceased having appeared in person and by James Lansing, his counsel, and having filed his claim for expenses paid by him and for compensation in making such sale, which claim was duly verified and is allowed by the surrogate:

It is ordered, adjudged and decreed that of the proceeds as aforesaid paid into court, there be paid to said

C B, widow as aforesaid, in lieu of her dower, the sum of twenty-two hundred dollars, and to said X Y, said executor, for his expenses and compensation the sum of thirty-nine and $\frac{50}{100}$ dollars, and to James Lansing his counsel, twenty-five dollars, and that the remainder, amounting to seven thousand seven hundred and thirty five dollars and fifty cents, be distributed *pro rata* among the creditors of the said deceased who have proved their claims as shown in the schedule hereto annexed showing the amount of the claim by each creditor as proved and the sum payable to each.

       Witness ...., surrogate, and the seal
[SEAL]   of said court the day and year first above written.

                    ...., *Surrogate.*

SCHEDULE REFERRED TO IN THE FOREGOING DECREE.

Amount paid into court, ...		$10,000 00
There shall be paid to C B, widow,	$2200 00	
" " " X Y, executor,	39 50	
" " " J L, attorney,	25 00	
		2264 50
And the remainder,.................		$7735 50

Shall be distributed to the creditors who have proved their claims as follows :

	Claims proved.	Distribution.
J L,....................................	900 00	450 00
A R,....................................	250 00	125 00
J D,....................................	2000 00	1000 00

If the executor or administrator, shall have paid debts in the course of administration, beyond the

assets which came to his hands, he shall have the
right to be re-imbursed out of the proceeds of the
sale, being considered the equitable assignee of
such claims. (*Livingston* v. *Newkirk*, 3 John. Ch.,
318.) But if the proceeds are not sufficient to pay
debts in full, the executor or administrator as above,
gets only his *pro rata* dividend with other creditors.

It would seem (S. L., 1863, chap. 400), that any
sum which may have been found due to the executors or administrators, upon the settlement of
their accounts, after applying thereon the proceeds
of the personal estate of the testator or intestate,
shall be paid in full, before distribution shall be
made among the creditors.

§ 43. If, after payment of debts and expenses,
there be any overplus of the proceeds of the sale, the
same shall be distributed among the heirs and devisees of the testator or intestate, or the persons
claiming under them, in proportion to their respective rights in the premises sold.

This distribution may also be provided for, in the
decree of distribution, the surrogate adjudicating
upon the rights of the heirs, devisees, or the persons claiming under them, and passing upon their
claims.

§ 44. (2 R. S., 107). Any securities which shall
have been taken on the sale of any real estate, shall
be delivered to the surrogate, and kept in his office.

He shall collect the money due thereon from time to time, and shall distribute and apply the same among the creditors whose debts were established before him, in the same proportion as herein directed respecting moneys arising on such sale.

§ 45. (2 R. S., 107). The securities taken by any surrogate, on the investment of a principal sum at annual interest, to satisfy a dower claim, shall be kept in his office as part of his official papers, and be delivered to his successor; and it shall be the duty of the surrogate to collect such interest, and pay the same to the person entitled thereto.

§ 46. After the death of the person entitled to such interest, the principal sum so secured shall be collected, and after deducting the costs and charges of the surrogate in the management, collection and distribution thereof, the residue shall be distributed among the creditors of the deceased, who shall have established their debts previous to the original investment of such principal sum, in the same manner, and with the like effect, as herein provided, for the distribution of the proceeds of the sale of real estate.

§ 47. If there be any surplus remaining after such distribution, it shall be divided among the heirs and devisees of the testator, or the heirs of the intestate, or the persons claiming under them, in proportion to their respective rights in the premises sold.

§ 1. (S. L., 1850, ch. 150.) Whenever any portion of the surplus moneys brought into the surrogate's office, as the proceeds of the sale of real estate, shall belong to a minor, or belong to any person who has a temporary interest in the said moneys, and the reversionary interest belongs to another person, the Surrogate's Court shall make such order for the investment thereof, and for the payment of the interest and of the principal thereof as the Supreme Court is authorized or required by law to make in analogous cases.

§ 2. The investments that shall be made by virtue of this act, shall be secured by mortgage upon unincumbered real estate within this state, which shall be worth at least double the amount of such investment, exclusive of buildings thereon, in the name of office of the surrogate, and he shall keep the securities as he now is required by law to keep other securities belonging to his office, and the interest and principal shall be distributed by and under the direction of the surrogate, in conformity to the order under which the investment shall be made, and to the person or persons entitled thereto.

Surplus Moneys on Mortgage, or Judgment Sale in certain Cases, to be paid to the Surrogate.

(Chap. 658, Laws of 1867). Whenever there shall remain any surplus moneys, arising from the sale of any lands or real estate, of which any deceased person died seized, by virtue of any mortgage or other lien, given by, or obtained against such person during his life, the person or corporation holding such surplus, shall pay it to the surrogate of the county having jurisdiction of the estate of such deceased person, within thirty days after the sale, and the surrogate's receipt shall discharge the party receiving the surplus.

The surrogate, on application of a creditor, or the personal representatives of the deceased, shall pay out the money in the same manner, and by the same proceedings, as if the moneys arose from the sale of the real estate of the deceased for the payment of debts, under the order of the surrogate.

§ 60. (2 R. S., 110.) The several surrogates shall record in books to be provided by them, for that purpose, all orders and decrees by them made upon any proceedings before them in relation to the sale of real estate, and shall file and preserve all papers, returns, vouchers and documents connected with such proceedings.

CHAPTER XIX.

PROCEEDINGS BY CREDITOR TO COMPEL MORTGAGE, LEASE OR SALE OF REAL ESTATE.

The provisions of the statutes, authorizing and regulating the proceedings by a creditor to compel the mortgage, lease or sale of the real estate of a testator or intestate, for the payment of his debts are found in chap. 466, of Laws of 1837, § 72, *et seq.*, as amended in 1843, 1847, and again in 1873. They provide as follows :

If, after an executor or administrator shall have rendered an account, either voluntarily on his final settlement, or upon the order of the surrogate on the application of a creditor, it shall appear that there are not sufficient assets to pay the debts of the deceased, any creditor whose debt is not secured by a judgment, mortgage or other express charge on the real estate, may apply to the surrogate for an order, that the executor or administrator show cause why he should not be required to mortgage, lease or sell the real estate of the deceased for the payment of his debts.

This application may be made, notwithstanding the lapse of three years from the granting of letters, and it may be made by one who has obtained judgment against an executor or administrator for a debt against the deceased, and such judgment, after a trial at law upon the merits, is *prima facie* evidence of such debt before the surrogate.

But no real estate, the title to which shall have passed out of any heir or devisee of the deceased, by conveyance or otherwise, to a purchaser in good faith and for value, shall be sold by virtue of the provisions of this act, or of title four, chapter six, part two of the Revised Statutes, unless letters testamentary or of administration upon the estate of said deceased shall have been applied for within four years after his death, nor unless application for such sale shall be made to the surrogate, within three years after the granting of such letters testamentary or of administration, provided the surrogate of any county in this state, had jurisdiction to grant such letters of administration.

And provided further, that the period during which an action may be pending in favor of any creditor, against any executor or administrator, for the recovery of any debt or claim, against the testator or intestate, shall not be part of the time limited for making such application to the surrogate for such sale ; provided the plaintiff in such

PETITION OF CREDITOR FOR SALE.

To Hon. ...., Surrogate of the county of ....

The petition of ...., of the.................. of ...., respectfully shows as follows :

Your petitioner is a creditor of ...., late of the .... of ...., deceased, intestate, said intestate having died indebted to your petitioner, in the sum of .... dollars, and interest, upon a promissory note, made by him to your petitioner, or order, dated the ...... day of.................., 1873, and payable ninety days after date. Said claim is justly due to your petitioner, no payments have been made thereon, and there are no offsets against the same to the knowledge of your .petitioner, and the same is not secured by judgment, mortgage upon, or expressly charged on the real estate of the said deceased.

Letters of administration of the goods, chattels and credits of the said .... deceased, were duly issued by the surrogate of the county of .... , on the ...... day of ...., 1873, to .... of the ...., and the same still remain in full force as your petitioner is informed and believes.

On the .... day of.................., last, past, the said .... rendered an account of his proceedings as such administrator, which said account has been settled before the said surrogate, and it appears from the said account, upon such settlement, that there are not sufficient assets to pay the debts of the said deceased.

The said intestate died seized of the following described parcels of real estate, valued at the sum respectively affixed to each parcel, and occupied or not occupied as hereafter stated as to each ; that is to say (describe each parcel and names of occupants and value).

.... is the widow, and .... and ...., are the heirs at law of said ...., deceased, and all reside in the .... of..............

Your petitioner, therefore, prays that the surrogate will grant an order for the said ...., administrator as aforesaid, to show cause why he should not be required to mortgage, lease or sell the real estate of the said deceased, for the payment of his debts, and that such other or further proceedings, according to law, may be thereupon had, as may tend to the relief of your petitioner and the payment of his claim aforesaid.

Dated, December 1, 1874.

(Signed), ...

.... county, ss :

.................., being duly sworn, says that the foregoing petition, by him subscribed, is true of his own knowledge, except as to the matters which are therein stated on information and belief, and as to those matters he believes it to be true.

Sworn, etc.

(Signed), ...

ORDER THAT ADMINISTRATOR SHOW CAUSE.

At a Surrogate's Court, held in the county of
................., at the surrogate's office,
in the ..... of ...., on the ......
day of ...., 1874.

Present — Hon. ...., Surrogate.

In the matter of the real estate

of

..................., dec'd.

On reading and filing the petition of ....,
a creditor of ...., late of the ....
of ...., deceased, in testate :

Ordered, ..., administrator of the goods,
chattels and credits of ...., late of the ....
of ...., deceased, intestate, personally be and
appear before the surrogate of the county of............,
at his office, in the .... of ...., on
the ...... day of .... next, at ten o'clock in
the forenoon, then and there to show cause why he
should not be required to mortgage, lease or sell the
real estate of said deceased, for the payment of his
debts.

..................., *Surrogate.*

§ 49. (2 R S., 108.) Such order shall be served
personally on the executor or administrator to
whom it shall be directed at least fourteen days
before the day therein appointed for showing cause.

On the return of such order, the executor or administrator may set up, in bar of the application,

any matter of defense which may exist to the claim of the petitioner, or to the right of the petitioner to the relief asked.

§ 50. If no cause to the contrary be shown, the surrogate shall order notice of such application to be served and published, in the same manner as hereinbefore directed, on the application of an executor; and if, at the day appointed in such notice, the surrogate be satisfied of the matter specified in the fourteenth section (as above quoted), he may order such executor or administrator to mortgage, lease, or sell so much of the real estate of which the testator or intestate died seized, as shall be sufficient for the payment of the debts established before him.

The *notice* provided for in this section, is the order to show cause, to all parties interested.

ORDER THAT PERSONS INTERESTED SHOW CAUSE.

At a Surrogate's Court, held in the county of ...., at the surrogate's office in the .... of ...., on the ...... day of ...., 1874.
Present — Hon. ...., Surrogate.

> In the matter of the estate
> of
> ...., deceased.

An order having been heretofore made, on the application of ...., of the ...., a cre-

28

ditor of ...., late of the .... of ....,
deceased, intestate, requiring ...., the administrator of the goods, chattels and credits of said
deceased, personally to be, and appear before our surrogate of the county of ...., on this day, to
show cause why he should not be required to mortgage,
lease or sell the real estate of the said deceased, for
the payment of his debts, and the said administrator
having appeared, and having shown no cause to the
contrary:

Ordered, that all persons interested in the estate of
said deceased, appear before the surrogate of the county
of ...., at his office in the .... of
................., on the ...... day of ....,
187–, at ten o'clock in the forenoon, then and there to
show cause why authority should not be given to the
said administrator to mortgage, lease or sell, so much
of the real estate of the said ...., deceased,
as shall be necessary to pay his debts. It is further
ordered, that all persons having claims against said
deceased, may appear and exhibit, and prove such
claims at the time aforesaid, before said surrogate.

................., *Surrogate.*

On the day appointed in this order, the proceedings will be the same as those heretofore detailed
in the return of the like order, issued upon the
application of the executor or administrator, and
creditors may appear and prove their claims, with
the same effect as on the return of that order.
(See *ante.*)

But if the surrogate shall be satisfied, that all of the personal estate applicable to that purpose, has been applied to the payment of debts, and that debts exist which are not liens or charged upon the real estate, and that the executor has complied with the requirements of the fourteenth section, he shall order a sale of real estate.

The surrogate may make the order of sale upon the petition of the creditor, although all the administrators have not united in making or returning an inventory. (*Wood* v. *McChesney*, 40 Barb., 414.)

ORDER FOR SALE ON THE APPLICATION OF A CREDITOR.

At a Surrogate's Court held in the county of .... at the surrogate's office in the city of ...., on the ...... day of ...., 1874.

Present — Hon. ...., Surrogate.

In the matter of the real estate
of
................., deceased.

An order having been heretofore made by the surrogate of the county of ...., on the application of ...., of the .... of ...., a creditor of ...., late of the ...... of ...., deceased, intestate, requiring ...., the administrator of the goods, chattels and credits of said intestate, to appear before the said surrogate, on the ...... day of .... last, to show cause why he should not be required to mortgage, lease or sell the real estate of said intestate, for the payment of his debts, and the said administrator, having appeared, and shown no cause to the contrary; and thereupon, the said surrogate having made a further order, directing all persons interested in the estate of said ...., deceased, to appear before him on this day, to show cause why authority should not be given to the said administrator to mortgage, lease or sell so much of the real estate of the said ...., deceased, as shall be necessary to pay his debts, and on reading and filing satisfactory proof by affidavit, of due publication of said order, and of the due service thereof, on every person in occupation of the premises of which a sale is desired, on the widow and heirs-at-law of the said deceased, and the said administrator having appeared this day, in person and by ...., his proctor, and .. .., and ...., heirs-at-law, having also with the said .. .., petitioner, appeared, and the proper proceedings, in due form of law, having been thereupon had, and the surrogate, upon due examination, being satisfied that the said administrator has fully complied with the provisions of the statute, concerning the power and duties of executors and administrators in relation to the sale and disposition of the real estate of the testator, or intestate ; that the debt of the said ...., and other debts presented and proved before the said surrogate, and which the said surrogate has adjudged valid and subsisting against the estate of the said deceased, and for the purpose of satisfying which, application is made to mortgage, lease, or sell, the real estate

of the said deceased, are justly due and owing, and
that they are not secured by judgment, or mortgage,
or expressly charged on the real estate of the said deceased, and that the same amount to ....
dollars, and .... cents, and that the personal
estate of the said deceased is insufficient for the payment of such debts, and satisfactory evidence having
been given, that the said administrator has proceeded
with reasonable diligence in converting the personal
property of the said deceased into money, and applying
the same to the payment of debts ; and having inquired
whether sufficient moneys for the payment of such
debts aforesaid, can be raised by mortgage or lease of
the property of the deceased, or any part thereof; and
it appearing that the moneys required cannot be raised
by mortgage or lease, advantageously to the estate of
the said deceased, and the said ...., administrator as aforesaid, having executed a bond to the
people of this state, with sufficient sureties, approved
by the surrogate, in the penalty and with the conditions prescribed by the statute, which said bond is
filed with said surrogate, it is ordered that the said
..............., administrator aforesaid, sell the following
described real estate, whereof the said intestate died
seized, to enable him to pay the debts aforesaid, that
is to say. (Description.)

And it is further ordered, that the said administrator may give to the purchaser at such sale, of any of
the said real estate, a credit, not exceeding three years,
for not more than one half of the purchase money of
such real estate, purchased by him, to be secured by a
bond of said purchaser, and a mortgage upon the
premises to him sold. And it is further ordered, that

the said administrator make returns of all sales made by virtue of this order.

> In testimony whereof, the said surrogate has hereunto affixed his name, and the seal of this court, the day and year first above written.

[L. S.]

...., *Surrogate.*

§ 51. (2 R. S., 108.) Upon such order being granted and served on the executor or administrator, he shall mortgage, lease or sell as directed therein, in the same manner as if such order had been granted on his own application; the like bond shall be executed; the like notice shall be given, and the same proceedings had, in all respects, as before directed on the application of an executor or administrator, and the proceeds shall be returned to the surrogate in like cases, and distribution shall be made in the same manner.

§ 52. (2 R. S., 108.) If the executor or administrator neglect or refuse to serve and publish the notice required, or to do any other act necessary to authorize or carry into effect an order for the mortgaging, leasing or sale of the real property of the deceased, the surrogate may appoint a disinterested freeholder, who shall proceed in the same manner as directed in respect to such executor or administrator.

ORDER THAT EXECUTOR OR ADMINISTRATOR MAKE AND FILE BOND FOR SALE.

At a Surrogate's Court held in the county
of ...., at the surrogate's office in
the .... of................, on the ...... day
of ·················, 1874.
Present — Hon. ...., Surrogate.

In the matter of the real estate

of

...., deceased.

It appearing by the records of this court, that the
real estate of the deceased, is of the value of ....
dollars, and that it is necessary to have the same sold
for the payment of the debts of the said deceased, it is
ordered, that .... , administrator of the goods,
chattels, and credits of said deceased, in conjunction
with two sufficient sureties to be approved by the surrogate, execute a bond to the people of this state, in
the penal sum of .... dollars, conditioned as
required by law.   ...., *Surrogate.*

ORDER APPOINTING FREEHOLDER TO MAKE SALE.

At a Surrogate's Court, held in the county
of ...., at the surrogate's office
in the ...... of ...., on the ......
day of ...., 1874.
Present Hon. ...., Surrogate.

In the matter of the real estate

of

...., deceased.

On filing the petition duly verified of ....,
a creditor of the above named deceased, showing that

...., the administrator, etc., of the said deceased, has refused and still refuses to execute the bond required in these proceedings by the order of this court, and nominating ...., a disinterested freeholder, to make such sale, it is ordered that .... be appointed to make such sale, on his filing the bond required by law.

................, *Surrogate.*

The Interest of the Deceased in a Contract for Purchase of Lands may also be Sold.

The interest of the deceased in a contract for the purchase of lands, whether he was the original purchaser, or held the contract by assignment, may be sold on the application of the executor or administrator, or a creditor, in the same cases, and in the same manner as if he had died seized of such lands, and the same proceedings may be had for that purpose, as are directed above in respect to lands. (2 R. S., 111, amended 1847.)

Such sale shall be made subject to all payments thereafter to become due, and may be made subject to all payments due and unpaid, or to become due. In either case, the sale will not be confirmed by the surrogate, until the purchaser shall execute a bond, with sureties to be approved by such surrogate, in a penalty double the whole amount of such payments yet to be paid on such contract,

conditioned that such purchaser will make all payments unpaid for such land, and will fully and
amply indemnify the executors or administrators
of the deceased, and the heirs or devisees entitled,
against all demands, costs, charges and expenses,
by reason of any covenant or agreement contained
in such contract, or by reason of any covenant,
agreement or liability of the deceased, on account
of the purchase of such lands, and against all other
covenants and agreements of the deceased to the
vendor of such land in relation thereto. But if
there be no payments unpaid, or thereafter to become due on account of such contract, no bond
shall be required of the purchaser.

When the bond shall have been executed, or if
it shall not be necessary as above, the surrogate
will direct an assignment, by the executor or administrator, of the contract to the purchaser, who
shall thereupon have all the rights which the deceased would have had, if living, in relation to the
contract and the lands contracted for.

If a part of the lands so contracted for, may be
sold advantageously, and so that the proceeds of
such part will satisfy and discharge all the payments to be made for such land, according to the
contract, the surrogate may order such part only
to be sold, and in that case the purchaser shall not
be required to execute any bond.

The moneys arising from such sale shall be paid to the surrogate, and shall be disposed of in the same manner as directed in regard to proceeds of lands sold; but the claim of dower shall only extend to the annual interest, during the life of the widow, upon one-third of the surplus of the moneys arising from such sale, which shall remain after paying all sums of money due from the deceased, at the time of such sale, for the land so contracted for and sold.

§ 73. (2 R. S., 112.) The surrogate shall apply the residue of the moneys arising from such sale, in the first instance, to the payment of all sums of money then due from the deceased to the vendor of the lands so contracted, on account of such contract (when the lands are sold subject only to payments thereafter to become due), and shall then proceed to distribute the balance among the creditors of the deceased in the manner hereinbefore provided; and if there be any surplus after payment of debts and expenses, the same shall be distributed among the persons who would have been entitled to the interest of the deceased in the lands sold if such sale had not been made, or the person claiming under them, in proportion to their respective rights in the premises sold.

§ 74. Where a portion only of the land so contracted is sold, the executor or administrator shall execute a conveyance therefor to the purchaser, which shall transfer to him all the right of the deceased to the portion so sold, and all the right which shall be acquired by the executor or administrator, or by the person entitled to the interest of the deceased in the land sold at the time of the sale, on the perfecting of the title to such land pursuant to the contrct.

§ 75. Upon payment being made in full on a contract for the purchase of land, a portion of which shall have been sold according to the preceding provisions, the executors or administrators of the deceased shall have the same right to enforce the performance of the contract which the deceased would have had, if he had lived; and any deed that shall be executed to them, shall be in trust, and for the benefit of the persons entitled to the interest of the deceased, subject to the dower of the widow, if there be any, except for such part of the land so conveyed as shall have been sold to a purchaser according to the preceding provisions; and as to such part, the said deed shall enure to the benefit of the purchaser.

CHAPTER XX.

Statutory Provisions as to Sales by Executors under Power given in the Will, and as to Confirmation of Sales Originally made under Surrogate's Order.

§ 55. (2 R. S., 109.) Where any real estate or any interest, therein, is given or devised by any will legally executed, to the executors therein named, or any of them, to be sold by them or any of them, or where such estate is ordered by any last will to be sold by the executors, and any exe-'cutor shall neglect or refuse to take upon him the execution of such will, then all sales made by the executor or executors, who shall take upon them the execution of such will, shall be equally valid, as if the other executors had joined in such sale.

§ 57. Where by any last will a sale of real estate shall be ordered to be made, either for the payment of debts or legacies, the surrogate in whose office such will was proved, shall have power to cite the executors in such will named, to account for the proceeds of the sales, and to compel distribution thereof; and to make all necessary orders and decrees thereon, with the like power of enforcing them, as if the said proceeds had been originally personal property of the deceased, in the hands of an administrator.

§ 58. Any executor or administrator, or other person, appointed as herein directed, who shall fraudulently sell any real estate of his testator or intestate, contrary to the foregoing provisions, shall forfeit double the value of the land sold, to be recovered by the person entitled to an estate of inheritance therein.

§ 59. No offense, in relation to the giving of notice of sale, or the taking down, or defacing, such notice, shall affect the validity of such sale to any purchaser in good faith, without notice of the irregularity.

§ 60. The several surrogates shall record, in books to be provided by them for that purpose, all orders and decrees by them made, upon any proceedings before them in relation to the sale of real estate, and shall file and preserve all papers, returns, vouchers and documents connected with such proceedings.

§ 61. Wherever a sale of any real estate has heretofore been made, by virtue of an order of the Court of Probates, or of any surrogate, and a conveyance executed in pursuance thereof, but without the concurrence of any discreet person besides the executor or administrator, as heretofore required by law ; and wherever any conveyance has been executed, or shall be executed in pursuance of such sale, without setting forth at large the order of the surrogate directing such sale, or the order confirming the same, the said irregularities may be rectified, and the sales confirmed by the chancellor of the state. (Supreme Court.)

§ 62. Upon any application to the chancellor, (Supreme Court) for confirmation of such sales, he shall direct a reference to a master in chancery (referee) to examine and report touching the proceedings on such sale, and whether any heirs or devisees of the real estate sold, or persons claiming under them, reside within this state.

§ 63. Upon the coming in of the master's (referee's) report, notice shall be published for eight weeks successively in the state paper, of such report being filed, and requiring all persons interested, to appear before the chancellor (Supreme Court) at such time and place as he shall have directed, to show cause why such sale and conveyance should not be confirmed.

§ 64. If it appears by the master's (referee's) report, that any heirs or devisees of the real estate sold, or any person claiming under them, reside within this state, then a copy of such notice shall be served on such heirs or devisees, or persons claiming under them, either personally or by leaving the same at their usual dwelling place, in case of their absence, at least fourteen days, before the time appointed for such hearing.

§ 65. If upon the hearing of such application, and the examination of the proceedings, it shall appear to the satisfaction of the chancellor (Supreme Court) that the said sale was made fairly, and in good faith, he shall make such order for confirming the sale and conveyance, as he shall deem equitable, and such sale and conveyance shall from that time, be confirmed and valid, according to the terms of the order.

CHAPTER XXI.

Guardians and Wards.

Guardians, are persons having, by reason of their relation or by appointment, the care and custody of infants, during their minority.

Their relation to their wards is one of trust and confidence, so much so, that they cannot, in any beneficial transaction substitute themselves for their wards.

Guardianship by relation, arises under the provisions of the statute.

§ 5. (1 R. S., 718.) Where an estate in lands shall become vested in an infant, the guardianship of such infant, with the rights, powers and duties of a guardian in socage, shall belong

1. To the father of the infant;

2. If there be no father, to the mother;

3. If there be no father or mother, to the nearest male relative of full age, not being under any legal incapacity; and as between relatives of the same degree of consanguinity, males shall be preferred.

§ 6. To every such guardian, the statutory provisions that are or shall be in force, relative to guardians in socage, shall be deemed to apply.

§ 7. The rights and authority of every such guardian shall be superseded, in all cases where a testamentary or other guardian shall have been appointed, under the provisions of the third title of the eighth chapter of this act.

Guardianship in socage arose, when socage land, or lands held upon the payment of certain services, other than military services, descended to an heir of a tenant of such lands under fourteen years of age.

The provision is inoperative in this state, and the distinction of guardians, as such, in socage, is a mere legal curiosity.

Guardians may be appointed by the father or mother, by the Supreme Court, or by the surrogate.

§ 1. (2 R. S., 150, amended by laws of 1871, chap. 31.) Every father, whether of full age, or a minor, of a child likely to be born, or of any living child under the age of twenty-one years, and un-married, may, by his deed or last will duly executed, or, in case such father be dead, and shall not have exercised his said right of appointment, then the mother, whether of full age, or a minor, of every such child, may, by her deed or last will duly exe-cuted, dispose of the custody and tuition of such child during its minority, or for any less time, to any person or persons in possession or remainder.

§ 2. Every such disposition, from the time it shall take effect, shall vest in the person or persons to whom it shall be made, all the rights and powers, and subject him or them to all the duties and obligations of a guardian of such minor, and shall be valid and effectual against every other person, claiming the custody or tuition of such minor, as guardian in socage or otherwise.

§ 3. Any person to whom the custody of any minor is so disposed of, may take the custody and tuition of such minor, and may maintain all proper actions for the wrongful taking or detention of the minor, and shall recover damages in such actions, for the benefit of his ward.

He shall also take the custody and management of the personal estate of such minor, and the profits of his real estate during the time for which such disposition shall have been made, and may bring such actions in relation thereto, as a guardian in socage might by law.

Such guardians, appointed by deed, or by will, are subject to the supervision of the Supreme Court, as the successor of the Court of Chancery. It may compel them to account from time to time, and may, for cause, remove them. The surrogate also has jurisdiction to compel an accounting by testamentary guardians, as will presently be noted. It is optional, however, with the persons appointed by will or by deed, whether they will accept the trust, but if they do so accept, there is no discharge except for good cause shown, by the Supreme Court. Acceptance of the trust, may be inferred from some act done by the guardian appointed, or assuming some care of the minor's estate, or some direction of his conduct.

A guardian, wherever or by whomsoever appointed, is limited as to the exercise of his power to the state wherein the appointment is made. The appointment is an act of jurisdiction dependent upon the situation of the person or the property, within the territory of the state. This authority is not limited to the cases of citizens of the state. (*McLoskey* v. *Reid*, 4 Brad., 334.) But it is difficult to conceive that a father, resident in one state, may not appoint a guardian of his infant child with authority over real estate in another state. The authority granted is as great as the authority of the father, and the substitution is complete.

But it was held that a guardian appointed by a foreign court, was not entitled to receive from the administrator here, the portion of his ward, and that a legacy to the minor, must be paid into court and invested as we have heretofore considered in relation to legacies to minors, unless the guardian shall be appointed here. (*McLoskey* v. *Reid, sup.*)

So the rule that one may become an executor *de son tort*, applies also to guardianship, and it was held that an agent of an administratrix, who from mere friendship, assumed to act as guardian of infant heirs, and received rents and profits of their real estate was chargeable with interest thereon, not as agent of the administratrix, but as guardian. (*Mason* v. *Roosevelt*, 5 Johns. Ch., 534.)   So a father or any other person, who enters upon a minor's lands or takes possession of his personal property, may be treated by the minor as a guardian, and compelled to account as such. (*Sherman* v. *Ballou*, 8 How., 304 ; *Van Eppes* v. *Van Deusen*, 4 Paige, 64.)

The authority of two or more guardians is joint, and that of each extends to the entirety, *per my et per tout*, so that should one die, the authority continues in the survivor. (*People* v. *Voyron*, 3 Johns. Cas., 53.)

The Supreme Court will, upon petition, appoint a guardian for a minor, and control him in the exercise of his duties ; will compel him to make suitable provision for his ward, to account when necessary, and remove him for cause, as in case of a testamentary guardian ; will audit his final account, and discharge him from his trust.

The guardian appointed by the Supreme Court, continues until the majority of the infant, and is not controlled by the election of the infant, when he arrives at the age of fourteen years.   (*Matter of William Nicoll*, 1 Johns. Ch. Rep., 25.)

We will proceed to consider the appointment or allowance by the surrogate. When the minor is under the age of fourteen years, the surrogate is said to *appoint* the guardian, but when the minor is fourteen years of age, or upward, he makes choice of his guardian, and petitions for his allowance, and the surrogate is said to *allow* the choice of the guardian.

§ 4. (1 R. S., 150 as amended by Laws of 1870.) If no guardian for any such minor shall have been appointed by the father or mother, by deed or will, every such minor, of the age of fourteen years, may apply by petition to the surrogate of the county where the residence of such minor may be, for the appointment of such guardian as the minor may nominate, subject to the approbation of the surrogate.

The residence of a minor, is determined by the residence of the parent; if but one survive, then of *that* parent. (*Brown* v. *Lynch*, 2 Brad., 214 ; *Matter of Hughes Infant*, 1 Tucker, 38.)

But this residence, must be actual, not legal, to confer jurisdiction upon the surrogate. (*Matter of Pierce*, 12 How., 532.) So when a guardian was appointed in one county for a minor under the age of fourteen years, and the guardian changed the residence of the minor into another county within this state, it was held that an application

by the minor for a subsequent appointment must
be made in the county of the new residence. (*Ex-parte* v. *Bartlett*, 4 Brad., 221.) But a relative, not
a guardian, by the mere removal of the minor,
cannot change the legal residence of the minor.
(*Matter of Hughes*, 1 Tuck., 38.)

The petition should state the age and residence
of the minor, and the name and residence of the
person nominated as guardian, and should be signed
by the minor.

There should also be appended a consent of the
person nominated to serve if appointed, and an
affidavit of some person acquainted with the facts,
that the petition is true, stating the amount of the
personal property of the minor, and the annual
value of the rents and profits of his real estate.

FORM OF PETITION BY MINOR OVER FOURTEEN YEARS OF AGE.

To Moses Warren, Esq.,
      Surrogate of Rensselaer county:

The petition of A B, of the town of Lansingburgh,
in the county of Rensselaer aforesaid, respectfully
shows : That your petitioner is a resident of the county
of Rensselaer, and is a minor over fourteen years of
age ; that he was sixteen (16) years of age on the 15th
day of May last ; that your petitioner is entitled to certain property and estate, and that to protect and preserve the legal rights of your petitioner, it is necessary

that some proper person should be appointed the guardian of his person and estate during his minority. Your petitioner therefore nominates, subject to the approbation of the surrogate, C D, of the town of Lansingburgh aforesaid, the maternal uncle of your petitioner (or, in no way related to your petitioner), to be such guardian, and prays his appointment accordingly. And your petitioner, &c.

Dated, April 15th, 1874.

(Signed),   A B.

Rensselaer county, ss:

A B, the foregoing petitioner, being duly sworn, says that he has read the foregoing petition, and knows the contents thereof, and that the same is true, to the best of his knowledge and belief.

A B.

Sworn before me, this ...... day }
    of ...., 1874.   }

CHAS. J. LANSING,
Justice of the Peace.

Consent of Person to be Appointed.

I, C D of the town of Lansingburgh, consent to be appointed the guardian of the person and estate of the above named minor during his minority.

Dated, April 15, 1874.

C D.

AFFIDAVIT AS TO PROPERTY.

Rensselaer county, ss:

E F, of the town of Lansingburgh, in said county, being duly sworn, says that he is acquainted with the property and estate of the above named minor ; that the same consists of personal property only, which does not exceed in value the sum of five hundred dollars; (that the same consists of real and personal estate; that the value of the personal estate of said minor does not exceed the sum of five hundred dollars), and that the annual rents and profits of the real estate of said minor, do not exceed the sum of fifty dollars, or thereabouts.

E F.

Sworn this 15th day of April, }
  1874, before me, }

        CHAS. J. LANSING,
           Justice of the Peace.

§ 8. (2 R. S., 151.) Before appointing any person guardian of a minor, the surrogate shall require of such person a bond to the minor, with sufficient security, to be approved by him, in a penalty double the amount of the personal estate, and of the value of the rents and profits of the real estate, conditioned that such person will faithfully, in all things, discharge the duty of a guardian to such minor, according to law, and that he will render a true and just account of all money and property received by him, and of the application thereof, and of his guardianship, in all respects, to any court having cognizance thereof, when thereunto required.

§ 9. The bond so taken, shall be retained by the surrogate among the papers of his office, and in case of any breach of the condition thereof, may be prosecuted in the name of the ward, although he may not have arrived at full age, by his next friend or guardian, whenever the surrogate shall direct.

BOND OF GUARDIAN.

Know all men by these presents, that we, John Dean, Samuel Stiles and John Doe, of the city of Troy, in the county of Rensselaer, are held and firmly bound unto James Dean of the city of Troy, aforesaid, a minor, in the sum of two thousand five hundred dollars, to be paid to the said James Dean, his certain attorney, executors, administrators or assigns, to which payment, well and truly to be made, we bind ourselves, our and each of our heirs, executors and administrators, jointly and severally, firmly by these presents.
Sealed with our seals, and dated ⎱
     this 15th day of April, 1874. ⎰

....

The condition of this obligation is such, that if the above bounden John Dean, shall faithfully, in all things, discharge the duties of a guardian to the above named James Dean, a minor, according to law, and shall render a just and true account of all moneys and property received by him, and of the application thereof, and of his guardianship, in all respects, to any court having cognizance thereof, when thereunto required, then this obligation to be void, otherwise to remain in full force and virtue.

JOHN DEAN.   [L. S.]
SAMUEL STILES.   [L. S.]
JOHN DOE.   [L. S.]

Rensselaer county, ss :

Samuel Stiles and John Doe, of the city of Troy, in said county, being severally sworn, depose and say, and each for himself say, that he is worth the sum of two thousand five hundred dollars, over and above all debts due from, or liabilities incurred by him.

SAMUEL STILES.
JOHN DOE.

Sworn before me, this 15th }
    day of April, 1874. }

..........................,
Justice of the Peace.

State of New York, } ss.
    Rensselaer county, }

On this 15th day of April, 1874, before me personally appeared John Dean, Samuel Stiles and John Doe, to me known to be the persons described in and who executed the foregoing bond, and severally acknowledged that they executed the same.

.........................,
Justice of the Peace.

Endorsed.
    Approved.
        ...., Surrogate.

The petition being satisfactory, and the bond having been approved and filed, the surrogate enters in his special minutes an order for the appointment.

ORDER FOR LETTERS OF GUARDIANSHIP.

At a Surrogate's Court, held in the county of ...., at the surrogate's office in the ...... of ...., on the ...... day of.................., 1874.

Present — Hon. ...., Surrogate.

In the matter of the person and estate

of

A .... B .... , a minor.

On reading and filing the petition of A B, of the town of ...., in said county, from which it appears, that the said A B is a minor, over the age of fourteen years and under the age of twenty-one, and has no testamentary guardian and is possessed of certain property, and asking for the appointment of .... as the guardian of his person and estate; and on reading and filing the consent of said .... to be so appointed: And the said .... having filed his bond in due form of law to said minor with a penalty and sureties approved by the surrogate : It is ordered that the said .... be appointed the guardian of the person and estate of said minor until he shall arrive at the age of twenty-one years, and that letters of guardianship issue accordingly.

.................., *Surrogate.*

And thereupon the surrogate issues letters of guardianship, in the name of the people, in conformity with the order.

But if the minor be under the age of fourteen years, the proceedings are not so simple.

§ 5. (2 R. S., 151). If such minor be under the age of fourteen years, any relative, or other person in his behalf, may apply to the surrogate of the county where such minor shall reside, for the appointment of a guardian of the minor, until he shall arrive at the age of fourteen years, and until another guardian shall be appointed. Upon the making of any such application, the surrogate shall assign a day for the hearing thereof, and shall direct such notice of the hearing to be given to the relatives of the minor, residing in the county, as he shall, on due inquiry, think reasonable.

PETITION FOR GUARDIAN, MINOR UNDER FOURTEEN YEARS, BY MOTHER.

To ...., Esq.,
       Surrogate of the county of .... :

The petition of Sarah Dean, of the city of Troy, in the county of Rensselaer, respectfully showeth that your petitioner is the mother of James Dean, a minor; that said minor resides in the county of Rensselaer, and is under fourteen years of age; that said James was ten years of age on the 14th day of August last past; that said minor is entitled to personal property to the value of about four hundred dollars, as your petitioner is informed and verily believes, and that he is also seized of certain real estate, the annual rents and profits whereof do not exceed the sum of fifty dol-

lars, and to protect and to preserve the legal rights of
said minor, it is necessary that some proper person
should be duly appointed the guardian of his person
and estate.

Your petitioner, therefore, prays that you will appoint John Dean of the city of Troy, in the county of
Rensselaer, the guardian of the person and estate of
said minor, until he shall arrive at the age of fourteen
years, and until another guardian shall be appointed.
And your petitioner will ever pray.

Dated, this 15th day of April, A.D. 1874.

SARAH DEAN.

Consent.

I, John Dean of the city of Troy, county of Rensselaer, do hereby consent to be appointed the guardian
of the person and estate of the above named minor
during his minority.

Dated, this 15th day of April, A.D. 1874.

JOHN DEAN.

State of New York,   }
    Rensselaer county, } ss.

Sarah Dean of the city of Troy, the above petitioner,
being duly sworn, deposes and says, that the matters
set forth in the foregoing petition are true, as she is
informed and verily believes.

SARAH DEAN.

Sworn before me, this 15th day }
    of April, A.D., 1874.   }

MOSES WARREN,
Surrogate.

It will be observed, that the notice is to be served
on such relatives only as the surrogate shall direct,

and if the applicant be the person to whom the surrogate would direct notice to be given, and he is satisfied that the appointment is for the interest of the minor, the surrogate will assign the hearing for the same day and proceed with the appointment. (*Wilcox* v. *Wilcox*, 22 Barb., 178.)

But it may occur that the petition is made by some one more remotely related to the minor.

PETITION FOR GUARDIAN, BY RELATIVE, NOT ENTITLED.

To ...., Esq.,

     Surrogate of the county of ....:

     The petition of ...., of the .... of .... in the county of ...., respectfully shows: That your petitioner is the maternal uncle (or the friend, as the case may be), of James Dean, a minor; that the said minor resides in the county of .... and is under fourteen years of age, and was ...... years of age on the ...... day of ...., last past, as your petitioner is informed and believes; that the relatives of said minors in said county of .... are .... his mother, and .... his brother of full age, and ...., his maternal aunt; that said minor is entitled to personal property of the value of about .... dollars, and that he is also seized of certain real estate in this state, the annual rents and profits whereof do not exceed the sum of .... dollars (if the statements are not according to the personal knowledge of the petitioner say, as appears by the affidavits hereunto annexed), and to protect the legal rights of said minor, it is necessary that some proper person should be duly appointed the guardian of his person and estate.

Your petitioner, therefore, prays that you will appoint .... of the .... of ...., in the county of ...., the guardian of the person and estate of said minor, until he shall arrive at the age of fourteen years, and until another guardian shall be appointed.

Dated, this ...... day of ...., 1872.

(Signed), ...

.... county, ss :

.................., being duly sworn, says that the foregoing petition, by him subscribed, is true of his own knowledge, except as to the matters which are therein stated on information and belief, and, as to those matters he believes it to be true.

(Signed), ...

Sworn, etc.

Add Consent of Guardian to be appointed and affidavits as to property if necessary.

ORDER FIXING HEARING, AND FOR NOTICE.

At a Surrogate's Court held in the county of ...., at the surrogate's office in the ...... of ...., on the ...... day of ...., 1874.

Present — Hon. ...., Surrogate.

In the matter
of
.................., a minor.

On reading and filing the petition of ...., praying for the appointment of ...., as guard·

ian of said minor, and it appearing therefrom that
.................., and ...., are relatives of said
minor, resident in this county: ordered, that the ......
day of ...., be assigned for hearing the said
matter at the surrogate's office in the .... of
.................., at ten o'clock in the forenoon, and that
at least six days' notice in writing, be given by said
petitioner to said relatives, of the time and place of
such hearing.

(Signed), ..., Surrogate.

NOTICE OF HEARING TO RELATIVES.

Surrogate's Court,.................. county.

> In the matter
> of
> ...., a minor.

Take notice, that a petition has been presented to
the surrogate of the county of ...., for the.
appointment of ...., a guardian of the person
and estate of said minor, and that the said surrogate
has assigned the .... day of ...., at ten
o'clock, A.M., at his office in ...., as the time
and place of hearing the said matter.

(Signed),
.................., Petitioner.

To ...., mother, and
..................,
..................,
of said minor.

The subject as to who shall be appointed the guardian of an infant, is not to be lightly considered by the surrogate. Formerly, under the Revised Statutes, an order of preference was created, providing for the appointment : 1, of the mother ; 2, the grandfather on the father's side ; 3, the grandfather on the mother's side ; 4, either of the uncles on the father's side ; 5, either of the uncles on the mother's side ; 6, any one of the next of kin to the minor, who would be entitled to a distributive share in his personal estate, in case of his death. But in 1830, the sections were repealed, leaving to the surrogate a large discretion. The surrogate, therefore, acting as the chancellor formerly would do, will see that all the safeguards which the law has thrown around the infant, to prevent an injudicious appointment shall be regarded. (*White* v. *Pomeroy*, 7 Barb. Ch., 640.)

For it depends upon the guardian, whether the infant shall be trained for a station of honor and respectability, or whether he shall be surrounded by such influence, as to plunge him into profligacy and ruin.

The surrogate will, therefore, consult the interests of the infant, rather than even his wishes, or the wishes of those desiring the appointment. (*Bennett* v. *Byrne*, 2 Barb. Ch., 216.)

The requirements of the statute as to the notice

30

to be served only on such relatives as the surrogate shall think reasonable (§ 5, *sup.*), does not relieve the surrogate from the duty of making inquiry, for the purpose of ascertaining who are the relatives of the infant residing in the county, and of requiring notice to such, and so many of them as may be deemed reasonable, to secure the proper attention to the rights of the infant (*Underhill* v. *Dennis*, 9 Paige, 202), and if he omits to make the proper inquiries, or to cause the near relatives to be notified, the appointment may be set aside. (Id.)

The relatives are not summoned as parties, but to give information upon the matters to the surrogate. (*Kellinger* v. *Roe*, 7 Paige, 362; *Cozine* v. *Horn*, 1 Brad., 143.)

But while it is imperative that a day shall be assigned for the hearing, he may assign the day on which the petition is presented, if he shall determine that notice to the relatives need not be given. And where there is nothing to show that this course was not taken, it will be presumed that the surrogate assigned the day of the application for the hearing. (*Wilcox* v. *Wilcox*, 22 Barb., 178.)

If the surrogate shall be satisfied with the person nominated, and the bond required shall be filed (as to form of bond see p. 457, *ante*), an order will be entered for the appointment and letters will be issued accordingly.

ORDER FOR APPOINTMENT.

At a Surrogate's Court, held in the county
of ...., at the surrogate's office
in the ...... of ...., on the ......
day of ...., 1874.
Present — Hon. ...., Surrogate.

In the matter

of

..................., deceased.

A petition of ...., having been heretofore
presented to the surrogate, asking for the appointment
of ...., as guardian of the person and estate
of the above named minor, until he shall arrive at the
age of fourteen years, and until another guardian
shall be appointed, accompanied with the consent of
..................., to be so appointed, and it appearing
that certain relatives of said minor reside in said
county; now on reading and filing proof of the due
service of notice of the hearing in this matter, on such
relatives, and none of them appearing (or, and
..................., appearing, and the surrogate being satisfied of the propriety of the application), and the said
..................., having filed his bond to said minor
with a penalty, condition and sureties approved by the
surrogate: Ordered, that said .... be appointed the guardian of the person and estate of said
minor, until he shall arrive at the age of fourteen years,
and until another guardian shall be appointed and that
an appointment issue.

..................., *Surrogate.*

§ 6. (1 R. S., 137, amended chap. 341, Laws of 1870, and chap. 708, Laws of 1871.) The surrogate to whom application may be made under either of the preceding sections, shall have the same power to allow and appoint guardians, as is possessed by the Supreme Court, and may appoint a guardian for a minor whose father is living, upon a personal service of notice of the application for such appointment upon such father, at least ten days prior thereto, and in all cases he shall inquire into the circumstances of the minor, and ascertain the amount of his personal property, and the value of the rents and profits of his real estate, and for that purpose may compel any person to appear before him and testify in relation thereto.

§ 10. "Every guardian so appointed by a surrogate, shall have the same power as a testamentary guardian, and every person so appointed guardian of a minor, under the age of fourteen years, shall continue guardian of such minor, and shall be responsible as such, notwithstanding the said minor may arrive at the age of fourteen years, until another guardian be appointed, or such first guardian be discharged according to law."

But any minor who may have had a guardian appointed by the surrogate before he arrived at the age of fourteen years, may, on arriving at that age, petition the surrogate for the allowance of another guardian, and on proof of the facts, the surrogate will make a new appointment accordingly.

We may here remark again that, although guardians in socage and other guardians, are mentioned in the statutes and in the books upon the subject, there are virtually but two guardians, viz; guardians appointed by the will or deed of the father, and guardians appointed by the Supreme Court or the surrogate, and the powers and duties of each of them are the same.

The guardian is entitled to the custody and control of the person of his ward, to the same extent as a father, under the supervision of the court, and his duty is to attend to the proper care, nurture and education of his ward, in a manner suitable to his condition in life. He shall not permit him to remain in idleness, if able to earn his support by his own industry, if he do so permit him, he will not be allowed for his support in such idleness, but he will be allowed the expenditures necessary to educate him for future usefulness, and his support while so educating him. (*Clark* v. *Clark*, 8 Paige, 152.)

Though a father is liable for necessaries furnished to his child, without his consent, because he is bound to support him and is entitled to his services, yet a guardian is not so liable. (*Cole* v. *Ward*, 4 Watts & Serg., 118.)

In case the guardian abuse the power he has over the person of the ward, the court will interfere and remove him, if necessary.

In relation to the personal estate, the power of the guardian, and consequently his duty, extends only to the collection and investment of it in good, permanent securities, and the receipt and expenditure of the income for the necessary care, nurture, education and clothing of his ward ; and for the purpose of such collection, he may sell such personal property as he may think perishable, and for the interest of the minor. (*Field* v. *Shieffelin*, 7 Johns. Ch., 150.)

He may arbitrate for his ward. (*Weed* v. *Ellis*, 3 Caines, 253.) He may settle with executors for a legacy due to his ward and find him until an error be shown on accounting. (*Dakin* v. *Deming*, 6 Paige, 95.) He may assign a bond and mortgage belonging to his ward, without leave of the court. (*Tuttle* v. *Heavy*, 59 Barb., 334.) He may bring actions relative to the personal property of his ward. (*Thomas* v. *Bennett*, 56 Barb., 197.) He may collect money due to his ward and give discharge and receipt and receive payment of money secured by bond and mortgage before it is due and give a proper satisfaction piece. (*Chapman* v. *Tibbits*, 33 N. Y., 289.)

His power and duty in regard to the real estate,

is to lease it and receive the rents and profits thereof, and after paying the taxes and for the necessary repairs, to expend the surplus for his ward as above, when necessary, or invest it, and suffer it to accumulate for his benefit. (*Genet* v. *Tallmadge*, 1 Johns. Ch., 561.)

It is his duty to lease it, if possible, and if he willfully neglect to do so, or occupy it himself, he will be accountable for the fair value of the rents and profits. He can lease only for a period ending with the minority of his ward. (*Field* v. *Schiffelin*, 7 Johns., 154.)

A guardian occupying for a minor heir, whose ancestor's debts are not paid, and receiving rents, is not liable for rents applied to the maintenance of the heir prior to due notice or application from the ancestor's creditors. (*Thompson* v. *Brown*, 2 Johns. Ch., 619.)

He may maintain trespass for entry on his ward's land. (*Holmes* v. *Seeley*, 17 Wend., 75.)

The general guardian has no right to purchase his ward's real estate, even though a special guardian was appointed. The sale is not absolutely void, but voidable, and where the ward suffered eighteen years to elapse without impeaching the conveyance to the guardian, it was held that he waived the objection and affirmed the sale. (*Bostwick* v. *Atkins*, 3 N. Y., 53.)

If on foreclosure sale of his ward's land, the guardian purchase as such, the only effect is to merge and extinguish the mortgage. (*Low* v. *Purdy*, 2 Lans., 422.) But it seems that if he purchase with his own funds, he may stand as assignee of the mortgage. (Id.)

It is the duty of the general guardian to provide for the infant's support, maintainance and education, out of his estate, notwithstanding he has a father living, if the father is poor and unable to support him. For sums expended for that purpose he will be allowed on the settlement of his account. (*Clark* v. *Montgomery*, 23 Barb., 464.)

Guardians are not entitled to expend moneys derived from insurance on his ward's buildings in the rebuilding of them. (*Hazzard* v. *Rowe*, 11 Barb., 22 ; *Copley* v. *O'Neil*, 39 How., 41.)

He has no power to mortgage or sell the real estate, but may make, as guardian, an application to the Supreme Court (the infant if over fourteen years of age joining therein), that a special guardian be appointed to sell the real estate at any time it may become necessary for the support, etc., of his ward, or advisable for the reason that the same is unproductive in proportion to its value, or that it is depreciating in value ; and the court, if satisfied of the propriety or necessity of the sale, will allow it, and direct the least price at which it may be sold.

And whenever it shall appear to the Supreme Court, by due proof, or on the report of a referee appointed for the purpose, that any infant holds real estate in joint tenancy, or in common, or in any other manner which would authorize his being made a party to a suit in partition, and that the interest of such infant requires that partition of such estate should be made, such court may direct and authorize the general guardian of such infant to agree to a division thereof, or to a sale thereof, or of such a part of the said estate, as in the opinion of the court shall be incapable of division, or as shall be most for the interest of the infant, to be sold.

It is a sufficient ground for this last proceeding, that the real estate is held jointly or in common with adults, and that the value of the estate is small in comparison with the expenses of a partition suit, to which it must otherwise be subjected.

These proceedings are specially and fully treated in Crary's Treatise on Special Proceedings, and in Barbour's Chancery Practice, which see.

§ 20. (2 R. S., 152.) Every guardian in socage, and every general guardian, whether testamentary or appointed, shall safely keep the things that he may have in his custody, belonging to his ward and the inheritance (the real estate) of his ward, and shall not make or suffer any waste, sale or destruction of such things, or such inheritance, but shall keep up and sustain the houses, gardens and other appurtenances to the lands of his ward, by and with the issues and profits thereof, or with such other moneys belonging to his ward as shall be in his hands, and shall deliver the same to his ward, when he comes to his full age, in as good order and condition, at least, as such guardian received the same, inevitable decay and injury only excepted; and he shall answer to his ward for the issues and profits of real estate received by him, by a lawful account.

§ 21. If any guardian shall make or suffer any waste, sale or destruction of the inheritance of his ward, he shall lose the custody of the same, and of such ward, and shall forfeit to the ward thrice the sum at which the damages shall be taxed by the jury.

But the guardian shall not be held to repair from his own moneys, where the income of the estate of his ward is insufficient, although such insufficiency is a good ground for an application to the Supreme Court for a sale.

The relation of the guardian to his ward is one of confidence, and the guardian can not in any way derive benefit from the funds or property of the ward, beyond his fees. If he compromise a claim against his ward, or purchase a debt against him at a discount, it will be for the benefit of his ward only. (2 Kent's Com., 229.) He cannot substitute himself for his ward in any beneficial transaction, although if he do so put himself in place of his ward, and a loss accrue, he himself will have to bear it.

If he purchase land in a sale where his ward is interested, and take the conveyance to himself, his ward, on coming of age, may, if he elect, claim the benefit of the purchase. If he settle a debt due to his ward and take a promissory note, running to himself, he will be held accountable for it, whether it be collected or not; otherwise, if he take the note to himself as guardian.

If the guardian use the moneys of his ward in trade, the ward may elect, on coming of age, to take either the profits of the trade, or his money, with compound interest, to meet the profits. If he neglect to invest the money of his ward after a reasonable time (and he is usually allowed six months), he must pay interest, and in case of gross neglect he will be charged compound interest.

The proper rate of interest is six *per cent* with annual rests, adding to the principal at each rest. (*King* v. *Talbot*, 40 N. Y., 76; see also 2 Wend., 77; 8 Barb., 48.)

He may not employ an agent or attorney, at the expense of his ward, to do those acts which he ought to do himself, such as the collection of rents, &c. ; his commissions are for such services. If he have his ward in his own family, he will be allowed a reasonable sum for his board, if the ward does not earn enough to remunerate him. (*Rait* v. *Rait*, 1 Brad., 345.)

But a guardian, being the father, supporting his child and ward according to his own means and station in life, cannot be allowed for such support. (*Matter of Kane*, 2 Barb. Ch., 375.)

A guardian may not expend the capital of his ward, but only the income, except under the direction of the Supreme Court, which will, upon the petition of the guardian, if considered necessary and advisable for the interest of the minor, authorize the guardian to expend so much as may be directed, in support and education, especially education, wisely considering this in the highest degree important.

A guardian, however, acting within the scope of his powers, like an executor or administrator, is bound only to fidelity and ordinary diligence and prudence in the execution of his trust, and his acts, in the absence of fraud, will be liberally construed. (*White* v. *Parker*, 8 Barb., 48.)

A guardian appointed in another state, can not receive of an executor or administrator in this state, a legacy or distributive share to his ward; but, to acquire the right, he must be appointed in this state and give the proper security. And a guardian appointed in this state, has no power over the real estate of his ward situated in another state.

Their rights and powers are strictly local and cannot be exercised in other states. (*Morrill* v. *Dickey*, 1 Johns. Ch., 156 ; Story Conf. Laws, 414.) Nor have they any authority over the real property of their wards, situate in other countries ; for such property is governed by law *rei sitœ*. (Story Ibid., 414, 417.)

We have already seen, that a legacy to a minor, of fifty dollars or under, may be paid to his father, for the use and benefit of such minor; but when the legacy exceeds that sum, the same may be paid, under the direction of the surrogate, to the general guardian, who must first give security to the minor, to be approved by the surrogate, for the faithful application of such legacy ; and this security is additional to that previously given on the appointment, unless that so previously given, was estimated especially in view of the legacy.

When a distributive share is to be paid to a minor, the surrogate may direct that it be paid into court, and invested under his orders; or he may direct that it be paid to the general guardian. A general guardian has the same powers in relation to the collection of a legacy or distributive share by actions or proceedings before the surrogate, that his ward would have if of full age.

CHAPTER XXII.

Accounts of Guardians. How Compelled to Account, and how Removed, or Relieved of their Trust.

Guardians appointed by deed, or by the Supreme Court, are subject to the jurisdiction of that court, and may account personally to their ward, on their coming of age, or may be compelled to do so by the court. The court on petition, or after action brought, will appoint a referee to take and state the account, and will compel the attendance of witnesses, and on the coming in of the report will confirm or modify it, according to the facts.

But the Surrogate's Court has no jurisdiction of that class of guardians, but guardians appointed by the surrogate must account annually to him, and he must supervise their accounts.

§ 57. (S. L., 1837.) Every general guardian appointed by the surrogate, shall, annually, after such appointment, so long as any part of the estate or the income or proceeds thereof remain in his hands or under his control, file in the office of the surrogate appointing him, an inventory and account, under oath, of his guardianship, and of the amount of property received by him and remaining in his hands, or invested by him, and the manner and nature of such investment, and his receipts and expenditures, in the form of debtor and creditor.

GUARDIANS' ANNUAL ACCOUNT, ETC., AND INVENTORY.

Inventory.

Surrogate's Court, Rensselaer county :

```
In the matter
      of
A ...... :.B........., a minor.
```

A just and true inventory of the estate and effects of the above named minor on the first day of April, 1862:

Cash received of C D, executor,
    etc., of C D, deceased,.............. $350 00
1861.   Dr.
John La Fountain, bond and
    mortgage, $200, interest one
    year, $14, ... 214 00
R. Thompson, bond and mort-
    gage, $300, interest six months
    $10.50, ... 310 50
Ten shares Central Rail Road
    stock par value $1000, actually
    worth,   830 00
House and lot No. 164 Fulton
    street, Troy, valued at,............. 800 00
Farm in Sand Lake valued at, 2,000 00
                           ——— $4,504 50

ACCOUNT.

J K, Guardian, in Account with A B, a Minor.

1861.   DR.

April 1, To interest on La Fountain mortgage,........... $14 00

Oct. 1, To interest on Thompson
mortgage,................. 21 00

1862.

Feb. 1, To dividend Central Rail
Road, 3 per cent,........ 30 00

To 3 quarters' rent house
164 Fourth street,...... 180 00

March 1, To 1 year's rent farm,
in Sand Lake, ... 200 00
                                                                ———— $445 00

CONTRA.

1861.   CR.

April 10, By board paid J H, 26
weeks at $2, ... $52 00

July 1, By clothing purchased of
J N, ... 10 00

9, By hats purchased of
G F, ... 50

Oct. 1, By board paid J H,
26 weeks, ... 52 00

10, By clothing of J N,...... 15 00

Oct. 1, By repairs No. 164
Fourth street,........... 8 50

1862.

Feb. 10, By taxes 164 Fourth
street, ... 11 00

By taxes farm in Sand
Lake,....................... 22 00

31

April 1, By interest on $350, un-
invested 6 months,.....   12 25
Commission for receiv-
ing income 2½ per cent
on $445, ...   11 12
Commission on paying
out income 2½ per cent
on 195.37,..................   3 87
Balance due estate,........   234 64
──────
$445 00

Rensselaer county, ss :

J K, of the city of Troy, being duly sworn, says
that the above is a just and true inventory of the whole
real and personal estate and effects of the above named
minor, so far as the same have come to his knowledge,
and a just and true account of his guardianship, and
of the amount of property received by and remaining
in his hands, invested by him on account of the said
minor, and of the manner and nature of such investment, and also his expenditures on account of the said
minor and his estate (since his last annual account to
this court).   J K.

Sworn before me, this 2d }
    day of April, 1862.   }
                        M W, *Surrogate.*

§ 58. (S. L., 1837, chap. 460.) Every surrogate
shall annex to, and deliver with each appointment
of a general guardian made by him, a copy of the
preceding section (in relation to filing annual accounts), and shall file in his office all accounts and
inventories before mentioned ; and in the month

of February in each year, shall examine all such accounts and inventories as shall have been filed in his office for the preceding year.

§ 60. (S. L., 1837, ch. 460.) If, on such examination, the surrogate shall be satisfied in any case, that the interest of the ward requires that a more full and satisfactory account should be given, or that such guardian should be removed, or in case any guardian shall neglect to file such inventory and account for three months after the same should have been filed, such surrogate shall proceed against such guardian (and cite him to show cause why he should not be removed). But such surrogate may discontinue such proceedings, or such guardian filing in his office an account and inventory satisfactory to said surrogate, and on payment of all costs which may have accrued in consequence of such neglect.

§ 11. (2 R. S., 152.) Any guardian appointed by any surrogate, may be cited to account before the surrogate who appointed him in the same manner as administrators, upon the application of any ward, or any relative of such ward, and, on good cause being shown, may be compelled to account in the same manner as an administrator. And, upon a wards arriving at full age, he shall be entitled to compel such account without showing any cause. (*Seaman* v. *Duryea*, 11 N. Y., 324.)

§ 12. Every guardian of a ward who shall have arrived at full age, and every guardian who shall be superseded in his trust by another guardian, may apply to the surrogate who appointed him, for a citation to his ward, or to such new guardian, to attend the settlement of his accounts; which citation shall be issued by such surrogate, and be served in the manner and at the time herein directed (fourteen days, personally) in the case of proceedings for the removal of a guardian.

The petition made by the guardian, should state the jurisdictional facts; the appointment by the surrogate and the arrival of the ward at full age, or the superseding of the guardian, and pray that proceedings be had for the settlement of his accounts.

Instead of procuring a citation in these cases, the parties may voluntarily appear before the surrogate, and proceedings will be had the same as on the return of the citation.

The form of the account differs so little from the account filed by an executor or administrator on final settlement (see *ante*), that it is not deemed necessary here to present one. The proceedings, in all respects, except the mere matter of form, resemble the proceedings of a final settlement.

The guardian should file his account in full; which should give dates and names of parties to whom payments may have been made, and should charge the guardian with the whole of the personal property received by him, and with all interest received or for which he is liable, for funds uninvested after six months from the receipt of such funds. It should also contain the reasonable expenses of the guardian, which are regulated by the same rule as the allowance for expenses of executors and administrators and his commissions.

It was held in *Morgan* v. *Morgan* (39 Barb.), that a guardian performing services outside of his official duties, for the benefit of his ward, as where he personally made repairs on the real estate, bestowing his personal labor, was entitled, on settlement, to a fair allowance for such services.

But in *Morgan* v. *Hamas* (49 N. Y., 667), the rigid rule as to executors and administrators, that however beneficial their services to the estate; however onerous the trust, they could be allowed only commissions. The case then of *Matter of the Bank of Niagara* (6 Paige, 213), must be considered as overruled.

The commissions for receiving and paying out moneys, are the same as allowed to executors, to wit : five per cent on all sums up to one thousand dollars ; two and a half per cent on sums above one thousand dollars, up to ten thousand dollars, and one per cent on all sums above ten thousand dollars.

And in making his annual account, as well as on settlement, the guardian may charge five per cent or two and a half per cent, as the sums may demand, on his receipts and disbursements for each year.

But an investment, or reinvestment of the fund from time to time, is not such a paying out of the trust fund as entitles the guardian to commissions for paying out the same; nor is he entitled to charge a commission for collecting or receiving back of the principal of the fund which he has so invested. (*Matter of Kellogg*, 7 Paige, 265.)

He should also file all vouchers received by him, and verify the whole by his oath; and the accounting will be conducted, in all respects, like an accounting by executors or administrators, and may be contested in the same manner.

When the proofs are all in, the surrogate will make a decretal order settling the accounts of the guardian and directing the payment of any remainder in the hands of the guardian, to the ward. This decree can readily be formed from the decree on final settlement of the accounts of an executor. (*Ante*, p. 340.)

Should the decree be against the guardian, a certificate thereof may be filed in the clerk's office so as to make it a lien against his real estate, and an execution may be issued thereon. The payment may likewise be enforced by attachment as in the case of an executor, or after return of execution unsatisfied, by suit upon the bond of the guardian.

The decree may be discharged in the same manner as a decree against an executor or administrator. (For form see *ante*, p. 366.)

§ 13. Appeals from the final order of the surrogate on the settlement of a guardian's account, may be made to the Supreme Court, in the same manner and time (three months), and with the same effect as in case of administrators.

The *guardian*, whether appointed by the surrogate or *by will, may be removed.*

§ 14. (2 R. S., 153, as amended 1873.) On the application of any ward, or of any relative in his behalf, or of the surety of a guardian, to the surrogate who appointed any guardian, or to the surrogate before whom any last will and testament containing an appointment of a guardian, shall be, or shall have been proved, complaining of the incompetency of such guardian, or his wasting the real or personal estate of his ward, or of any misconduct in relation to his duties as guardian ; (or, by § 45, chap. 460, Laws of 1837 ; that the guardian has removed, or is about to remove from the state), the surrogate, upon being satisfied by proof of the probable truth of such complaint, shall issue a citation to such guardian, to appear before him at the day and place therein specified, to show cause why he should not be removed from his guardianship.

PETITION TO REMOVE A GUARDIAN.

To the Surrogate of the county of .... :

The petition of .... of the ...., of ...., respectfully shows :

That on or about the ...... day of ...., 187.., one .... was duly appointed by the surrogate of said county, the guardian of the person and estate of ...., a minor; that the said .... entered upon his trust and assumed control of the person and estate of said minor.

And your petitioner further shows that since his appointment, as aforesaid, the said .... has become incompetent and an unsuitable person to perform the duties of such guardian, by reason of habitual intemperance in the use of alcoholic liquors (or, that the said .... has wasted and continues to waste, and misapply the estate of said minors, or other cause); that your petitioner is one of the sureties of said .... as such guardian (or, a relative of said minor) ....

Your petitioner, therefore, prays that an examination may be had in the premises, and that a citation issue to the said .... to the end that he may be removed as such guardian and his appointment revoked.

Dated, this ...... day of ...., 1872.

(Signed), ...

Rensselaer county, ss :

..................., being duly sworn, says that he has read the petition by him subscribed and that the same is true of his own knowledge except as to the matters which are therein stated on information and belief and as to those matters he believes it to be true.

(Signed), ...

Sworn before me this 25th }
   December, 1874.   }

...................,
Notary Public.

ORDER FOR CITATION THEREON.

At a Surrogate's Court, held in the county of ...., at the surrogate's office in the ...... of ...., on the .... day of ...., 1874.
Present—Hon. ...., Surrogate.

In the matter of the person and estate
of
..................., a minor,

On reading and filing the petition of ....,
one of the sureties of ...., the guardian of the person and estate of the above named minor, setting forth, that the said .... has become incompetent by reason of intemperance and praying for his removal (or, that the said .... has removed or is about to remove from this state).

Ordered that a citation issue to the said ....,
requiring him to appear in this court to show cause
why he should not be removed from his guardianship.
.................., *Surrogate.*

The insolvency of the guardian, or one of his
sureties, is cause for removal. (*Matter of Cooper*, 2
Paige, 34.)

Gross intemperance of the guardian, is also good
cause. (*Kettletas* v. *Gardner*, 1 Paige 488.) The
guardian was removed for misconduct, in having
trusted his ward's money to his brother-in-law, on
personal security. (*Matter of Mary O'Neil*, 1 Tucker,
34.)

§ 15. Such citation shall be served personally on
the guardian to whom it may be directed, at least
fourteen days before the return thereof; or if such
guardian shall have absconded or concealed himself, so that such citation cannot be personally
served, it may be served by leaving a copy thereof
at the last place of residence of such guardian (or
if the guardian has removed from the state, the
citation may be served by publishing the same in
the state paper for four weeks). (S. L., 1837, ch.
460, § 47.)

§ 16. The surrogate, at the day appointed for
showing cause, and on such other days as he shall
appoint, shall proceed to inquire into the alleged

complaint, and shall grant subpœnas to compel the attendance of witnesses to any person applying; and if satisfied of the incompetency or misconduct of such guardian (or that he has removed or is about to remove from this state), he may, by an order to be duly entered in his minutes, remove the said guardian from his trust.

ORDER FOR REVOCATION.

At a Surrogate's Court, held in the county of ...., at the surrogate's office in .... of ...., on the ...... day of ...., 1874.

Present — Hon. ...., Surrogate.

In the matter of the person and estate

of

..................., deceased.

On filing the citation heretofore issued in this matter, returnable this day, with proof of the due service thereof on .... the guardian of the above named minor, and the said .... not appearing (or, the said .... having appeared), and the surrogate being satisfied, after hearing the proofs and allegations of the parties of the truth of the matters stated in the position of .... in this matter, It is ordered that the said .... be removed from the office of guardian of the person and estate of said minor, and that his appointment heretofore made be revoked.

.... , *Surrogate.*

§ 17. Upon such removal being made, the surrogate may proceed and appoint a new guardian, in the same manner as if no guardian had been appointed.

An appeal may be had from any order removing a guardian, or appointing one, or refusing to make a removal, within six months from the making of such order, but no appeal will affect such order until the same be reversed.

So, if a guardian on being ordered to give new sureties, fail to do so, he may be removed.

§ 46. (S. L., 1837, ch. 460.) Whenever it shall be made to appear to any surrogate that the sureties of any guardian are becoming insolvent, that they have removed or are about to remove from the state, or that for any other cause they are insufficient, and he shall be satisfied that the matter requires investigation, he shall issue a citation to such guardian, requiring him to appear before such surrogate at the time and place therein to be specified, to show cause why he should not give further sureties, or be removed from his guardianship ; which citation shall be served in the same manner as the citation mentioned in the last preceding section (personally fourteen days, or by leaving at his place of residence) is required by that section to be served.

PETITION THAT GUARDIAN GIVE NEW SURETIES

To the Surrogate of the county of .... :

The petition of .... of the town of .... respectfully shows :

That your petitioner is a relative of ...., a minor, of said .... of ....: That on or about the ...... day of ...., 1869, one .... was appointed by this court the guardian of the person and estate of said minor, and on such appointment ...., and .... united with said .... as sureties in his bond filed in this court to said minor. That your petitioner is informed and believes that ...., one of said sureties, is becoming, or has become insolvent, as your petitioner is informed and verily believes (or has removed, or is about to remove from this state ; or, that the said sureties are insufficient, for the reason that the estate of said minor has increased very much in value since appointment of such guardian). Your petitioner, therefore, prays that your honor will investigate the matter to the end that the said .... should give further sureties, or be removed from his guardianship.

Dated, this ...... day of ...., 1870.

(Signed), ...

.... county, ss :

................., being duly sworn, says that the foregoing petition by him subscribed is true.

(Signed), ...

Sworn before me this ...... }
    day of ...., 1874. }

....

Clerk of Surrogate's Court.

ORDER FOR CITATION TO GIVE FURTHER SURE-
TIES, ETC.

> At a Surrogate's Court, held in the county
> of ...., at the surrogate's office
> in the .... of ...., on the ......
> day of ...., 1874.
> Present — Hon. ...., Surrogate.

In the matter of the person and
estate

of

..................., a minor.

On reading and filing the petition of ....,
in behalf of said minor, setting forth that ....,
one of the sureties of ...., the guardian of
said minor, is about to remove from this state : Ordered
that a citation issue to the said ...., requiring
him to appear in this court, to show cause why he
should not give further sureties, or be removed from
his guardianship.

................., *Surrogate.*

§ 47. On the return of the citation, or at such
other time as the surrogate shall appoint, he shall
proceed to hear the proofs and allegations, and if
it shall satisfactorily appear that the sureties are
for any cause insufficient, the surrogate may make
an order requiring such guardian to give further
sureties, in the usual form, within a reasonable
time, to be prescribed by the surrogate.

ORDER FOR ADDITIONAL SURETIES.

At a Surrogate's Court, held in the county of
..................., at the surrogate's office,
in the ...... of ...., on the ......
day of ...., 1874.
Present—Hon. ...., Surrogate.

In the matter of the person and
estate

of

...., a minor.

On the return of the citation issued to ....,
the guardian of the person and estate of said minor,
with due proof of the service thereof on said ....,
and the said ...., having appeared, and it
appearing that ...., one of his sureties has
removed from this state: Ordered, that said ....
give further sureties, approved by the surrogate, in a
bond in a penalty of $................. , to said minor
within .... days from this date.

................., *Surrogate.*

§ 48. If such guardian neglect to give further
sureties to the satisfaction of the surrogate within
the time prescribed, the surrogate may, by an order
to be duly entered in his minutes, remove such
guardian from his trust.

ORDER REMOVING GUARDIAN, FOR NEGLECT TO GIVE SURETIES.

At a Surrogate's Court, held in the county of ...., at the surrogate's office in the ...... of ...., on the ...... day of ......, 1874.

Present — Hon. ...., Surrogate.

In the matter of the person and

estate

of

.................., a minor.

An order having been heretofore made in this matter on the ...... day of ...., requiring ...., the guardian of the person and estate of said minor to give further sureties within .... days from that day; now on reading due proof of the service of said order on the said ...., on the .... day of ...., 1872, and the said ...., having neglected to give such further sureties :

Ordered, that said ...., be removed from his trust as such guardian, and that a revocation issue under the seal of this court, of the letters heretofore granted to him.

.................., *Surrogate.*

Any person interested may appeal from any order in these proceedings, within six months from the making of the order, and the guardian so removed may be required to account immediately, on the application of the new guardian, the ward, or any relative of the ward.

CHAPTER XXIII.

RESIGNATION OF GUARDIAN.

As the Court of Chancery, in the exercise of its supervisory power over guardians, permitted them, when they become incapacitated to discharge their duties, or to resign when the interests of their ward required it; so the statute permits the surrogate to accept the resignation of a guardian.

§ 51. (Chap. 460, Laws of 1831.) A guardian may apply to the surrogate by whom he was appointed, for liberty to resign his trust, setting forth the reasons why the application is made, verifying the same by his own oath, or otherwise.

He may show for such cause, his physical disability, arising from age or illness, his removal, actual or contemplated, to a distance from where the property of his ward is situated ; the marriage of his ward, if a female, or any other cause which would render it for the interest of the infant that he should resign.

32

PETITION OF GUARDIAN TO BE ALLOWED TO RESIGN.

To the Surrogate of the county of .... :

The petition of ...., of the ....
of ...., respectfully shows :

That heretofore your petitioner was, on the ....
day of ...., 1868, duly appointed by the surrogate
of said county, the guardian of the person and estate
of ...., a minor, and has, as your petitioner
verily believes, conducted himself honestly in the execution of his trust.　That ...., and ....,
are the next of kin of said minor, residing in this
county above the age of fourteen years.

That your petitioner is desirous of resigning his
trust as such guardian, for the reason that he has removed from this state (or is about to remove, or,
other cause), and he prays that he may be permitted to
render an account of his proceedings as such guardian,
to the end that a successor may be appointed and your
petitioner may be relieved therefrom.

Dated, this ...... day of ...., 1874.

(Signed),　..................

.... county, ss :

.................., being duly sworn says that the foregoing petition by him subscribed is true.

(Signed),　..............

Sworn before me, this ...... day ⎤
　of.................., 1874.　⎦

§ 52. (S. L., 1837, chap. 460.) Such surrogate,
in his discretion, may thereupon issue a citation to

the ward, requiring him to appear at a time and
place to be therein mentioned, and show cause why
the guardian should not be at liberty to resign his
trust. The citation shall be served by delivering
a copy to the ward, at least ten days before the
return day thereof. Notice of the proceedings
shall also be given to the next of kin of the ward,
if there be any of the age of discretion, in the
county of the surrogate.

ORDER FOR CITATION THEREON.

At a Surrogate's Court, held in the county of
...., at the surrogate's office
in the .... of ...., on the
...... day of ...., 1874.
Present — Hon. ...., Surrogate.

In the matter of the person and
estate
of
..................., a minor.

..................., the guardian of the person and estate
of the above named minor, having presented his petition to the surrogate, setting forth that he has conducted himself honestly in the execution of his trust,
but has removed from this state : Ordered that a citation issue to said minor, and to his next of kin residing in this county, requiring them to appear and
show cause why said .... should not be at
liberty to resign his trust.
...., *Surrogate.*

§ 53. On the return of the citation, and proof of the service of the notice, the surrogate shall appoint some discreet and competent person to appear and attend to the interests of the ward in the premises, who shall consent in writing to such appointment. Any other person, who shall be desirous to do so, may also appear on behalf of the ward.

The appointment of some discreet and competent person to attend to the interests of the ward, is the appointment of a special guardian, the order for whose appointment, and whose consent, will be identical with those papers on the proof of a will, and may be found *ante.*

§ 54. The guardian shall then proceed to render to the surrogate a full, just and true account in writing, of all his receipts and payments on account of the ward, and of all books, papers, moneys, choses in action and other property of the ward, which may be in the hands or under the control of the guardian, and shall verify the same by his own oath, and such other evidence as shall be satisfactory to the surrogate.

The account rendered in this proceeding, differs in no respect from the same rendered upon the arrival of the minor at full age, and the remarks heretofore made upon the latter apply with no less force to the one at present under consideration. The form to be used can readily be adopted from the account of an executor or administrator on final settlement.

§ 55. " If the surrogate shall be satisfied that the guardian has, in all respects, conducted himself honestly in the execution of his trust; that he has rendered a just, true and full acccount, and that the interest of the ward would not be prejudiced by allowing the guardian to resign his trust, he may thereupon proceed, in the mode prescribed by law, to appoint a new guardian for such ward, and order that the former guardian deliver over all the books, papers, moneys, choses in action, or other property of the ward, to such new guardian, and take duplicate receipts for the same.

The proceedings upon the appointment of the new guardian will be identical with those already treated of. If the minor is under fourteen years of age, the appointment will be on the application of some relatives and on notice. If the minor be fourteen years of age or upwards, the appointment will be on the petition of the minor. The order for delivery to the new guardian may be in the following form.

ORDER FOR DELIVERY OF ASSETS TO NEW GUARDIAN.

At a Surrogate's Court, held in the county of
.............., at the surrogate's office in
the city of ...., on the ....
day of ...., 1872.

Present—Hon. ...., Surrogate.

> In the matter of the person and
> estate
> of
> ...., a minor.

It appearing to the satisfaction of the surrogate,
that ...., guardian of the above named minor,
has in all respects, conducted himself honestly in the
execution of his trust; that he has rendered a full,
just and true account, and that the interests of the
said minor would not be prejudiced by allowing the
guardian to resign his trust, and .... having
been duly appointed guardian of said minor in place
of said .... :

Ordered that said ...., who has accounted,
deliver over all the books, papers, money, choses in
action, or other property of said minor, appearing in
his hands by his said account to the said ....,
and that he take duplicate receipts for the same.

................, *Surrogate.*

§ 56. On delivering one of the said receipts to
the surrogate, to be filed in his office, the surrogate

may enter an order that the former guardian, on his own application, has been permitted to resign his trust, and that he is thereupon discharged from any further custody or care of the ward or of his estate. But nothing therein contained shall preclude the ward or his new guardian from having a further account from such former guardian, in relation to all matters connected with his trust, before he was permitted to resign the same; and in relation to all such matters, the sureties of the former guardian shall remain liable in the same manner and to the same extent as though such order had not been made.

ORDER PERMITTING GUARDIAN TO RESIGN.

At a Surrogate's Court, held in the county of ...., at the surrogate's office in the ...... of ...., on the ...... day of ...., 1874.
Present, Hon. ...., Surrogate.

In the matter of the person and estate of ...., a minor.

..................., guardian of the above named minor, having heretofore petitioned this court to be allowed to resign his trust, and the said minor having been cited, and such further proceedings having been had that the said .... rendered his account as such guardian, and A B having been appointed guardian of said minor in place of said ...., and the said .... having, according to the order of this court, delivered over to the said A B all the books, papers, moneys, choses in action or other property of said minor, and having filed in this court one of the receipts taken therefor :

Ordered that the said ...., on his own application has been, and is, permitted to resign his trust as guardian for the said minor, and he is discharged from any further custody or care of said minor, or of his estate.

................., *Surrogate.*

CHAPTER XXIV.

Dower of Widow, and how Admeasured.

Dower, is the estate which the widow of a deceased person takes in the lands of her husband, being a life estate in one-third of the lands whereof he was seized of an estate of inheritance at any time during the marriage. (1 R. S., 740.)

And a widow can be barred of her dower, only by her own act, as by uniting with her husband, in conveying the land, by ante-nuptial settlement; by acceptance of a devise or bequest, in lieu of dower, or by conjugal unfaithfulness; but to make this last effectual, a divorce, must be derceed against her for adultery, in the life time of her husband. (1 R. S., 741.)

And the widow of an alien entitled to hold real estate, if she be an inhabitant of this state at the time of his death, is entitled to dower in the same manner as if such alien had been a native citizen. (§ 9.) Also any woman, being an alien, who has heretofore married, or who may hereafter marry a citizen of the United States, shall be entitled to dower, within this state, to the same extent as if a citizen of the United States. (S. L., 1845, ch. 115.)

The general rule given by the statute above quoted, is, however, subject to some restrictions. Thus, if a husband exchanges lands, the wife not uniting in the conveyance completing the exchange, she shall not be entitled to dower in both, but shall make her election; and if she shall not commence proceedings to recover her dower in the lands given in exchange, within one year after the death of her husband, she shall be deemed to have elected to take her dower in the lands received in exchange. (1 R. S., 740; 7 Barb., 633; 12 Barb., 537.) And where a person mortgages his lands before his marriage, his widow shall not be entitled to dower, as against the mortgagee, or those claiming under him, but shall be entitled to dower as against every other person.

When a husband alone executes a mortgage for purchase money, his widow will not be entitled to dower, as against the mortgagee or those claiming under him, but shall be entitled, as against all other persons; and if the lands so mortgaged be sold under such mortgage, the widow will be entitled to dower in any surplus remaining after payment of the mortgage, and the costs and expenses of sale, and shall be entitled to the interest or income of one third of such surplus, during her life.

A wife may cut off her incohate dower, by uniting in the conveyance of land with her husband during the marriage, or, before her marriage, by consenting to receive a settlement, either in lands or money, as a jointure or provision in lieu of dower. If such settlement be made without her assent, or a testamentary provision be made to her, in lieu of dower, she shall have one year after the death of her husband to elect whether she will take the settlement, or the provision of the will, or her dower in the lands; and if she do not commence proceedings for the recovery of her dower in the lands within one year, she will be deemed to have accepted the settlement, or the testamentary provision in lieu thereof. (1 R. S., 742.)

A petition filed by a widow, for admeasurement of dower, is not the commencement of proceedings for the recovery of dower, as contemplated by the statute, and is not evidence of the election of a widow to take dower instead of a testamentary provision. Nor is a letter to the executors, that she rejected the provisions of the will, and that she did thereby " elect to claim dower," such an election. (*John Walton's estate*, 1 Tuck., 10.)

Where a widow is entitled to dower in her husband's lands, and is not bound to elect whether to take a settlement or testamentary provision in lieu thereof, within one year after her husband's death, she may demand her dower at any time within twenty years after such death ; but, if at the time of such death, she be under the age of twenty-one years, or insane, or imprisoned on a criminal charge or conviction, the time during which such disability continues shall not form any part of the said term of twenty years.   And in case of recovery of her dower, shall be entitled to receive damages for withholding it, to the extent of one-third part of the annual value of the mesne profits of the land for not exceeding six years.   (1 R. S., 742.)

A widow may bequeath the crop in the ground of the land holden by her in dower (§ 25, 743), and in default of any testamentary disposition, it would go to her administrator.

The dower interest of a widow may be ascertained and admeasured, either by an action in the Supreme Court, or by special proceedings upon the petition of a widow, or heirs or persons claiming under them, to the Supreme Court; or to the County Court of the county where the lands are situated, or to the surrogate of the same county. When the lands are situated in the city of New York, the proceedings may be had in the Court of Common Pleas of that city, and in the city of Buffalo, in the Superior Court, when the premises are situated in that city.

Under the former practice, a bill in equity could be filed in the Court of Chancery, seeking as relief, the admeasurement of dower and the adjudication of the title to it, and an action could undoubtedly be maintained in our Supreme Court, seeking the same relief.

But we think that it is judicious in all cases, to apply for admeasurement of dower, when the extent of the dower only is questioned. When the right to the dower is to be litigated, an admeasurement before ejectment brought, simplifies the proceedings, and confines them to the single issue of the title.

When admeasurement is sought, Surrogate's Court is to be preferred, where all the lands in which dower is demanded, lie in one county, from the fact the court is always open and notice may be given for any day. Where, however, the lands lie in different counties, and dower is demanded in all, the proceedings must be had in the Supreme Court.

The statutory provisions are as follows:

§ 1. (2 R. S., 488; 3 R. S., 5th ed., 791.) "Any widow who shall not have her dower assigned to her within forty days after the decease of her husband, may apply for admeasurement of her dower (to the courts specified above), specifying therein the lands to which she claims dower."

She may apply by petition, notwithstanding a partition suit has been commenced of the premises, to which suit she is a party. Her title, after admeasurement, is superior to that of the heirs of her deceased husband; and if she can secure admeasurement before decree of sale, she is entitled to the fruits of her diligence, and after admeasurement, she may enjoy it and it will not be affected by a decree of sale. (*In re Achsah Sipperly*, 44 Barb., 370.)

§ 2. "A copy of such petition, with notice of the time and place when it will be presented, shall be served at least twenty days previous to its presentation, upon the heirs of her husband; or, if they are not the owners of the lands subject to dower, then upon the owners of such lands claiming a freehold estate therein, or their guardians, where such heirs or owners are minors.

PETITION FOR DOWER, BY WIDOW.

To the Surrogate of the county of Rensselaer:

The petition of M B, of the town of Schodack, in the county of Rensselaer, respectfully shows: That she is the widow of A B, late of said town, deceased; that she was lawfully married to said A B, in his life time, and lived with him as his wife until his death, on the 15th day of June, 1860; that the said A B, at the time of his decease, was seized of an estate of inheritance of and in the following lands and premises, situated in the said town of Schodack, bounded and described as follows : On the north by lands of Barent Van Hoesen, east by lands of said Van Hoesen and Joseph Hare, south by lands of Joseph Hare, and west by lands of James Van Voorhies, containing one hundred acres, be the same more or less.

Your petitioner further shows : That A B, and C B, children and heirs of said A B, deceased, claim to own said premises, and your petitioner verily believes that they are the owners thereof, subject to your petitioner's right of dower.

Your petitioner therefore prays that an order be made for the admeasurement of her dower in said lands and premises and that three reputable freeholders may be appointed for the purpose of making such admeasurement. And she shows that A B, the said child and heir of said A B, deceased, is a minor under the age of twenty-one years and over fourteen years old, and having no general guardian.

Dated Schodack, April 1, 1862.

M B.

 E S S,
  Attorney for Relator.

Rensselaer county, ss :

M B, the petitioner above named, being duly sworn, says that the foregoing petition, by her subscribed, is true of her own knowledge, except as to the matters which are therein stated on information and belief; and as to those matters, she believes it to be true.

M B.

Sworn before me, this 1st day   ⎫
 day of April, 1862.   ⎬

    M R,
   Justice of the Peace.

NOTICE TO HEIRS OR OWNERS.

To C B, and A B, heirs-at-law of A B, late of the town ·of Schodack, deceased, and all others claiming a freehold in the lands described in the annexed petition.

Take notice, that a petition, of which the annexed is a copy, will be presented to Moses Warren, Esq., surrogate of the county of Rensselaer, at his office in the city of Troy, on the 25th day of April, 1862, at ten o'clock in the forenoon of that day, and that a motion will be then made that the prayer of the petition be granted.

Dated, April 3, 1862.

M B.

E S S,
Attorney for Petitioner.

§ 3. " Such notice may be served personally, on any party of full age ; or upon the guardians of minors ; or by leaving the same with any person of proper age, at the last residence of such party or guardian, in case of his temporary absence ; and if any such heir or owner be a resident out of this state, the service of such notice may be upon the tenant in actual occupation of the lands, or if there be no tenant, by publishing the same, for three weeks successively, in some newspaper printed in the county where such lands are situated.

§ 4. Where such heirs or owners are minors and have no general guardians (within this state), the court or surrogate, on application of the widow, shall appoint some discreet and substantial freeholder a guardian of such infants, for the sole purpose of appearing for and taking care of the interests of such infants in the proceedings, and the notice of application, and all notices in the subsequent proceedings shall be served on the guardian so appointed, whether the infant reside in the state or not.

ORDER APPOINTING GUARDIAN FOR MINORS.

At a Surrogate's Court, held in the county of ...., at the surrogate's office, in the .... of ...., on the ...... day of ...., 1874.

Present—Hon. ...., Surrogate.

In the matter of the dower
of
...., a widow.

............., claiming to be the widow of ...., late of the town of ...., having filed her petition for the admeasurement of her dower, and it appearing that .... and ...., heirs-at-law, of said deceased, are infants interested in the real estate described in said petition :

Ordered, that ...., of the .... of ...., a discreet and substantial freeholder, be appointed guardian for said infants, for the sole purpose of appearing for and taking care of the interests of such infants in the proceedings in this matter.

................., *Surrogate.*

33

§ 5. Notice of the application for the admeasurement of dower, and all notices in the subsequent proceedings shall be served on such guardian, whether the infant reside within the state or not.

§ 6. After the expiration of forty days from the death of any husband, his heirs, or any of them, or the owner of any land subject to dower, claiming a freehold estate therein, or a guardian of any such heirs or owners, may by notice in writing, require the widow of such husband to make demand of her dower, within ninety days after the service of such notice, of the lands of her deceased husband, or of such part thereof, as shall be specified in such notice.

NOTICE TO WIDOW, TO DEMAND DOWER.

To Mrs. M B, widow of J B, late of the town of ...., in the county of ...., deceased.

You are hereby notified, that you are hereby required to make demand of your dower in the following described lands, of your deceased husband in which the undersigned claims a freehold estate to wit: All that (description), within ninety days after the service of this notice upon you.

Dated ...., December 29, 1874.

(Signed), J D.

§ 7. If such widow shall not make her demand of dower within the time specified in such notice, by commencing a suit, or by an application for admeasurement, as herein prescribed ; or if such widow shall not make such demand within one year after her husband's death, although no notice to that effect shall have been given ; the heirs of the husband of such widow, or any of them, or the owners of any land subject to dower, claiming a freehold interest therein, or the guardian of any such heirs or owners may apply by petition to the Supreme Court, or to the County Court of the county where such lands are situated, or to the surrogate of the same county, for the admeasurement of the said widow's dower of the lands of her husband, or of such part thereof as shall be specified in the said petition.

§ 8. A copy of such petition, with notice of the time and place of presenting the same shall be served personally on such widow, twenty days previous to its presentation.

The petition and notice can readily be framed from the petition of a widow heretofore given and the notice annexed thereto.

§ 9. (Id.) Upon application being made, either by a widow or by any heir or owner, or by the guardian of such heir or owner, the court to whom the same shall be made may, upon hearing of the parties, order that admeasurement be made of such widow's dower, of all the lands of her husband, or of such part thereof as shall have been specified in the application.

The proofs on this hearing are, the seizin or ownership of the husband, in the lands specified; which, when no opposition is made, is evidenced by possession with claims of title, and the marriage of the deceased with the widow.

Marriage, in this state, is a civil contract, requiring no especial ceremony, and the essentials are, the consent of parties capable in law of contracting. (2 R. S., 138). This consent may be proved as having been given at a ceremony of marriage performed by a civil magistrate, or by a minister of the gospel, or it may be inferred from circumstances, and the long continued conduct of the parties. This last, be it borne in mind, will not prove the fact that the contract had been actually made, but will be merely circumstantial.

Long continued cohabitation, until the death of the alleged husband, the woman being received and treated as his wife, is *prima facie* evidence that a marriage had taken place. (*Young* v. *Foster*, 14 N. Y., 114.)

But the evidence being merely circumstantial if it be proved that the cohabitation was meretricious, the presumptions in favor of marriage fail, for cohabitation may be continued for base purposes, no less than in honorable marriage.

§ 10. Such court or surrogate shall thereupon appoint three reputable and disinterested freeholders, commissioners for the purpose of making such admeasurement, by an order which shall specify the lands of which dower is to be admeasured, and the time at which the commissioners shall report.

ORDER FOR APPOINTMENT OF COMMISSIONERS.

At a Surrogate's Court, held in the county óf ...., at the surrogate's office in the ...... of ...., on the ...... day of ...., 1874.

Present — Hon. ...., Surrogate.

In the matter of the dower
of
..................., a widow.

On reading and filing the petition of the above named widow, praying for the admeasurement of her dower in the lands therein described, and proof of the due service of a copy of said petition with notice of the presentation of the same, and it appearing by proof duly taken, that said petitioner is the widow of ...., late of the .... of ...., deceased, and that the said .... was in his lifetime seized of an estate of inheritance in the lands therein described. Now on motion of ...., attorney for the petitioner:

Ordered, that ...., and ...., three respectable and disinterested freeholders, be and they are hereby appointed commissioners, for the purpose of making admeasurement in the following described land. (Description.)

And it is further ordered that said commissioners report to this court their proceedings, on the .... day of ...., then next.

.................., *Surrogate.*

§ 11. (2 R. S., 489.) The commissioners so appointed, before entering upon their duties, shall be sworn, before the surrogate who appointed them, or before some officer authorized to take affidavits, that they will, faithfully, honestly and impartially discharge the duty and execute the trust reposed in them by such appointment.

OATH OF COMMISSIONERS.

Surrogate's Court, ... county.

| In the matter of the dower |
| of |
| .... , a widow. |

We do severally swear that we will faithfully, honestly and impartially discharge the duty and execute the trust reposed in us as commissioners appointed by the surrogate of the above named county, to admeasure the dower of the above named widow.

(Signed),   A B.
C D.
E F.

Sworn before me, this 28th }
December, 1874.   }

..................,
Justice of the Peace.
Rensselaer county.

§ 12. If the persons so appointed commissioners, or either of them, shall die, resign, or neglect or refuse to serve, others may be appointed in their places, by the court or surrogate who appointed the first commissioners, and shall take the same oath.

§ 13. The commissioners so appointed shall execute their duties as follows :

1. They shall, if it be practicable, and in their judgment for the best interests of all the parties concerned, admeasure and lay off, as speedily as possible, the one-third part of the landse mbraced in the order for their appointment, as the dower of such widow, designating such part with posts, stones, or other permanent monuments. (As amended, 1869, chap. 433.)

2. In making such admeasurement, they shall take into view any permanent improvements made upon the lands embraced in the said order by any heir, guardian of minors or other owners, since the death of the husband of such widow, or since the alienation thereof by such husband, and if practicable, shall award such improvements within that part of the lands not allotted to such widows, and if not practicable so to award the same, they shall make a deduction from the lands allotted to such widow, proportionate to the benefit she will derive

from such part of the said improvements as shall be included in the portion assigned to her.

3. They shall make a full and ample report of their proceedings, with the quantity, courses and distances of the land admeasured and allotted by them, to the widow, with a description of the posts, stones and other permanent monuments thereof, and the items of their charges, and in case it be not practicable, nor in their judgment, for the best interest of all parties concerned, to admeasure and lay off the one-third part of the lands and premises embraced in the order for their appointment, and designate such part, with posts, stones or other permanent monuments, then they shall so report; and also make full and ample report of all the facts of the case, to the court by which they were appointed, at the time specified in the order for their appointment.   (As amended S. L., 1869, chap. 433.)

4. They may employ a surveyor with necessary assistants, to aid them in such admeasurement.

§ 14. The court or surrogate appointing such commissioners, may, upon their application, or that of either party, enlarge the time for making their report, and may, by order, compel such report, or discharge the commissioners neglecting to make the same, and appoint others in their places.

REPORT OF COMMISSIONERS.

> In the matter of the dower
> of
> M......... B.........

To Moses Warren, Esq.,
　　Surrogate of Rensselaer county :

The undersigned, A B, C D, and E F, commissioners appointed by the surrogate of said county of Rensselaer, by order dated the 25th day of April, 1862, to make admeasurement of the dower of M B, above named, widow of A B, late of the town of Schodack, in said county, deceased, in the land and premises described in said order, and situated in said town of Schodack, do respectfully report: That having first been duly sworn, faithfully, honestly and impartially to discharge the duty and execute the trust reposed in us by said appointment, we met on said premises on the 30th day of April, 1862, to discharge the duty and execute the trust aforesaid; having first given notice of our intention so to meet, to M B, C B, and J H, guardians of A B, who did appear at said time and place. Whereupon we caused a survey to be made of the premises, and a map to be made thereof, which map and survey is hereto annexed.

And we do further report, that we have admeasured and allotted to the said M B, for her dower in the said lands and premises, the one-third part thereof, which is bounded and described as follows : (*describing by metes and bounds, and designating the permanent monuments*), being the part designated on the said map, hereto annexed, by the letter A, and included within the red lines.

The items of the charges of said admeasurement, including our fees, are as follows:

Two days' service for each commissioner, $2 per day for each,..............................	$8 00
One days' service of S D G, surveyor,...........	5 00
Paid for chain and flag bearers, one day each, $2 per day,...	4 00
	$17 00

Witness our hands, this 12th day of May, 1862.

A B,
C D, } Commissioners.
E F,

§ 15. (2 R. S., 90). Such report shall be filed and entered at large in the minutes of the court to which the same shall be made, or in a book to be provided by the surrogate for that purpose, when made to him.

§ 16. The court or surrogate, to whom such report shall be made, may, at the time appointed for receiving the same, or at such other time to which the hearing shall have been adjourned, on good cause shown, set aside the said report, and appoint, as often as may be necessary, new commissioners, who shall proceed in the manner hereinbefore directed ; and if not set aside, the said court or surrogate, shall, by order, confirm the said report and admeasurement.

§ 17. (2 R. S., 491.) The admeasurement so made and confirmed, shall, at the expiration of thirty days from the date of such confirmation, unless appealed from, be binding and conclusive, as to the location and extent of the said widow's right of dower, on the parties who applied for the same and on all parties to whom notice shall have been given, as hereinbefore directed. But no person shall be precluded thereby from controverting the right and title of such widow, to the dower so admeasured.

But it may occur that it would be injurious to lay off and admeasure the dower and provision for such a case is made by chap. 433, Laws of 1869.

In case said commissioners shall report, that it is not practicable, or, in their judgment, for the best interests of all the parties concerned, that the one-third part of the land or premises embraced in the order for this appointment, be admeasured and laid off, with posts, stones or other permanent monuments, then the said court or surrogate, may, upon competent evidence being adduced, as to the net rental value of such lands, or premises, order and decree that a sum equal to one-third part of such net rental value, be annually, or oftener, paid over to such widow, during the term of her natural life, as and for her dower, in such lands or premises; and such widow may sue for, recover, and collect, such sum of, and from the owner of such lands or premises, during the natural life of such widow.

If, at any time, it shall appear to the Supreme Court, or to the County Court of the county in which such lands and premises are situated, or to the surrogate of the same county, upon the application of any party interested, that the net rental value thereof has materially increased, or diminished, such court or surrogate, may, upon a hearing of all proper parties in interest, of which they shall have had due and proper notice, order and decree that such sum be correspondingly increased or diminished.

An appeal may be brought to the Supreme Court, within thirty days from the confirmation of the report of the commissioners, and unless it is so brought, the admeasurement shall be binding and conclusive, as to the location and extent of the said widow's right of dower, on the parties who applied for the same, and on all parties to whom notice shall have been given. But no person shall be precluded thereby from controverting the right and title of such widow to the dower so admeasured, and the widow may bring an action of ejectment, when she will be obliged to show the seizin of her husband, her marriage and his death, and the defendants may controvert those facts, and show any other facts which could cut off the right of the widow to her dower.

Upon receiving or recovering possession of the land so admeasured to her, such widow may hold the same during her natural life, subject to the payment of all taxes and charges accruing thereon subsequent to her taking possession, and may occupy or lease the same. (§§ 18 and 19.)

She may bequeath the crops in the ground at her decease. (1 R. S., 743.) Or, in default of a testamentary disposition, they would go to her administrator.

The costs and expenses of the admeasurement, taxed by the surrogate, or by a judge of the court in which the proceedings are had, shall be paid equally, one half by the widow, and one half by the adverse party (§ 20), and these costs like all other costs in the Surrogate's Court shall be taxed and allowed, as formerly in the courts of Common Pleas.

CHAPTER XXV.

APPEALS.

An appeal lies from the decision of a surrogate within the time regulated by statute, formerly to the chancellor, now to the Supreme Court.

From an order allowing or denying probate.

§ 55. (2 R. S., 66, as modified 1847, ch. 280.) After any will of real or personal estate, or of both, shall have been proved before a surrogate, any devisee or legatee named therein, or any heir or next of kin of the testator, may within three months thereafter, appeal to the Supreme Court from the decision of the surrogate, either admitting such will to record or probate, or refusing the same; and upon such appeal being filed with the surrogate, it shall stay the recording, or the probate of such will until it be determined.

§ 1. (S. L., 1871, chap. 603.) Appeals, when taken from the decree or decision of a Surrogate's Court, declaring the validity of a will and admitting the same to probate, shall not stay the issuing of letters testamentary to the executors, if in the opinion of the surrogate, the protection and preservation of the estate of the deceased require the issuing of such letters, but such letters shall not confer power upon the executor or executors named in the will to sell real estate, to pay legacies, or distribute the effects of the testator until the final determination of such appeal.

§ 56. (2 R. S., 66.)   The party filing such appeal, shall, at the same time, execute and file with the surrogate a bond in the penalty of one hundred dollars, to the people of this state, with such sureties as the surrogate shall approve, conditioned for the diligent prosecution of such appeal, and for the payment of such costs as shall be taxed against him, in the event of his failure to obtain a reversal of the decision so appealed from.   No appeal shall be deemed valid, until such bond be filed.

APPEAL FROM DECREE OF SURROGATE.

Surrogate's Court, county of Rensselaer :

In the matter of proving the
will and testament
of
Eugene Bendon, deceased.

A sentence and decree of the county judge of Rensselaer county, acting as surrogate, having been pronounced and entered in this matter on the 14th day of April, 1871, whereby it was decided, ordered, adjudged and decreed that the instrument in writing propounded for probate in this matter by Thomas Sausse, one of the executors named therein, bearing date the 25th day of July, 1868, is the last will and testament of Eugene Bendon, late of the city of Troy, in said county, deceased, above named, and as such is valid as a will of real and personal estate, and whereby the same was admitted to probate and ordered to be recorded as a will of real and personal estate, and we, Thomas Bendon and Annie Kelly, heirs-at-law and next of kin to the said Eugene Bendon, deceased, feeling aggrieved by the said decree, we, the said Thomas Bendon and Annie Kelly, do hereby appeal from the said sentence or decree to the Supreme Court, and pray that the pleadings, proofs and proceedings in the said matter may be transmitted to the Supreme Court to the end that such order may be made thereupon as shall be just.

THOMAS BENDON,
ANNIE KELLY.

Dated, July 3d, 1871.

BOND ON APPEAL.

Know all men by these presents, that we, Thomas Bendon, and Annie Kelly, as principals and ....
and ...., of the city of Troy in the county of Rensselaer, as sureties, are held and firmly bound unto (naming the respondents to the appeal), in the sum of (not less than one hundred dollars), lawful money of the United States, to be paid to the said (respondent). To which payment well and truly to be made, we bind ourselves, our heirs, executors and administrators, jointly and severally, firmly by these presents.

Sealed with our seals, and dated the }
third day of July, A. D., 1871. }

Whereas the above named Thomas Bendon and Annie Kelly, have appealed to the Supreme Court from the sentence or decree of the county judge of the county of Rensselaer acting as surrogate of said county, admitting to probate a certain paper writing purporting to be the last will and testament of Eugene Bendon, late of the city of Troy, in said county, deceased, which said sentence or decree is dated the ...... day of . ..., 1871.

Now the condition of this obligation is such that if the said Thomas Bendon, and Annie Kelly, or either of them or their heirs, executor or administrator, shall prosecute this said appeal to effect, and shall pay all acts that shall be adjudged against them, by the Supreme Court on such appeal, then this obligation to be void, otherwise to remain in full force and virtue.

(Signed),

THOMAS BENDON. [L. S.]
ANNIE KELLY.   [L. S.]
.... [L. S.]
.... [L. S.]

Rensselaer county, ss :

On this ...... day of ...., 1871, before me personally came Thomas Bendon, Annie Kelly, ... and ...., to me known to be the same persons described in, and who executed the foregoing instrument, and severally acknowledged that they executed the same.

(Signed), ...,

Justice of the Peace.

Endorsed.

I approve of the within bond, as to form, manner of execution, and the sufficiency of the sureties therein.

(Signed),

................., *Surrogate.*

34

Rule fifty-one of the Supreme Court also provides as follows:

On an appeal from the order, sentence or decree of a Surrogate's Court, the party appealing shall file a petition of appeal, addressed to the court, with the clerk of the county in which the order, sentence or decree appealed from was made, within fifteen days after the appeal is entered in the court below, or the appeal shall be considered as waived; and any party interested in the proceedings in the court below, may thereupon apply to this court *ex parte* to dismiss the appeal with costs. The petition of appeal shall briefly state the general nature of the proceedings, and of the sentence, order or decree appealed from, and shall specify the part or parts thereof complained of as erroneous. And where the appeal is from the sentence or decree on the settlement of the accounts of an executor, administrator or guardian, if the appellant wishes to review the decision on the allowance or rejection of any particular items of the account, such items shall be specified in the petition of appeal; or the allowance or disallowance of any such items shall not be considered a sufficient ground for reversing or modifying the sentence or decree appealed from.

The respondent, in his answer to the petition of appeal in such case, may also specify any items of the account as to which he supposes the sentence or decree is erroneous as against him and in favor of the appellant. And upon the hearing of the parties upon such appeal, the sentence or decree may be modified as to any such items, in the same manner as if a cross-appeal had been brought by such respondent. The appellant may have an order, of course, that the respondent in the petition of appeal answer the same, within twenty days after the service of a copy of the petition of appeal and notice of the order, or that the appellant be heard *ex parte*. And where the respondent is an adult, upon filing an affidavit of such service upon the attorney of the respondent, if he has appeared either in this court or in the court below, by an attorney of this court, or upon the surrogate, if he has not appeared by such attorney, and that no answer to the petition of appeal has been received, the appellant may have an order of course, that the appeal be heard *ex parte* as against such respondent.

Where the respondent is a minor, if he does not procure a guardian *ad litem* upon the appeal, to be appointed within twenty days after the filing of the petition of appeal, the appellant may apply to a justice of this court *ex parte*, for the appointment of such guardian. And if the minor has appeared by his guardian *ad litem* in this court, the appellant may have an order of course that the guardian *ad litem* of the respondent answer the petition of ap-

peal within twenty days after service of a copy
thereof and notice of the order, or that an attachment issue against such guardian.   When a petition
of appeal is filed, if it has not been served on the
adverse party, the respondent may have an order
of course that the appellant deliver a copy of the
petition of appeal to the attorney, or to the guardian *ad litem* of the respondent, within ten days after
the service of notice of such order, or that the appeal be dismissed; and if the same is not delivered
within the time limited by such order, the respondent, upon due notice to the adverse party, may
apply at a special term to dismiss the appeal with
costs.   Upon the hearing of any such appeal as is
referred to in this rule, it shall be the duty of the
appellant, to furnish the court with a copy of the
petition of appeal and of the answer thereto, if an
answer has been received, and a copy of the proceedings below, including a copy of the appeal as
entered.

PETITION OF APPEAL TO SUPREME COURT.

SUPREME COURT.

Thomas Bendon and Annie Kelly

against

Thomas Sausse and Peter Brannan, as executors of the will of Eugene Bendon, deceased, Catharine Kean, Bernard Kean Caroline O'Sullivan, Mary A. McGovern, Anna Brennan, Maria Nugent, the Society of St. Vincent De Paul, of Troy, St. Vincent's Female Orphan Asylum, the Troy Orphan Asylum, and the Catholic Male Orphan Asylum.

To the Supreme Court:

The petition of appeal of Thomas Bendon and Annie Kelly, appellants in the above entitled cause, by McClellan & Lansing, their attorneys, respectfully shows to this court:

That the said appellants are heirs-at-law and next of kin of Eugene Bendon, late of the city of Troy, deceased;

That the said Eugene Bendon died at the city of Troy on the ...... day of ...., 1870, aged seventy-two years and upwards, being, at the time of his death, the owner of real and personal property of the value of fifteen thousand dollars and upwards;

That after the death of the said Eugene Bendon, and on the 22d day of September, 1870, Thomas Sausse, named as one of the executors of the paper writing hereinafter mentioned, produced before the surrogate of the county of Rensselaer, and propounded to him for proof as a will of real and for probate as a will of personal estate, a certain paper writing purporting to be the last will and testament of the said Eugene Bendon, deceased, bearing date the 25th day of July, 1868;

That the appellants, your petitioner, and each of them, duly appeared before the said surrogate and contested the validity of said alleged will and its admission to proof or probate aforesaid;

That the proceedings before the said surrogate were duly continued from time to time, and on the 14th day of April, 1871, E. Smith Strait, Esq., county judge of Rensselaer county, acting surrogate, made and entered a decree in the matter aforesaid, in substance, that said paper writing, so propounded as aforesaid is the last will and testament of said Eugene Bendon, deceased, and ordering that the same be admitted to probate, and be recorded as a will of real and personal estate.

And your petitioners, the said appellants, allege that the whole and every part of the said decision, order, judgment and decree (except such portion thereof as relates to the costs of the respective parties) is erroneous, improper and illegal, and they have, in consequence, duly appealed to this honorable court.

And the appellants, your petitioners, pray that said decision, order, judgment and decree of said acting surrogate, and every part thereof, except as aforesaid, may be reversed and annulled.

And the appellants, your petitioners, further state that the persons, institutions, societies and corporations intended to be made defendants, respondents and parties to the said appeal, are as follows:

Catharine Kean, Bernard Kean, Bernard Bendon, Caroline E. O'Sullivan, Mary A. McGovern, Anna

Brennan, Maria Nugent, the Society of Saint Vincent De Paul, of Troy; the Troy Orphan Asylum, Saint Vincent Female Orphan Asylum, the Catholic Male Orphan Asylum, Thomas Sausse and Peter Brannan, as executors of the will of said deceased.

And your petitioners pray that the persons, institutions, societies and corporations above named may answer this petition of appeal pursuant to law and the practice of this court, and that a hearing may be had on this appeal, and your petitioners may have such further or other relief in the premises as to the court shall seem just and equitable.

Dated, July 3, 1871.

ANNIE KELLY,
THOMAS BENDON.

McCLELLAN & LANSING,
Attorneys & of Counsel.

Rensselaer county, ss :

On this 3d day of July, 1871, before me personally appeared the above named Annie Kelly and Thomas Bendon, and severally made oath that they had heard read the foregoing petition of appeal and know the contents thereof, and that the same is true of their own knowledge, except as to the matters which are therein stated on information and belief, and as to those matters they believe it to be true.

DANIEL DUNN,
Com'r of Deeds, Troy, N. Y.

ANSWER TO PETITION OF APPEAL.

SUPREME COURT.

Thomas Bendon and Annie Kelly,
  Appellants,

     against

Thomas Sausse and Peter Brannan, executors, etc., Respondents.

These respondents in answer to the petition of appeal herein, admit that a decree or sentence of the date, tenor and effect in the said petition of appeal set forth, was made by the surrogate of the county of Rensselaer :

And these respondents are advised and believe, and submit that such decree or sentence is just and equitable.

These respondents, therefore, pray that the said sentence or decree of the surrogate of the county of Rensselaer may be affirmed, and that the said petition of appeal may be dismissed by this honorable court, with costs to be adjudged to these respondents.

JOHN MORAN,
Attorney for Respondents.

The proceedings are further regulated by statute.

§ 90. (2 R. S., 608.) Appeals from the decisions of surrogates, by which any will of real estate shall have been admitted to record, or any will of personal estate shall have been admitted to probate, or by which any such will shall be refused to be admitted to record or probate, to the Supreme Court, shall be made within three months after such decision made and entered, in the manner and with the security specified in the first title of the sixth chapter of the seventh part of the Revised Statutes.

The manner of appealing and the security, we have before given at full length.

§ 104. (2 R. S., 609.) Appeals may be made from the orders, decrees, and sentences of surrogates, in all cases, to the Supreme Court, except appeals from orders concerning any admeasurement of dower.

§ 105. Such appeals from the decree of a surrogate, for the final settlement of the account of any executor, administrator or guardian, shall be made within three months after such decree shall have been recorded.

§ 106. Such appeals from the order of a surrogate, for the appointment of a guardian, or for his removal, or upon a refusal to make such removal, shall be made within six months after such order shall have been entered.

§ 107. In all other cases not hereinbefore specified and not otherwise limited by law, appeals from the order, decrees, and sentences of surrogates, to the Supreme Court, shall be made within thirty days after such order, decree or sentence shall have been made.

§ 108. (2 R. S., p. 610.) No such appeal shall be effectual until a bond be filed with the surrogate, with two sufficient sureties to be approved by him, in the penalty of at least one hundred dollars, to the adverse party, conditioned substantially, that the appellant will prosecute his appeal to effect, and will pay all costs that shall be adjudged against him by the Supreme Court.

§ 109. Every such appeal, when perfected, except in the cases specified in the next two sections, shall suspend all proceedings on the order appealed from, until such appeal be determined, or until the court to which the appeal shall have been made shall authorize proceeding thereon.

The cases in which the appeal does not stay proceedings are appeals from appointment of collector; from order directing sale of perishable property; from order appointing appraisers, and from order for service or publication of notices.

Appeals from commitment of an executor, administrator or guardian, or from commitment for disobedience to subpœna shall not stay proceedings unless the appellant shall give a bond in the penalty of one thousand dollars.

§ 118. (Page 611). Appeals to the Supreme Court from the orders of surrogate and the decisions of the County Courts, confirming or vacating any admeasurement of dower, shall be made within thirty days after such order or decision made, upon giving a bond as required by law.

An appeal does not lie from the surrogate's order appointing admeasurers of dower, but only after filing the admeasurer's report. (*Gardiner* v. *Spikerman*, 10 Johns., 368.)

The court has no power to enlarge the time for appealing, fixed by statute. (*Stone* v. *Morgan*, 10 Paige, 615.)

Where an executor on being ordered to account does so, and an order is entered thereon without citation to parties interested, so as to make it a final settlement, an appeal must be made from the order in thirty days. (*Guild* v. *Peck*, 11 Paige, 475.)

So also a decision of a surrogate confirming probate after allegations against a will, must be appealed from in thirty days. (*Williams* v. *Fitch*, 15 Barb., 654.)

Upon the question as to who may or may not appeal, we will cite the following cases.

A devisee or legatee may appeal from an order admitting a will to probate, notwithstanding that he was a petitioner for probate and he is not estopped by his petition. (*Vandermark* v. *Vandermark*, 26 Barb., 416.)

Parties to a proceeding to prove a will and codicils, who if the will is proved take nothing under the codicils, and whose interests are therefore unaffected whether the codicils be proved or not, may nevertheless appeal from an order admitting the codicils to probate. (*Parish* v. *Parish*, 42 Barb., 274.)

Legatees may intervene in the proceedings for probate before the surrogate and may do the same on the appeal; but if they do not intervene, and a final judgment is rendered declaring the invalidity of the instrument propounded as a will, they cease to be interested parties and cannot appeal from the order annulling the record and awarding costs against the executor, and directing him to file an inventory. The executor thus represents the legatees, and they are bound by his acts. (*Marvin* v. *Marvin*, 11 Abb. N. S., 97.)

But a legatee who is not a party to the proceedings for probate, may appeal from the order refusing probate; and this without leave of the court. (*Lewis* v. *Jones*, 50 Barb., 645.)

A husband cannot appeal in his own name from a decree allowing probate, by virtue of his wife being one of the next of kin. (*Foster* v. *Foster*, 7 Paige, 48.)

One whose interest is determined, ceases to have a right to prosecute an appeal, as where an heir at law apparent prosecuting an appeal, a posthumous child is born to the decedent. (*Reid* v. *Vanderheyden*, 5 Cow., 719.)

In proceedings for the sale of real estate, a purchaser who bid off the property, can appeal from an erroneous order of the surrogate setting aside the sale. If an appearance before the surrogate was necessary to constitute him a party, the administrator appearing in behalf of himself and the purchaser is sufficient. (*Delaplaine* v. *Lawrence*, 10 Paige, 602.)

If the surrogate denies an application for the appointment of a guardian of a minor, and the applicant appeals, the minor must be made respondent. The relatives of the minor who approved the appointment are not the proper parties respondent as to the appeal. (*Kellinger* v. *Roe*, 7 Paige, 362.) But it seems it is not necessary, in all cases, to make the infant a party, on an appeal from an order appointing or removing a guardian. (*Underhill* v. *Dennis*, 9 Paige, 202.)

On an appeal from a decree, all persons interested, (as those to whom sums were awarded by the surrogate), should be made parties; although they were not parties before the surrogate. (*Willcox* v. *Smith*, 26 Barb., 316.)

Parties interested in the establishment of a will, may intervene on an appeal from a decision against it ; but must come in by petition in the proper form, and make themselves parties to the proceedings before they can take any part therein. (*Foster* v. *Foster*, 7 Paige, 48.)

INDEX.

35

552 INDEX.

37

38

39

Milton Keynes UK
Ingram Content Group UK Ltd.
UKHW020912290324
440282UK00017B/20